M.R.

Mercy
In Pursuit of the Truth about the Death of Yvonne Gilford

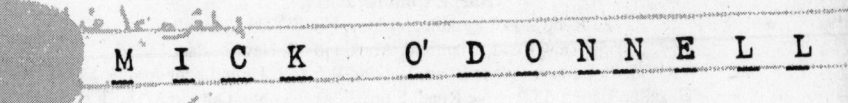

MICK O'DONNELL

HarperCollinsPublishers

For Liam,
the truth is not always what we'd rather it be.

HarperCollins*Publishers*

First published in Australia in 1999
by HarperCollins*Publishers* Pty Limited
ACN 009 913 517
A member of the HarperCollins*Publishers* (Australia) Pty Limited Group
http://www.harpercollins.com.au

Copyright © Michael Allan O'Donnell 1999

This book is copyright.
Apart from any fair dealing for the purposes of private study, research, criticism or review, as permitted under the Copyright Act, no part may be reproduced by any process without written permission.
Inquiries should be addressed to the publishers.

HarperCollins*Publishers*
25 Ryde Road, Pymble, Sydney, NSW 2073, Australia
31 View Road, Glenfield, Auckland 10, New Zealand
77–85 Fulham Palace Road, London W6 8JB, United Kingdom
Hazelton Lanes, 55 Avenue Road, Suite 2900, Toronto, Ontario M5R 3L2
and 1995 Markham Road, Scarborough, Ontario M1B 5M8, Canada
10 East 53rd Street, New York NY 10032, USA

National Library of Australia Cataloguing-in-Publication data:

O'Donnell, Mick.
Mercy: in pursuit of the truth about the death of Yvonne Gilford.
ISBN 0 7322 6464 2.
1. Gilford, Yvonne. 2. Parry, Deborah. 3. McLauchlan, Lucille.
4. Murder - Investigation - Saudi Arabia. I. Title.
364.152309538

Cover photographs: Courtesy of the Gilford Family and Alex Garipoli

Printed in Australia by Griffin Press Pty Ltd on 79gsm Bulky Paperback.

9 8 7 6 5 4 3 2 1   99 00 01 02

About the author

Mick O'Donnell has worked as a Sydney-based journalist in newspapers, radio and television for 20 years. For the past nine years he has been a producer of current affairs television for the Australian Broadcasting Corporation and the Seven Network, covering many domestic and international stories. He first travelled to Saudi Arabia during the Gulf War in 1990.

Acknowledgments

Thanks must go to Mr A. Rahman N. Alaholy, former Saudi ambassador to Australia, who arranged the author's initial visit to Saudi Arabia, and to The Law Firm of Salah Al-Hejailan, which sponsored the second visit. Neither of these parties requested or received any special treatment in reports of the Gilford case or this book. The assistance of many named informants is, I trust, acknowledged by their appearance in the narrative. There were many others who provided information and chose not to be named, for reasons of privacy or personal and employment security. Many thanks to them, in particular to the Saudi nationals who provided invaluable help in difficult political circumstances.

Professionally, thanks go to Greg Barbera, Alex Garipoli, Paul Barry, Anthony McClellan, Jackie Nesbitt, Alison Black and Virginia Haussegger.

Thanks also to Sophie Lance, Jill and the staff at Hickson Associates.

Thanks especially to Annette and the boys, from their often-absent but entirely devoted husband and father.

Contents

1/ Phone calls 1
2/ Night 5
3/ Death 9
4/ Joke 18
5/ Confessions 36
6/ Frank 60
7/ The White Ladies bury Yvonne 84
8/ Familiar faces 91
9/ Lawyers 97
10/ Rationale 105
11/ Saint Therese and the missing budgies 113
12/ Appeal in the dark 120
13/ We go 124
14/ Dead letters 144
15/ Kayf 149
16/ Frank at home 154
17/ Doubts? 156
18/ The grasshopper in gaol 165
19/ Complicity 169

20/ Doing time 171
21/ Tactics 175
22/ Breaking news 178
23/ Betrayal 187
24/ Deal done 200
25/ We go again 205
26/ Fishmongers 208
27/ False accusation 219
28/ Brangwen 227
29/ Consultant 232
30/ Hotel blues 240
31/ Wedding bells 245
32/ White lady from Louisiana 247
33/ Dundee 266
34/ Pride and prejudice 271
35/ Who guards the guard? 296
36/ Moon 299
37/ After 303

Chapter 1

Phone calls

On the phone a youngish, gruff-voiced Australian woman is describing an execution. Or rather, the moments after an execution. She had stumbled into a crowd one day, in the shopping district of Al Khobar, an eastern oil town in Saudi Arabia. Pushing through the cloaked forms of Saudi men (in white) and women (in black), Kathryn Lyons made out the object of the crowd's attention: the beheaded body of a man, lying on a plastic sheet in the noonday sun.

Kathryn was confronted with the result, though not the moment, of execution. Is that why she can describe this grim experience in such unmoved tones? Or is it because she is used to the blood and gore of human parts, working as she does in a major hospital nearby? Kathryn is a lab technician at the King Fahd Military Medical Complex, a prestigious hospital in the kingdom's Eastern Province.

Six weeks earlier, one of Kathryn's colleagues, an Australian nurse, died in her room at the hospital, the victim of a frenzied stabbing. Kathryn's anger about the murder has deepened into hate.

Later, after our telephone conversation, I will stumble on this same square, where executions are held at midday on Fridays. There's a pedestrian overpass, so shoppers can cross the busy thoroughfare in safety. Taxi drivers in *keffiyah*, the white or red-and-white scarves sported by most Saudi men, call for trade in the square, metres from the scene of many officially sanctioned deaths. A municipal fountain splashes there, as benign as in any square in any sleepy town anywhere in the world. Women walk with plastic bags of groceries. No one stares at the spot where blood has spilt.

On the phone, Kathryn describes the moments after a public beheading in an understated monotone. 'It was just there, next to the Coke machines, the body without a head.' Actually, Coke is banned in Saudi Arabia for its links to Israel; they are Pepsi machines. 'Then they wrapped it in a blue sheet with pink roses and put it in the ambulance.'

Kathryn's cool recollection of these details evokes the banality of this violence. She didn't see the sword raised, glinting in the sun of the square. She was still shopping at the moment of death. I have seen it only on videotape, yet it sickened as few screen images still can. The crowd gathered, in hundreds, around the white-clad form of the condemned man. Passive, drugged no doubt, the victim kneels. The executioner gesticulates, as if performing, lazily, for the crowd. The sword distantly flashes its fascination several times as the man who wields it walks up and down, preparing. The moment comes so casually, the shock is in its sudden, sickening finality. One man has killed another, by order of the king. The subjects look on and learn the reality of divine justice, as prescribed in the holy book, the *Koran*.

Kathryn hasn't grown to adulthood, as these crowds have, with the simple presumption of the justice of this act. Her own country has banned execution for 30 years now. Yet she doesn't condemn a justice abhorrent to her own culture. Now, on the phone, her own violence follows. 'I hope they get what they deserve,' she spits.

Kathryn is talking about her former colleagues: two nurses, a Scot and a Briton, who worked with her at that same hospital. They have been accused of the murder of Australian nurse Yvonne Gilford. Kathryn wants them dead for that brutal deed. If it happens, their execution will take place in that same square, under the clock, near the Pepsi machine, in Al Khobar.

How could a woman as apparently level-headed as the phlegmatic, rugby-playing Kathryn Lyons seek such a brutal vengeance? Why does she believe in the guilt of Lucille McLauchlan and Deborah Parry, the nurses who have so stoutly proclaimed their innocence? And why would one Australian seek vengeance for a fellow countrywoman in such vehement terms? Many questions remain in this strange tale. Some of the answers may follow.

Another telephone call. It's late in Australia. The children, here at home, are asleep, thankfully undisturbed by the midnight ring. The man's voice, through the international crackle, is familiar. Stan McLauchlan. We've met once, there in Al Khobar, when he made his forlorn plea, via our television camera, to the man who holds his daughter's life in his hands.

Tonight, Stan is desperate. He is ringing with an unabashed demand in his usually controlled Scots brogue. 'We want your help, Mick.' Stan wants me to talk to the dead woman's brother, to appeal to this man he's never met, for mercy. Stan knows that if his daughter, Lucy, is found guilty of murder, only the family of the dead woman can save her from the executioner's sword. He's not allowed by his lawyers to approach the family directly. His letters haven't been passed to the obscure, bearded man in Australia who holds the power of clemency under Saudi law. With the lawyers for the conflicting parties in this bitter case not even speaking with each other, Stan has turned to the only people he knows who are in friendly contact with both sides: the television team from Australia which has attempted, vainly thus far, to prompt a dialogue between the two. It's an almost pathetic reaching-out to a journalist he barely knows on the other side of the world. But as my own children sleep, I can understand his need to try any means to save his daughter.

Stan has no good reason to trust anyone from the media. Like all the street-level players in this real-life soap, he and his family have been plagued by the slavering hounds of the press. Now, as he did when he spoke to our camera in Saudi Arabia, he turns to us again in desperation, having no other avenue. 'Please tell him, Mick, that my daughter didn't do this.' Stan cannot understand how a man of his own age and class can believe the calumny against this man's sister and his own daughter. 'If he knows his own sister wasn't a lesbian, then he must know the rest of the case is bollocks.'

Would I talk to the brother in Australia, asks Stan. Would I try to convince this man that the two women accused of his sister's murder are innocent?

I assure Stan that I have tried, many times, but will do so again. And I remind him that the worst thing to do with this besieged country man in South Australia is to push too hard. If Frank Gilford — the brother — is to relent, is to grant mercy to the alleged killers, he will do so in his own time and not at the behest of ranting journalists. At the other end of the line, in Saudi Arabia, Stan McLauchlan mutters his thanks. His desperation has come from his latest visit to his daughter in gaol. After many weeks in a squalid cell, her spirits are falling; hope is nowhere in sight.

These telephone calls from strangers: one, in hate, wanting the murderers to be murdered by the king's executioner; one, in desperation, wanting to stay the executioner's hand. I felt for both callers, yet, as a journalist, I wanted more for them to keep talking, revealing their feelings, for this was a story few would see from the inside. Both sides demanded the true story be told; neither conceded any truth in the other's protestation of guilt or innocence. And so, over many months, in pursuing the truth about the death of Yvonne Gilford, I wandered between these two poles, from belief in guilt to belief in innocence — and back again. This is the story of my own pendulum of belief and where it finally came to rest.

Chapter 2

Night

The night comes down on the compounds of Saudi Arabia, enveloping these scattered modern encampments in the *kayf* of the early evening. 'The soft night-breeze wandering through starlit skies and tufted trees, with a voice of melancholy meaning,' wrote the great British traveller Richard Burton, who ventured to the kingdom in 1853. Burton described this feeling of *kayf* as 'the savouring of animal existence; the passive enjoyment of mere sense; the pleasant languor, the dreamy tranquillity'. The long summers have conditioned the Saudi Arabs to welcome the laziness of evening: 'the trouble of conversations, the displeasures of memory, and the vanity of thought' falling away as the night breeze comes in.

In the compounds, now in the brief winter of 1996, the people turn away from the night and the desert, looking inwards, to themselves and their fellows. You can be happy here, if you don't fight the languorous pace of the desert but allow it to wrap you in its soporific charms. Thought becomes impossible; meditation inescapable.

The guests of the desert people don't know better: they fight the heat, the isolation, the loneliness of the great desert spaces and the feeling of not belonging in a land of alien custom. They fill their lives with trivia and television; parties, illicit bars, gossip. Violence is possible here. Hatreds swell in the heat of the summer, are nurtured in the longer nights of the mild winter, without reason or reference to the polite ways of home. The guests stick to their own kind; so, often, it is Pakistani fighting Pakistani, European in private war with fellow European.

The people, the Saudis as well as their guests, are found mostly in these compounds, reminiscent of the old circles of tents, scattered across the sands. Small groups, sticking to one another, knowing each other's business. The lack of privacy is tribal; you belong to the group. Everything you do affects your fellows. Your violence is violence which sweeps up all in the tribe.

The King Fahd Military Medical Complex some miles out of the three-city conurbation of Dhahran, Dammam and Al Khobar in the Eastern Province, is a compound, an encampment of tribes, living too close to one another. In the West, the closest comparison might be a university or a mining town. All have come from somewhere else; the thing that has brought them here binds them in its pursuit but doesn't make them one.

Here, at the military hospital, 2000 people live and work at close quarters: the single men's quarters, single women's, the married quarters, the VIPs'. The guests, the strangers, have come from many parts of the world. The Filipinos have little in common with the Britons, and there is mutual suspicion. The Brits whisper about prostitution among the Filipinas; the Filipinas find their dorm-mates snobbish and close them out. Petty disputes erupt and smoulder under the veneer of Western-style professionalism.

The buildings are brown and bland, modern but not flash. They squat, prefabricated around courtyards, softened by stands of Australian eucalypts. To her building, number 44, Yvonne Gilford has brought with her a little Australian/South African informality. It's she who has begun the practice of draping the bushes around the single women's quarters with washing, hung to dry quickly in the desert heat. Others follow suit, the colours of women's blouses and skirts giving the compound a slightly raffish, more human air.

Yvonne Gilford. A quiet, gentle woman, whom others notice more for her self-sufficiency than outgoing sociability. She isn't a drinker or a party-goer, though both are on offer here. The expats have brought their habits from home, continuing them despite Saudi prohibitions. So Yvonne is a walker, a swimmer, a cyclist, a thrifty saver.

Even now, in the cooler season, the days can swelter. This night, the night of December 11, 1996, comes just like any other for Yvonne in her six months here. Yvonne, having been to borrow videos after work, makes her way to her building. The dormitory buildings house small units, known as *efficiencies*. Some of the staff jokingly refer to them as *deficiencies*. In Building 44, there are only a few women home. Others are on shift at the hospital, at the pool for the women-only session or visiting friends. Yvonne's bed-sit is room 3A, on the ground floor, at the back. There is a small table and three chairs, a coffee table with its own chair, some cupboards built in, a cooker in the space by the door, just off the small bathroom. Yvonne's room is scattered with mementos of her many years of travel. In a letter to her best friend in South Africa, Yvonne has written of her first impressions: 'Flat was fair but floor filthy ... hopefully at some stage it will be painted as some of the walls are a bit grubby — won't hold my breath.' She has sketched her small block ('only 16 units in my block as only 2 floors'), as well as the flat. These are cramped quarters, but adequate. A meticulous person, Yvonne describes in detail what the hospital has provided for her simple living and comfort: '2 side plates, 2 dinner plates, 2 dessert plates, 2 glasses, 3 large saucepans ...', enough for herself and a visitor, '...fry pan, colander, chopping board, carving knive'... The misspelling draws attention to this detail in the inventory. A humdrum detail — everyone has a carving knife.

Yvonne's window is open, by custom, to let a friend's cat in and out. The nurses are soft on the cats. Some are wild but spend their days lying lazily around the dormitory buildings, hoping for a feed. When word gets out that the cats are to be culled, soft-hearted, impractical nurses hide them in their rooms until it's safe. Fifty metres away, with a view of Yvonne's window, is a guard post, manned at all hours.

A friend drops in. A feisty Scot, Lucille McLauchlan has been here only a few months. She shares a bicycle with Yvonne. They often spend time together, the older Australian woman offering motherliness to the 31-year-old Briton. They chat about the videos. Lucy is the last person acknowledged to have seen her friend alive. She says she left soon after, back to her own room in the adjacent building.

There, in Building 43, joined to Yvonne's but with a separate entrance, another Australian nurse, Rosemary Kidman, has just come in from her shift. She, too, is a cat-lover, and shares the care of Purdy with Deborah Parry, an English nurse, who lives just across the corridor on the first floor. Their apartments, like Lucy's, are identical to Yvonne's, with personal idiosyncrasy possible only in the placement of the couch-bed, the scattering of souvenirs and the degree of cleanliness. Debbie's is messy. Rosemary's is neat. Lucy's is spotless: the bath, the stove, the walls.

Debbie has been here only three months, from her native England. She's 37, unmarried. Her family has been touched by tragedy too often. Her mother, father, brother-in-law and brother all died unexpectedly. Rosemary, in her fifties, is a single mother, from Western Australia's Perth. She's here to escape the boredom of suburbia.

Rosemary and Debbie are in the habit of tapping on each other's door for a chat. They have keys to each other's room for convenience in letting the cat come and go. Tonight, Rosemary steps across the corridor to say hello. They chat about the humdrum of the day. Rosemary doesn't stay long and returns to her room and her mail. There's a letter from the woman who owns the cat, recently married and returned to Canada, talking of coming back to collect the animal. Rosemary worries that this will upset Debbie, who now sees Purdy as her own. She steps back across to Debbie's room to pass on the news. Debbie is in her nightgown, sleepy. They exchange a few words and wish each other goodnight. Rosemary goes to bed and sleeps until morning.

Back in Yvonne's building, the long corridors, dim-lit, are quiet. Some of the single women are staying off-compound with friends. Some are at work. Noise in any of the rooms is muffled by thick walls, solid doors. No one hears a thing when, some time during this night, violence comes.

Chapter 3

Death

Who will tell us what happened that night? If we take any personal account for this first narrative, it will be tainted by subjectivity, suspect. Even the official reports are now clouded with suspicion, the outside world failing to trust the Saudi police and judicial systems.

We have to begin somewhere. Let's start with the police. Their succinct description is in a letter to the medical authorities: Dhahran Police Letter No. 21/13/1369/S. It's dated 2/8/1417. The Saudis use the Hejiran calendar, based on the year Mohammed declared his holy war for possession of the sacred city of Mecca. For those in the West, who date great events and small from the birth of Jesus Christ, this letter was written on December 12, 1996 — the day of Yvonne Gilford's death.

> About 8.30 A.M. on Thursday, 2/8/1417, we were notified by the security officers at the King Fahd Medical Complex that one of the nurses had been found dead in her room, No. 3A, Building No. 44 of King Fahd Medical Complex. We directly moved to that place. The deceased was found lying on the floor of her room. Her head was on the east side and her legs were on the west, close to and on the east side of the bed. She was wearing a shirt with designs on it together with brief shorts. The shirt was pulled up towards the top of her body. There were several stabbing injuries on various parts of the body and one of these was to the back of the right thigh. There was also an incised wound on the right side of the waist as

well as several other stabs of various sizes on the back of the deased. There was a blanket over her head. When that blanket was removed, we found beige trousers belonging to the deceased, a brassiere, white socks and a small pillow, all stained with blood. There were also several stabs on the left front as well as in the middle of the deceased's neck. There was a stab to the right front of the neck. There was also an incised wound on the forehead and blows to the right eye, nose and mouth, which were covered with blood. The forensic doctor appointed by you came and he carried out the preliminary examination at the sites. Apart from some blood splotches around the dead body and near to the kitchen sink, no other traces of violence or resistance were seen. The door and the windows in the room showed no sign of damage. It appeared that the name of the deceased is Yvonne Roseanne Gilford, of Australian nationality, and she was 56 years of age.

Pretty much as phlegmatic as police descriptions anywhere. No sign of bias or subjectivity. Just the facts. Interpretation has to wait for Dhahran Police Letter No. 21/13/2/882/S, 13 days later:

I want to inform you that after investigation and questioning of the two accused, Lucille McLauchlan informed the investigator that on Wednesday evening/Thursday morning (the night of the murder), at 1:A.M. she received a telephone call from Yvonne Roseanne Gilford telling her that Deborah Kim Parry was in her room and refused to leave and she asked her to come to her room to assist in convincing Deborah Kim Parry to leave and she went immediately and she tried to solve the problem. She said that there was a sexual relationship between Yvonne and Deborah and that Yvonne wanted to terminate that relationship, while Deborah objected. She further added that the discussion continued until 4:A.M., when both Yvonne and Deborah became upset and thereupon Deborah threw a kettle at Yvonne's face, pursuant to stand up and she slapped her on the face twice. She went on to say that Deborah entered the kitchen, fetched a knife and stabbed Yvonne several times and she remembers that these stabs were just below Yvonne's left breast she believes. She added that Yvonne fell down and Deborah continued to stab her on the neck and the upper part of her back. She further added that Yvonne was making a noise from her mouth, whereupon Lucille placed a pillow upon her face in order to prevent her from making a noise, until she died. Lucille told the investigator that after they were sure Yvonne was dead, Lucille and Deborah cleaned the place, rearranged the room and wipe [sic] away any traces adding that Deborah was injured at the lower part of her back when she was pushed by Yvonne. She also added they stole Yvonne's cash card and left the room around 5:A.M.

Deborah Kim Parry was also interrogated and her statements were identical to those of Lucille. Deborah mentioned that she could not remember some of the stabs because she did not know what she was doing. Their confessions were legally endorsed.

Is that the truth? Don't we know that police are frame-up artists the world over (as well as having a clunky writing style)? What about the Guildford Four, the Birmingham Six, the host of convicted now appealing their sentences in Australia following the uncovering of police corruption in the Wood Royal Commission? Never trust a copper.

So who will tell Yvonne's story? What about the doctor? Everyone trusts a doctor. Over on the telly, here in a Sydney loungeroom, there's a British murder series on. It's fashionable now, in popular novels and television, to dwell on the gruesome minutiae of forensic medicine. The armoury of tools is awe-inspiring: DNA matches, electronspectroscopy, the gathering of the most minute fibre particles to match a suspect to a scene or a victim. Generally the rigorous and hard-nosed scientist or medico, diligently toiling over the high-tech tools and the dismal subject matter, hides somewhere a heart of their own. In tonight's showing, the hero, a doctor, is a Scot. He's working over a body, cheerfully wielding a scalpel in a post-mortem, telling his assistant the dead man now has no friends but them. It's up to these forensic medical sleuths to find the truth of their dead. Let's hope Yvonne's last doctor has such a worthy creed.

Dr Abdulmonaim Abou Al-Fatouh Abou Al-Malati, a forensic medicine specialist at the Ministry of Health of the Eastern Province, never knew Yvonne in life. Here at the Dammam Central Hospital, early on Sunday, December 22, it falls to him to conduct the autopsy on a middle-aged nurse from Australia. He has at hand the notes of his junior, who visited Yvonne's room at lunchtime on the day of the murder. The doctor who carried out the forensic inspection there found a scene much as described by the police in their letter, with a few more bare details:

> Her left leg was straight and her right leg was bent, approximately 90 degrees. The floor of the room, the deceased's body and clothes were covered with blood. The deceased was holding some hair of light colour and varying length. One hair was approximately 9 cms long.

Sounds objective, no hint of interpretation. He describes what Yvonne was wearing, the few human details barely bringing personality back to this woman, so recently a healthy, happy person with plans and hopes, now reduced to the role of a victim in an official report:

> Long sleeved shirt of light brown colour and a white background, Woolworth brand, size 8, with five white buttons affixed to the left side of the shirt and five buttonholes, stitched with black thread, on the right side of the shirt.

White buttons, black thread. Who among us guesses what we'll be wearing in case of sudden death? Was this a favourite shirt of Yvonne's or something she shrugged on for sleep? Had she chosen its colour, its cut, with care or with little thought? She can't tell us now. The forensic doctor fills his report with the last little facts of her life, so pertinent to police and forensic scientists and ferreting lawyers, probably of tiny or no meaning to the woman herself. If Yvonne could speak now, would she shout in anger: forget the trivia of the colour of my shirt and buttons; think instead of how I felt as I died, in terror, on the floor of my own small room, my sanctuary.

In black and white, in the Medical Report on Case No. 250/417TSH, there is no hint of that terror, that feeling. Only the nerveless remark that cuts in the shirt matched the injuries on the deceased. Only facts:

...
b) Cotton underwear size 10 (BHS brand) with some blood stains, but no cuts.
c) Small metal earrings, light yellow in colour with a white stone, affixed to both ears.
d) We found on her neck the following:-
   1. A thin necklace, light yellow in colour, and a short metal chain of the same colour joined to it.
   2. A thin necklace, light yellow in colour: hanging from the necklace was an empty locket.

Had Yvonne bought the jewellery for herself, treats hard-earned in long months of nursing? Or were these treasured gifts from those she loved? Why was the locket empty? Had it ever contained the tiny picture of a sweetheart? The report doesn't tell us. The medical investigator merely notes what was there on a woman's dead body, then sends the clothes to the Criminal Evidence Department 'for further investigation of the cuts and the blood and for semen testing', and the jewellery to Dhahran Police.

Yvonne's body, like her clothes and jewellery hers no longer, goes to the Dammam Hospital, where it lies today, under the detailed and professional examination of Dr Abdulmonaim. But perhaps twelve hours after the murder, his colleague carried out The External Forensic Examination of the Body of the Deceased. This doctor, unnamed in the report, conscientiously noted that 'the face, the neck, the chest and the abdomen had dried out and the limbs were starting to dry out and were pale. The toenails and fingernails were affected with cyanosis.' The dictionary tells us this is 'morbid blueness of the skin'. The doctor describes this as the body of 'a female in her sixties'. Unfair to Yvonne, who looked youthful in life. He allows himself one small adjective bearing a hint of how what he sees affects him: 'External examination of the body of the deceased showed the following recent and vivid injuries ...' *Vivid.* Perhaps it's a technical term of his trade. It certainly understates the shock of his list on first and later readings. Newspaper accounts will confuse the number of stab wounds — some say 13, some say 15. This is because the report describes, in fact, 29 separate wounds, and whether they are all stabs or attempted stabs or blows is perhaps open to interpretation. Their descriptions are various:

14 / Mercy

A. The Head and Face
...
4. A horizontal incised wound approximately 4 cms long on the top of the forehead and about 3 cms below the hair ...

B. The Neck
...
2. A diagonal incised wound, approximately 2 cms long and approximately 7 cms above the left side of the neck base ...
6. A contused wound on the right side of the chin, approximately 2.5 cms long, with a small bruise, dark red in colour, each 1 cms long, on the right side of the lips.

C. The Chest and Abdomen
...
6. A diagonal linear abrasion, on the top left part of the stomach, approximately 12 cms long ...

D. The Back
1. A vertical stabbing wound, approximately 1 cms long and 2.5 cms to the right of the centre line of the back and approximately 23 cms beneath the neck base ...

E. The Upper and Lower Limbs
1. Several small linear bruised abrasions of dark red colour on the right hand and a small linear bruised abrasion of the same colour on the right forearm ...

The list goes on and on: incised and contused wounds, linear abrasions, stabbing wounds. Any lay person would simply say Yvonne was stabbed and/or beaten all over her body. Brutally. Cruelly. And that this was no thought-out crime. This was frenzy. This was a crime of passion. But today, ten days after the murder, it's time for the autopsy. The Forensic Medicine Specialist, Dr Abdulmonaim, looks deeply, not just at the surface. His examination reveals an equally assaulting array of internal wounds. We should all be spared the detail. There's enough in one paragraph of The Opinion:

5. The death resulted from stabs which penetrated the heart, lungs, liver, spleen and right kidney causing heavy bleeding and pneumothorax in the chest and dramatic collapse of breathing and blood circulation.

Does he use the word 'dramatic' to include his feeling for what happened to this woman he never knew? Probably not. Dramatic in the technical sense. Drama in the emotional, melodramatic sense is left to the reader to find in the doctor's description of 'the instrument suspected of having been used in the incident'.

The police called Dr Abdulmonaim in to Dhahran Police Station on a Saturday in January 1997 to see 'whether or not the instrument has been used to cause the injuries'. The doctor describes it for us:

> The instrument consisted of a knife 'Rose — 85, super stainless steel' made in Japan. It has a brown handle 13 cms in length, fixed by three yellow metal screws having a diameter of 0.5 cms. This handle is fixed to a white metal blade with a sharp edge and 19 cms in length. The widest part of the blade is the one fixed to the handle and is 3.6 cms wide. The width gradually decreases to form a sharp point.
>
> The knife appears to the naked eyed to be absolutely clean and free of any suspected polluted materials. It is in a good condition.

What these 'polluted materials' may have been isn't clear. Anyway, the doctor concludes that the injuries 'might have been caused by the suspected knife which has been examined by us'.

There is much that Dr Abdulmonaim's report doesn't tell us, but it contains the skeleton of all the drama that was to follow. Even the swirling politics that washed over this sad, distant death are hinted at in his 17-page document. He refers to a letter from the governor of the Eastern Province, Prince Mohammed:

> We have to pay special attention to this matter and keep us informed of the results of the investigation.

Special attention indeed. Not since the furore over the British television screening of the program *Death of a Princess*, a dramatised account of the execution of a Saudi princess, in 1980 had there been such a point of contention between these major trading partners, the United Kingdom and the Kingdom of Saudi Arabia. The charging of two British women with the dreadful murder of Australian Yvonne Gilford was to prove a nightmarish labyrinth for the governments of all three countries.

Over on the telly, the fictional Scots forensic medical specialist, Dr McCallum, takes some time out from scalpels and mortuary slabs to talk to a friend from his neighbourhood. He has just done an autopsy on her husband. Here is a medical scientist with a human touch. The scandal of the husband's murder has hit the papers.

The woman's lover is suspected, and her relationship with that man has been splashed in the press. 'It's unfair. You don't recognise yourself when somebody writes about you. They never get it quite right, do they?' Our medico agrees. 'No, they don't.'

Chastening words for any journalist setting out to find the human — and, hopefully, truthful — side to a notorious murder story. But in deference to the shifting sands of the desert surrounding the compound where she died, Yvonne Gilford's murder story is not a simple one which can be cleared up by the exacting and precise technicalities of forensic medicine. It's not that the Saudis lack science. Dr Abdulmonaim's report refers to the knife and Yvonne's clothes being examined by the professionals at the Criminal Evidence Department of the Eastern Province. How thorough their work was we may never know. No report has been released through the court which tried Lucille and Deborah. The blood and urine tests mentioned in the medical report reveal nothing of note: 'They were free of alcohol, drugs, poisonous and prohibited materials.' Vaginal and anal swabs, subjected to 'Fluorence Iodine Tests', proved negative, according to Dr Abdulmonaim's report.

So, in the end, where you stand in this mystery depends on your position in the politics and prejudice surrounding Yvonne's murder. If for you, the Saudi system, based as it is on the religious *Sharia* law, is corrupted by its lack of openness and the rigours of Western-style cross-examination, then you will scarcely believe the concise conclusions summarised in the doctor's report. If you trust the Saudi law but believe that Saudi men would assume, as a matter of course, that an unmarried woman of a certain age must be a lesbian, then you will doubt at least the motive imputed. But why not suspend all your doubts, political stances and prejudices for a little, as Yvonne herself perhaps would have, and search for some kind of truth in the human traces of her tale? Given that the Saudi system is so closed, given that there have been no blinding flashes of forensic truth publicly disclosed to preclude all doubt, you have no choice but to meet as many of the personalities in this story as you can, sum up the assertions and personality of each, and make your own decision based on your own, flawed, human response. Yvonne is described by many as open-minded, not prejudicial towards race or creed. Perhaps she could have been the kind of objective observer, dispassionate but able to recognise human warmth, which so many of us in journalism fail to be.

Now that Dr Abdulmonaim is finished with Yvonne's remains, he can write in point eight of The Opinion: 'If this report is satisfactory, we agree that the body can be buried.' So Yvonne leaves him now, this doctor who sought the truth of her demise in science, and travels back to her homeland, to South Australia's sleepy Adelaide in the hot summer of January 1997. There we can meet not the forensic Yvonne but Yvonne the woman, as known to her friends and family. But while her body finds release, those entangled in her murder remain, here in Saudi Arabia, awaiting the more uncertain fate of the living.

Chapter 4

Joke

Did you hear the one about the Scot, the Englishwoman and the Australian? They went to the bank and ...

The nationalities make it sound like the classic three-headed joke. Depending on your own origin, you can make any one of the three the butt of the mirth — most likely, the Australian. In Australian corrupt police parlance, a 'joke' is a pay-off, the profit from complicity in crime. You may be thinking that in this case the Australian was Yvonne Gilford. But this joke — alleged crime — came after Yvonne's death and at her expense. The Australian we're talking about now we'll call Caroline Ionescu. Caroline had had an inkling since she was a young girl that, one day, she would end up in Saudi Arabia. So she was here, nursing at the King Fahd, when Debbie and Lucy turned up. She hadn't had much to do with Debbie — didn't warm to her. But she was friendly with both Yvonne Gilford and Lucille McLauchlan. Her friendship with Lucy threw her into an intense and uneasy triangle with the Scot and her English friend for one telling week after the murder.

Caroline is not a small woman. She has a mop of thick, curly brown hair and she likes a chat. She went to school in Adelaide, the capital of Yvonne Gilford's home state of South Australia. So when she met Yvonne in Dhahran, they had something to chat about. They would walk, some mornings, around the compound perimeter, Yvonne faster than her more substantial companion. 'She'd get ahead and I'd catch up,' Caroline remembers. They would meet twice a week to walk, sometimes jog. Caroline remembers Yvonne as a nice woman with a wide vocabulary, a reader. They would talk, on their walks, about 'how hot it was, hospital work, keeping fit, books we were reading'. Caroline was reading James Patterson detective novels, Yvonne more widely but also the pop stuff, Tom Clancy, Dean Koontz. Yvonne would talk about walking, swimming, bike-riding (she shared a bicycle with Lucy). 'Yvonne trained at the Royal Adelaide Hospital and I'd worked there, so we had something in common.' Yvonne's accent, Caroline remembers, was polite Australian, with a South Australian slant. That means she'd say 'skool' instead of the 'skewl' of broader Australian accents.

Today, Caroline speaks of her fellow Australian with sadness and respect. But let's not forget she was a closer friend to Lucy. She talks of the grief of losing Lucy as a friend. 'I still have no malicious thoughts or anything towards Lucy and Debbie. I feel very sorry and sad for what they're going through.' Her first reaction after the two were arrested was:

Why did they detain them? They're innocent, they're innocent. Nothing I saw directly after the murder made me think that anything was amiss with those people. Except Debbie's behaviour progressively got more erratic and she became more anxious, like she'd lost the plot. She was away with the fairies. You couldn't keep her in the one spot for more than five minutes. She would be up and moving, always: 'I haven't slept; I'm taking tablets.'

It's still very difficult to believe two Westerners conspired to murder this woman. Or that it was done spontaneously. For one woman to murder ... but for two, in Saudi Arabia where you know the rules, I just find that difficult. But if I had to really think about it I would look at the situation where Debbie — her behaviour changed. She became obsessed. She was thinking, it's the Filipino Mafia and she was going around to all the Filipinas trying to get information if there was a Mafia gang on the compound and who was into moneylending. Was it security? She was just very forceful, very pushy.

This is how Caroline talks, fast and furious. A bit flighty. One minute she's telling us she couldn't believe in Lucy and Debbie's guilt; the next, she's suggesting that Debbie's weirdness after the murder is suspicious. In a witness box, she would be unreliable. Yet she is all we have to confirm or deny much of Lucy and Debbie's movements and behaviour after the murder. Perhaps Caroline's leaps between condemnation of and support for the two accused women will suffice as a kind of objectivity. Until we know more.

Caroline can tell us something about each of the women at the centre of this story. Debbie's room was 'a mess'. Rosemary Kidman's was 'like your Mum's place'. Lucy was 'fanatical about cleanliness'.

> *She used disinfectant and detergent everywhere. The bathroom would be glistening, the stove scrubbed inside, outside, upside down. Her room was always fresh even though she was a smoker. I said, 'God, your place is so clean. You should come and do mine.'*

In the days and nights after the murder, the single women in the compound stuck together, huddling in each other's rooms, talking, not sleeping. They were frightened, confused. This was the second murder on the compound in eighteen months. The murderer of a Filipina nurse, Liberty da Gusma, had never been found. Now, there was paranoia, anxiety, as the women speculated, cut off from the world. Lucy and Debbie were on opposite shifts but spent time together when Debbie had days off. Caroline had the same shifts as Lucy, so was often in her company. One night, Australian nurse Rosemary Kidman contacted an Australian journalist in Jerusalem, Nigel Vincent, to make sure the world knew what was happening.

'It is terrifying to think there is someone walking around the compound who has done this,' Rosemary told the reporter from Sydney's *Daily Telegraph*. 'Yvonne was viciously killed. She had to fight for her life. This murder must be solved.'

Caroline was also quoted: 'We want to make sure this murder is not swept under the carpet. Yvonne's room was right beside the security guard gate, yet no-one saw what happened. We are a very small community of people here. To have two murders of single women in two years is very frightening. We just don't feel safe.'

The newspaper report described the nurses as 'too scared to be identified' and said they claimed Saudi police had been careless with evidence and were refusing to tell staff anything. Sheets taken from the murder scene had been discarded on the pavement outside Yvonne Gilford's room. 'This is supposed to be evidence,' one of the nurses had said.

Caroline remembers that night:

> *The reporter rang Rosemary back to tell her what he was going to print. I was down in Lucy's room and Debbie came down. Rosemary rang and said, 'He's ringing back in five minutes. Come up and hear what he's going to say.' They'd all listened on the speaker phone and he'd asked if there was anything they wanted to correct. Caroline did: there were eleven Australians on the compound, not fifteen. The others said nothing. I said, 'Lucy, Debbie, have either of you got anything to add about this murder?' God knows what they were thinking.*

Let's colour Caroline's memories with her admission that she didn't really like Debbie:

> *Her personality didn't really click with me. I went out of my way to avoid her. When we were on night shift, I'd sit outside near the fountain if I knew she was having lunch in the cafeteria [the nurses refer to their midnight meal break as lunch], because I didn't like her personality.*

On first meeting, Debbie had told Caroline the story of the many deaths in her family. 'It's hard enough living in Saudi Arabia without having someone thrust that in your face in the first five minutes. We all want friends and that sort of thing, but you just don't go about doing it the way she did.'

These observations may, of course, say more about Caroline than Debbie. She admits as much. 'A lot of people liked Debbie, that's the thing. But I just didn't click with her, so I thought it better to stay away from her.' But Lucy was different.

> *I hadn't known Lucy for long prior to the murder. Maybe six weeks — sitting in the cafeteria for lunch, dinner. She went to the swimming pool. She'd recently bought a bike with Yvonne and she was going to help me buy a bike. And I was getting to know her. She was meant to be getting married in January and going to Bahrain. I go to Bahrain quite a lot, so I was helping her out with that sort of thing.*

Bahrain is known to many expatriates in the Eastern Province as 'the pub at the end of the causeway'. An island state, it is joined to Saudi Arabia by the 27-kilometre King Fahd Causeway. Bahrain is an Islamic country but not nearly as strict as Saudi. You have no trouble getting a drink there. Many women don't wear the cover-all of *abaya* and veil. It's an escape valve for the wealthy foreign workers in the Saudi kingdom.

Caroline and Lucy shared a broad sense of humour, even after the murder.

> *Her fiancé Grant sent over these jokes about Scottish girls. They were really funny. And it was a way of laughing for a change, instead of being so serious and intense and scared. We sat down on night shift at lunchtime, just laughing our heads off. It was stress release.*

So even in the days immediately after the murder, Lucy could laugh and be herself? 'Yeah. She always seemed very controlled and composed to me.' Before and after the murder.

'We were both smokers, so that made it easier. After the murder I smoked a lot more in her company. She smoked a lot more than me.' A pack a day after the murder.

Lucy hadn't mentioned to Caroline that she'd left trouble behind her in Britain. Even today, Caroline is surprised that Lucy is really facing charges of stealing from a dying patient back in Scotland.

Lucy hadn't talked of money troubles but was 'always sending money home'. Caroline had the impression that it 'had to be there by a certain date'. She hadn't been aware that Lucy had borrowed money from Yvonne.

> *I knew Debbie had bills, because she was always going on about them after the murder happened. We were going into town on the Wednesday morning [the day prior to the arrest]. She said to me, 'Caroline, have you saved much money since you've been in Saudi? You've been here a while.'*

Caroline had told her she'd been able to save, as well as go on a couple of holidays. 'She was very interested in knowing my saving patterns.'

Caroline had been with the two accused women on shopping trips to town in the days before their arrest, and her evidence regarding their banking transactions was central to the police case. Those who support the women's innocence believe the police used Caroline's recollections of bank visits to insert elements of fact into the fiction of their confessions. Those who believe in their guilt will see Caroline's story as confirmation of Debbie and Lucy getting their hands on Yvonne's money.

'We got paid on the Monday after the murder,' says Caroline. This was December 16, four days after Yvonne's death. 'That's why Lucy and I went into town on the Monday evening.' First, they'd gone to the Saudi Hollandia Bank in Al Khobar. There they'd both cashed their hospital-issued Saudi Hollandia Bank cheques. 'Then we went and had coffee. After that, we went to the Al Raji Bank where she said she wanted to telex money back to her account in Scotland for Grant.'

Caroline had observed Lucy filling out the forms and going through the telex process, although she hadn't noticed the amount involved.

> *She told me she had basically sent all her money. After the Al Raji Bank, we went down to the Al Shola Mall where she bought two coffee cups. It was getting close to the second call to prayer and we decided we'd go out for dinner at the Pattaya Chinese restaurant, which is just near the mall. After we'd eaten, we decided to go for a walk because we were both quite full — even though we'd hardly eaten in the last few days. We went for a walk around the block and she said she needed to find an auto teller machine so she could withdraw some money. And I said, 'OK.' First we went to the Al Raji Bank, but the autoteller machine wasn't working, so then we went round to the Arab National Bank, behind Al Shola. She went in while I waited out on the footpath. She had her Bank of Scotland Visa card, or MasterCard, and she said she wanted to try and withdraw some money from it. She hadn't done it before and wanted to see if it worked. And obviously it did.*

Or could she have had Yvonne's card?

> *From what I heard later, yes, that's true. The only way you'd know is if you didn't see any transactions on her Bank of Scotland card bank statements, which have never been given to the police, from what I've heard, to confirm what I've said.*

Caroline slips easily between the presumption of innocence and the various stories she'd heard from other hospital staff after the women were arrested. Another nurse, Brangwen, had been with Lucy once before the murder when Lucy had used her Bank of Scotland card at one of the banks. This didn't tally with Lucy claiming to Caroline that she hadn't used the card in a Saudi bank before. 'She had done it before and she knew where the banks were. She'd told me she didn't know where any of the banks were.'

But let's not stray into after-the-event wisdom. Let's stick to exactly what Caroline knows of what happened in that week after the murder.

> *So, we went to the Arab National Bank and she withdrew the money. Then we went back into the Al Shola Mall and we did some shopping. I bought Chanel eye cream, because I had big black bags under my eyes and I thought, 'If Chanel won't work, nothing will.' Lucy bought Clinique make-up, about four or five different types, as well as a few things from another shop.*

The next day, Tuesday, December 17, Debbie was due to work night shift. 'We got her off on sick leave,' says Caroline.

> *I stopped her from working. I'm sorry to say this, but she couldn't have looked after post-renal transplant patients. I made her go to Casualty, see a doctor and get sick leave. I said, 'Debbie, you're not working. You can't work.' She was losing it. Not that I'm a doctor, and I hate to pass judgment, but as a friend and a colleague.*

Lucy and Caroline had gone with Debbie into town, to the Al Rashid Mall. More up-market than the Al Shola, this is a mall like any in the West, with bluff, featureless walls hiding a glossy interior and surrounded by acres of carpark. Caroline recalls:

> *It was just on prayer call and we went up to get some food, because I hadn't eaten since the previous night. Lucy hadn't either. I went and got my food and I came back to where Debbie was and Lucy was walking off in the distance. They were at McDonald's, you see. Debbie said Lucy had gone to withdraw more money from a bank. At*

> *the time I didn't think it very unusual. I knew that she'd withdrawn money the night before. Not that it's any of my business. In my head I went, 'Oh, maybe she didn't withdraw enough. Maybe she's going to spend some money tonight.'*

When Lucy returned to their table at McDonald's, Caroline asked if she'd managed to do her banking. 'Yes, I have,' was Lucy's reply. At that stage, Caroline still wasn't suspicious about Lucy's bank visits. Her mind was on getting away from Debbie, who was in a constantly frenetic state.

> *'I really can't have her hanging around me,' I said. 'If you two want to go off shopping, please go ahead. I'll just sit down. I'm really exhausted.' I hadn't slept. I didn't really want to be there, but it was good to be out of the compound. But Lucy said, 'No, no. I want to go shopping with you. I don't really want to be around her either.'*

So they went off shopping without Debbie.

> *Lucy went down to the next clothes shop and she spent about eleven, twelve hundred riyals, which is about $400. She bought a watch. I think she bought some more make-up or perfume, or something to that effect.*

What about Debbie's shopping?

> *She bought a tapestry. She was also obsessed with getting a film developed, getting this photo enlarged and framed. She was apparently seeing this guy; I think she'd only seen him once or twice before. Jeremy, I think his name was. She became obsessed with getting this film blown up and framed to give him for Christmas. Every time I'd see her she'd say, 'I have to go and get this film blah blah blah.' I'd say, 'There's a photo place down there. You'll find frames in there. Go there, do that — it's over. That's it. No more.' Shut up about it, you know? I thought, she's been going out with this guy for two weeks; getting a photo blown up, what sort of relationship is this? She didn't end up getting it blown up that night.*

Caroline is telling this story a year later, safely back home in Australia. She tells of the speculation later that Debbie had been trying to cover up the alleged lesbian relationship with Yvonne by talking about Jeremy and the photo.

The three nurses went home together to the hospital in a taxi after the evening's shopping. Caroline remembers an odd moment during the journey: 'I was so tired. I had my hand across my stomach, holding the door handle, trying to fall asleep. And then Debbie turned round to Lucy and said something, the most odd thing. "Lucy, it's really good. We've exhausted her. Really, we've exhausted her."' Caroline imitates Debbie's voice, low and heavy, as she relates this.

> *I kind of like went to myself, 'Forget about it, you're imagining things. Don't even think about what that was, Caroline. Stop thinking. You're tired — go to sleep.' I moved over so not one part of my body touched her.*
>
> *When we got back to the compound, psychologically I must have picked up something because when I tried to take my hand off the door handle my fingers were like etched into the handle. She had frightened me, subconsciously, without me really realising it. I got out and I was shaking. I didn't think anything, that she had murdered anybody or anything. I just thought that was a really odd, odd statement to say to somebody.*

Caroline checks herself. 'But then I could have misinterpreted it. Debbie might just have been saying, "It's great, we've exhausted her. Now she'll be able to go home and sleep." But just the way she said it'... Caroline shudders with the memory of that taxi ride.

How reliable is the account of this eyewitness? Has she embellished her own recollections in the hindsight of the arrest and subsequent conviction of her former friends? For much of Lucille McLauchlan and Deborah Parry's behaviour in that week, we have only Caroline Ionescu as character witness. She's excitable, a talker — but she's all we have.

Were the women's purchases extravagant? 'I honestly didn't think so,' Caroline responds.

> *I'm a bit of an extravagant spender myself when I want to spend. Lucy obviously hadn't bought much for her apartment. She'd only been there a while, and I think*

> she'd only received one or two cheques. One cheque you just want to blow anyway. And it wouldn't surprise me doing that, 'cause I've done it myself. She was buying a few more things, but I didn't see it as excessive. Though if you look at it in terms of monetary value, you could probably say, 'Gee, you spent a lot of money.'

On the Wednesday morning, the day before the two women were arrested, staff at the hospital were called together for a security meeting. 'They were asking for changes and increases in security for us,' Caroline explains.

> Well, Lucy and Debbie just went right off the wall with all these suggestions. Like, putting curtains up in the ends of the corridors. I turned round in that meeting and said, 'Debbie, wouldn't you want reflector glass at least, so that you can see out and feel a sense of freedom?' She was saying, put a buzzer next to the bedhead in case someone breaks into your room. Those rooms are so hard to break into. You can't break in unless you've got a jackhammer. She was just full on: change security, change security.
>   Debbie's behaviour just got so erratic and so peculiar. One time she was really losing it; she was like blah blah blah blah, talking a hundred miles a minute and talking really high-pitched. I grabbed her by the shoulders and said, 'Debbie, take a deep breath and calm down. It's OK.' And she said, 'I'd better go and take another tablet.' So I said, 'Do what you need to, darlin', but it's OK. Just relax, relax.'

What pills was Debbie taking? 'She told me it was called Bromazopine [sic]. I don't know what that is. I never looked it up.' (Bromazopan is a benzodiazepine drug, in the same family as Valium, prescribed for anxiety.) Had Debbie taken medication before the murder? 'One of the girls at Employee Health told me that Debbie had come down for strong medication.' Caroline didn't ask what the medication was. 'It's not my business,' she says now — oddly, given how much of Lucy and Debbie's business she *is* prepared to talk about.

On the Wednesday morning, Lucy had asked Caroline to come shopping again.

> 'Oh, Lucy,' I said. 'You're looking very dressed up this morning. Your hair's nice, you've got make-up on, you're looking very smart. Are you going out?' You know, me being curious and nosy. And she said, 'Yes, I'm going into town. Would you like to come?'

Caroline had been missing sleep and so declined. But Lucy was insistent. 'Oh, I'd really like you to come in. I'm going in with Debbie. She has to send some money home and she doesn't know how to telex it.' Caroline, who describes herself as someone with 'a bit of a generous heart', relented.

> So we went back to my room for my money and my bag. They'd already organised a taxi. Lucy had never been in my room before. She never went and visited other people. People always had to come to her, and I didn't mind going to her room. So it was really odd her coming into my room. I felt really uneasy. I don't know, it's just a weird thing. She was like, very looking around. It was just weird. I don't know how to describe that feeling.

Caroline's words come out in a tumble, running over each other. 'I just thought I'd throw that in,' she says.

'We went down and met Debbie at Security Gate 26. The taxi hadn't turned up. That's when Debbie started asking me about how I do my banking, how I felt my saving skills were. She turned round and said, "Are you a good saver? Do you think you're a good saver? Are you a good saver? I think you're a good saver." That was her voice,' says Caroline, speaking fast, high-pitched. '"It's a nice day. Don't you think it's a nice day?" And I'd say, "Yes, it *is* a nice day." She'd go, "Yes, it *is* a nice day, don't you think?"' Caroline, describing this manic behaviour, re-enacts it.

> We go in. I go to a jewellery shop near the Saudi Hollandia Bank. Lucy and Debbie went to the bank. Debbie had her pay cheque. Cashed it, apparently had an argument with the teller behind the counter, that's what Lucy told me. Then she told Lucy to go away, she didn't need her help after all. So Lucy went to the coffee shop which was near where I was. It just turned into this big

> *drama. So what happened was, I turn up at the coffee shop, Lucy's there, then Debbie turns up. Two other people from the hospital were there and we're all having a talk.*

Caroline slips in and out of the present tense with the drama of it all. Perhaps she likes telling the story.

> *Because we were eating so erratically, everyone was losing weight around this time. If you were eating, you'd eat something substantial, to keep yourself going. For energy. Being a nurse, you know these sorts of things. For breakfast, Debbie ordered this chocolate banana split thing with lots of chocolate ice-cream. Really inappropriate food for waking up in the morning. Or, who knows, she could have been up all night. I think she was. Whereas Lucy and I and the others, we'd have something like a sandwich, trying to be healthy. I said to her, 'Why don't you have something healthy?' She went, 'Oh, no. This is what I want.' Then next minute, after she finished that, she just got up, walked out the door, didn't say goodbye, didn't say anything — just left. I said, 'Lucy, where's Debbie gone?' 'Oh yeah, she's going out to get something or buy something, and then she's going off to meet some friends.' I never saw her again after that.*
>
> *After we'd finished there, we were going to Al Shola and we stopped in at the Ten Riyal Shop. Lucy wanted to pick up something. When she came out, I said: 'Lucy, one of the [nursing] supervisors [Deslyn Marks] told me, "Caroline, be really careful. It might be somebody you know."' I'd just remembered that Deslyn had said it to me the day before. Lucy looked at me and said, 'What do you mean?' I said, 'That's what I was told: be careful, it might be someone I know.'*

Lucy's response was dramatic, Caroline recalls. 'She said, "I have to go to the toilet, I feel really sick." She almost dropped her pants immediately. "I'm gonna be sick, I'm gonna be sick."' Lucy had insisted on rushing back to her apartment in the compound. Later, Lucy told Caroline she'd had diarrhoea.

That night, the night before Lucy's arrest, she and Caroline had walked to work together and had coffee, laughing at Grant's Lochie girl jokes. Working different wards, they'd met for the midnight meal in the cafeteria. There, carrying their trays from the bain-marie to a table, they'd met Captain Asiri, hospital security chief. 'Hi, girls,' he'd said.

> *I said, 'Hi, Captain Asiri. How's things going? Hear any more news about anything?' — you know, keeping up a conversation. He said, 'Do you know of anyone that put a thumbprint next to the peephole in Yvonne's door?' I said, 'What? I don't know what you're talking about.' And we left. It was the oddest statement.*

It had been as if the captain were pushing for a reaction. Caroline and Lucy met again in the morning at shift's end. 'I said to Lucy as we were walking home, "I'll give you a call later on. Are you going home to sleep now?" She said, "Yes." So I get home. About 8 am I rang her, just to wish her a good sleep. She didn't answer her phone.' Caroline continued to ring every five minutes until a quarter to nine. 'I tried ringing Debbie as well. I went to bed.'

What Caroline couldn't know just then was that instead of going to bed, Lucy had gone into town with Debbie. As Caroline slept, her friends were being taken into custody. And now it was Caroline's turn.

> *About 11 I get a phone call [from Nancy Hasham, the nursing coordinator]. 'Caroline, you must come down to Captain Asiri's office immediately. They're sending a car to pick you up.' It sounded really urgent, so I got dressed in clothes you would never wear anywhere. I forgot my glasses. I get there. There's a man in a ghutra and thobe [the Arab robe and headdress] with a walkie-talkie.*

Captain Asiri ordered Caroline to sit. She needed to go to the toilet. After refusing at first, he relented when she insisted in her forceful, Australian way. 'I speak my mind. So, next minute I have a male police officer coming into the toilets with me. I'm thinking, "What's going on?"' On her return, she barraged the captain with questions; he eventually revealed she was to be taken to the police station. Caroline made a big fuss about going back to her room to get her glasses, but the police officer refused: 'Come on, come on, you're coming with me now.'

> *So I go off to the police station. The first thing I do is pull out my cigarettes. Sitting in this room with all these men around. Light one up. 'You can't smoke here.' I said, 'I'll smoke wherever I want, thank you very much.' You know, very determined Caroline. Dunhill Lights.*

As Caroline reaches for her cigarettes in her bag, she finds the glasses she thought she'd left in her room and starts laughing to herself at the fuss she'd caused back at the hospital. 'They must have thought I was off my head,' she says. 'I'm puffing away and next minute I'm taken into this room. An office. You've got chairs, a long red leather couch, books.' Later, her suspicion that Lucy and Debbie are in the adjacent offices is confirmed.

> *I had an inkling. The doors were closed. I knew something was going on. That's when the questions started. A young guy that's quite plumpish. He remembered me because I looked after a guy that shot some police officers down at Half Moon Bay. That was in the intensive care unit a couple of months before. He said he remembered me because I was very determined in my job. I'd said to him [when he wanted to question the wounded offender], 'You can't come in now, I'm doing this. You stand outside until I've finished my job.'*

Now, on his turf, it was the policeman's turn to be determined. 'I'm doing *my* job now, Caroline,' he said.

> *An hour into the interview, it was taking too long, so he told me to write my statement down. I had three interpreters in my room from the hospital. Bashir, Samir and Ali Showedi, the head. And I turned around to Ali Showedi — I didn't even know he worked at the hospital — and I said, 'Am I going home tonight?' He said, 'Yes, you're going home tonight.'*
>
> *I could trust Samir. In the sense that he isn't a Saudi. He's a teacher by trade. When they were doing my interpretation they wanted to get my Australian*

> *personality, so he could get the right Arabic tone in it. That's why I trusted him.*

Samir and the other interpreters struggled with Caroline's idiomatic English and Australianisms. 'I'd have to explain step by step,' she says. 'They were interested in every word. I'd say, "I'm really stoked", or "I went and grabbed my sunnies".'

Major Hamed, the fiendish figure described by Lucy in her report of police duress, also appeared during Caroline's interrogation. But she reports no mistreatment by him or any of the other officers. He said to her, 'We have to be not 100 per cent certain but a thousand per cent sure. You will not lie. If you lie, we will know.'

Caroline took the mickey out of the police. 'I said to Major Hamed, "I have a red bra and green undies on for Christmas. Do you want to have a look?"'

> *As the interview got longer, I knew there was something going on with Lucy and Debbie. Because of the questions that they asked me. The main questions that I had to concentrate on were what I had done from the time the murder happened to the time I was in the interview at the police station. And also what did I know of the relationship between Lucy and Debbie and Yvonne, and Lucy and Debbie in particular since the murder had happened.*
>
> *I said I couldn't tell them what the relationship was, because I never saw them as a threesome together. I said what Debbie's behaviour was like since the murder. I said what Lucy's behaviour was like. I said Debbie was away with the fairies. And they wanted to know the meaning of 'away with the fairies'. I said, 'How about "lost the plot"?' And I said, 'You know when you read a book and you don't know what's going on? That's how I found Debbie.' I also said Debbie was a very caring, kind woman. She was.*

The police told Caroline that they had watched for her safety as they followed her on her trips to town with Debbie and Lucy.

> *On the bottom of my statement [as translated into Arabic] I wrote, 'I do not speak Arabic, I do not write Arabic, I do not understand Arabic and I do not know if this is an*

actual true interpretation of what I have said.' I needed something to back me up.

I was treated extremely well. I was given water, I was given food, cigarettes. I was able to go to the toilet freely. I could stop the interview at any time. I was a bit overwhelmed, of course. There were at some stages up to ten people in the room. And people coming in, looking at you and walking out. I just thought if that was a Western place, that would happen to you as well. I had no mental abuse, no physical abuse, no psychological abuse. I was very scared, because inside you think, 'Oh, my God. Maybe I'm getting set up', because I'd already been interviewed twice during that week at the hospital. It was my first trip to the actual police station. I was scared and I had to go to the toilet quite a few times and had diarrhoea and I was constantly drinking a lot of water. But that was out of sheer nerves more than anything.

Some time during that day, Caroline heard Debbie in the adjacent office.

She was yelling. I don't know exactly what she was saying, but she was yelling. I heard her say, 'No, no, no.' I'm thinking, 'What's going on in there?'

One of the last questions I was asked was did I know about a lesbian relationship going on with any of them. I said, 'No, I didn't.'

This hadn't been mentioned during Caroline's two interrogations at the hospital. It suggests the police had only just concocted the lesbianism idea that night, or that they had just heard it in Lucy's confession, next door.

This was at the end of a long day, 13 hours in the police station. Caroline had been on night shift the previous night and had less than two hours' sleep before she was called in for questioning. She was exhausted.

I tried to see Lucy at the end of that. I really did. I wrote a note to Ali Showedi [the interpreter] to give to Lucy. I wrote, 'Keep smiling, keep your chin up. Just tell the truth and you'll be right.' And then what happened, as I was leaving, her door was open, so I pushed it open even more and walked in.

As she describes this, Caroline re-enacts her movement, pushing towards Lucy and calling her name, her determination apparent. She mimes a desperate, pathetic, reaching motion, Lucy calling back.

The look of horror on her face, of her trying to grab out to me, is the last image I have of Lucille McLauchlan. I cannot get that image of her out of my head. Pleading for me to help her. I couldn't touch her. I was taken out immediately and the door was closed. And I said, 'I'm not going anywhere until I see her again.' I said, 'Is Debbie OK?' Even though I didn't really care about Debbie; it was just out of humanness. I said, 'Tell Debbie I'm thinking of her.' I didn't want to leave without those two girls.

Some days later, back at the hospital, says Caroline, she saw one of the interpreters who had been at the police station that day. 'Samir told me that he heard Lucy's confession and she just confessed, no problem.'

Much later, Debbie's family will claim that Caroline, in an interview with British lawyer Michael Dark several days after her interrogation, was much more critical of the police. According to the family, Caroline had reported that the police were flicking her eyes during the interview. 'No, they never did that to my eyes,' she says now.

The family claims Caroline went to the British Trade Office in Al Khobar to report her own mistreatment and spoke to the British women's lawyer because she was suspicious of the Saudi police's motives. Caroline denies this.

What I was mainly concerned about was giving Michael Dark as much information as I told the police, so that Lucy and Debbie could have a fair trial. That's why I went and saw Michael Dark as soon as I could. But I had no one flicking my eyelids. I had no one pulling my hair. If someone flicked my eyes, I can tell you the Australian consul would know about it. I mean, I would be broadcasting that to the world. I've got a fairly strong personality. If what I know is true, I will back up my truth.

Back at the hospital, following her 13-hour interrogation, Caroline rings fellow Australian Rosemary Kidman. Rosemary is awake, though it's after midnight. She invites Caroline around, to hear her tale of the day. In the small bed-sit, with Purdy the cat sitting on Rosemary's pyjama-clad lap, Caroline recounts the hours of questioning. She says nothing of mistreatment. Rosemary and Caroline take photographs of each other, to record the moment, the end of a long week since the murder. Caroline looks tired, but fine; there's no hint of any police harassment.

Chapter 5

Confessions

Confession of our faults is the next thing to innocence.
— Publilius Syrus, *Moral Sayings (1st Century BC)*,
translated by Darius Lyman

Every violation of truth is not only a sort of suicide in the liar, but is a stab at the health of human society.
— Emerson, 'Prudence', *Essays: First Series* (1841)

A lie always needs a truth for a handle to it.
— Henry Ward Beecher,
Proverbs from Plymouth Pulpit (1887)

As Caroline and Rosemary relaxed, their friends, Deborah Parry and Lucille McLauchlan, lived the worst fear of their lives back at the Dhahran Police Station.

We know that Lucy is the strong one, Debbie the weaker. Right? So who confessed first? According to the document which records her shame, Lucy had confessed within twelve hours of her arrest; Debbie held out until the next day. This contrast was later to raise the secret ire of Deborah Parry's family. Today, both women would read the quotations above with anger, believing them to be assumptions of their guilt. But these moral jibes of the sages could equally be turned against the Saudi captors of the accused women, should the women's later claims of duress prove true.

The confessions of the two women, written in Arabic, signed in English, thumbprinted, countersigned and stamped, are exotically obscure. They hide the truth. They are, at best, an amalgam of the angry urgings of police investigators and the desperate compliances of weary, frightened prisoners. At worst, they are the lies of the women married to the lies of the Saudi police. You're going to have to make up your own mind, reading between the lines of cultural difference, of translation and retranslation, of the power imbalance of captor and prisoner.

[Translation]

>Thursday, 9/8/1417AH
>[that is, December 19, 1996] at 7.15 pm
>
>Confession
>
>I, Lucille McLauchlan, of British nationality, 31 years of age, holding passport No. D12659214 issued in Glasgow on 24/3/1994, a Christian, a sister at King Fahd Military Hospital of Dhahran, being fully competent hereby confess voluntarily as follows:
>
>On Wednesday 1/8/1417AH corresponding to 11 December 1996, at 1:00 o'clock after midnight, and while I was in my room, I received a telephone call from the deceased, Yvonne Gilford of Australian nationality, who lived in apartment No. 3A, building No. 44, King Fahd Military Hospital of Dhahran, who asked me to visit her in her apartment and informed me that the Deborah Parry 'Dibi', of British nationality was also there. It appeared to me that she was confused, and I told her that it was already late in the night. However, I noticed that she was irritated and, because of that, I left my building and went to her apartment in the neighbouring building. I knocked at her door and she opened the door for me. Dibi was there and they were discussing their lesbian relationship which was not as active as it had been. She told me that Dibi refused to leave Yvonne's apartment. They asked me to intervene and assist them in solving the problem. We sat and talked about the problem until it was 4.45 a.m. when both of them got upset.
>
>Consequently, Dibi took a metal kettle which was there on the kitchen table. There was no water in that kettle. She threw the kettle at Yvonne. The kettle fell at Yvonne's face. Yvonne was hurt and fell down. Dibi kicked her on the

face. While the victim was lying on the ground, Dibi once again entered the kitchen and fetched a kitchen knife of the type used for slicing bread. Meanwhile, Yvonne stood up and Dibi stabbed her on the chest whereupon Yvonne fell again on to the ground. Thereafter, Dibi sat on her and stabbed her several times on her neck and back; (before that and when they started to quarrel and before Yvonne was hit by the kettle, Yvonne pushed Dibi who fell on a green small table and consequently got hurt). Thereafter, Dibi took hold of a pillow which was lying at a short distance on the ground and put that pillow on Yvonne's face in order to prevent her from crying and that has caused her death. I have witnessed that event without doing anything. Thereafter, Dibi left the victim's body. I was terrified from what I saw and told Dibi that if Yvonne was able to talk to anybody we would be discovered. Dibi was relatively less irritated than me and said:

' Now we have to clean the place.'

She entered the kitchen and started washing the same knife which she used in the stabbing. Thereafter, she dried that knife and placed it either in a drawer in the kitchen or on the kitchen table. Then she entered the bathroom, collected a white towel and cleaned the blood on her hands. She also used the same towel in cleaning the knife and the metal kettle, which I placed on the cooker after I had tried to fix its broken arm. Then I took a wet piece of cloth, which was lying on the washing machine, and cleaned the blood on my left hand. Then, I threw that piece of cloth which fell near Yvonne's body. Thereafter, I and Dibi, went to my flat and cleaned the traces of blood which appeared on our clothes. I remained in my flat and Dibi went to her flat and each of us took a bath and washed our clothes in order to remove any traces of blood.

Two days later, Dibi informed me that she had in her possession Yvonne's automatic machine card and she knew the secret number assigned for that card. Dibi did not tell me how she came to know that secret number. She suggested to me to go and withdraw money from Yvonne's account. I told her that we might be discovered by the police. She said that was impossible. We actually went on three consecutive days and withdrew on each time

SR5,000. The first time and the second time, it was me who withdrew the money. Dibi withdrew on the third time. On the fourth time which was the last, I withdrew SR5,000, whereupon I was caught by the police while I was there at the bank. I had in my possession Yvonne's automatic teller machine card. Dibi informed me of the secret number of that card which is 4663. I remitted some of the amounts which we have obtained to my account in Britain and I sent part of it by mail to my mother in Britain.

The reasons for committing the crime is that Dibi loved Yvonne and did not want anybody else to share that love. I have not reported the crime because I was terrified, and I hereby sign this confession.

This odd four-page document is written in Lucy's plain hand, a readable print which leans slightly to the left, undersigned in her less intelligible script and countersigned by a host of men: Ali bin Jumah Al-Sowaid and Al-Bashir Ibrahim Hasabalah, both translators from the hospital, Abdullah Al-Ahmari, member of the Disciplinary Board, Ahmed Sulaiman Al-Amri, investigator, and Captain Saud M. Al-Toraigi. It was later signed by a judge at the court of Al Khobar when Lucy was brought before him to confirm the confession was hers.

The list is a small hint of the bewildering array of strangers who confronted Lucy during her interrogation. The language in the confession is surely nobody's. That is, nobody speaks or writes like that in their natural voice. Lucy's lively letters home reveal a voice that is informal, challenging; not the contrived nonsense of 'meanwhile', 'thereafter', 'consequently' and 'Dibi was relatively less irritated than me'. Months later, a host of legal and technical experts would examine this confession for signs of coercion. You can find them, if you look. Much of the document is clearly dictated. It's doubtful that Lucy would be capable of contriving such language even if she wanted. In Western jurisdictions the niceties of tape-recording, and even videotaping, of confessions have been introduced. Not so here in the Dhahran Police Station. Does any of this confession sound like the genuine revelations of a guilty woman? One thing stands out, especially in the light of reading Debbie and Lucy's later confessions. The blame is all on Debbie. She started the fight, she rained the blows down on Yvonne. Lucy was a non-participant bystander, guilty only by dint of inaction and silence. A minimalist confession. Later, that is to change.

But let's cut now to a couple of different voices: first, the voice of Lucille McLauchlan in May 1997. Then, she wrote a cover note to a long statement of her claims of confession under duress written by her fiancé, Grant Ferrie:

> This is a true account of how I was treated by the police and I told this to Grant Ferrie and to my parents when they came to see me in Dammam ... I was terrified of what the police would do to me and also I believed them when stated I would not be subject to Shariah law and that I would be sent back to the UK in 2–3 weeks. This is why I wrote what the police requested and told me to write, although it was completely untrue.

What follows, in the 'Precognition of Grant Ferrie (30) of Dundee', is indeed a harrowing account of Lucy's claims of what happened to her during the police interrogation. Lucy has signed all 47 pages.

> At the police station she was put into an office type interview room and they took her handbag away from her. At that time in that room there were six police officers present all male police officers in the room with her ... One of the police officers a Major Hamed starts speaking to her because he is able to speak better English than the rest and he tells her to take her abaya off which is the black robe that women wear in that country over their clothes. Once she had removed that she had her hands handcuffed behind her back. This Major Hamed kept leaving and re-entering the room. By this time it is about 9.30am and she asks why she is being detained and she is told by Major Hamed to shut up.
>
> Major Hamed sat beside her and put his hand on her thigh. He said to her 'I know you know who killed Yvonne and made her soul leave her body'. He then said 'We know Debbie told you it was her, she has told us this'. He then said to her 'How did you get Yvonne's credit card and when did you decide to take her money and why are you protecting Debbie'. Lucille replied, 'I don't know what you are talking about and Debbie did not kill Yvonne'. Hamed

replies, 'I know all about you'. He said that they had received a fax from back home, meaning Britain, telling them that Lucille is a thief and a harlot. By this time she is obviously very frightened and very concerned about what is going to happen to her. Then Hamed stands up behind her and pulls her hair so that her head tips right back and says to her 'Major Abdul Rachman thinks you're pretty and he is not as nice as me'. He says to her 'If I leave you alone with him he will lock the door so no one can help you'.

He let go of her hair and in front of her was Major Abdul Rachman touching his penis. It is obvious he has a hard on. By this time she is terrified of what is going to happen and Major Hamed leaves the room and comes back in with her handbag.

He takes out a bank credit card and a bundle of money and counts out 5,000 Saudi riyals. The card is Yvonne's. He tells Lucille to pick it up, however she refuses and because she refuses she gets a few slaps across the face and the back of the head. Because of this treatment she picks it up.

Hamed then says to her 'All we want is your co-operation'. He states, 'I know you didn't kill Yvonne but I want you to write a statement Debbie killed her and I helped steal the money'. Lucille refuses and says 'You can do what you want to me but I am not saying that'. Hamed replies, 'Yes you will or you will be sorry'. He says to her that if she co-operates she will be home in one or two weeks and will not go to jail. He sounded very convincing when he said this. Lucille again refused and said 'You can't make me'.

...By this time it was about 10.30am. She was then told to stand and not allowed to sit down and then told to remove her sandals.

...By this time she is desperate to go to the toilet and she informs them that if she doesn't go to the toilet she will probably wet herself and Hamed started laughing at this.

Lieutenant Khalid keeps coming up and asking her if she has ever had an Arab. He is very fat and had body odour and Lucille refused to answer him. He then started standing on her toes which was obviously very, very painful. She then asked for a lawyer and was informed that the 2 police are the lawyers in Saudi. She then asked to see someone from the British Embassy.

...Another one of the police officers, she doesn't know his name, kept poking her in the forehead which meant that the back of her head was banging against the wall behind. Because of what he is doing she is feeling nauseous and Hamed keeps pulling her hair and saying, 'You will co-operate'... They all kept saying to her 'Britain is trash and Islam rules'.

...By this time it is about mid-day and her legs are aching as she has not been allowed to sit down. The handcuffs which they have put on her are too tight and they are also hurting her.

...Hamed keeps going over again saying to her 'All you have to do is co-operate and you will be home in one or two weeks' and he keeps saying, 'No problem, no problem' when he says that. He told her the reason it wasn't a problem is that Yvonne is a Christian and wasn't a Muslim.

...Lucille was thinking to herself while this was going on and she couldn't understand why anything had happened to Yvonne because she was a nice person. However the police then started to talk about Yvonne and they described her as a lesbian, a money lender and a person who drank a lot.

Lucille was very surprised at all of these accusations as she didn't think that Yvonne was any of these things.

Hamed then started telling her that Debbie had been telling them lots of things. He then left the room and came back in a few minutes later and said 'Debbie has told me that she threw a kettle at Yvonne' and 'Debbie has told me that she punched Yvonne in the face' and then they said that Debbie had said she had stabbed Yvonne and they demonstrated where Yvonne had been stabbed. They then said that Debbie had placed a pillow over Yvonne's head after she had stabbed her in order to kill her as she was still alive.

...The police are so convincing that she is beginning to have doubts in her own mind about whether Debbie did do it or not. Hamed then says to her 'If you don't co-operate we will get evidence to say that you killed Yvonne'. Lucille says to him 'You don't have any evidence' and Hamed says to her 'I could put your things and your fingerprints anywhere I want. If you want to co-operate all you have to do is say you had Yvonne's bank card and that Debbie killed her'.

...At that stage she wasn't sure of the time but she thinks it was probably round about 2.00pm ... by this time she is begging to be allowed to go to the toilet. Her hands are swollen because of the handcuffs and her feet are swollen because of the fact that she has been standing all this time ... and then she did wet herself and she was wearing grey joggers and it was obvious that she had wet herself and Hamed and his colleagues thought it was hilarious and they all started laughing at her.

He then took the handcuffs off her and pulled her out of the room. She was marched past about twenty young police officers who were walking along the corridor. She was then put into the men's toilets and Hamed gave her her abaya robe and told her to take off her trousers and wash herself which she did.

She also had diarrhoea at this point ... a fat man came in and took away her pants and her joggers while she was washing her hands. He said to her 'Sister no problem I wash. You do what Hamed tells you to please. He is a big problem be good sister'.

...By this time all she is wearing under her abaya is her tee-shirt and she is terrified of what is going to happen to her ... we had decided there was no point in her remaining on the pill while she was working over there and she was terrified in case these police officers might rape her and she would end up pregnant.

Hamed then took her back to the interview room ... He then tells her to take her abaya off again and she refused to do this. He slapped her three or four times and then went behind her back and twisted her arm up behind her back.

...Lucille was scared that he was going to break her arms so she agrees to take off her abaya and she is left wearing nothing but her tee-shirt and she is then put in a chair with her hands handcuffed behind her back.

By this time Major Hamed, Major Abdul Rachman and Lieutenant Khalid are all around her and then another police officer with two stars on his shoulders kneels in front of her and opens her legs. Hamed then says to her 'Do you want to start writing or does the first lieutenant take his trousers off'. Lucille could tell from the attitude of the Lieutenant that he was itching to do something to her and had actually started to take his trousers off.

There were two other police officers apart from the ones I have already mentioned in the room and they started cheering. Either Hamed or the first lieutenant lifted her tee-shirt up and started making comments about her white marks which is obviously where she hadn't been burned by the sun and he had his hands on the inside of her thighs.

Hamed was actually touching her breasts while the lieutenant did this. Lucille then said 'If you stop touching me and let me put my abaya on I'll write whatever you want'.

Lucy claims she was then allowed to put her *abaya* back on, the handcuffs were taken off, and she was given a bottle of water and a packet of cigarettes. Retching now, she was taken to the toilet again and had more diarrhoea.

Hamed then supplied her with a writing pad and paper which had dates and times on it, which are the times that Lucille and Debbie are alleged to have used Yvonne's credit card to obtain money. Hamed then said to her, 'I will tell you what to write', and that once she had written it he would check it and if it was all right they would write it in a blue book. He then said to her, 'If you cooperate and be a good girl then no one will touch you or fuck you.'

The confession we've already seen followed. Is this tale of extreme coercion true? Only Lucy attests to this police behaviour towards her. Three interpreters who were in the room with her at various times during that long day report no such brutality. But there is another voice, the voice of the woman who may have supplied the times on Hamed's list of when the card was used. The voice of Caroline Ionescu is an authentic one, unmediated by police wanting a quick and tidy result or by translators struggling with the alien idiom of police syntax. Not cleaned up by a lawyer in Scotland wanting the best for his client. Caroline, who was interrogated in the office next to that where Lucy sweated, heard nothing from Lucy's room. She did hear Debbie, calling out in the room next door on the other side. Most of it was unintelligible, something like 'No, no.' Was this a woman responding to threats or merely strongly disagreeing with suggestions police were putting to her? Caroline couldn't be sure.

While the account she gave Grant Ferrie is the fullest, Lucy also wrote her own retraction, five months later, denying her confessions and describing the police mistreatment. She says she was approached at the Arab National Bank at around 8.30 am by three men in *ghutras* and *thobes* and a man in trousers and a jacket. When she was taken to the police station she was confronted by six policemen: 'Major Hamed, Major Abdulrahman, Lieutenant Khalid, a young lieutenant, Colonel Zharani, another policeman — he was small and fat.'

Lucy gives a similar version to what she told Grant, though some of the detail is more graphic:

> Hamed told me that I had Yvonne's bankcard and showed me my handbag which had been taken off me outside the bank. He took a green bankcard out of my handbag and 5000 SR. He told me I was a thief and a harlot and he knew all about me.
> ...They stamp on my feet every 10–15 minutes. Hamed and another policeman feel and poke my breasts ... Colonel Zahrani puts his hand between my legs and laughs when I start crying. One of the policemen has a plastic spatula type thing. He uses it to kill flies. He hit me on my arms and the top of my legs with it until I stop crying ... my feet are stamped on, my breasts and private parts are felt so I stop crying ... one of the policemen kneels between my legs and states via Hamed he wants me to give him oral sex. I have had enough as I am 100% positive I am very close to being raped. I agree to write a statement.

And so she does. After making her first confession that night, Lucy is taken before a judge who asks her, through an interpreter, if her confession is true. She agrees it is. But in her retraction, Lucy claims she has done this because of the threats of Major Hamed:

> I am warned very BLUNTLY if I say anything to the judge in court I will be taken back to Dhahran Police Station and the treatment will be 100 times worse than before. Hamed also tells me the judge will not believe me anyway as the police and the courts are one. I do as he asks at court.

According to Lucy's retraction, her mistreatment continues:

> I am taken to Dammam Prison. It is now approximately 0130 on 20th December 1996. I have been awake for 32 hours. The investigation continues until 25th December 1996. I am taken to the police station every day at approximately 0800 until approximate 1200 midnight. I am slapped and sexually abused repeatedly every day. Never when the interpreters are present ...
>
> This is why I did not tell the court at the time of the investigation my statements was [sic] lies. I am telling the truth now. Please do not punish me for being afraid.

What about Debbie? Apparently, she hadn't confessed until after Lucy. In her own retraction, written months after, she also describes serious mistreatment on that long day of their arrest:

> Approached in Al-Shola mall by a man in a thobe and told to come with him; taken outside and bundled into a white car; very, very frightened at this point as no explanation was given to me and told to 'shut-up' ... Taken to Dhahran Police Station and taken into an office where there were 4–6 policemen. I did not know where Lucy was ...
>
> I was informed that I had killed Yvonne and they said that they knew I was having a lesbian relationship with her and that I was a very bad person. I was sobbing with fear at this point as I had not killed anyone and Yvonne was my friend and colleague. They kept on telling me to 'shut-up' and that I was 'British trash' and was a killer.

The abuse that follows in Debbie's description is very similar to the account in Lucy's retraction:

> Major Hamed kept on coming in and out of the room and pulling my hair and slapping my face ... I was told to remove my abaya at this point and the police continually touched my breasts and private parts. One of the policemen whilst kneeling in front of me with his hands on my thighs ... was licking his lips and asking me 'Who initiated the sex with you and your girlfriend, Yvonne?' I kept on saying that I was not a lesbian and had boyfriends;

they said 'No, you son of a bitch, you are a killer and used
to lick Yvonne until you killed her'. All this time they were
rubbing my thighs; I thought that I would be raped by them
all; I was so, so frightened as they undid some of my skirt
and touched my skin on my legs; I was so very frightened.

Some of Debbie's account is quite odd and seemingly unrelated to her history:

The police were laughing at me and saying you are a
British trash you have killed other people; we know from
Interpol; we have details here that you have tried to kill
patients by doing many bad things; you are a bad person.
You killed a lady last time you were here under a different
name.

Debbie describes being beaten on the throat, being refused water and the toilet, and having requests for lawyers and the British embassy denied.

For a long period of time I heard policemen shouting and
a lady crying. I did not know if this was Lucy at this point.
Later that night I realised that it had been her all the time.

Debbie says that she, too, was in fear of being raped or killed. And that, like Lucy, she was promised she would be home in two weeks if she confessed.

Several times a policeman held a cigarette close to my
eyes and I could feel the heat, it was unbearable.

After about 12 hours, Debbie says, she was

...told to remove my clothes or they would do it for me. I
removed them myself and they all surrounded me. One
knelt down with his head just between my knees and
removed some pubic hair with scissors. They said if I
move they would cut me. I think I was left undressed for
approximately one hour but I am not sure. During this time
my breasts were poked, fondled and pulled which caused
great pain and touched my private parts [sic].

> I still would not write as they asked me to and so they made me stand against a wall with my hands behind my back and Lucy walked into the room and said 'Debbie stabbed Yvonne in the neck, back and chest'.

This assertion later angered Debbie's family. They felt that Lucy had pushed Debbie into her own eventual confession.

> At this point I could see that Lucy had no trousers on as her abaya was open at the bottom. She was then taken out again and I then realised that it had been her that I heard crying ... At approximately 0130 hours I was pushed into a police car and taken to Dammam Central Prison ... Put into solitary cell with running water and with a padlock on the door.

Guilty or innocent, Debbie's fear at this stage can barely be imagined. Yet, she hadn't yet confessed. Only when she is returned to Dhahran Police Station at eight the next morning does she relent:

> I cannot take any more so I agree to write whatever the police wanted me to even though it was all lies. Prior to cooperating I was constantly pushed against a wall and pull [sic] forward with a hard tug using my headscarf. This was also continually flicked in my face. My feet were also stamped on by two policemen.
> I continued to cooperate until the investigation was completed on December 25 1996.
> Please remember I was alone, very, very frightened and desperate to go home to my family.

Debbie made two confessions, which differ on some points, particularly the extent of Lucille's involvement. The first, undated, is written in capitals, with her thumbprint on each page. While her writing is plain, the signature, 'Deborah Kim Parry', is more elaborate, with flourishes in the D and the P.

> I went to Yvonne's apartment as I had been having a lesbian relationship with her since not long after arriving at the hospital and saw her every day. We talked and watched television for a while until I went to my room to

change into my black jeans and pink T-shirt. I washed and showered whilst there and also washed my hair and fed the cat. When I went back to Yvonne Gilford's room she told me that Lucille McLauchlan had visited earlier. Yvonne and I sat and talked again until she told me that she wanted to end our relationship, as she had found someone else. I was upset and cried for a long time, eventually Yvonne rang Lucille McLauchlan in her room as she did not know what to do. Yvonne let Lucy in the door of her apartment, this was at 1a.m. in the morning. We talked for a long time amongst ourselves, and then the argument became out of control. Yvonne Gilford became aggressive and Lucille hit her in the face. I was pushed over a small table by Yvonne Gilford, I bruised my buttocks. I then stood up and took a kettle from the stove and threw it, it broke, as it had hit Yvonne on the head. She was dazed, but very angry, as was everyone. I took a bread knife from the kitchen draw [sic]. It had a serrated edge and stabbed Yvonne, as to what I thought was only three times, I was not aware of any more. They were to her chest, neck and back. Lucille and I were panic stricken at this stage, as Yvonne was hurt, but still alive, Lucille McLauchlan took a pink, floral cushion and pressed it onto Yvonne Gilford's face until she stopped breathing, she was lying half on her back and half on her side at this stage. We were surprised that security had not heard any noise from inside of Yvonne's apartment at this time as it is very quiet in the compound in the early hours of the morning. It must have been approximately 0400 hrs in the morning by this time. I was surprised to have hardly any blood on my clothes. I had a cut on my left hand at this point, which Dr Daoud later commented on at work. In the apartment the knife was washed and returned to the draw [sic]. It was dried on a white towel from the bathroom by one of us. I was not sure if Lucille had also been involved in a lesbian relationship with Yvonne Gilford of Building 44, although she had a boyfriend in England, but that does not mean anything. The broken kettle was wiped also using the white bathroom towel, it may have been a hospital towel and returned to the bathroom. The small table was picked up by Lucille after she had suffocated Yvonne with the cushion, either pink or floral. I returned the silk flowers to the television set, which was on the video that Yvonne had recently bought. The coffee cups, tea cups and cutlery that we had used that evening were washed by us and placed in the appropriate cupboards and draws [sic]. We left Yvonne Gilford's room, that is myself and Lucille McLauchlan at around about 0500 hours in the morning. We both had abayas on at this time. It was cool outside and we often wore abayas on the compound. Before leaving the room the telephone was disconnected from the wall and Lucille McLauchlan took Yvonne Gilford's bank card and person number (pin number) from her wallet which was on a cabinet between the lounge and kitchen. It was a wooden cabinet. Lucille looked through the peep-hole in the door at this time to make sure that no one was around. We were very, very frightened at this point as it was all an accident. We momentarily spoke in Lucille McLauchlan's room until approximately ten past five in the morning. We discussed the awful accident. I returned to my room as I was on duty at 0700 hrs in the morning and had to wash my clothes and have a shower and hair wash before leaving. The next few evenings were either spent talking to Lucille McLauchlan or on night duty. My cut on my left hand was very painful and my left buttock was bruised. On the evening of the 16th of December, 1996, Lucille McLauchlan had gone into the bank in Khobar and drawn out money. She gave some to me. We both went to Al Rashid shopping mall on the evening of the 17th December, 1996, I think it was and drew more out. This was a Tuesday evening. We shopped and ate there. I bought sewing materials and a new watch as did Lucille McLauchlan. I also bought two new rings and a new red and white nightshirt. I collected photographs for one of my friends here. Caroline left us when we went to the bank machine. We went home by limousine. We then again went to Khobar, Shola Mall, on the morning of the 19th December, 1996, which was a Thursday and once again drew out money from the machine. I bought items for my cat in the pet shop. In total Lucille had eight thousand Saudi Riyals and I had seven thousand Saudi Riyals. I bought several material items with this. I bought a new continental quilt set, one for my room and one for use if I went to the people I am friendly with. I bought many small things, such as a rug for my room and some new French underwear that I bought at Al Rashid Mall. The most money went on the underwear as this cost six hundred and ninety Saudi Riyals and a gold chain and palm tree which I bought also at Al Shola Shopping Mall on the first occasion. I do not know what Lucille McLauchlan did with her money. On one occasion I changed my own salary at the bank with Caroline and Lucille having had coffee at the Vienna Coffee Shop in Khobar. I telexed approximately two thousand Saudi Riyals to the National Westminster Bank in Alton in Hampshire, England. I have the rest of my salary in my handbag at the police station. On several of these occasions Lucille McLauchlan and I parted to do our own shopping. On the morning of the 20th December [she means the 19th], 1996, Lucille McLauchlan went to the bank machine and I went into Al Shola Shopping Mall. This is where I was arrested in the north part of the mall and escorted to the police station in Dhahran by an ununiformed policeman ...

What can we say about this account? The shopping trips generally accord with Caroline Ionescu's recollection. But then the police had interviewed Caroline for many hours. If they were forcing Debbie to write a false confession, they could have used Caroline's timeline as a guide. The most striking point is where Debbie's confession differs from Lucy's, implicating Lucy in the suffocation of Yvonne. Lucy's original confession had laid all the blame on Debbie.

In Grant Ferrie's 'Precognition' recording Lucy's claims of police abuse, he describes Lucy being taken back to the Dhahran Police Station on Saturday, December 21:

Hamed then crouches down in front of her and pats her knees and says there is a little problem. He says that he now wants her to say that she helped kill Yvonne with Debbie. Lucille asks why he wants this and he tells her it is because people say Yvonne was strong and if a female killed Yvonne then there must have been two of them.

According to Grant, Lucy refuses and Hamed threatens her again: 'I can hurt you if you don't co-operate.'

> Hamed then takes the pants that she was wearing the first time she was in the interview room out of a drawer and puts them on the desk. He then says to Lucille, 'first of all we are going to Yvonne's apartment' ... She is then taken back to the hospital and taken to Yvonne's apartment. She has to stand pointing at a kettle while she has her photograph taken and then standing pointing at a bread knife and having her photograph taken again. She was also made to touch the knife.
>
> She notices that there is blood all over the carpet and the place has a smell of death.

Back at the police station,

> Hamed now tells her that Debbie has said that she stabbed Yvonne and that Lucille suffocated her and stole her bank card and they split the money.

At first, Lucy refuses to write a statement saying that she has suffocated Yvonne.

> The first lieutenant whose name she doesn't know hits her across the back of the head and she falls over. She then gets up onto her knees and he stands in front of her and unzips his trousers. He has an erection and she closes her eyes and says to Hamed, 'Okay, okay'.

According to what Lucy has told Grant, as he writes in his 'Precognition', the next two days are spent in rewriting drafts of the confession, with physical and emotional abuse continuing. On the Sunday,

> Hamed tells her that Debbie is being stubborn and Lucille says to him, 'You told me that she had confessed'. He says 'Debbie is blaming you for everything'.

Lucy writes again, with Hamed supervising.
Not all of these many versions of Lucy's confession have

survived, but it is clear that she was told to make additions to her original confession:

> The first stab — Yvonne was standing facing Debbie as she came out of the kitchen. Debbie came towards Yvonne and stabbed her under her left breast. Yvonne fell to the ground. Debbie sat on top of Yvonne and stabbed her in the neck then on her right upper back. This is [sic] the stabs I actually saw. After Yvonne was dead Debbie and myself cleaned the bread knife used to kill Yvonne. Debbie did this and dried it with a white towel. The kettle was wiped with the white towel. I picked up the broken green table and put it between the two tables in Yvonne's room. I cannot remember cleaning any other area of Yvonne's apartment.

That addendum is signed and thumbprinted and then, as if the police have had an afterthought, for good measure:

> I Lucille McLauchlan would like to state that I was a partner by suffocating her with the pillow on the morning of December 12th, 1996, which caused Yvonne's death. I am truly sorry for my actions and the part I played in this murder. I sign for what I have just written.

In yet another version of her confession, Lucy says that her own relationship with Yvonne was 'mother/daughter' rather than lesbian. She writes of Debbie refusing to leave Yvonne's apartment.

> Yvonne at this time very frankly told Debbie that the relationship was over and that she wanted her to leave her apartment and not come back. At this point Debbie went berserk. She was very angry. Also I must state at this point that Debbie had been since I arrived in Yvonne's apartment acting strange. I mean by this she appeared to be on some kind of medication. I do not know if this is true or not. Debbie went into Yvonne's kitchen and picked up the kettle which was sitting on the stove and threw it at Yvonne. It hit Yvonne on the forehead. Yvonne fell to the ground at this point. I picked her up and she seemed dazed. I slapped her twice on the face to see if she was

conscious which she appeared to be at this time. I was screaming to Debbie that I would call security if she did not leave the apartment now.

Then she describes her own panic as Debbie stabs Yvonne, she's not sure how many times. Yvonne

> ...was still making noises from her mouth. I placed a pillow over her face to stop her making a noise. If security had come at this point to Yvonne's apartment I honestly believed they would think that I had stabbed Yvonne. I held the pillow over Yvonne's face until she stoped making a noise. I would like to state at this point that the pillow was actually a cushion...

In this version, Lucy describes Debbie as being very calm as she cleans up. Then they both take Yvonne's wallet and remove the bank card.

> We memorised her P.I.N. number which was 4663 with the intention of removing money from Yvonne's bank account.

They go to Lucy's apartment, Debbie stays for a couple of minutes. It's now around 5.10 am.

> I took off my pyjamas and my abaya and put it in the washing machine. I went to my apartment and had a shower. I put my t-shirt and my sweat pants on. I then made coffee and just sat in my room.

As if prompted by Hamed, Lucy writes in the margin:

> I must add I held the cushion over Yvonne's face until she was suffocated.

In her original confession, Lucy had claimed it was 'Dibi' who had used the pillow to suffocate Yvonne. Not much solidarity there. And, remember, according to Debbie in her retraction, it was Lucy who first cracked, walking into the room where Debbie was being interrogated at the police station and saying, 'Debbie stabbed Yvonne in the neck, back and chest.'

Lucy's description of the knife in this confession differs little from that described in the medical report:

> ...a brown handle 13 cms in length ... fixed to a white metal blade with a sharp edge and 19 cms in length. The widest part of the blade is the one fixed to the handle and is 3.6 cms wide. The width gradually decreases to form a sharp point.

Lucy's description is of

> ...a bread knife. The handle was brown approx 5cm long. The blade was silver in colour and about 20cm long. It was approx 3cm wide from the handle but narrowed to the tip to a point.

It's not hard to believe that she is quoting a policeman who is quoting the medical report.

Lucy told Grant that now Hamed had a problem

> ...because Lucille's statement is thirteen pages long and Debbie's is only three. She is then taken into the room where Debbie is and she has to read her statement to Debbie. Debbie is totally distraught and she can hardly write and Debbie has to write down what Lucille is saying so that the statements are the same. Debbie is very upset and Lucille tells her 'Look let's just get it finished and we'll get out of here.'

By the time Debbie makes her confession on Monday, December 23, she too is stabbing her friend in the back, so to speak, now accusing Lucy of stabbing, as well as suffocating, Yvonne.

> ...at 2:00a.m. Yvonne telephoned Lucille McLauchlan and requested her to come to a room. I was with her at that time. Yvonne requested me to have lesbian relationship with her. I refused her request. When Lucille came to us I was crying because of the request of Yvonne to have lesbian relationship with me. As a result of my refusal Yvonne was nervous. Lucille tried to cool down the situation. But Yvonne also requested Lucille to have lesbian relationship with her.

Lucille also refused her proposal. Lucille slapped Yvonne on her face. Yvonne fell on a small green table which was in the room and as a result thereof the table was broken. Yvonne got up and pushed me away and as a result thereof my back collided against the chair ... meanwhile, all of us were shouting. I took a metal jug from the table and threw it towards Yvonne. The jug hit the left side of her head. Yvonne fell as a result of the hit. She got up and went to the kitchen and brought a knife [the bread knife] from the drawer of the kitchen. A fight took place. Yvonne was brutally excited and she was trying to stab us with the knife. I pushed her towards her bed she fell on the bed [sic]. When she fell on the bed she was injured by the knife. She got up again and tried to stab us by the knife. Again she fell and injured herself by the knife in her thigh. Lucille and myself tried to push Yvonne towards the bed. At that time I was slightly injured in my left hand by the knife which was in the hand of Yvonne. Also Lucille was injured in her right thigh by the knife which was in the hand of Yvonne. When we pushed her again towards the bed the knife fell from her hand. Lucille took the knife and stabbed Yvonne on her back. Also I took the knife and stabbed Yvonne. I cannot remember the number of stabs. This happened within a short time. We were very confused and scared. All this happened while we were trying to defend ourselves from Yvonne. As a result of the fighting and hitting there was blood on the ground and the bed. Some of the flowers fell on the ground. We requested Yvonne to stop her acts. Time was late when she died. I tried to make sure that she was still alive. So, in order to check the pulse of her heart I put my finger on her neck. There was no pulse. Lucille and myself laid her on the ground in order to help her but we could not do anything because she was already dead. While we were cleaning the room and the bed, a small pillow fell on the face of Yvonne. We did not use that pillow to smother her. After that I picked up the knife and washed the blood. Lucille dried the knife with a piece of cloth. Lucille put the knife in the drawer of the kitchen. The knife was of a brown handle. We placed the flowers back on the TV. Using the kitchen washer we washed the blood off our hands ... We arranged the bed ... We quickly departed to my room. We,

> Lucille and myself sat together speaking for approximately one hour in my room, say up to 3:00 or 3:30a.m. I prepared myself to go to work in the morning. Lucille was free and therefore she washed my clothes and her clothes ... I was dressed in ... black jeans trousers and purple tee shirt ... The motive behind the quarrel and fighting [which] caused the death of Yvonne was her request to have lesbian relationship with me and Lucille. I no [know] nothing about the banking card of the deceased. What I know is that you told me that you have found the card with Lucille using the same in one of the bank's teller [sic] in Al-Khobar.

The glaring inconsistencies in these various versions would make great grist for a cross-examiner's mill. Is it all a fabrication of the police? Was it Yvonne who committed the first act of violence, or Debbie? Did Lucy stab Yvonne or not? Did she use the cushion/pillow on Debbie, or, as Debbie says, did it just fall on Yvonne? Was Debbie really unaware that Lucy had the bank card? The handwritten confession Debbie made is not too far from her own style, particularly the way she writes 'very, very painful' and 'very, very frightened' for emphasis. The printed versions of the confessions of both women read as what they probably are: the stilted wording dictated by police, written in English by the women, translated into Arabic and then back into English.

No Western court would be happy with these confessions. A judge in Britain or Australia would not allow a jury to convict on the strength of them, without corroborating evidence. But to the Islamic courts of Saudi Arabia, a confession is everything.

On Christmas Eve, the two women are taken before the *Sharia* court in Al Khobar to confirm their confessions. According to Grant Ferrie's 'Precognition':

> ...there are two judges there this time. One is the same judge as before and the other is an important looking man and there is a younger man with them. They ask her if her statement is true and she says it is ... They are taken into the court at different times from each other and they both do as they have been told to do and at 1.00pm approximately they are taken back to Dhahran Police Station where she has a very brief meeting with Lawson Ross from the British Embassy.

This is the women's first contact with the outside world for five days. That afternoon, the police tell them again that if they stick to the story of how they killed Yvonne they will be home in a couple of weeks.

Lucy and Debbie twice went before *Sharia* judges in the days after their arrest and confirmed their confessions. To this day, this fact has obscured the existence or lack of forensic and other evidence which might convince a Western court. While the police letters suggest the crime scene was wiped clean, it would seem inconceivable that a crime of such frenzy would not result in damning, if microscopic, scientific clues. Yet, even as it accepted the flawed confessions, the *Sharia* court never deigned to release information on what other evidence was available to it, be it scientific or even the statements of witnesses to the behaviour of the accused before and after the murder.

On Christmas Day, both women are taken back to the hospital for a videotape session. Several staff recognise them in the carpark. A couple of friends call out good wishes. One woman screams abuse.

In Yvonne's room, the women are made to hold a knife and a kettle and 're-enact' the crime. In Lucy's account to Grant, she says she and Debbie are very upset by this and that Hamed tells them if they don't cooperate in making the video they will be put in the men's section of the prison. Debbie later told her family that the re-enactment seemed so ludicrous they descended into giggles. The tape never surfaced in court and has certainly not been released publicly.

On December 28, Lucille and Deborah are taken to Dammam Central Police Station, where they meet Tim Lamb from the British embassy. As Lucy later told Grant, Lamb informs them that they

> ...are in big trouble and they will not be allowed home soon. Lucille looks at Hamed and asks him why he lied and he just smiles at her. She tells Tim that the whole story is lies and retracts the confession that she has made... Debbie also tells Tim the same...

When we visited Dammam Central Police Station for the Channel Seven *Witness* program six months after the confessions were made, Major Hamed denied the claims of intimidation.

The police had their own video crew filming us as we interviewed Hamed, who sat nervously swivelling in his chair. Was his nervousness due to having to speak in unaccustomed English, to having to perform for his superiors and the half-dozen other police gathered in the room, or to his simply being unused to having his actions questioned? Who knows? He would not comment on the investigation, confining himself to bland defences of the Saudi system: 'We think ours better than trials in any other country in the world.' He didn't look like a nasty, nurse-beating and terrorising hard-nosed cop. But then I wasn't alone, naked and at his mercy.

Chapter 6

Frank

Word of the murder came through the press for most of us, trickling out in the days before Christmas 1996. The details were obscure.

Frank Gilford, Yvonne's brother, heard at the same time as the rest of us. He was resting from the weekly routine of his busy courier service on Sunday, December 14, when an Australian Broadcasting Corporation journalist called to get his response. The ABC had heard the news from one of Rosemary Kidman's daughters in Sydney. Rosemary had rung her daughters to make sure the Australian Department of Foreign Affairs and Trade and the media knew of Yvonne's death. She had been worried it would be hushed up, like the 1995 murder of a Filipina nurse at the hospital.

The ABC's Sunday morning report was soon flashing around the world, through a network of Yvonne's friends. In Johannesburg, Sue Taylor was woken at 5 am by Penny, another of Yvonne's close friends and the mother of two of the children Yvonne had 'adopted' in South Africa. Sue remembers screaming, 'No, no, no!', waking her husband and 10-year-old son. Young Matthew wandered in, frightened to hear his pragmatic mother so upset. 'Aunty's been killed.' A quiet boy, Matthew withdrew into his shell. Yvonne had always treated him as if he were *her* son too. Sue got through to the hospital in Saudi and spoke to an American who confirmed the dreadful news. Sue couldn't believe it. By coincidence, on the same weekend, the doctor who ran the recruitment agency which sent Yvonne to Saudi had been murdered in a Johannesburg home break-in. To Sue, the world suddenly seemed out of control, full of violence.

The Australian Department of Foreign Affairs and Trade, which had known of Yvonne's murder for two days by then, announced that it 'regretted the delay' in informing her family, but claimed it had had trouble contacting Frank Gilford. Frank told his 84-year-old mother, Muriel, on the Sunday night. Monday's papers ran the story on page one. *The Sydney Morning Herald* reported that

> An Australian official from the Australian consulate in Riyadh, Saudi Arabia, has travelled to Saudi Arabia to assist in finding out the details of the murder of Australian nurse Yvonne Gilford, who was reportedly suffocated, stabbed and bashed with a hammer at the King Fahd Military Hospital.

The Age, of Melbourne, spoke to Frank, who 'described his sister as a bright and bubbly person who knew the risks involved with her posting'. What risks? This was the first hint of the alarmist obscurantism of so much of the reporting that was to follow. The dangerous mystery of the Orient.

On December 14, the Saudis announced their 65th execution for the year: a Saudi national, for the murder of his wife. Could this be the alleged risk of living in the Kingdom of Saudi Arabia? Surely the peculiarly oriental risk of the sword was for the murderers, not the victim, who lived a rather ordinary life in the rather humdrum routine of a hospital compound. On December 15, two more men faced public beheading in the kingdom, this time an Egyptian for murder and a Pakistani for drug smuggling. Such announcements by the Interior Ministry are routine:

> With God's help, Gholam Murtada Haji Ahmed Baksh, a Pakistani national, was arrested when he tried to smuggle narcotic tablets into the Kingdom inside his stomach. Following investigations, he was indicted with his crime. He was arraigned before a court which convicted him of smuggling narcotics and sentenced him to death as a punishment. The sentence was upheld by the Appeal Court and the High Judiciary Council. A Royal decree was issued to carry out the court's religious sentence. Gholam Murtada Haji Ahmed Baksh was beheaded in Jeddah today.

The crucial sentence concerns the Royal decree and the religious sentence, signifying the special nature of law and punishment in Saudi Arabia. The king has ultimate power, but only as sanctioned by Islam and its *Sharia* courts. As news of the identity and nationality of the accused in Yvonne's murder got out, journalists in Britain and Australia began to see the elements of a good story. Executions, religious law — exotic and dangerous.

On December 18, *The Guardian* in London reported that Saudi Arabia was

> ...preventing at least 20 Britons from leaving the country because of an investigation into the murder of an Australian nurse at a Dhahran hospital. The Britons, along with some 40 other Westerners, including Canadians, Australians and Americans, are being denied their passports by the authorities, sources at the King Fahd military hospital said last night. Many have been questioned by Saudi police.
>
> 'What concerns us is that we are being held against our will,' complained one British employee who missed a flight home on Monday. 'They are refusing to release our passports. The chances of getting on another flight before Christmas are nil.'
>
> A Filipina nurse was stabbed to death in 1994 but that case was never solved.
>
> Saudi Arabia is sensitive about dealing with Western expatriates because of the strict application of Islamic law. Relations with Britain were scarred in the late 1970s over the case of Helen Smith, a British nurse who was killed during a party in Jeddah.

On Friday, December 20, another Saudi was beheaded, in Riyadh, for murder — the 68th execution for the year. That routine death highlighted the stakes when, two days before Christmas, the British Foreign Office made the following announcement:

> We have been informed by the Saudi authorities that two female British citizens are being detained by the Saudi police who are investigating the murder of an Australian nurse.

The Mirror reported that a

> ...Foreign Office spokesman last night said it had informed relatives of the two nurses but refused to name them.

Now all the elements of a great news story were in place: Britons wronged by strange Saudi system.

Dundee, perched on the Firth of Tay in Scotland, was wintry cold when the deeply phlegmatic Stan McLauchlan took the call from the Foreign Office. A doughty union official, he was rocked by the news of the arrest of his much-loved daughter, Lucille. Ann McLauchlan, more openly emotional than her husband, was quick to tears.

In the English country township of Alton, Hampshire, bad news was no stranger on the home phone of the Ashbee family. Deborah Parry's sister Sandra Ashbee had buried her first husband, her brother, her mother and father in quick succession. Now her one sister was in big trouble. Jonathan Ashbee, Sandra's bearded and earnestly careful husband, slipped quickly into the role of the family's father–protector, seeking to comfort his inconsolable wife. Their four children, deeply attached to their Auntie Debbie, knew something was wrong; they weren't told what.

By now, Yvonne had become 'the last of the Florence Nightingales' in the press, after she was thus described by an old friend in South Africa. The identities of the two accused nurses were still secret, though the British press was making much of the fact that they had been locked up for Christmas. The Foreign Office and the women's families kept mum, but then, on Christmas Eve, *The Times* in London reported:

> One of the women was last night identified by sources at the King Fahd Military Medical Complex in Dhahran as Deborah Parry. She is thought to be 36 and to have family in the Midlands. The other nurse, also single and in her 30s, was named by the same sources as Lucy or Lucille Mclaughlin [sic] from Scotland.

The same report carried the key facts:

> Under Sharia — strict Islamic law — the women could face execution by beheading if convicted. Clemency is in the hands of the bereaved family: a murderer is spared only when they indicate a willingness to forgive, usually after the payment of compensation.

And:

Human rights organisations expressed concern over the women's treatment. Amnesty International said: 'Torture is frequently used by the Saudi authorities to extract confessions and the nurses might face months on remand before coming to trial.'

Frank Gilford's first response to the news that 'clemency is in the hands of the bereaved family' is low-key: 'We've still got that vacant empty feeling after Yvonne's death. It's still hard to believe,' he told the Sydney *Daily Telegraph* that Christmas Eve. 'He said he had no strong feelings on whether Yvonne's killers should be beheaded,' the paper reported. 'You have got to abide by the laws of the country you are in, but even if the killers spend the rest of their lives in a Saudi prison that would be a just result,' were Frank's words.

In Britain, the first rumblings of outrage over Lucy and Debbie's arrest were being heard. On Christmas Day the Sydney *Daily Telegraph* quoted the director of the human rights organisation Fair Trials Abroad, Stephen Jakobi:

> When British people go to work in Saudi Arabia, they are in effect signing away their liberties in return for a large salary.
> Saudi Arabia is one of those countries for which international treaty protection does not run. This is in keeping with the Saudis' contempt of [sic] foreigners' rights.

Christmas Day in Dundee was a miserable affair. Stan and Ann McLauchlan's grandchildren couldn't play outside their father's home in Broughty Ferry with their new bikes. The place was crawling with media. The family knew little about Lucy's fate, although that same day in Dammam, her thoughts were with them. *The Scotsman* later published her Christmas Day letter from gaol:

> Me and Deb are maybe going to have to say things which are not accurate to get out of here. Please remember this ... Jail is bearable. All female even the warden. Me and Deb are together so we're not alone. I'm devastated and afraid but honestly I'm OK.

The news that Christmas wasn't good. *The Herald* of Scotland was able to shout on page one: 'WE WON'T SAVE KILLERS FROM BEHEADING — NO MERCY FROM VICTIM'S FAMILY'.

By now, Frank, back in South Australia, had hardened in his opinion. 'Frank Gilford, brother of nurse Yvonne Gilford, says he will not prevent the maximum sentence being carried out,' reported *The Herald*.

> Mr Gilford told reporters: 'Whoever did this did not give clemency to my sister and I don't think I would offer clemency, bearing in mind the way my sister was murdered.'

Already the press were dividing on national lines. *The Herald*'s sympathy was clearly with its local Scots family:

> The horror and anguish at the arrest of Ms McLauchlan was etched on her parents' faces on Christmas Day ...
> Miss McLauchlan's father, Stan, 52, said: 'My daughter has dedicated her life to nursing and the care of others and she graduated as student nurse of the year. Anyone who knows her will know she is incapable of the charges that have been made against her' ... He and his wife Ann plan to fly to Saudi as soon as they receive more information.

The National Health Service Trust, which runs Dundee's public hospitals, put out a statement confirming that a 31-year-old nurse called Lucille McLauchlan was dismissed when training in May 1996 'for gross misconduct following police investigation'.

The Herald quoted Stan McLauchlan as expressing bewilderment at this allegation:

> My daughter has dedicated her life to nursing and the care of others. She graduated as a student Nurse of the Year, and has won an award for her nursing ability ... Lucy left the National Health Service after the unit in which she worked for four years was closed. The nature of her job changed and the lack of career opportunities led her to opt to work as a nurse overseas.

Pathetically, Lucy's family was unaware of, or refused to acknowledge, the serious allegations she faced even before the murder.

The paper described Stan as 'a well-known and respected figure in Dundee, where he was shop stewards' convener of the Robb

Caledon shipyard and then the Kestrel Marineyard ... currently unemployed but sits on industrial tribunals.' A sympathetic figure in industrial Scotland. Stan told *The Herald*:

> I have spoken on the phone to my daughter since her arrest, but only very, very briefly. She has assured us of her innocence and said that she was being well-treated.

The Scotsman summed up the political pressures involved in the case, outlining the 'special relationship' between London and the Saudi capital, Riyadh:

> Contracts worth £15 billion for the purchase of 120 British Tornado strike aircraft, minehunter warships and other military equipment have already been signed. British defence industries hope the eventual value of sales to the Saudis, including tanks and Hawk training aircraft, will top £53 billion.
>
> The Foreign Office and Defence Ministry will hope that the contracts provide leverage to soften the harsh court procedure in what Human Rights Watch Middle East has described as 'one of the most singularly undemocratic nations in the world'.

In Hampshire, the media had not yet discovered that Deborah Parry's closest family were under 'Ashbee' in the phone book. Christmas was no less depressing for all that. A 'colleague' of Debbie, in Dhahran, spoke with the London *Daily Telegraph*:

> Miss Parry had suffered a series of family tragedies in recent years, losing her parents, brother and brother-in-law. 'She had been very lonely and only arrived here four months ago. But she was so happy to have settled and found new friends.'

Into the swirl of media hostility lurched the quiet, bearded figure of Frank Gilford. In Australia, the press, radio and television were in Frank's ear, on his doorstep. Little sympathy for him was ending up in print. Under Saudi law, the reporters told him, he could say yea or nay to the death penalty for anyone found guilty of his sister's murder.

Yea, was his simple answer. Frank knew nothing of Islam, could barely give word to his own grief. And here was the world asking him to pronounce on the accused in a murder, in obscure circumstances, under a strange legal system, across the globe. It wasn't hard for the journalists to glean colourful, almost rabid responses. Backed up into their small kitchen, Frank and his wife Laurel were, without realising it, shovelling grist for the media mills. They now had a standard line for inquiring reporters: 'If you do something wrong in a foreign country, you have to abide by the rules and punishments of that nation.'

Headlines began to reflect the two dominant themes of the coming months: Saudi brutality (apparently endorsed by the recalcitrant Frank Gilford) and the innocent suffering of the British nurses:

'LASHINGS OF DESERT LAW AND ORDER' — Sydney *Daily Telegraph*, December 27
'NO ROOM FOR MERCY FROM THE SYSTEM THAT DEALS IN DEATH' — London *Daily Telegraph*, December 28
'BRUTAL NATION RULED BY THE SWORD' — *Scottish Daily Record*, December 12

These typified the picture of Saudi Arabia, while accounts of the accused women, despite the Dundee allegations against Lucy, generally expressed sympathy:

'ACCUSED NURSE "NOT CAPABLE OF HURTING ANYONE"' — *Irish Times*, December 28
'FAMILY PLEADS FOR HELD NURSE — MURDER — CONCERN GROWS FOR ACCUSED' — *Western Morning News*, December 28
'CAUGHT IN A DESERT STORM' — *Scotland on Sunday*, December 29
'SAUDI DEATH CASE NURSE CARED FOR QUEEN MUM' — London *Mirror*, January 2, 1997

And by December 28, *The Scotsman* was reporting that Lucy had confessed in the hope of an early return home.

Frank Gilford was now claiming to have 'pretty conclusive evidence' against the two British nurses, according to the Scottish *Herald*. It reported Frank as saying they were caught on Saudi security cameras using Yvonne's credit card. Frank didn't reveal where he got this information, and in fact the alleged video has never been produced. According to defence lawyers, police eventually conceded that the video they had was from their surveillance camera outside the Arab National Bank, not from a conventional closed-circuit security camera. Frank's information probably came from *Al Hayat*, the Saudi-owned newspaper published in London. On December 26, it published an account quoting 'police sources'. The paper obviously did have good sources, though some of the information was less than accurate. It revealed that the two nurses had confessed to murdering Yvonne unintentionally. But the claims that Yvonne had been stabbed five times and hit with a hammer bear little relation to the official medical report. *Al Hayat* mentioned the security video cameras and claimed the murder occurred after a party attended by Debbie and Lucy, who were said to be good friends of Yvonne.

By December 30, *Al Hayat*'s 'police sources' had improved their act. Now, the hammer was replaced by the teapot as one of the murder weapons, the kitchen knife was mentioned, and the claims of lesbian sex and moneylending emerged. *Al Hayat* reported that the two women had confessed and that the fingerprint of one of them had been found in Yvonne's flat. It claimed the two had taunted Yvonne that she was an 'old lady'. It was suggested that the police leaks were in response to the stinging criticism of the Saudi legal system in the British press.

On New Year's Eve, some of the details of the claims against the two accused became officially public, to the extent that they were published in the official Saudi News Agency, quoting an unnamed senior police official: 'A personal dispute ensued between Deborah and the Australian nurse, prompting Deborah to resort to violence, stabbing the victim. Lucille helped to deliver the last blow by smothering her,' it said.

The Saudi ambassador in London, Dr Ghazi Algosaibi, now went to the press with his claim that the women would get a fair trial. 'This trial by the Press is not helping anyone, least of all the two nurses and their families,' he said. 'The court will examine the case thoroughly and fairly. The nurses will have ample opportunity to defend themselves, and access to legal representation ... Even if they are found guilty, the death sentence is not automatic.'

The claim that the women would have defence lawyers was surprising, given that lawyers were by no means a regular fixture in Saudi criminal courts. While it was common for the accused to have a family member or other respected figure to appear with them in court, the concept of a defence lawyer was unheard of. What was little-known then was that Dr Algosaibi is a close friend of Salah Al-Hejailan, the Saudi commercial lawyer who had just been hired by the accused women.

While this name was to become a regular feature in press reports in the new year, for the moment the ambassador merely announced, 'The women have already appointed a very prominent Saudi lawyer who speaks English fluently and who will have access to them and will attend court sittings.' The powerful alliance between ambassador and lawyer had swung into action.

The British Foreign Office, with one eye on human rights and the other on British trade interests, announced that Dr Algosaibi's comments were 'helpful'.

At this early stage, Frank could still express a less than rigid view. Under 'BROTHER MAY SPARE SAUDI NURSES' on December 29, the British *Sunday Times* reported Frank as saying:

> 'After the trial, I might consider an appeal for clemency.' An act of mercy could prepare the way for 'blood money' to be paid to the victim's family for the loss of their relative. Gilford, however, said he would be 'insulted' by such an offer. 'My sister's life was worth more than money,' he said. 'Any clemency would be out of compassion for the families of the two women.'

The Scotsman, in Edinburgh, was among the first to use the popular headline 'The Shadow of the Sword' and upped the odds by disputing Frank's illusion that the women would not be beheaded:

> This year so far, the Saudi authorities have executed 68. Ominously for the two British nurses ... at least three were women. Two Pakistani females lost their heads early this month for attempting to bring heroin into the Kingdom ... A Saudi woman died for killing her husband, despite evidence that she had been abused by him over a period of time and was in fear of her life.

It wasn't long before everyone had an opinion of Frank Gilford. To the eye-for-an-eye brigade, he was a hero; to civil libertarians, the anti-Christ. Some of us took little notice. It was just another murder story. At the office there was gossip. Some wondered if this was a story we should look at. The *Witness* program, Australian Channel Seven's weekly current affairs flagship, had been through its infant year, 1996, in crisis. The presenter, probably Australia's best-known journalist, Jana Wendt, had publicly fallen out with the network management and the program's executive producer. Now, in early 1997, Jana had gone and the staff were reeling, wondering if we had a future.

Researcher Mick O'Regan shut the door on the office gossip and started phoning Frank Gilford. But Frank had had enough of journalists. Sorry, we're not doing any more.

Executive producers don't like researchers taking 'no' for an answer, so Mick was dispatched to South Australia and drove the few hours through the beautiful Clare Valley wine district to Jamestown. Being hospitable country people, the Gilfords opened the door to Mick on their shady verandah, asked him in, got to like him and said 'yes', they would do an interview with *Witness*.

A week later, the crew was on its way to South Australia. Briefed by Mick (researchers generally get left out of the fun of the actual filming), the new *Witness* presenter Paul Barry, sound guy 'Big Al' Garipoli, cameraman Craig 'Gadgets' Watkins and I drove up through the stubble of the newly harvested wheat fields to see Frank and Laurel.

In the car on the way, the chat revealed our ignorance. His quotes in the papers made Frank look a nasty, bloodthirsty man. Therefore, he *must* be. Laurel seemed worse. Our sympathies, like those of most journalists, were generally for a liberal approach to sentencing, certainly not reflexively in favour of the death penalty. We weren't expecting to like the Gilfords, though Mick O'Regan had.

First impressions seemed to confirm first prejudices. Frank and Laurel were already heartily sick of the media. Mick had evidently only just surmounted their reluctance to undertake this interview. We arrived, pulling into the Gilfords' grassed yard behind their two courier vans. This was a modest house, low-slung like many Australian bungalows, with a verandah front and back. Behind the house, two bitser dogs lazed, raising only a desultory growl at our appearance. In a row of cages beyond the clothes line, budgies, cockatoos and rarer birds made a racket. A very tall radio mast stretched up by the paling fence. Wired to it, halfway up, was a tin cut-out of a magpie, painted black and white. Down the back of the block were the vegie gardens and chook pens. As I stepped up to the fly-wire door to the back of the house, I could see Frank and Laurel having their sandwiches for lunch in the dusky kitchen. The ABC one o'clock bulletin was on, loud.

The welcome wasn't exactly a hearty one. I offered to wait out the back until they'd finished and was surprised when they agreed. This wasn't looking good. After ten minutes and a lot of patting the dog and looking at the budgies, they called us in. We met a man in his late fifties, with a bushranger beard and deep-set eyes. The rest of Frank followed his belly and his opinions and words seemed even further back. Laurel was a woman of similar age and approaching similar girth, with short, greying hair and troubled eyes — and a ready wit, we soon found. One friend described her as cloaking her lack of education in humour. She loved to play jokes on journalists. She claimed once that Frank had a black belt in karate. This seems not to be the case.

In the kitchen, their attempt at haughty disdain for city journalists soon melted. Country hospitality, in Australia as anywhere else, is a difficult tradition to shrug off. Once they got to see we weren't slavering for juicy morsels of their souls, Laurel first, then Frank, took to us. As we set up lights, a favoured blue budgie flew around the kitchen, obviously a stranger to its cage. It flew past a plaque on the Gilfords' kitchen wall: 'My house is clean enough to be healthy and dirty enough to be happy'. Laurel had a loaf fresh out of the benchtop electric bread baker. With butter and jam and Nescafé, we were soon into the photos of Yvonne and the anecdotes about our less-worthy colleagues. It's a shameless thing to do, join in your interviewees' grumble about other journalists, but we all do it.

Those with an axe to grind on Frank's pain have said some cruel things. That Frank wasn't close to Yvonne, that he'd barely seen her in the 20 years of her travelling life before she died. And that Frank and Yvonne were worlds apart in character and experience. Some of that is true, but it doesn't do justice to the bond between them. That day, in January 1997, their closeness was clear to us, chairs, camera and microphone drawn up to the Gilfords' kitchen table, with the photo albums out.

There is a photograph of Frank and Yvonne as kids, at maybe six and three, something like that. The photo is old enough to be sepia. The children are blonde and sweet. If you can tell anything from a photograph, you can tell that these kids are close. It's not clear where this picture was taken, probably at 'Erudina', the outback property in South Australia's Flinders Ranges where they grew up.

Frank showed us shots of the country, rugged, remote. Out there, there's no preschool or playgroup or kids down the road. The two little blondies had only each other to play with and love and learn from. They had a large world to roam in, those thousands of hectares of the station, amongst the sheep, the scrub and the flies. And they did it together. As they grew older, yes, their paths diverged. Frank stayed bush, while Yvonne went to town. She went to the 'big smoke', Adelaide, the state capital, a provincial but substantial city of about a million. Frank worked on various properties, rode horses and motorbikes. Yvonne studied nursing at the Royal Adelaide Hospital, and developed a taste for people and faraway places. Their bond remained.

In a letter to a friend a few months before Yvonne died, you can read that bond in simple words: 'Had a letter from Frank. Mum giving them a hard time. Says she doesn't want to stay where she is — poor Frank.'

Clearly, Yvonne depended on her brother. To him fell the burden of sustaining their mother, Muriel, when she developed Alzheimer's disease and moved to a senior citizens' home after their father's death.

On her way from her 20-year stint in South Africa to her new job in Saudi Arabia, Yvonne had spent some weeks in South Australia, catching up with Frank and her mother. She became close to Frank's wife, Laurel, despite the differences in their background. Laurel is a small-town woman, who ran the Jamestown bakery on her own for many years after her first husband died. She's a respected woman around town, liked for her strength of will and her gutsiness in carrying on alone, with kids to raise, running the business. Frank, too, had been married before. When he and Laurel married several years ago, it was a partnership approved all round by family and Jamestowners. Two battlers united.

A strong woman, Laurel had had her troubles. Perhaps it was years of grief and strain that brought her some of the symptoms of schizophrenia. Voices. You can see the pain and bewilderment in her eyes as she describes this today. Yvonne helped her. Unsatisfied with the efforts of the local doctor in dealing with Laurel's condition, Yvonne gave her advice about where to seek other help. Yvonne must have done this with care, without bossiness. Any hint of condescension would surely make Laurel bridle. As she recalls the generosity of her sister-in-law, Laurel, a woman who embodies that clichéd Australian trait of laconicism, is in tears. She will not hear a word against Yvonne. 'For the short time I knew Yvonne, she was a sweet, delicate, loving person. She wouldn't hurt a kitten. Yvonne and I got on well, at first sight. She was very caring. She supported me a lot, 'cause I wasn't very well. Yvonne was always there for me.'

Frank, a man of few words, has trouble voicing a description of, and his feelings for, his sister: Was she like him? 'No, she was better looking than me,' he says in his loungeroom. Laurel laughs.

Frank: 'No, she was hard to describe — pleasant, bright, really enjoyed life sort of business, you know. Well, what do you say ... ?'

Laurel: 'Very adventurous girl.'

Frank: 'She loved what she was doing, and she made the most of her life while she was doing it.'

As our talk turns to Yvonne's death and those accused, it becomes clear that Laurel is more vehemently in favour of the death penalty than Frank. 'Dehead 'em,' she mutters out of the corner of her mouth. Frank tries to be more diplomatic, in response to Paul Barry's on-camera questioning.

'Would you choose capital punishment?'

'Yes, I would.'

'And what about you, Laurel?'

'Yes, I would go along with that, definitely. They had no mercy on Yvonne, what they done. And if they're found guilty, let them have what comes to 'em.'

In contrast to many of their published statements, here, Frank and Laurel were quietly adding a rider to their calls for the damnation of the accused. 'If they're found guilty' were Laurel's words. It was clear that Frank and Laurel didn't want to be seen as closed-book simpletons giving knee-jerk reactions. Up to that time, and in the coming months, that was often how they were painted. Yet, if you looked for it, you could find sympathy in their souls. Any journalist could walk in here and elicit a rabid comment. Many did. But if you probed their hearts, especially Frank's, you'd find troubled waters.

In the first place, Frank hadn't much idea of what his legal rights were in Saudi Arabia. Pointing to headlines about 'the man who holds the sword' he was dismissive of reports which placed him in absolute control over Lucy and Debbie's lives. He repeatedly maintained that their fate would be up to the Saudi legal system, not him. He didn't want the power he was claimed to have. This was wishful thinking. As events were to prove, he did indeed have power over life. Today, he was at pains to show that he had support for his pro-death penalty stance. He showed us two piles of correspondence, perhaps a thousand letters. This, in the first month of the story. The letters against him were outnumbered three to one by his supporters. 'Support on my side is a lot bigger than what I would have expected,' says Frank, holding up the pro-pile. He reads from a few:

> I hope you won't give clemency to the two nurses who apparently murdered your sister. Your sister is dead and can't tell her side of the story. If they are freed they will sell the story and become rich at your sister's expense.

So Frank Gilford, by the beginning of 1997, had become the lightning rod for Australian public opinion on the death penalty, just as he would, in a more extreme way, in Britain later in the year. His dilemma came close on the heels of the 1996 mass murder of tourists and staff at Tasmania's Port Arthur. The trial of the prime suspect in the Oklahoma bombing case, Timothy McVeigh, was due soon and Britain was still in shock from the Dunblane murders of the year before. If ever the pendulum of public opinion was to turn back towards capital punishment in Australia, this could well be the time.

The renegade, ex-Liberal independent politician Pauline Hanson had made a name for herself by speaking out against the Australian orthodoxy of tolerance. She found many followers, especially in the bush, for her stance against support programs for Aboriginal people and against the bipartisan political approach which had promoted multiculturalism in this country for a dozen years. Late in 1997, she was to promote the idea of a referendum on the death penalty. In the meantime, Frank was many people's idea of heartland Australia, either salt-of-the-earth good sense or redneck conservative, depending on your point of view.

Capital punishment was on the statutes in most Australian states until soon after Ronald Ryan was hanged on February 3, 1967, in Melbourne's Pentridge gaol for the murder of a prison warder during an escape attempt. Public opinion at the time wasn't entirely clear. The Federal Cabinet considered holding a referendum but never did. In 1967, the Federal Attorney-General, Nigel Bowen, quoted Gallup opinion polls which suggested that support for the death penalty for those convicted of murder had dropped from 67 per cent in 1955 to 42 per cent in 1965.

During the debate over the sentencing of Ryan, these days known as 'The Last Man Hanged', among Australia's 16 daily newspapers, only one supported the decision to hang Ryan, while eight were against. The remainder were uncommitted.

Queensland had abolished capital punishment in 1921. After the controversy over Ryan's death, the other states soon followed suit.

In 1994, an attempt to promote a United Nations' resolution failed amid opposition from many non-aligned and Islamic states. The resolution would have asked countries to consider restricting the use of capital punishment and to work towards an eventual moratorium for the death penalty. Italy and Ireland were the strongest promoters of the failed resolution. The United States, which so often sees itself as the leading proponent of human rights in the world, was muted in the debate, with many of its own states committed to the death penalty.

Britain retains the death penalty for treason and piracy on the high seas. Its last hanging was in 1964. The European Union has banned capital punishment for its member states.

Commenting in *The Irish Times* on the 1997 outrage over Saudi Arabia's proposed hanging of two British women, Kevin Ryan wrote:

> The last lawful public beheading in Europe occurred before thousands of spectators in Paris in 1939, well within the lifetime of the present Saudi king. The last beheading in Europe was in France in 1977, and the victim then was an Arab, Hamida Djandoubi. And last June we passed — though nobody noticed — the 25th anniversary of the last legal flogging in Britain. So much for the superiority of European judicial and penal culture over that of the Arabs.

Frank Gilford's weighing of his correspondence may have been a distorted measure of Australian public opinion. Certainly, the major political parties retain a consensus against the practice. Even the most conservative senior party — the Nationals — in one of the most conservative states — Western Australia — has rejected calls for a referendum on reintroducing the death penalty. Yet, the rise of Pauline Hanson and her One Nation Party were to question the old assumptions about tolerance in Australian society. Perhaps Frank and Laurel, in their apparent support for capital punishment, represented an emerging groundswell of support for the ultimate penalty.

Through 1997, Frank and Laurel — and many others — would make all manner of claims about the way Saudi justice could be administered. Even by January, Frank was confidently asserting blithe claims which later proved false. Women wouldn't be executed in public; they would go before a firing squad, not an executioner with a sword; it was up to the Saudi state, not the family of the accused, to impose the death penalty. Frank clung to such claims as a way of shielding himself from the blast of responsibility and acrimony turned on him from around the world.

In fact, he did have the right to see the death penalty imposed on his sister's murderer(s). Frank had become the first individual Australian to be given the right to uphold or waive execution for murder of a family member. But most Australians, including Frank and his family, were not only speaking a different language to the Saudis who gave him that right, they were not even talking in the same room. The average Saudi takes capital punishment as a given, endorsed in the holiest of books, the *Koran*. There are no opinion polls of Saudis to gauge their devotion to this tenet, but any traveller in the kingdom will find Saudi subjects' commitment to the teachings of Islam almost as natural and automatic as breathing air.

Qisas, the right of retaliation, emerged from the tribal ways which Mohammed had to deal with in the Arabian peninsula in the eighth century. A mandated and strictly controlled dispensation of 'an eye for an eye' was a way of avoiding blood feuds. Rather than one murder leading to many, further violence after one murder could be forestalled by one, sanctioned, execution. While many Moslems would maintain it is blasphemy to suggest that any of the edicts Mohammed had whispered to him from Allah's messenger had an earthly origin, it's not offensive to point out that *Qisas* was a very practical form of justice in the war-stricken time of the Prophet (peace be upon him).

Even that January, so soon after the murder, Frank did know enough to recognise his central dilemma. It was this: all or nothing. He could push all the way for the death penalty, but he couldn't negotiate for anything less. He couldn't say, 'I, as the brother and closest responsible relative, seek five years' hard labour for the convicted.' At that stage he eschewed the money option of so-called blood money, a concept alien to him. Which left him with, probably, the death penalty or bugger-all. From what he'd heard, in the event of a victim's family waiving death, the convicted generally received a very light state-imposed gaol sentence or simply walked free. That, to him, didn't seem like justice.

Some media commentators had begun to perceive the depths of his dilemma. David Edgar, the British author and playwright, wrote in the British *Guardian*:

> ...victim power is a benign form of lynch law. It is bad for civil liberties, in that it places decisions that should be taken by disinterested professional strangers in the hands of people who are understandably and properly dominated by feelings of anger and vengeance. It is bad for the victims and their families, in that it asks them to put a value on the life of someone they knew in the currency not of their own grief but someone else's punishment.
>
> Islamic law appears to be asking Frank Gilford to choose between sending two women to a barbaric death or devaluing the importance of the life of his sister.
>
> It is not a position in which he — or any other grieving person — should be placed.

This was all very well for David Edgar, but the fact of Frank's fate was that he found himself with Saudi victim power granted by destiny, not choice.

A more informed observer was Hosnein Esmaili, a lecturer in Islamic jurisprudence at Sydney's University of New South Wales, who wrote in *The Australian* newspaper that Frank's refusing to take up his role in the *Sharia* court

> ...would bewilder Saudi authorities. Without the relatives' formal demand for a permitted punishment, there can be no penalty for murder under Islamic law.
>
> Yvonne Gilford's relatives cannot achieve their very Australian desire for 'justice' without adopting an un-Australian stance: the personal quest for retaliation ... Frank Gilford's preference is for a lengthy prison sentence for the alleged murders, a sentiment clearly based on Australian notions of fair punishment.
>
> However, prison is a State punishment and is not available as a personal demand. Rather, under Islamic law, the relatives must choose between the options of the death penalty, forgiveness or the demand of *diah*, or blood money. The Government is permitted to add its own punishment, such as imprisonment or lashing, but will only do this if it feels that the criminals are so especially wicked that the form of retaliation demanded by the victim is inadequate. Any prison sentence is likely to be mild by Australian standards.

This was just the outcome Frank feared. He told us that a short prison sentence simply wouldn't be justice for his sister. It was difficult to disagree.

On two other points in his lecture to Australian readers on Islamic law, Hosnein Esmaili proved less reliable. He wrote that a 'withdrawn confession cannot be used as evidence of intentional murder'. He also claimed 'defendants are only likely to be convicted of second-degree murder', because 'Islamic jurists are suspicious of circumstantial evidence'. In the event, the court accepted the confessions and convicted Deborah Parry of intentional (or first-degree) murder.

The most intriguing aspect of Esmaili's assertions concerns not Islamic law in Saudi Arabia but that 'the quest for personal vengeance' was somehow 'un-Australian'. Perhaps he's right, although plenty of Christian-dominated and Anglophone societies, including Australia, have through much of their history condoned the death penalty for murder.

In a survey of recent historical trends on the issue in *The Australian* newspaper, Nicholas Rothwell reported that Australians have, by and large, moved even further away from support for the death penalty than at the time of Ryan's hanging in 1967. In mid-1995, Victoria, the state which pulled the noose around Ryan's neck, conducted a detailed opinion survey on sentencing laws. Even though the state government's questionnaire was distributed through a tabloid newspaper, only 13 per cent of respondents supported the death penalty. Writes Rothwell:

> The range of polls by private organisations has been relatively consistent. In the two decades following Ryan's death, support for capital punishment fluctuated between 45 and 70 per cent. But a detailed study for the Institute of Criminology in May 1986 found a much lower level of approval — 26 per cent of a large sample for the death penalty for murder.

Even after the Port Arthur massacre in 1996, in which the killer Martin Bryant gunned down staff and tourists, response in terms of calls for public vengeance was muted. As Rothwell reports,

> Throughout the aftermath of the crime, one was struck, as one still is, by the great restraint and care of public

discussion. At Martin Bryant's sentencing last November, there was an understandable plea by one of his intended victims, Carolyn Loughton: 'All Australians should now look at a debate on the reintroduction of capital punishment for mass murder.'

Yet this appeal was received by the country in a kind of crushed silence, so general did the acceptance seem to be of another view. The view that the way to respond to an impulse of universal violence was to rise beyond it, to display a different reaction: not revenge, but alert conscience, for what — the question seemed to hang unanswered, unanswerable — in such circumstances, would constitute retribution?

Instead, the country — in a surprising consensus of state and federal governments — went the other way and legislated gun control. Rothwell quotes criminologist Dr Paul Wilson, Dean of Social Sciences and Humanities at Queensland's Bond University, contending that Australian views may be influenced not just by the political consensus against capital punishment, but by awareness of certain recent spectacular miscarriages of justice — such as the conviction of Lindy Chamberlain (the woman whose baby was stolen by a dingo) — that could have led to the execution of the wrong person.

Rothwell also points to the hanging of bushranger and self-styled Irish-Australian republican Ned Kelly in 1880 as leaving a deep national distrust for civil vengeance. Although he was a robber of banks and shooter of police, Kelly has grown in popular consciousness into a heroic figure who still stands in his home-made armour in defiance, not only of the real police bullets at Glenrowan, but also of repressive colonialism.

Father John Brosnan, the priest who accompanied Ryan to the gallows in 1967, celebrated a mass in 1980 on the centenary of Ned Kelly's death. Brosnan, now a campaigner against euthanasia, says: 'We are never less adequate than when we try to punish, whether the baby in the cradle or the murderer on the gallows.'

All of this tends to suggest Esmaili has a point and that Frank Gilford's sample of letters on his kitchen table is unrepresentative of the wider Australia.

After our quiet little interview in Jamestown that day in January, we told Frank we weren't going to put his views to air before we had a chance to speak to the families of the accused women and to the Saudis. To be ready, though, we asked him and his wife to go through the little television charades which have become a ritual of our professional lives. We needed footage to round out our report on this beleaguered family. I whispered to Craig Watkins that we could do something with the cages and the birds. He laughed, thinking I was joking about such a laboured metaphor. I wasn't, being one for direct images. Sighing, Craig obliged. Perhaps overcome by the crassness of my vision, he failed to notice as he was packing up his lights in the kitchen that his big 10 kW lamp had melted the Gilfords' fridge-door handle. He had been using the bright white of the fridge to bounce some light on to Frank and Laurel in the interview. They didn't notice, either. Anyway, there we were in the backyard, getting Frank to hold tiny birds in his big worker's hands and then free them towards the camera. Laurel even agreed to be filmed bolting the cage doors, careless of the prison analogies. The truth was they were very gentle with their birds, had names for them all, and could catch and free them at will, without harming them. Frank, shot low and past his big belly, looked more the gentle giant than the cruel executioner.

Frank and Laurel run a local courier service, driving documents and parcels from the rail connection at Port Pirie to local businesses and homes. They work hard, with an early start each day. Today, a Sunday, they agreed to be filmed in the main street of Jamestown, as if they were making deliveries. As always, we had them go through the motions several times, shot from different angles. Friends by now, they endured this tedious business without complaint. At one stage I took Frank aside to ask him if he would sign an exclusivity agreement, at the behest of our executive producer. Frank said he would rather keep our arrangement on an informal level and declined a meagre offer of payment. This was somehow a relief. The idea of paying people to keep their mouths shut is still an uncomfortable one for a recent refugee from public television. And as Frank was later to show, he couldn't keep his mouth shut anyway.

Paul and I offered to help the Gilfords however we could, perhaps with contacting lawyers in Saudi Arabia. At this stage, Frank had only had limited advice from the lawyers of the Australian Department of Foreign Affairs and Trade. He hadn't yet selected a Saudi firm from among the suggestions made by Foreign Affairs.

This may have been why Frank, at that time, seemed less hardline than when he later spoke under the guidance of lawyers in Riyadh. We promised to at least send him any interesting articles on the case we came across. We parted with warmth and with warm words about Laurel's bread. Frank agreed that we could come to Adelaide a week later to film Yvonne's funeral. Her remains were being flown home that week.

The day after filming with Frank Gilford and his family in Jamestown in January, I wrote to the Saudi embassy in Canberra with a request for permission to visit Saudi Arabia and report on the Gilford case. We hoped that now that we had established a strong — and apparently exclusive — relationship with Frank, the Saudis would see us as having a useful stake in the story.

Before I made the request, we sought advice from specialist Middle East journalists on the best way to obtain such approval. The universal opinion was we hadn't a hope. *The Independent*'s Robert Fisk, seen by many as the doyen of Middle East hands, said the Saudis almost always said no to foreign journalists' visits and it would only be possible through the back door, with the sponsorship of a Saudi business. Such an approach appeared impractical. The nature of the case necessitated being open about our work. We wanted to see the places where Yvonne had lived and worked and openly question the accusers of Lucy and Debbie.

When seeking visas to closed countries, journalists invariably grovel. In this case, given the uproar in the British press, the obvious course presented itself: stress the things that aligned Australia and Saudi Arabia and distanced both countries from the Brits: 'Living here in a former British colony, we are aware of the sometimes overbearing assumptions made in Britain. The British media can be relentless and one-sided in pursuit of a story; in this story it seems both the Saudi and Australian perspectives are pushed to one side.' Colleagues in Britain and Australia might puke at this, but persuading the distant officials of an obscure bureaucracy is an arcane and delicate art.

The next thing was to quote the Saudis back at themselves. Any official in any Information Ministry office wants to hear supplicant journalists reflecting back the reluctant visa-issuing nation's view of itself.

The most prominent spokesman for Saudi Arabia in the West in recent years has been Dr Ghazi Algosaibi, the ambassador to Britain. In a clever article in *The Independent* published in the first week of the furore over the British nurses' arrest, he fought back against the drubbing the Saudi *Sharia* court system had received. He criticised the lack of informed thought in British reports in which

> ... readers learnt that it was up to a victim's family to insist on retribution or pardon. No one stopped to ponder this rather strange legal phenomenon, handing the power of life and death to the relatives of the victim.
>
> In fact, murder in the *Sharia* is a personal crime; the state is bound to respect the wishes of the victim's family. Each year in Saudi Arabia, many killers are pardoned by the families of the victims, but this is hardly noted by the Western media, interested only in the number of executions. All students of Islam know that the *Koran* did not introduce the principle of retribution, but merely reaffirmed what the Old Testament said.
>
> What the *Koran* did introduce was the concept of pardon. The *Koran* gives relatives of a murder victim the absolute right to insist on a 'life for a life'. Yet the *Koran* heaps praise on those who forgive and pardon. All this does not sit well with the common media image of a 'brutal' *Sharia* and so it is consistently ignored.

Aside from the fact that I desperately wanted to get into Saudi Arabia to produce a report on what was to become one of the big stories of 1997, to some extent I agreed with Algosaibi. It is fascinating that the *Koran* gives powers to victims' families. At just this time in our own courts in Sydney there were fledgling attempts at introducing the concept into our adversarial system. Under new legislation, the victims of a crime could make a statement to the sentencing judge to explain the effects the crime had had. The judge could take the relative pain caused into account when making a decision on the severity of sentence.

So, in all my correspondence with the Saudis, from that very first letter, I have always stressed this interest in the power of mercy granted by the *Koran*. In the first letter, I quoted from Algosaibi's interview with John Ware on the BBC *Panorama* program *Death of a Principle*: 'When you repeat words like "barbaric" and "disgusting" you make no effort to understand a civilization different from yours. You colonized the world for centuries and it is time that this era came to an end. Why do you want to impose on us a new cultural colonization which is no less vicious than the old military colonization?'

Sending off such letters, you have to wonder whether anybody actually reads them. I was heartened months later when, standing outside an Al Khobar mosque one evening, an official from the office of the governor of the Eastern Province told me he had enjoyed reading my letter. He was smiling a smile which made it unclear whether he'd enjoyed what he believed to be the concurrence of our views or enjoyed seeing through my self-seeking stratagems.

Many journalists later asked how we managed to become the only Western media allowed in to cover the story. The answer is, I still don't know for sure. Maybe I got an A for grovelling. Or maybe the Saudis genuinely wanted to see conciliation between the families of the victim and the accused and thought we were the best chance of a conduit. Anyway, they let us in.

The call came one morning in March when I was scurrying around Canberra chasing some story about shady dealings in the South Pacific. The then ambassador, Abdul Rahman Alaholy, called on my mobile phone. In my surprise I almost knocked over Mick Dodson, the disgruntled Aboriginal Commissioner for Social Justice, who was in a grumpy hurry to get to another futile Native Title meeting with Prime Minister John Howard.

The ambassador said that our request for visas had been approved and I need only send application forms for our team to the embassy. I quickly called the office to let them know. The office failed to be as excited as I was; the story had gone off the boil. And my enthusiasm was a little premature. It was to be another four months before the promise of visas would finally come good.

Chapter 7

The White Ladies bury Yvonne

If this were fiction, you'd know Yvonne by now. She'd have been painted and shown to you, drawing your sympathy. But in life, we don't hear about obscure people like Yvonne Gilford until after the event that brings them fame. By then, they are marked by the circumstances of their notoriety: in this case, the gruesome facts of Yvonne's death. Yet, there is always a person beyond the one now stamped 'Victim'. It's sad that we'll never think of Yvonne except as the nurse who was murdered, allegedly by her fellows, in a strange country far from home.

For some time, Yvonne Gilford was known to the world by one photograph, showing her as a nurse just after graduation. I warmed to that picture. It's very similar to one of my aunt, Helen, who would have been Yvonne's age now, had she not died in a car accident in the 1960s. The pictures of them both are formal, touched-up, and with those crisp old nurses' caps, rather nun-like. Not wimples, but those pointy things, about to take off, like the flying nun. Helen used to call me 'Buster' and knitted me a green jumper. Sentimentally silly to warm to Yvonne on the strength of a photograph her friends didn't like, but Yvonne's life and death are about to absorb much of my own for the next year.

It's a Saturday and it's hot in that dry, South Australian way. We're not so far from the dry pastoral lands of Yvonne's childhood and beyond that the inland deserts of this country, so far from the sandy place of her death. We're early, the reporter Paul Barry, Quentin on camera and Big Al on sound, with myself as the nervously scurrying producer.

Television crews and funerals are not a happy mix. You always feel intrusive. That's because you always are. I've promised Frank Gilford that we won't be, any more than necessary. But a camera needs to see and a congregation faces to the front. The camera is going to have to move up into eyesight of the bereaved.

The Heysen Chapel, named for the Australian pastoral landscape artist Hans Heysen, is part of a complex, Centennial Park. There are enough chapelettes and gathering spaces to have a couple of services going at once. It's a recent brick-and-glass place with views out to the extensive, eucalypt-scattered grounds. Though we're well early, Yvonne is here before us, her coffin waiting up by the altar, that Florence Nightingale photograph perched atop it. I fuss around chasing the funeral directors. They're the White Ladies and they are what the name says. Only women, all wearing white in business-like jackets and skirts. The leading White Lady today, Julie, has white hair to go with the rest of the ensemble. Clever marketing, I guess, the white and the women contrasting with the usual sombre chaps in black and grey. It's a chain that's spread across the country. Julie suggests we place the camera near the organ, under the staircase. Or up in the gallery. Great spots for pics of the backs of heads. We set up lights and leave them burning, hidden behind pillars in the hope the mourners won't notice when they arrive.

They do begin to arrive, gathering in the grounds and around a coffee urn. Producers spend their lives causing themselves embarrassment, which I do now, asking various people if they are Sue Taylor. Sue is coming today from New Zealand; from the country town of New Plymouth, where she grew up. She is — was — Yvonne's best friend. After they met in New Zealand in 1972 — Yvonne was there to try working in a strange country for the first time — they decided to travel together. Their odyssey took them to Britain, where they both worked as nurses for several years, and to many other countries before they both moved to Johannesburg and settled down. Sue married, Yvonne didn't. Yvonne became a de facto aunt to Sue's son, Matthew, and the children of other friends. Sue has told me on the phone that no one knows Yvonne better than she. So we've arranged to meet her here, at the funeral, and to interview her afterwards in pursuit of the Yvonne beyond the old-fashioned photograph.

A shortish woman with dark glasses, pearls, a dark dress with white trim and buttons, down to the nape blonde hair and a few more pounds than she wants, agrees that she is Sue Taylor. We talk, briefly, as the service is about to begin, and arrange to meet again afterwards. She is friendly but a little distant, preoccupied. Her friend's death is staring her in the face.

It's a subdued service but the chapel is full. Family, of course, and many people who knew Yvonne before her travels. She trained here at the Royal Adelaide Hospital and worked at the Memorial. Propped against the coffin is the formal portrait of Yvonne from her younger nursing days. A studio shot, touched up and coloured. She looks prim, proper. The Reverend Dr Peter Ryan from Glenelg Uniting Church officiates. He does his best, but he didn't know Yvonne. It's a relief when Sue Taylor steps up to the rostrum to deliver her eulogy. She reaches past the formal portrait to the memory of the friend she loved. 'Her unbelievably good commonsense and enjoyment of life always amazed me. Here was a person who genuinely only saw the good in others.'

It's the speech of a friend accustomed to teasing and being teased. Not over-respectful, full of light, humorous reminiscence. Yvonne's intolerance of Sue's shoe obsessions, and so on. It's obvious they were close. Later, Sue confesses she left out the last bit of her eulogy, embarrassed among Yvonne's family and other friends. The omitted couple of lines refer to a favourite movie the two friends shared — *Beaches*, with Bette Midler. It's a Hollywood weepie about two friends, one the star, the other in her shadow. Yvonne and Sue identified with the characters; Yvonne the shy one, Sue the upfront — yet the gregarious performer depending on her friend's implicit support.

The service is winding up with a vocalist, a woman from the parish, perhaps, who sings wholesome Christian songs, not hymns. The close family are in the first pew as the camera creeps up for a glimpse of their grief. There are no floods of tears, but pain is evident in the faces of Frank Gilford, his wife Laurel, and their adult children. Yvonne's father has preceded her. Tiny, beside Frank, is their mother, Muriel, in her eighties and with Alzheimer's now. Despite the memory lapses, she knows her daughter is dead. Hers is the annoyed glance at the camera.

We dash outside to film the guard of honour of nurses from the Memorial as the White Ladies carry the coffin to a grey hearse. It's only two minutes' drive to Yvonne's resting place and we're there ahead of the crowd. Frank and his family gather under a green tarpaulin by the grave. There are long-leaved gum trees close by to shade some, but most stand in full, strong sun to hear the words of the minister as Yvonne's coffin is lowered: '... washing Yvonne's footprints from the shore.' A niece clutches the framed portrait. There are flower petals for all to scatter and it's soon over. I have to disturb the family privacy to make arrangements to ferry Sue back to old Mrs Gilford's house when we've finished with interviews.

We drive Sue off around the cemetery grounds, in search of a quiet spot and a seat. We find somewhere by the duck pond; but where camera crews go, noise follows. Ducks, lawnmowers, water-sprinklers, all conspire to invade the intimacy of interviews. It's a noisy world. Sue has just left the funeral of her closest friend, but she needs to talk. She has brought photographs and letters. Her voice is well-tinged with a South African edge these days, though there's a little of the old Kiwi creeping back in. She's gracious. There's no sense of having to drag things out of her.

'This is the last photograph I took of her before she went to Saudi Arabia,' says Sue, handing over a snap of a slim woman in a cotton, armless shirt. Tribal-looking beads hang heavy around her slim shoulders. Yvonne's hair is blonde, short. Earrings. She could be much younger than her 56 years. Her glance to the camera is quite direct, perhaps carrying a little hurt.

Paul, our reporter, comments how different Yvonne looks to the Florence Nightingale portrait of her training years, until now the world's most commonly seen image of her.

'Well, that was 30-odd years ago,' says Sue. 'She turned into a much more attractive person.'

Other photographs show Yvonne on their travels, with tribesmen in Tunisia, nursing in England and South Africa. Sue reminisces, some of the anecdotes strangely prescient. In England, years ago, they had been on a bus once, passing Holloway prison. On a whim, they had decided to apply for jobs there. During their three-month stint, Sue met a prisoner who seemed quite nice. One of the warders referred Sue to the prisoner's file. The name on the file was 'Myra Hindley'. The Moors murderer. The notorious child murderer who had committed her ghastly crimes in the 1960s, whose wide-eyed photograph had become Britain's most famous personification of evil. But who could seem 'quite nice' to a stranger, a nurse, in her prison. Clearly, to Sue, this was a lesson in all not being what it seemed on the surface. Innocence could not be assumed from first appearances. Yvonne, who by Sue's account was a more trusting soul than she, never met the famous murderer.

At another time, during their three years in England, Yvonne had found a job as nurse–companion to the mother-in-law of Adnan Kashoggi, the Saudi businessman and arms-dealer. Yvonne had taken Sue along as her guest to a family dinner. 'Fascinating,' Sue recalls, 'though I'm not really into chauvinistic men. Blowsy, if you know what I mean; show-offy, garish, but quite generous.' Certainly an introduction to the wilful ways of the Saudi rich.

Together, Sue and Yvonne travelled to 29 countries, with their base in Britain. In 1976, a nursing employment agency recruited them to go to South Africa. Their passage was booked the week Soweto schoolchildren began to burn the Afrikaner schools, in protest against the race-based education system. The agency rang Sue and Yvonne, worried that they might pull out if they were seeing the images of violence on television. They went anyway, loved the place, and stayed for 20 years.

Sue and other friends married and had children. Yvonne had various male friends and one long relationship, with a man called Owen Joyce. Yvonne's friends didn't like him. They never married, despite his proposal shortly before she left South Africa. Childless herself, Yvonne became a very close 'auntie' to her friends' children. In 1996, Yvonne had decided to take up the job in Saudi Arabia to save enough to set up a small cake-decorating business back in Adelaide. She'd long been an enthusiastic baker of cakes for friends' birthdays, and especially for the children. Some of her cake designs had won awards in South Africa.

Sue Taylor is not a silly or narrow woman. She has been about. She knows of the assertions of lesbian affairs and relationship break-ups as motive for the murder. She wouldn't be shocked or upset, she says, if her friend had been a lesbian; she just knows that wasn't the case.

Her own belief that the police case against the British women is correct is based on money. Yvonne had been writing her letters just before the murder. In July 1996, Yvonne wrote of a lot of new staff due to arrive in August, including '2 English'. Presumably, these two were Lucy and Debbie. Three weeks before the murder, Yvonne told Sue on the phone she was going to lend them money. 'She said, "At the moment I've lent the English girls some money."' Sue assumed these were the same 'English' staff mentioned in the letter and that one of them was, in fact, the Scot, Lucy McLauchlan. 'I said that you should never lend money to people you don't know.'

Sue Taylor had known of Yvonne's financial affairs, because she had power of attorney for Yvonne in South Africa. Yvonne had arranged a double-shuffle with an English friend who was moving with her husband from South Africa to Perth. The plan was for Yvonne, as an Australian national, to send some of her money to Perth for the friend, who would in turn reimburse Yvonne in her South African bank account. But, says Sue, 'the money hadn't come to them yet from Yvonne'. This meant there was plenty of money available through Yvonne's bank cards, should anyone try to obtain it. Sue says that Yvonne had reassured her friends in Saudi that if they ran short of money because of late pay, she could help out. 'She'd said, "Don't worry, because I haven't sent any money out yet." Maybe that's how they knew who to target.'

Yvonne's letters to Sue are peppered with references to money, mostly housekeeping chat about costs of a computer, a sound system. She generously offers to buy presents for Matthew, Sue's 10-year-old son who calls her 'Auntie'. 'Will get the computer if you think it will be of benefit to him and will try and find one of the South African girls going home to take it for me.' Yvonne wants to know which games to get for Matthew and whether Sue can have Yvonne's old camera fixed for him.

Sue is convinced that Lucy and Debbie became aware that Yvonne had money while they, like many other staff at the hospital, had little or none. On October 14, Yvonne wrote to Sue: 'Pay late again this month so there are a lot of disgruntled staff — fortunately it doesn't affect me as have put some in a bank account here and will when I've got a reasonable amount transfer it out but at least I don't have to worry if pay day is late.'

By phone, Yvonne had asked Sue to warn the nurse recruitment agency that prospective staff should have their financial commitments secured well in advance of coming to Saudi because of the chronic delays in pay. In the days before the murder, Yvonne had told Sue she'd written to her since the October letter. Perhaps Yvonne did write of troubles at the hospital, of friction with other staff, even of problems with security guards. If she did, Sue was never to read of it. The letters never arrived by mail, and the personal effects sent back with Yvonne's body to her family contained nothing for her friend. Sue is left to wonder whether the murderer(s) destroyed her last link with her friend.

Now, in her grief in Adelaide, the more-worldly Sue is at one with Frank and Laurel. She wants justice. 'I think the crime, whoever committed the crime, deserves the full justice of the country.' No worries about taking another life? 'No. I say it, I think, because Yvonne was very strong. She looks very frail, but she was a very strong person. And I think what was done to her must have taken a terrible, terrible fight and for that it makes me very angry.'

Our interview takes place through the cries of the ducks and the occasional roar of a lawnmower, the only interruptions to this intimate, five-person memorial to a woman four of us never met. In a television interview you can meet a stranger intensely, ask questions that only lovers would ask on a first date. It's not quite real, but it's more intense than most of the encounters of everyday life. It is constantly astounding how much newly met interviewees will reveal of themselves and their lives. It's a confessional, that little cocoon of people, gathered in a semicircle around the subject. Not only the reporter, who is engaging most directly with the person being interviewed, usually with piercingly direct eye contact, but with the cameraman and sound recordist as well as the producer. Sue enjoyed it, if talking about a bitterly missed friend's death can be enjoyable. Often the demands and attention of film crews allow expression of feelings somehow suppressed by the delicacy of family and friends.

Yvonne seemed to be there.

Chapter 8

Familiar faces

January 13, 1997. Jonathan Ashbee, Debbie's uncle Terrie Knight, Lucy's father and mother, Stan and Ann McLauchlan, and Lucy's fiancé, Grant Ferrie, are off to Saudi Arabia. They have permission to visit their loved ones.

Jon and Terrie cast their eyes around the departure lounge at Heathrow airport, looking for Stan and Ann. At this stage, only the McLauchlans have appeared in the press. They should be recognisable, but they're nowhere to be seen. Minutes pass, everybody boards. Jon still can't see them. He'd like to say hello; they're in the same boat, with a family member facing death in a strange country. There's an announcement over the P.A. Would Mr and Mrs McLauchlan come to the gate? More minutes pass and Jon and Terrie board. As they're fastening their seatbelts the captain's voice comes over the speakers. Would Mr and Mrs McLauchlan make themselves known to the cabin staff? There's movement at the door. A middle-aged man and woman head down the aisle, eyeing the Arab faces of three-quarters of the passengers. The man, clearly the worse for wear, lifts his voice to address the plane: 'Fucking Arab bastards,' in a broad Dundee accent. This is Stan McLauchlan. The flight has been delayed four hours. British Airways had kindly offered the McLauchlans the hospitality — including the bar — of its executive lounge. At least now, Jon knows who to say hello to.

Once the flight gets under way, he and Terrie walk up to the McLauchlans' seats. 'Are you Mr and Mrs McLauchlan?' Ann bursts into tears. Stan pulls Jon down to his level and gives him a big kiss. 'So good to meet you.'

The next morning, in Dhahran, Stan is a different man; far from the effusive character of the night before. 'Devastated,' Jon later recounted. Jon, too, is less than effusive. He has never been to the Middle East before. If his sister-in-law can be arrested and imprisoned by the Saudis, why can't he? It's a subdued foursome that meets lawyer Michael Dark in the busy entrance hall. Michael is the urbane British gent with his shell-shocked charges. Jonathan lights up a cigarette, desperate after eight hours on the plane. Michael gently chastises him. No smoking during Ramadan.

Later, at the Dammam Police Station, all are nervous. Stan, whether from concern for his daughter or the rigours of the flight and BA hospitality, is ashen-faced. They're ushered to the police general's office. Lucy and Debbie have been ferried from the Dammam Prison — they don't know why — and are sitting by the office door. As they see their families, they're shocked, jumping up in elation. They think they're going home. Not so fast. Jon and Terrie hug Debbie. Stan and Ann hug Lucy. Jon goes to Lucy, arms out for a hug. She stares at him, straight in the eye, a stern Scots stare, and shoves out her hand. She's not letting any strangers close.

The two families part to catch up separately. In their interview room, Terrie and Jon have spotted the closed-circuit camera and the hidden microphone. To gain a little privacy when they wish to discuss something confidential, Jon and Terrie sit on the desk to obscure the camera's view and Terrie swings his leg to brush against the mike. Soon the police come in to move them. Debbie bursts into tears, 'Do you know what they've done to me? I'm going to tell the world.' Jon says, 'Deb, we're being taped.'

Lucy writes of the meeting to friends back in Scotland:

> I saw them on Saturday and Sunday for a couple of hours each day. Brilliant but a bit weird. It was very emotional. I couldn't think of a bloody thing to say at first — very unlike me as you know. Mum looks great as did Grant. It was great seeing him. Only problem was I wanted to come home with him — got quite upset, but as my dad says I've got good strong Scottish blood in me so I'll be fine.

Throughout their months in gaol, Lucy has been the strong one, Debbie close to the edge.

Deborah Parry fled to Saudi Arabia on the back of an ultimatum. For months, in England, she'd been in love with an older man, Stuart.

Stuart had just emerged from the break-up of a long-term marriage. You know what they say: the first woman a divorced man becomes involved with is inevitably part of his transition to his new life. He'll go on to someone else. Debbie wanted more from Stuart. He was unable to give it. She said, 'Alright, I'll go to Saudi Arabia then.' Once having made the threat she felt she had to follow through. Despite the drastic failure of a previous stint in the Saudi capital, Riyadh, in 1993, she was committed to going, cutting off her nose to spite her face.

When he heard of her arrest, Stuart, now involved with another woman, rang the Ashbees in concern. He apologised for intruding but offered whatever support he could. His new relationship wasn't going so well. He pined for Debbie. 'He's devastated. He just can't believe it,' says Sandra, 'and to think that she might suffer the death penalty.' Sandra and husband Jon had been matchmakers for Debbie and Stuart, through some other friends. 'They'd got on so well; they liked the same things. I think perhaps if he'd met her a year later'... Sandra and Jon sigh for what might have been. 'It got very intense very quickly and I think he found it too much to handle.'

What else? When Deborah Parry went to Saudi in August 1996 she was fighting with her only sister, her only surviving sibling, Sandra. They were fighting because Debbie's previous boyfriend, Roger — in fact, her fiancé of 10 years — was now married and had children of his own. Paul was godfather to a couple of Sandra's kids; quite natural when he was engaged to Debbie. But now that their relationship was well over, there was a question of loyalty. Debbie didn't want Sandra and her family to continue their relationship with Paul. It's a common thing in break-ups.

So when Debbie was arrested, she and Sandra weren't on speaking terms. She felt that Sandra would want nothing to do with her, now that she was in disgrace and blackening the family name. How wrong could she be? Sandra and her husband Jonathan stuck to Debbie like glue, if that were possible given that they were in England and she in Saudi. Every six weeks or so, Sandra and Jon travelled to Saudi to see Deb in the police cells in Dammam. They became her lifeline.

While Sandra acknowledges that she and Debbie would fight as much as any two close sisters, here was a case of adversity uniting a small and vulnerable family.

Deborah Parry was born in the small Hampshire town of Alton. Her early childhood, with her older sister and younger brother, was spent in the nearby village of Farringdon. Debbie began to speak of becoming a nurse when she was five. When she was seven, their father's work as a pilot took him and his wife to Switzerland. The children lived with their grandmother for a while, then Debbie and Sandra went to a convent school near Alton. They were Anglican, not Catholic, but it was a good school and they had aunts nearby. Their mother was unwell. Debbie finished her schooling at the local Eggers Grammar school, while Sandra stayed on at the convent.

Debbie's favourite things concern the small family she lives with, on and off, in Alton: her sister, Sandra. Her brother-in-law, Jonathan Ashbee. Their four children: Alex, the 11-year-old eldest daughter from Jon's previous marriage; Jon junior, aged four; Ben, aged six; and three-year-old Maddie. Debbie is happiest doing simple things, especially taking her favourite, Ben, to a cafe in the Alton high street for a doughnut and milkshake.

Debbie is a gentle person, says her sister. Though she's allergic to wasps, she won't have them harmed. 'She won't let me kill a wasp. She says, "Come on, let's just shoo it out of the house."'

She's self-critical, especially about her appearance. She doesn't like photographs of herself, because she thinks she comes across as horsey. In fact, she has a bright smile, though you could read her eyes as a little intense, a little Princess of Wales-ish. Debbie's faltering self-image was imposed by her father, a stern man, insistent on the right way of doing things, a stickler for correct form. One of Debbie's friends in the Saudi hospital later claims that Debbie told her her parents were alcoholic. Debbie was in awe of her father, perhaps frightened. Sandra relates a memory of their father. Their brother, Keith, had been talking at the table. She mimes the motion of her father banging his hand down on the table surface, reprimanding his son. An unremarkable recollection really, except for the fact that Sandra even thinks of relating it. You can see her reliving their father's authoritarian thrall as she tells the story.

Even before her imprisonment, Debbie suffered from claustrophobia.

When Debbie was in her late teens, in 1978, her younger brother, Keith, was killed in a motorcycle accident. He was 16. Ten months later, her mother, Eunice, died in a drowning accident during a boating holiday. Their father died of a heart attack in 1987. While Debbie and Sandra were still reeling from these untimely deaths, Sandra's first husband, John Osgood, died suddenly from a brain haemorrhage. In 1989, Debbie herself was in a serious road accident. Sandra says, 'It was touch and go for two or three months. I thought I was going to lose her.'

During her time in her Saudi prison cell, the occasionally suicidal Debbie often wishes she had died in the car crash.

Feisty. That's the word they use to describe Lucille McLauchlan. Her letters to friends and family back in Dundee, published in *The Scotsman*, are full of fight and crack.

> The situation here is starting to look more promising. About bloody time. Thank god I've got all of you behind me back home — I don't know what I would do without you all. Jean, you were saying you were at Scottish Slimmers. Come and stay with me here. Weight loss is no problem take my word for it — shit yourself thin diet. (only kidding).
>
> I will say now no matter what happens here I will come home with a clear consciounce [sic].
>
> Yvonne was my friend — really nice lady. She looked after me when I came to Saudi. Now she's being dragged through the gutter along with me and Debs. Well I will have the last say in this matter be assured of that. I think I'm OK because I'm not afraid anymore. I've done nothing wrong and knowing this helps me cope. That's about all the drivel from the jail front.

After Menzieshill High School in Dundee, Lucy went to the Nursing College at Ninewells Hospital up on the hill over the River Tay. She graduated as a state-registered nurse at Stracathro Hospital in Brechin, Angus, in 1991. Her father, Stan, says she was Student Nurse of the Year. Lucy's one brother, John, three years younger than her 31, is also a traveller, working on an oil rig in Indonesia.

They're a close family — Lucy living at home with Stan and her mother, Ann, until she went to Saudi Arabia in 1996 — though none of them seem to know of the troubles which came during her stint at the King's Cross Hospital's infectious diseases unit back in Dundee. Even now they won't talk about the allegations against her in her hometown.

Lucy's fiancé, Grant Ferrie, works as a tyre-fitter in a Dundee plant.

While her defence lawyer, Salah Al-Hejailan, tempted his clients to take advantage of gossip about Yvonne, both Debbie and Lucy have always appeared true to their dead friend.

> All I will say and this upsets me most is that Yvonne was my friend, a kind, caring lady who looked after me when I came to Saudi Arabia. For people to say I did this to her, Freda, makes me very angry. She's being dragged through the gutter along with me and Debbie. Never mind Freda, I'll have the last say on this matter.

She's writing about claims in the Scots *Daily Record* which paint Yvonne as running a moneylending racket, complete with enforcers. The source for the *Daily Record* story is later found to be a crank.

Is Lucy's response gritty loyalty, or an elaborate cloak to hide her complicity in Yvonne's murder?

Caroline Ionescu, Rosemary Kidman and an American friend of Debbie's, Catherine Wall, tried to visit the two women in prison soon after the arrest. Caroline had shampoo, conditioner and a note for them: 'Tell the truth, keep smiling and stick to your guns.' Stopped at the gate, Caroline made a fuss. Finally allowed to see an official, they were told it was the wrong visiting day and hour.

Trying again some weeks later, Rosemary and Caroline were again turned away, the prison officials saying that police had ordered no visitors. Undeterred, Caroline had the taxi driver take them to Dhahran Police Station to see Lieutenant Colonel Al-Zamil, officer in charge. One of the police, Major Hamed, had said to them, 'You know they wouldn't have been charged if they were not guilty. Why do you want to go and see the murderers?' Caroline had stamped her foot and replied that Lucy and Debbie were friends and innocent until proven guilty.

In June Caroline had tried again, only to be refused once more.

Chapter 9

Lawyers

The odd, often amusing and as-often tragically confused relationship between Salah Al-Hejailan and his two British women clients began much as it continued. On New Year's Day, 1997, his words appeared in the press to mark his appointment to Debbie and Lucy's defence the day before. Asked about their possible execution, he told the London *Daily Mail:* 'I believe this will just not happen — we are looking at this death as accidental and not premeditated.' The problem with this statement, from their point of view, is that it contradicted the basic tenet of their own stated defence: innocence. Here was their own lawyer, cited by the British Foreign Office as a good local man with excellent English, unconsciously contradicting his own clients. Rather than a simple statement of their innocence, Salah Al-Hejailan was allowing for the possibility that the two women may, in fact, have caused Yvonne's death, albeit accidentally.

On the same day, Reuters quoted the British consul in Saudi Arabia, Tim Lamb, who had just been to see Deborah and Lucille in the Dammam Central Prison. The women had broken down, the report said, when told they would likely be there for a long time. 'Deborah Parry told the consul that she wanted to withdraw her confession.'

The confused disparity between Salah Al-Hejailan's statement and the retractions of his clients could perhaps be explained by the fact that he'd not yet met them, nor closely examined their case. He told Reuters that the *Sharia* law would ensure the nurses received a fair trial, adding that the case was an opportunity for the world to learn about Saudi Arabia's legal system.

'I will plead the case in court out loud and in writing. There will be cross-examination of the witnesses. It is almost the same system as in the West,' he said. This, of course, wasn't true. The two systems were vastly different, and there never was to be any cross-examination. At this stage, however, Al-Hejailan was cheerily putting the best gloss on things. Along with the Saudi authorities, he saw himself as a can-do man who would fix this political problem between the Saudi and British governments.

> Lawyers from my office are going to Dammam on Saturday ... I will also go of course. They will make the preliminary interviews, take down the circumstances, prepare the basic things.

In fact, Salah Al-Hejailan didn't see his famous clients for several months. Other lawyers from his firm, notably the British lawyer Michael Dark, became frequent visitors to the women. But Salah Al-Hejailan is a man accustomed to dealing with what he feels are larger, weightier matters. Murder charges against two Britons, while interesting for their publicity factor, were small beer compared to the common coinage of his flourishing practice in international commercial law.

Salah is a large man, preoccupied with his larger-than-life status. One colleague describes him as accustomed to dealing with the heavyweights of American and British political and business life: Secretaries of State, Foreign Secretaries, the chairmen of oil and other firms seeking to do business in Saudi. And, says the colleague, Salah believes he has the measure of the large men of the West. 'He has seen them talk principle and practise personal interest.'

It would be wrong to see such a man as so pragmatic that he has lost the essence of his own Islamic upbringing. That would be a shallow interpretation of a complex character's world-view. Just as the avowedly committed Christians Salah has met in his high-flying political and business encounters could be seen as chequered in their actual practice of Christian precepts, prepared to compromise for personal gain and aggrandisement, Salah is a Moslem with a practical bent, though in the end a Moslem, a Saudi Moslem male.

So, for him, the presumptions of his gender, his creed and his nationality necessarily override his opportunistic dabbling in Western-style talk of human rights. Like most Saudis, for him it would be natural, almost automatic, to assume the guilt of the accused, particularly when the accused were women, particularly Western women. From the outset, the imperative in the case was to find a practical solution for a thorny entanglement between politics, international trade and the hubbub of the Western press. And he was just the man for the job.

For Lucy and Debbie, sitting frightened in their cell, all this was distant, unfathomable. As they began to plead their innocence to family, friends and the larger world, they had no choice but to place their faith in a man they'd never met, manipulating a system they couldn't comprehend. In one key respect he was their best advocate. Amid all the world's clamouring about the principles and issues in the case, he was one of the few who saw that this was a practical problem needing a practical solution.

In Saudi — as anywhere, of course — connections count. And Salah Al-Hejailan is well-connected. His youngest brother, Mustapha, is adviser to Saudi billionaire Prince Al-Waleed bin Talal. His oldest brother, Jamil, is the general-secretary of the Gulf Co-operation Council, the peak body representing the Arab Gulf states. Jamil was prominent in Paris during the Gulf War as ambassador to France. A younger brother, Mohammed, took up his posting last year as ambassador to Australia and New Zealand. Salah's brother-in-law, Al-Ghazzawi, was Minister of Information during the 1960s and 1970s. Hence the appearance of Salah's sister, Salwa Majdia, in the first Saudi television broadcasts in 1965.

Robert Lacey, author of the definitive examination of Saudi society and politics, *The Kingdom* (published in 1981), explains the political significance of those broadcasts. The relatively liberal King Faisal had introduced them against the wishes of the conservative religious sheikhs. Prince Khalid ibn Musa'id, a born-again Moslem who had turned from his playboy ways in Europe to religious zealotry at home, led a band of extremists in a violent assault on the television station in Riyadh. In a rare example of direct confrontation between religion and state, the king ordered his chief of police to fire on the leader of the demonstrators. Prince Khalid, the king's nephew, was shot dead. There had been similar religious opposition to the introduction of radio in the 1920s.

The alignment of Salah Al-Hejailan with the moderate forces of change continues today, to the extent that he has used the Gilford case as a vehicle for expressing reformist views on the legal system. This couldn't happen without high-level protection and patronage. The extent of this can be gauged by the lineage of Salah's wife. Her uncle, Abdullah Suleiman, was the first Finance Minister of the modern Saudi state and signed the first Saudi oil concession, with Standard Oil of California, in 1933. Her father was Abdullah's deputy. This crucial early deal set the pattern of Saudi engagement with the can-do Americans over the head of faltering, short-sighted British indifference to the men of the desert.

Salah's family, however, did benefit from dealings with the Brits. His father was a horse-trainer who sold racehorses to the British in Cairo in the 1940s. Salah himself studied law in Cairo in the 1950s, a time when many modern Saudis gained a more liberal and pragmatic world outlook. There he met Dr Ghazi Algosaibi, the man who was to become his ally, as ambassador to Britain, in the Gilford case. In his younger days, Algosaibi wrote a book, the title of which can be translated as *Open House*, which described his experiences as a student in Cairo. Despite the libertarian suggestion of the title, it would be a large overstatement to describe these men as Saudi beatniks. Their embrace of liberal Arab and Western mores is always tempered by an ultimate deference to the tighter religious and political strictures of Saudi life. To this day, Salah expresses a preference for the romantic melodramas of the Cairo cinema of the 1940s and 1950s over the contemporary product of Hollywood. His sons tease him about this old-fashioned taste, but he insists the clean-cut, well-dressed stars of his favoured genre are 'much nicer'.

Salah's own ascendancy came with the decline of Egyptian influence in the Saudi kingdom. Egyptian legal expertise had long been favoured by the Saudi royals, and lawyers from Cairo wrote and interpreted Saudi law for the Saudi kings. But when the Arab socialism of Egypt's President Nasser challenged the survival of Saudi traditional monarchy in a military confrontation on the Yemeni border in 1962, the Egyptian advisers were promptly kicked out of the kingdom. Salah, with his grounding in Egyptian jurisprudence, was perfectly placed to step into the vacuum as legal adviser to the King's Council of Ministers. The political and business alliances he made in that position have served him ever since.

These days, says one of this worldly and confident legal lion's colleagues, Salah Al-Hejailan maintains his thriving legal practice largely as an inheritance for his sons. There is little that he hasn't seen or done in the rarefied world of Saudi and international commercial law. His sons are treading faithfully as cubs in the lion's footsteps. The eldest, Hassan, is still in his twenties but is practising in the Riyadh office of The Law Firm of Salah Al-Hejailan and has often visited the British nurses and taken part in their court appearances. One of Hassan's brothers is studying law in London; the other is studying high-level private investigation in California. The firm looks set to be a major force in the Riyadh legal world for a good time to come.

The international practices in Riyadh ally themselves with prominent British and American firms. The prominent Briton in Salah's practice is Michael Dark, a discreet and reserved Englishman respected for his services to the British embassy and British interests in the kingdom. From the start of the Gilford case, Michael Dark looked less than at ease in his role as right-hand man to the unpredictable Salah. Well aware of the political and financial pressures on the case, Dark attempted to steer a middle course between the bombastic posturings of his boss and the sedate certainties of British law. Dark, now 52, has practised in Saudi Arabia for 12 years, leading a colleague to say he has 'become slightly desiccated by the sadness of staying in Saudi too long', cutting off his options. Having worked with Salah for so long, this colleague says, he has become dependent, with all the frustration and identity-paring that may involve. Dark has often seemed more at ease with his British colleagues who represent the families of Lucy and Debbie than with the multi-tongued, difficult-to-read firm in Riyadh. He was well aware of the need to placate both Saudi and British sensibilities. Even on that first day of the brief, New Year's Day, he was trying to play to both arenas, promising reporters calling the Riyadh office that the women would get a fair trial.

'I am confident the legal system here will produce a fair result,' he said, claiming that the country's legal system presumed innocence and demanded a case to be proven beyond doubt for there to be a conviction.

Also in Salah's battery of international talent are several Egyptian academic lawyers, their PhDs giving the firm a rich patina of credibility. More colourfully, the firm is flanked by a couple of Americans, the short but garrulous figure of New York litigator Bob Thoms being the most active in the Gilford case. Thoms has brought the pugnacious extremes of the adversarial United States' legal system to bear on the case, encouraging Salah Al-Hejailan in his more picayune shafts of inspiration, to the cost of Frank Gilford.

The blue corner, the defence (blue for the misery of their clients' plight), was rounded out by the firms representing the families.

In Birmingham, the prominent civil rights lawyer Rodger Pannone stepped in to help the Ashbee family in its pursuit of Debbie Parry's cause. Pannone was a former president of the Law Society in England and chaired its working party on international human rights.

In Glasgow, a man who had come fresh from his role as legal adviser to the victims of the Dunblane massacre, Peter Watson. Himself a phlegmatic Scot, Watson hired the Glasgow PR firm Media House to help spin the story the women's way. Pannone, with a deep pedigree in public interest advocacy, knew well how to play the media. He eventually placed his eggs in the basket of *Panorama*, the BBC's investigative television program. Unfortunately for both men, despite their undeniable skills, this was a case to be fought in a system outside their jurisdiction and influence.

The red corner (red for blood-seeking) was soon manned by a rival law firm in Riyadh. The International Law Firm is run by some young Saudi lawyers who see themselves as a potential match for the hubris and muscle of Salah Al-Hejailan. The firm is headed by Hassan Al-Awaji, the young son of a former government minister. It is aligned with the Cleveland-based firm Jones Day Reavis & Pogue, which produced the two American lawyers who entered the fray in the Gilford case. Yusuf Giansyracusa is a tallish West Coaster who converted to Islam after marrying a Moslem woman. He used to prosecute mobsters in San Francisco. A mob-busting convert. Surely a recipe for hard-line attitudes.

The most prominent firm-member in Yvonne's case was Jim Phipps. Jim, an owlish man in glasses, a bald pate and a scholar's beard, took a Fulbright scholarship in *Sharia* law before he entered practice in Riyadh. He's a Mormon with a strong belief in the absolutist strictures of the Islamic system. To him, an eye is definitely worth an eye.

Something about Jim appealed to Frank Gilford when the American flew to Australia and made the trek to Jamestown early in 1997. Probably the fact that Frank can't say no to someone who turns up with a genuine smile on his doorstep. And there has never been any hint that Jim Phipps wasn't genuine in his concern for his client. Frank hired Jim and the International Law Firm.

Back in Riyadh, Salah Al-Hejailan rang Jim's boss, Vern Cassin, and congratulated him on taking the Frank Gilford brief, offering cooperation. Salah says that all seemed friendly, at first. The extent to which relations between the firms has deteriorated can be gauged in the way one of the lawyers at The Law Firm of Salah Al-Hejailan now describes Cassin. 'He's a socialite who married a rich woman and likes going to embassy cocktail parties.' The two firms are bitterly dismissive of each other.

This acrimony goes back beyond the Gilford case. Several years ago, The International Law Firm poached one of Salah's best-earning lawyers. According to Salah, there was a question of some misplaced funds.

Before he joined The International Law Firm, Jim Phipps applied to Salah's firm for a job. They knocked him back. Despite that, says Michael Dark, Phipps rang him, offering to help out on Debbie and Lucy's defence. The next they heard, he'd signed up Frank for The International Law Firm.

Before the intervention of Frank Gilford's lawyers, friends Salah Al-Hejailan and Dr Ghazi Algosaibi were both trying to impress the British media with how neatly things could be sorted out. 'The death sentence will have to be asked for by the victim's family. If the family of the victim does not ask for it, the Saudi judge will not order it,' Al-Hejailan told Reuters.

'The relatives of a murder victim are the only ones who can insist on retribution. If they don't demand it, the court cannot impose the death sentence,' said Algosaibi, also to Reuters.

In those first days of January, both men hoped that Frank Gilford could quickly be brought around. That was before The International Law Firm showed its hand.

In response to the women's withdrawal of their confessions, Algosaibi commented, 'What I want to stress is that the only confession the court upholds is a confession that takes place freely in front of the court. Our police know this very well and it would be pointless to try to extract confessions by pressure.'

January and February of 1997 provided a brief window when there could have been a practical peace worked out between lawyers for the accused and the victim's family. In the midst of mixed reports on whether Frank would waive the death penalty, the comments of Al-Hejailan and Algosaibi provided hope for the women's families. Such hopes were short-lived. Within weeks, there would be open warfare between the Riyadh lawyers for Frank and for the women.

At the first hearing, Debbie and Lucy's passports were on the table before the three judges. All of the defence team thought this meant the two women were going home. The judge went through procedure, introducing all of the people in the room. He got around to James D. Phipps and asked what he was doing there. Phipps said, 'I'm speaking on behalf of Mr Gilford, brother of Yvonne Gilford. I've come to ask for the death penalty against Deborah Parry and Lucille McLauchlan.' Everything seemed to stop, a hesitation on all sides. The passports were put away. Although no evidence had been submitted, Jim Phipps made this demand specifically against Debbie and Lucy, not against *whoever* might be found guilty of the murder. Frank Gilford was later to say he had nothing against these two women in particular. He was waiting to see who was found guilty. Yet, his counsel was calling for them both to be put to death from the first day.

Lucy said to the judges: 'If we had told you our confessions were given under duress would you have sent us back to the police station?' The younger of the three judges replied: 'We ask the questions here.'

When I first spoke to Jim Phipps by phone in March 1997, he was already on the warpath, critical of what he saw as Salah Al-Hejailan's 'shenanigans'. He said Al-Hejailan wasn't experienced as a defence lawyer — that nobody in Saudi Arabia was, because there was no official role for lawyers in criminal cases.

Jim wasn't experienced either, despite his study of the *Sharia*. He sidestepped when I asked him about the supposed encouragement in the *Koran* for reconciliation. This was the man who had stood up in the Al Khobar court and demanded the death penalty for the two nurses. Now he conceded the Koran's focus on mercy.

What I didn't know then was that Jim Phipps' own tactics behind the scenes were about to explode in enmity and prevent any healing for many months.

Chapter 10

Rationale

On April Fools' Day 1997 came the bad news. The first and last chance for reconciliation before war had come and gone. The press release from The Law Firm of Salah Al-Hejailan gave a hint of the anger behind the scenes: 'We must express at the outset our shock and concern ...'

The cause of this shock was a press release issued the same day by the rival firm representing Frank Gilford, The International Law Firm. The release disclosed that Frank Gilford had rejected a private plea to him to waive the death penalty. 'We're not going to be pushed around by the defence lawyers or the press regarding what to do here,' said the statement released by his lawyers. 'I am surprised that their lawyers made this appeal before there has been a trial. It sounds to me as if their lawyers are admitting the nurses' guilt.'

On Saturday, March 29, Salah Al-Hejailan had sent Frank's lawyers a document headed 'Rationale for Early Waiver of the Death Penalty in the Gilford Murder Case'. This document's 17 pages amount to a passionate plea to Frank to reconsider his hard line on punishment for the nurses. It quotes Albert Camus, American and South African lawyers defending clients on death row, even the Pope. As Salah Al-Hejailan says in his press release, it is 'a thoughtful and considerate document', perhaps the only really respectful missive in the many months of sparring between the firms.

It was written mostly by the New York lawyer with Salah's firm, Bob Thoms, a person you wouldn't normally associate with heartfelt pleas for human rights. Yet it is an eloquent tract outlining the Christian and post-Enlightenment arguments against judicial killing.

Speaking to *The Independent* newspaper, Bob Thoms sounds personally stung by the quick rejection of the Rationale: 'We were hoping that Mr Gilford would consider its legal and philosophical arguments. We didn't intend to be pushy. We intended to be compassionate and caring.' Jim Phipps, one of Frank's lawyers in Riyadh, said Frank 'has simply said he will respect the outcome of the Saudi legal process. He also feels if you ain't guilty, then you don't need to make a plea for clemency.'

This was a clear sign of how hard Frank's lawyers were prepared to play. Jim Phipps, a man who prides himself on his knowledge of *Sharia* law, now proceeded to have a bet each way. The Western way is to wait for the court's verdict, with comment on a case prohibited by the *sub judice* rules. When Jim told the press that Frank was waiting for the outcome of the court case, he was adopting this Western standard. But in the Al Khobar court, he had already stood up and demanded the death penalty for Lucy and Debbie. That was definitely going the other way, the Saudi way, in which a victim's family is permitted to demand retribution, even before the court has given its verdict.

Now, in a further somersault, Jim Phipps slipped back into his Western lawyer's garb. When I called him from Sydney on April 2, he claimed the Gilfords had taken Al-Hejailan's appeal in the Rationale document 'as some kind of tacit admission of guilt. Why seek a waiver of the death penalty before there's a conviction?' he asked. 'At this juncture the Gilford family is not interested in discussion about forgiveness.'

Jim went on to describe some of the brutal detail of how Yvonne had been murdered, the many stabbings and beatings, the suffocation. 'The nature of the crime is hard to stomach,' he said. That was certainly true, but it is the responsibility of a lawyer to give the client precise advice about the law. And the law which applied here was Saudi law. One of its strong provisions is for early negotiation between the families of the victim and the accused. Even in this April 2 conversation, Jim was prepared to admit that. 'In Islam, there is a general desire to encourage healing, rather than enmity,' he acknowledged.

So on the one hand Jim Phipps was prepared to take the part of Saudi justice which allows for the victim's family to demand death for the accused before the accused are convicted. On the other hand, he wasn't advising his client to consider following the path of Koranic law which asks the aggrieved to consider mercy, also before a conviction. Instead, Jim and his colleagues were playing hard-ball American advocates, spinning the Rationale document to the press as some kind of admission of guilt.

If you actually read its seventeen pages, you'll find the words 'our clients ... protest their innocence'. Hardly an admission of guilt. The document explains why the appeal for clemency is made so early in the trial.

> We make this appeal and offer this Rationale before any court has given its verdict on the charges against our clients. This may appear surprising to a Western observer, but it is the invariable practice in an Islamic society and is just one small example of the difficulty of understanding a religion and culture which are not one's own.

Later, the Rationale points out that

> ...it is a recognized practice in Islam and in fact a requirement that goes without saying that contact with a victim's family, who may eventually control the fate of the accused, is to be established immediately upon the charging of the accused by the authorities ... we understand that some outside observers consider the practice of seeking clemency from the victim's family before the trial to be a 'high risk strategy' in that it could be misunderstood, so they say, as a pre-judgement of guilt ... on the contrary, it is the culturally accepted way of dealing with and properly channelling otherwise uncontrollable emotions in the aftermath of an alleged murder.

Given his depth of knowledge of the *Sharia* system, Jim Phipps was certainly not an 'outside observer'. He knew well enough that the appeal from Salah Al-Hejailan was a normal approach from the accused to the victim's family. He seems to have glossed over this in his comments both to his client and to the media.

The lawyers at Al-Hejailan's firm were not the only ones to be outraged by this ploy. The British ambassador to Saudi Arabia, Antony Green, had encouraged Salah Al-Hejailan to make his appeal to Frank Gilford in private and through his law firm. He had arranged a meeting with Jim Phipps and other lawyers from The International Law Firm to discuss the case on the morning of April 1.

Instead of keeping the appeal to Frank quiet, The International Law Firm rushed to condemn it as an admission of guilt. Late on March 31, the firm sent a draft of its press release condemning the Rationale to the ambassador for comment. It gave him one hour to respond. Though he rang within an hour, the press release had already gone out to the world's media, with its misleading claims. In a letter to Vern Cassin at The International Law Firm, dated April 2, Green condemns this move. 'Such a procedure is unprecedented in my experience as an Ambassador,' he writes.

> Your staff have suggested that the reason for the haste was a threat by Mr Hejailan's staff to address Mr Gilford directly. As I could have explained to you, I had a personal assurance from Mr Hejailan himself that any such approach would be conducted through you as Mr Gilford's lawyers.

Once again, the confusing mix of Western and Islamic legal practice emerged. In Islamic law a plea for clemency could be made directly to a family by someone associated with the accused — an uncle, a wise friend. In Western practice it is forbidden for the client or lawyers for one side to contact the client of the other.

The ambassador also blasted the text of The International Law Firm's press release.

> It selects short passages from a very long document in a manner that could give readers the impression that the two nurses are guilty. I cannot understand why a law firm would issue a statement of this kind before the trial has been held. I hope that you will issue a clarification to the effect that nothing in the press release should be read as prejudging the outcome of the trial.

Of course, no such clarification was given. The International Law Firm had, in fact, prejudged Lucy and Debbie. They may by now have had some evidence which convinced them of the women's guilt, but Western lawyers like Vern Cassin and Jim Phipps are well aware of the damage caused by prejudice to the accused in any trial. That principle went out the window as the near-blood feud between the law firms hotted up.

In the war of press releases, the dispute came down to this paragraph:

> Realistically, however, despite some alternative allegations or leads supported by written statements which appear to be credible, no coherent alternative theory has yet emerged for consideration by the police to account for Ms Gilford's death that might lead the Saudi Arabian authorities to drop the charges against Ms McLauchlan and Ms Parry.

This wasn't an admission of guilt but a statement of the bare truth of the desperate situation in which Lucy and Debbie now found themselves. It was true, now that they had withdrawn their confessions, that there were allegations of other possible suspects — though none that the police appeared to be investigating. In fact, once they had obtained their confessions, it appeared that all effective police work had ceased.

As Salah Al-Hejailan's own press release snorted, 'Mr Gilford clearly needs proper counselling and the benefit of a thoughtful exchange of views, not a hair trigger publicity machine.'

What The International Law Firm had perhaps sniffed — and taken unseemly advantage of — was the fact of a division in the defence ranks. The British lawyers for the families of Debbie and Lucy — as the families themselves — were wary of trying this 'Rationale for Early Waiver of the Death Penalty' approach. As they knew, the world simply didn't understand the niceties of Saudi law. Any dealing could and did look something like an admission of guilt.

The obverse of this was that dealing needed to be done. It would be done eventually, so why not now? Unfortunately, no one, save the pragmatic Salah Al-Hejailan, quite knew that then. Hence the months of pain on all sides that followed; pain that could have been avoided by a bit of pragmatic talking between the lawyers. From April Fools' Day on, the lawyers for both sides in Riyadh simply ceased talking to each other. Any communication henceforth would be through the disastrously distorting medium of the press release and whispers in journalists' ears.

Regardless of the merits or otherwise of the ill-fated Rationale, it does contain some fine words of argument against capital punishment, the most eloquent of which are Albert Camus' in his 'Reflections on the Guillotine', of 1957. Here, Camus rejects the 'crude arithmetic' of retaliation:

> But beheading is not simply death. It is just as different, in essence, from the privation of life as a concentration camp is from prison. It is a murder, to be sure, and one that arithmetically pays for the murder committed. But it adds to death a rule, a public premeditation known to the future victim, an organization in short, which is in itself a source of moral sufferings more terrible than death. Hence there is no equivalence. Many laws consider a premeditated crime more serious than a crime of pure violence. But what then is capital punishment but the most premeditated of murders, to which no criminal's deed, however calculated it may be, can be compared? For there to be equivalence, the death penalty would have to punish a criminal who had warned his victim of the date at which he would inflict a horrible death on him and who, from that moment onward, had confined him at his mercy for months. Such a monster is not encountered in private life.

The press release, written in an Islamic country in the midst of the most prominent case ever to cast one creed against another, does acknowledge, barely, that 'this view of course is at variance with deeply rooted beliefs in Islam'.

Yes, but not entirely. If the Christian imperative for mercy embodied in the reform of the New Testament is a rethink on the 'eye for an eye' of the Old Testament, we remember that those two big Ts are now bound in one book. So it is with the *Koran*. In one book we have divine words which do sanctify retribution. The same sacred book says that mercy is better than bald justice.

There's other good stuff in the Rationale. Justice William Brennan in *Furman v. Georgia* in 1972:

> The struggle about this punishment has been one between ancient and deeply rooted beliefs in retribution, atonement or vengeance on the one hand, and, on the other, beliefs in the personal value and dignity of the common man that were born of the democratic movement of the eighteenth century, as well as beliefs in the scientific approach to an understanding of the motive forces of human conduct, which are the result of the growth of the sciences of behaviour during the nineteenth and twentieth centuries.

It's odd to recall, of course, that the machine which motivated Camus' eloquence emerged from both the democratic and scientific developments Brennan refers to.

As Simon Schama in *Citizens*, his chronicle of the French Revolution, reminds us:

> In December 1789, Dr Joseph-Ignace Guillotin, deputy of the National Assembly, had proposed a reform of capital punishment in keeping with the equal status accorded to all citizens by the Declaration of the Rights of Man. Instead of barbaric practices which degraded the spectators as much as the criminal, a method of surgical instantaneity was to be adopted. Not only would decapitation spare the prisoner gratuitous pain, it would offer to common criminals the dignified execution hitherto reserved for the privileged orders. The proposal also removed the stigma of guilt by association from the family of the condemned and, most importantly, protected their property from the confiscation required by traditional practice.

It could be argued from this that it wasn't until the end of the eighteenth century that the self-glorifying West caught up in equality/morality with the Islamic world, which had applied quick decapitation to Allah's people since the eighth century. And, as the 1789 illustration reprinted in Schama's ephedrine-awake reminder of the bloody birth of modern democracy shows, the Republican French even raised a sword over the head of the condemned at these egalitarian executions. In their case, the sword was civilised by its once-removed use to sever the rope which held the blade before it dropped on the victim's neck. A sophistication not envisaged in Mohammed's book.

The Rationale, however, confined itself to the arguments of Judeo-Christian-based thought. In Saudi Arabia, its most controversial quotation was from a 1995 encyclical of Pope John Paul II, *The Gospel of Life*:

> The nature and extent of the punishment ... ought not go to the extreme of executing the offender except in cases of absolute necessity; in other words when it would not be possible otherwise to defend society. Today however, as a result of steady improvements in the organization of the

penal system, such cases are very rare if not practically nonexistent.

The International Law Firm aroused the Arabic press in Saudi Arabia to this reference to the Pope, as a way of undermining Al-Hejailan's standing at home. The suggestion was that there was blasphemy in quoting the Roman Catholic leader in a case where the *Sharia* had absolute hegemony. Several months later, this tactic backfired when Prince Sultan, the Defence Minister, became the first member of the house of Al Sa'ud to visit the Vatican.

The simple message of the Rationale was its clearest reference — to the opinion of Sister Helen Prejean, author of *Dead Man Walking,* that no government, let alone any person, is ever innocent enough or wise enough or just enough to lay claim to so absolute a power as death. And, the Rationale pointed out, 'the Gilford family are a part of the Western civilization and it would be inappropriate for them to take advantage of an Islamic religious tradition to which they do not belong'.

Had he been advised by thoughtful people who honoured the tradition from which they came, Frank Gilford might have been guided to see the sense in the other side's appeal. Frank himself is not a deeply educated man, more a quietly instinctive one. But he is no more a barbarian than any of the citizens of the Islamic and Western worlds; his later actions were to show he could be argued towards reason. What a pity those who should have had his best interests at heart didn't find a way to spare him the pain of the coming months, even if that involved the short-term pain of pointing out to him that a deal needed to be done.

Frank felt he couldn't bargain with the justice his sister deserved. In truth, he couldn't avoid such bargaining: the alternative would mean a life-or-death bargain with either too high a price — death for the British nurses — or one too low — a short gaol term. The only middle way involved money. And the only choice which involved no such bargaining in his heart was the one he never seemed to consider: opting out of his prerogative in the whole matter. Now, we would introduce him to someone who had taken that path.

Chapter 11

Saint Therese and the missing budgies

Therese Feeney chose forgiveness. Once a police officer, Therese is now a tour guide at an old abbey in a village in Ireland's County Roscommon. She is a woman who has seen her share of trouble. When we last spoke in late 1997, she was commemorating the 21st birthday of her little girl who had died at birth those many years before. This was something which drew us together, as I'd had a similar experience a few years ago.

We've never met, but have talked often by phone. Another producer from *Witness*, Ges D'Souza, went to Dublin to interview Therese for me in March 1997. Her story came to prominence in the wake of the British nurses' arrest, because 10 years earlier Therese had been in the exact dilemma Frank now faced.

Therese's sister, Helen, had been nursing in the Saudi city of Taif, from 1994 to 1996, when she was brutally murdered. Her friend of 10 years, fellow Irishwoman Monica Hall, was arrested for the murder with her husband Peter. Monica's story is dramatically similar to that of Debbie and Lucy. Arrested for the murder of a friend and nursing colleague, she later claimed to have been forced into a confession by police.

Monica also spoke to *Witness* in Dublin, although Therese declined to be filmed with the woman who had been convicted of her sister's murder. Monica told us her false confession had been obtained through 'psychological torture'. Denied contact with her embassy or her husband, Monica says she was kept for days in interrogation rooms without sleep until, 'I heard Peter's voice saying "I have signed your statement. What more do you want from me?", and this was followed by sounds of running water and more screams. I was shown a document that said Peter had killed Helen Feeney. I was led to believe that he was actually dead at one stage, so 56 hours into the interrogation I wrote and signed a statement saying "Yes, we both killed Helen Feeney."' Monica gave robbery as the motive. Now she made a plea to Frank: 'If Frank Gilford is watching this program, perhaps he can hear my descriptions of how confessions can be extracted through psychological torture because it is not something that happens every day but yet the result is the same — submissive, inert pulp.'

Like Debbie and Lucy, Monica claimed she had been told by her tormentors that she would be allowed to go home if she signed a confession. As in the case of Lucille, one of the accused was also facing criminal charges at home. Peter Hall, Monica's husband, told her during their imprisonment that he'd been charged with molesting an 11-year-old girl back in his home country, England. Monica says she was completely unaware of her husband's past. They had only been married five months when they were arrested.

A number of British journalists who published Monica's story have accepted it at face value. Therese Feeney does not. She still doesn't know whether or not Monica Hall killed her sister. Monica's trial ended in February 1988, 19 months after her arrest. A year later, she and her husband were told of their sentence — 10 years for him, eight for her.

Eight weeks later, as often happens at the beginning of the fasting month, Ramadan, the two were given a pardon by the king. 'The embassies came and told us that, yes, we would be released, but they didn't know when and there were two conditions. One, we were to write letters of thanks to the king, and the other was that there was to be no publicity. I agreed to both of those conditions because, as I saw it, I didn't have any choice. My mother was elderly and I was anxious to get home to see her.'

You may be wondering why there was no talk of the death penalty in all of this. Two-and-a-half years of gaol and they're out.

The reason is Therese Feeney. 'Saint' Therese, unlike her Australian counterpart Frank Gilford, travelled to Saudi Arabia and made a personal plea for clemency so that those accused of her sister's murder wouldn't be executed. 'An eye for an eye and a tooth for a tooth, et cetera, just never crossed my mind, although I have to admit that different stages of grief and anger occurred to other members of the family.' For Therese it was a straightforward decision based on faith. Her response to the question put to her in the Saudi court was automatic, almost catechismic.

> *Jesus taught when he was on earth the Lord's Prayer and in that are the words 'forgive us our trespasses as we forgive those who trespass against us'. He didn't say anything about forgiving if you were paid, or anything like that. He just said 'forgive', and so we forgave, and we were very blessed because ... by forgiving we were freed ourselves. We have a great sense of freedom.*

But Therese Feeney is not a saint in heaven. She's a woman among us who made an extraordinary decision. She recalled for us the day she heard of Helen's murder.

> *When you get news that somebody that you are close to is dead, your first reaction is unbelief, unbelief. I can remember, after telling my two daughters — who were quite young at the time and very close to their auntie — that she was dead, going outside into the yard and walking around the Land Rover in absolute disbelief. I don't know what I hoped to achieve by walking around the Land Rover, but it's what I remember doing and wondering how I was going to tell my father ... You see, one moment your life is perfectly normal — I remember I was cooking a chicken for Sunday lunch — and then the next, it's completely shattered and nothing seems real any more. It's just awful.*

In her grief, Therese seems just like the rest of us, not quite knowing how to deal with it. Yet in the quickness of her decision, she seems other-worldly, removed from ordinary life, saintly.

> *At all times we felt complete forgiveness towards whoever had murdered Helen. At her funeral, here in Dublin in the cathedral, prayers were said for her murderer or murderers and there was never any time when we wouldn't have had a spirit of forgiveness, so the realisation that we would be actively involved wasn't really a problem in that sense.*

Therese welcomed the aspect of *Sharia* law which gives the family of the victim a prerogative in determining the penalty.

> *I think it actually helped us, because our hurt as a family was being recognised and under Western law that isn't done. The family of a victim, even the hurt of a victim themselves, isn't legally recognised. So we found that helpful, not the fact that we had any power over whether somebody lived or died, but just the fact that our hurt was being recognised.*

Today, Therese sees Monica Hall on TV chat shows, talking about the case. She claims no bitterness.

> *When we went to Saudi Arabia, acting on behalf of my father, we gave the Halls forgiveness. Now that means giving them freedom, so if Mrs Hall wants to go on chat shows, if she wants to protest her innocence, that is her choice.*

It isn't hard to read between these lines that Therese has no certainty of Monica's innocence. As in Frank's case, there is an impasse between the accused and those who loved the victim.

Monica now lives in Dublin and, for the camera, moves about her small yard, placing feed in the birdhouse. It's winter, and there are no birds about. She lives alone. Her marriage to Peter Hall didn't survive the prison ordeal. Therese obliges our producer's request for some vision of her walking in a Dublin park, among scores of pigeons, ducks and swans on the pond. They're both women of mature age, both showing life lived long and hard enough in their faces.

Monica:

> *The experience has had a major impact on my life. I'm now seven-and-a-half years down the road from it. It has taken me six-and-a-half years to fully draw my breath after it. The difficulties that I had when I came home were astronomical, but they were at a level everybody else takes for granted. Opening and closing doors, handling keys, handling money, going out on my own, getting on and off a bus, noise, crowds, traffic.*

> *Supermarket shopping was a nightmare. I didn't know which tin of peas to pick off the rack. I just didn't have the ability to make that decision. All of those things were stripped away between the interrogation and the imprisonment, so it has been a very, very slow relearning of all of those faculties. There has been a lot of therapy. I have baby-sat myself through this experience so many times in the last six-and-a-half to seven years, but I've now accepted and hopefully integrated it into my life. It is part of my life's experience.*

Monica says she doesn't regret going to Saudi Arabia. Yet her face, still hardened by the years of grief and either guilt or wrongful accusation, tells the story of a penalty much beyond two-and-a-half years of gaol. This is a woman who still looks to be serving her sentence.

Like anyone seeking vindication and reconciliation, Monica asked to see the family of her murdered friend. 'I had a private meeting with Therese Feeney approximately two-and-a-half months after coming home, at my request. I told her the facts of the case and I said everything that I needed to say to her at the time.'

How did Therese respond? 'She listened to everything that I said.' Did Therese believe her? 'Well, that's a question you would have to ask her.'

As described by Therese, the meeting was less than a triumph of reconciliation.

> *After Monica Hall returned to Ireland, she made repeated requests to meet me. I didn't want her going to see my father, so in the circumstances I thought it was better if I met her. I met her in a hotel in Galway. She was accompanied by her cousin who was a solicitor. I asked for that. You couldn't actually say we talked. She asked to meet me, I listened to what she had to say, but it wasn't a normal conversation and when she finished what she had to say she asked me if I wanted to ask her any questions. I said I didn't want to appear flippant, which I didn't, it was a very serious matter to me, but I did want to know what happened to my sister's budgies because Helen had two budgies and she loved her budgies. And she told me she didn't know.*

Birds again. They seem to have some significance in this story. Frank's birds in his outback backyard. Monica's empty birdhouse. Therese walking among swans and missing the birds her sister loved. Were this a parable, those birds would tell us something.

The symbols in real life aren't so clear.

> *I didn't go to that meeting expecting to get anything from it. I had no wish to meet Mrs Hall. She had requested the meeting and I acceded to her request. Neither did I tell anybody about that meeting, not even my late father, my family. Nobody knew about that meeting until Mrs Hall spoke of us on television recently. I didn't tell my husband or my children.*

Why not? 'Because it wasn't something that I really wanted to do but thought, OK, if she keeps on asking, maybe it's better.'

Therese won't quite say that she believes Monica is guilty or whether her trial was fair. 'I'm not going to comment on that, because I don't want Mrs Hall coming back to me. I don't want to say anything that is going to start a seesaw. The tabloids will pick up what I say on your program.'

Therese offers, through the camera, a message for the Gilford family:

> *The Gilfords have suffered a very, very severe cross, just as we did, and I think they should seriously consider not adding to that cross themselves. They must think of their own inner-freedom for the rest of their lives and they must do what will give them that. But what I really want to say is that, through forgiving, we have got the most wonderful feeling of freedom. We aren't bitter and we don't have to carry that load around with us for the rest of our lives.*
>
> *We don't forgive and forget; we do remember, of course we remember, and we remember all the horror of it; but we can remember without any bitterness and that's what's important because my sister wouldn't have wanted her death to be in any way the death internally of any of us and so our lives go on.*

From her words now, it's clear that Therese harks back to her catechism days, the days when faith and life could be dreamed of in the parables she learnt as a child. But, as much as she would like it to be, her story isn't quite a well-formed parable. The perfectly formed story of forgiveness and reconciliation would require one, missing, ingredient. The missing bird has a name. Acknowledgment. Perhaps it should come from Therese herself, if her forgiveness truly is blind to guilt or innocence. Or perhaps it should come from Monica, if she is guilty, finally acknowledging the truth and throwing herself on the mercy and understanding of the family of her victim, her friend. One of these women is binding them both in a continuing sentence of doubt and mistrust.

The Feeneys hired no lawyers, the trip to Saudi Arabia cost the family £4000, a harsh tax on Therese's father but much less than what Frank Gilford faced.

As well as the walk with the ducks and swans, our Ges had Therese Feeney filmed on the phone to Frank Gilford. I set it up with Frank that Therese would call him. We didn't record the conversation between them. I hoped that Frank might benefit from talking with someone who had faced the same troubles he now did. He said he was happy to talk to her — and did, for many months afterward. She told him of her reasons for making her decision. He tolerated her, appreciating her concern but not her message.

Chapter 12

Appeal in the dark

Frank wasn't listening to Therese Feeney or journalists like myself who counselled against the death penalty. He was listening to Jim Phipps. From Riyadh, on the phone in May, Jim Phipps tells me that 'great care will be exercised' by the court. 'We've counselled Frank that he can rely on the court.'

Now the judges in the court have asked that there be conciliation between the nurses' side and Frank. They've adjourned for a couple of weeks to allow this to happen. Yet on Jim Phipps' side, despite his avowed support of the *Sharia* way, there's no hint of compromise, even of facilitating dialogue. Oddly, this is our best chance for access to all the parties. With no one talking to each other, perhaps we can slip in as intermediaries — and make a pretty good television program on the way.

In another Riyadh law office, Michael Dark is surprised when I call to say we've been given approval to come to the kingdom. He's interested to hear our impressions of Frank Gilford. I tell him Frank Gilford would be insulted by an offer of blood money.

Michael is frustrated. Jim Phipps and The International Law Firm have blocked access to Frank. He sounds just as frustrated by his clients. 'They're not saints,' he says. 'Deborah Parry is a very small, weedy little person who's had psychiatric problems for years. She'd jump if you said "boo".' Michael says he knows of the claims against Lucy back in Scotland.

Michael Dark explains that his firm can't criticise Saudi justice, despite the claims of the women to have been set up. 'Our position, with Salah as a leading lawyer in Saudi, makes it difficult to run down the system.' He mentions the unsolved murder from two years before. I ask for an alternative hypothesis for Yvonne's murder. He says he's had accounts from six or eight nurses who knew Lucy and Debbie at the hospital, all claiming harassment from the security guards. One guard had exposed himself to Yvonne, he says. One nurse had moved apartments because she was being pestered by a guard. After the murder, a number of the guards had been arrested. Yvonne had often left her window open for the cat, and her room was only 50 metres from a guard post.

Michael complains of the lack of evidence in the case, aside from the confessions.

I ask if we can see his clients. 'We're quite keen on you seeing the nurses,' he says, 'but we're bound to be cautious of allowing trial by television. I would like to try and get across to Frank Gilford and the Australian public that there are significant differences between Australian and Saudi law.'

He mentions that Salah Al-Hejailan is issuing a press release inviting Frank Gilford to come to Saudi Arabia at his expense. Salah wants Frank to meet the nurses and see the country for himself. I mention Frank's reluctance.

'I would quite like to use you,' Michael starts, then corrects himself and says, 'to ask you' to be a conduit to Frank. Michael is concerned that Jim Phipps is blocking information being passed to Frank, including the women's statements about their alleged mistreatment during their interrogations and confessions. 'I want to try and get through the Phipps filter. There are things we'd want you to say to Frank about the Saudi system if you come and look around.' Michael confides that he'd been thinking of sending an emissary directly to Frank, dodging Frank's lawyers. This had been just what The International Law Firm feared.

It's sounding like the women's lawyers will help us when we come to Saudi. The women's families will be there, too, on a visit, and maybe we can meet up. I arrange to meet Michael at Le Gulf Meridien hotel in Al Khobar.

A night or so later, a call comes at 3 am. I struggle to sound awake as Salah Al-Hejailan, in a big voice that sounds used to having its way, introduces himself. He has seen a letter, he says, from the acting Interior Minister, Prince Sultan, authorising our visit. We'll be allowed to interview the nurses, the governor of the Eastern Province, the chief of police, the works.

Salah talks of his offer to fly Frank Gilford to the kingdom. 'I will finance his trip,' says the lawyer, as if Frank will agree as a matter of course. I wonder if this offer is wise, given Frank's sense of his own independence. Salah has big ideas. He wants to suggest to Frank 'the foundations for what should be done next for his sister's memory'. Sounds like blood money dressed up as some kind of charitable trust. Salah says he doesn't want this to be misinterpreted as an admission of the nurses' guilt. 'They are innocent; they want to go to trial,' he says. He doesn't expect Frank to make a statement of forgiveness but a 'positive statement of reconciliation'.

It's hard to imagine the personalities of Frank and Salah coming to any such agreement. What the Saudi lawyer says casually would cause Frank serious affront: 'If he is insisting the two nurses are the killers, he must see that the confessions cast negative things on his own sister as a leading lesbian. The confessions are not complimentary to his sister.'

Salah, too, is talking of sending an independent messenger to Frank. Who would I suggest? He mentions a former British politician and an Australian lawyer who used to work in Saudi Arabia.

It's not clear what Salah wants from us, aside from advice on Frank which he doesn't look like taking. But it seems like a good idea to be in his good books: 'You will have my full support and cooperation,' he says, and adds he hopes to meet us when we come to Riyadh.

The next day, I talk to the Australian lawyer Salah mentioned. Anthony Abrahams is a man aware of his own importance to the general cause of human rights, wherever it may arise. As a member of the Wallabies, the national Australian rugby union team, he had led the players' boycott of South Africa in 1971. This is an unusual corporate lawyer, his heart well and truly on his sleeve. Abrahams had spent a couple of years attached to Salah Al-Hejailan's law firm in Riyadh.

Now, he takes it upon himself to coach me in how to deal with Salah, who he describes as 'a very big character with enormous charm. Bright but conscious of his power. He's used to dealing with half the US Cabinet and the heads of US companies.'

Why is Salah's firm taking the nurses' case? 'They're doing it pro bono,' says Anthony. 'All for nothing, except their honorary role with the British embassy.' He points out the politics of the case, 'taking place against a background of very big business between Saudi Arabia and the West, with companies like British Aerospace, and the bedding down of relations with Tony Blair.' Salah is trusted with 'getting this off the agenda as quickly as possible'.

Getting in the way of this, Anthony believes, is the old enmity between The Law Firm of Salah Al-Hejailan and The International Law Firm. 'Phipps should show more independence,' he says. 'It is morally controversial for the law firm to be taking the role it is.'

Anthony's anti-apartheid past gives him some high-falutin' ideas about intervening in this impasse. If I can handle Salah, who has a short attention span for people who bore him, 'you could be the person who saves these persons' lives'.

This seems a bit far-fetched, but it startles me into a sense of responsibility for these women I don't know. Also, it's nice to have everybody central to the case talking to us.

Chapter 13

We go

As we fly into Dhahran airport, we can see what the fuss is about. British military aircraft litter the tarmac on the long taxi into the terminal. Big trade is clearly at stake in this affair, which is ruffling the feathers of the Saudi–British relationship. As we step on to the stairs of the Saudi jet, the heat almost pushes us back. Jet-lagged in the late dusk, we meander with the other passengers into a terminal full of guest workers from Third World countries. Dhahran's terminal retains the scruffiness of another time, not like its awesome cousin in Riyadh. We're met by four or five gents in the common Saudi male dress of white *thobe* — a grandfather-neck white shirt that flows down to the ankles — and white or red-and-white *keffiyah* — the head scarf with a black cord. They're friendly in a bureaucratic kind of way. The short one, Hamad, reveals himself as the boss. He's from the local foreign desk of the Information Ministry. They help us through Customs — though not without the obligatory search of our gear for pornography — and minibus us to our hotel.

Though I'd been to Riyadh during the Gulf War in 1990, this is my first visit to the Eastern Province. All seems concrete and motorway in the dark.

The hotel, Le Gulf Meridien, is a French marble edifice on the corniche at Al Khobar. This is the shiniest of the three towns which have melded together on the mudflats of the Gulf shore. The vast lobby of the hotel could be anywhere, save for the man who dispenses coffee in tiny cups from a brass hook-spouted pot. Hamad promises to return early for 'your program', though it isn't at all clear what this might be. The others fall into bed while I slap myself into life to meet Michael Dark in the lobby. He's a slight man with slightly receding grey hair and an air of concentration. Even in his relaxed mode, he's wearing a blue blazer. He reveals that letters from the two women's families have gone to Jim Phipps, who hasn't passed them on to Frank. He's to meet the visiting British families later and will encourage them to see us during our stay.

'Our program' is even less clear when we wake and minibus to the Information Ministry office in downtown Dammam. This is a dusty but affluent place, the architecture the common white blocks of cement found throughout the Middle East. There are some seriously substantial villas in a stretch of town near the sea. We meet Hamad's boss, Jasim Al-Yaqoot, who shouts into his phone a lot and seems to have a lot of functionaries sitting about. We're directed through an ornate traditional Arabic door into a display area. They obviously bring foreign delegations here. There are photographs of ancient and modern sites — even some Bedouin tents — lining the wall. We're invited to watch 'the video', which turns out to be many minutes of Saudi industrial triumph. I leave the long-suffering crew, 'Big Al' Garipoli and Greg 'Babyface' Barbera, taking notes with Paul Barry while I step back through the gilded door to hassle Jasim.

It's soon clear that we won't get much done today. We can film some street life. Back on the Corniche, we shoot Saudis and foreign workers strolling and sitting on the sand. Signs prohibit swimming. There's a touching scene of a woman clad all over in black holding hands with her husband in white, sitting staring out to sea. Not all public displays of contact between men and women are prohibited, it seems, though what would be a commonplace shot elsewhere feels a little voyeuristic here.

Hamad, in the minibus, says we must ask his advice. He knows his country well and we must trust him. OK, I ask, can we film people in an old *soukh* in Dammam? It turns out that there is no rustic old marketplace in these new towns built on the back of the oil boom. He takes us to an area of narrow streets and fabric shops, manned by Pakistanis. There are gold shops, too, ostentatious gilt dripping in window displays. We are told not to concentrate on the women. Naturally, like any curious foreign crew, this is just what we want to do. I promise we'll stick to wide shots.

A group of tittering teenage girls, in black from head to toe, walks by, all flashing eyes. It is possible to flirt in an *abaya*, believe it or not. We watch the interactions of men and women on the street, head movements and eye flashes betraying an unexpected friendly but silent banter between the sexes.

A man walks by the camera and mutters to Hamad. Moments later there are ten police converging on us, chattering. We've transgressed, someone has complained to the *Muttawa*, the religious enforcers and they've called in the civilian police. Our offence? Taking pictures of women. I scurry around to the minibus to label a blank tape. Sometimes you can get away with handing over a blank if officious police and bureaucrats demand your footage. Young boys follow me, laughing and shouting *Amrika, Amrika*. By the time I return to the scene, the police have agreed to let us go, videotape intact. Hamad isn't happy.

In the van he confesses that the same thing happened when he brought a crew to the same place during the war. On the way back to the hotel, he incants verses from the *Koran*.

Later that night, we're having an abstemious dinner in the hotel's Lebanese restaurant when Hamad turns up with Jasim. They are distraught. If we don't hand over our tape, they will lose their jobs. Jasim is actually wringing his hands. Paul tells them we refuse to accept censorship. They say this isn't censorship but good relations. I try to distract Jasim by talking about Sydney and the Olympic Games. Hamad says he trusts me not to use the offending shots. We make no commitment and they depart looking worried. What will this mean for 'our program'?

Nothing, as it turns out. The next day, we're ferried to the hospital. 'The King Fahd Military Medical Complex', says the huge sign on the archway over the road. As we sweep into the compound, the first impression is of modernity. This looks to be a recently built complex, no more than 10 years old. Hamad drops off as we're placed in the safe hands of the military administrators. We sit around a board table and discuss the case and what we might be able to film. Lieutenant Colonel Zamil has taken over the top job at the hospital since the murder. Anyway, he assures us, he and his colleagues cannot be interviewed. They're bemused by our opposition to the death penalty and laugh when they talk about 'chop-chop square'. Yes, we can film the part of the compound where Yvonne lived.

The man in charge of public relations, a Major Abdulrahman, is suspicious, on principle. When we arrive at the block adjacent to Yvonne's, he has underlings strip the bushes of their colourful fruit: clothes spread in the sun to dry. I say we'd like to film this to show that the place is lived in. He thinks we're trying to make it look tatty. Upstairs, they insist on showing us the dryers in the laundry: proof that this is no cheapskate place. Then we're ushered to a room at the end of the corridor in this dormitory block. 'Just like Yvonne's,' they tell us. This is as close as we're going to get. We film that room, for all it's worth, Paul recording a piece to camera with the rider, 'In a room just like this one …' It's eerily atmospheric all the same. There is a coffee table equivalent to the one Debbie is alleged to have bruised herself on. There is the tiny kitchenette, source of the kettle and the bread knife. Over the peephole in the door, the last occupant has placed a little patch. Perhaps a wariness of other residents or of security staff?

While the others film in the tiny flat, I usher our large entourage into the corridor and try to keep the gossip to a whisper. Colonel Zamil fills me in on Saudi military discipline. When he went for his interview to join the Army, he says, he was asked the usual question to test his respect for authority. Some would be asked to empty the water from one bucket into another using a teaspoon. He was asked to shift the office wall twelve inches to the right. He goes through the motions on the wall of the dormitory corridor, demonstrating his compliance. He laughs, seeing I can't comprehend such unquestioning acquiescence. This is undoubtedly a culture of obedience.

As we leave the room 'just like Yvonne's' we find other small hints of life. Sandals left outside closed doors, a bicycle in the corridor. A newish sign on the security door urging residents to make sure it's closed. Outside, cats shelter from the blast of the noonday sun. We film the new barbed-wire perimeter fences which give the compound an air of a concentration camp. We're allowed to film Yvonne's block, though not her window at the rear of the building. Abdulrahman won't allow us to get a shot showing the proximity of the guards' post to the window.

Few people are about, some Filipinas waiting for buses to town in the heat. A few white-clad figures jumping off the bus on the way home. Some carry shady umbrellas.

We're taken to the recreation centre. We can film the pool, but there's no one there.

What about the cafeteria? Yes. This is in the main hospital building and a few foreign staff are still sitting over their trays. A Dutch woman waves angrily at the camera and leaves. We find a few Western women and start to film. No interviews, we're told. Paul starts to chat to Australian Kathryn Lyons and an American woman. We're ushered away. No interviews, but at least the ensuing altercation between Paul and myself and our minders makes entertaining footage.

We're allowed to film in the ward where Yvonne worked. Male Specialty One. An obliging patient with pins in his legs is wheeled up and down the corridor in a wheelchair for us several times. The American woman from the cafeteria does some business for us at the Nursing Station.

Abdurrahman wants us to come and have lunch. It will be served in the boardroom. But I've heard on the mobile phone that we can meet the British families if we come to the British Trade Office. Now. We gush our apologies and our thanks to our restrictive but otherwise genial friends. 'This is the Army. I have to do what I am told,' says Colonel Zamil.

Back on our own minibus with Hamad, we head to the Al Bustan compound in Al Khobar. The others head back to the hotel while Paul and I wait for the families. They're meeting in a room down the hall. Lawson Ross, the consular officer, says he'll put in a word for us. After five minutes, he emerges and says we can come in to put our case.

The room is smoke-filled and full of tired, worried faces. Grant Ferrie and Stan McLauchlan greet us in broguish Scots. Sandra and Jon Ashbee look the most weary.

Paul and I both make earnest pleas for a direct message to Frank Gilford. We talk about the man we know, that he's not a nasty fellow and responds to personal approaches. We explain his initial refusal to talk to us but his change of mind when our researcher turned up on the doorstep. The thing is to try to talk to Frank without anger, I suggest. 'I'm not angry,' says Stan, who certainly sounds it. 'I'm frustrated.'

Michael Dark has described Stan as possibly being a similar character to Frank. Gruff and independent. I can see it. We find the families' emotion transferring itself to us as we persuade them that, although they've decided not to do television interviews, this is their best chance to get close to Frank. As I hear my own words, I hope I'm right. Suddenly, the enormity of what these people face has hit home. Whatever they do, they explain, they worry it will be the wrong thing, that it might further prejudice Frank's mind against their loved ones. It could be worse if you do nothing, I suggest.

As the minutes melt into the Saudi afternoon and our satellite deadline approaches, the families are still not convinced. Stan and Grant can't understand how their letters to Frank weren't getting through. 'But you can talk to him through us,' we tried again. 'To Frank. It's not ideal, trying to reach him through television, but at least he would see you as real people. Letters he can ignore.' Lawson Ross ushers us out to wait again as Stan, Grant and the Ashbees agonise over their cigarettes. Should they do the interview or not? Making tea in the staff kitchen we count our chances as 50-50. Minutes later, Lawson calls us back into the room. The answer is yes. 'But don't do the dirty on us.' We make a time for the interview later in the day, here in the British Trade Office compound, in the villa where they're staying. We sigh our thanks and relief.

On the road, current affairs crews don't have too much time for cooling heels. Now we're off to a mosque to film Paul's introductions to the stories in this week's show. We've written scripts based on our earlier filming with the Gilfords and Sue Taylor, and with Therese Feeney and Monica Hall. Now, five months of work is coming to fruition. The sun's going down as we cruise around two elaborate-looking mosques, looking for the best vantage points. Hamad is perturbed when we settle on a stretch of open land with dirt mounds in it. Naturally, he thinks we're trying to make his town look grubby. Actually, we're sticking Paul on top of a mound so that he catches the last of the sunset and he's on a height level with the mosque in the background. Up there in his blue shirt he looks gorgeous. Perhaps it's the Oxford degree, but this guy has extraordinary confidence; it doesn't matter what mullock heap he's perched on in what strange land, he's still able to look like he knows what he's talking about. Of course, that's because he's been well-briefed by his producer ...

Now we tear back to the families' villa to record their interview. They're showered, and fresher than before, though quite agitated. Grant and Stan go first. 'Well, we still plan to get married as soon as she gets home,' says Grant, toning down his accent for Australians, 'sooner rather than later.' These are not effusive men and it's a struggle to get from them the feeling they evinced in our earlier chat. Stan talks of saying goodbye to his daughter at the police station. 'Obviously it was very emotional today, having to leave her. And I suppose that she'll be down for a day or two once we go. But she's a strong-willed girl and she'll bounce back again.

She knows herself that she's innocent and she has a clear conscience. And she's told us many times that she can live with herself because she knows she didn't do it.'

Grant: 'You ask anybody who knows her. There's no way she's capable of doing this — no way, it's not in her nature.'

I've promised to give Frank the whole interview, not just the bits we put to air. It seems so important that they reach out to Frank, given that they can't get their letters to him. Paul asks Stan, 'If you could say something to Frank Gilford, what would you say?' Stan responds:

> *The basis for the confessions, or the motive for the crime, is a lesbian relationship that has supposedly happened between the three girls. Now what I would like to say to Mr Gilford is, my daughter is certainly no lesbian and Mr Gilford himself I believe's on record as saying that his sister is not of that sexual persuasion. So it surely must register with him that if that's the motive for killing, then it's absolute nonsense.*

Now it's Sandra and Jon's turn. They both stub out cigarettes in the kitchen before taking the places of the others on the lounge. Jon, too, has a message for Frank. 'I would like to talk to Mr Gilford person-to-person and I would like to let him know the girl that I know. Because if he knows that girl, he will know she hasn't done this.'

Sandra: 'If he said he would be prepared to talk to us, I would be on the next plane out there. To tell him the type of person my sister was, is, and that she has no way, there's nothing in her that would make her do this.'

Jon: 'If he knew Debbie, the type of girl she is, then it would never ever cross his mind that she'd done it.'

Jon is on edge as he tells of his closeness to his sister-in-law. He laughs a little as he says she looks up to him as a father figure, even though she's slightly older. This is the man who has been carrying the weight of the case for the families. He's the diligent bank manager, the man who has the patience to deal with lawyers, the other family, his own distraught family, diplomats — and now the media.

In the stillness of the interview, it comes to a head and he breaks down. Paul tells him there's no hurry and we wait, for a moment, before it's clear that Jon can't go on. We all retire to the kitchen for five minutes so that he can have a smoke and recover. There's a camaraderie among everyone in that kitchen, a feeling that we are in amongst it at last and that maybe this will help to save two women's lives.

Back to the couch, and Jon and Sandra deliver their heartfelt entreaties to Frank. 'I pray to God every day,' says Sandra. 'And I know that Debbie's innocent. She has a clear conscience and I just hope the Saudi judicial system will see that.'

As they speak, it feels as though only a stony heart could resist them. They are prepared to travel to Australia to meet Frank at a moment's notice. We have to go, so we take addresses and promise to send copies of the interview. And also to speak to Frank on their behalf and to grill Jim Phipps on why he won't pass on their letters. Such an intense meeting in two short hours. Especially with the Ashbees, I feel a bond of responsibility.

We rush off again, back to the mosque. Now we lay our mini tracks to move the camera back and forth as Paul records more links. I phone Sydney to tell them we've got the goods and we'll be feeding, as scheduled, from the Dammam TV centre tonight. We're not allowed to film the praying men at the mosque except from the doorway. Aside from this we're made welcome, a Western camera crew not being an everyday sight in suburban Dammam. As men and boys arrive, they pass to the ablutions block to wash, an important part of Islamic ritual. At the door to the prayer hall, they slip off their sandals before they move in to touch their foreheads to the floor.

Outside, we record our links. We decide it's too ludicrous to film the silly introduction to some story about clowns on the steps of the mosque. Sometimes the bathos of television is too much. Prayers over, an elderly man emerges from the mosque, shouting. He's not angry, just emphatic. He's telling us, we're told by a man who interprets from the Arabic, that now we've been exposed to the wisdom of Islam we have no choice but to renounce our own faith and follow the true path. I thank him for his advice.

A long day is still in progress. Hamad tells us he's very careful about what he eats, despite his evident paunch, and scowls as we resort to some local version of Hungry Jack's on the way to the TV station. The station turns out to be a bit of a shack in a paddock. The manager has promised us all cooperation, but the hours slip by as Sydney keeps reporting problems with the vision quality. Each point in the relay — Sydney ground station, Riyadh uplink, Riyadh TV station and Dammam TV station — all say the problem isn't with them. Various suggestions are shouted through our Egyptian technician until finally all is delivered to Sydney by 4 am. Big Al and I, who have been feeding the tapes, rouse the others who have been sleeping on couches and we head for the hotel. At the gate to the TV station, sleeping guards suddenly discover their responsibilities and demand passports. We fall into bed at 4.30, only to be woken by Sydney radio stations at five. Word is out that we're the only film crew and journalists allowed into the country to cover the story, and that we've got the interview with the families.

Next day, or rather the same day with a few snatched hours of sleep, we're offered an audience with the police on the case. The others leave me at the TV station to try to arrange another feed while they go off to the Dammam Police Headquarters. My business done, I wander out on to the highway to hail a cab to town. This means half an hour in a daze in the noon sun. Finally, a man who has less English than my Arabic takes me to a police station in downtown Dammam. For a few minutes I have a sense of how it must have been for Lucy and Debbie among the strange men in blue and green uniforms. Unknowable, terrifying in guilt or innocence. But after several corridors and stairways and offices, a major tells me I'm at the wrong station and directs me to the headquarters. There I find the camera and lights already set up and Major Hamed and Lieutenant Colonel Al-Karmi are swivelling in their chairs.

During the interview they are nervous, polite and insistent on the dignity of themselves and their police force. These are not men used to the impertinence of journalists.

Paul asks them about the claims that they have harassed the women into confessing: 'It's not true. An investigation took place with no intimidation being done to these nurses. Everybody has a right to retract his confession.'

The police tell us they have evidence besides the confessions given by the two women. 'If there were no evidence, I will assure you they will not be arrested.'

Hamed refuses to show us the video taken of the accused women at the murder scene, saying that all the other evidence is with the file before the judges and we can't have access to it.

What about witnesses? We know that other staff at the hospital have been questioned by the police. Will their evidence form part of the case? 'There is evidence, but it's not eyewitnesses. You know, usually criminals, when they commit their crimes, try to avoid anyone seeing them.' Thanks for the tip, Major.

Major Hamed confirms that hospital security were questioned after the murder. 'They've been interrogated and we've come to the conclusion they have nothing to do with the case so they've been released.'

The defence lawyers had suggested that the type of test used in the post-mortem to establish whether Yvonne was sexually assaulted is a procedure now abandoned in the West. The major dismisses this assertion. 'We made the test and the result was negative. Each country has its own procedures and its own forensic lab and I think in Saudi Arabia we have the best forensic labs in the world.'

The officers can give us no timetable for the case. 'It's just like any case all over the world; it takes time. In Islamic law, we are all equal in front of the court, regardless of colour, tribe, religion, ethnic group. And I assure everybody that justice will take place in this case.'

Are the police upset that many in the West criticise the Saudi judicial system? 'They have their rules, their opinion. Saudi Arabia has laws from Islam. We think ours better than trials in any other country in the world.'

This session, in the artificial light of the television cameras, raises more questions than answers. Two vastly different ideologies, cultures, practices, conversing in the same room but not meeting at any point. No doubt Hamed presumes his questioners are stupid, asking silly questions. But if he refuses to discuss any evidence, there is no objective ground on which police and journalists can meet.

In the grounds of the police headquarters we film police and American-looking squad cars. It's not hard to make men in khaki uniforms with pistols look menacing. But to us, they're unfailingly polite, even providing a police car and driver to move in and out of shot on cue.

Greg Barbera films the hexagonal pattern of the barred windows. It's here the women come to meet their families every six weeks. If you assume that the Saudi legal system and its police are benign, the headquarters can look modern, efficient, businesslike. If you assume police brutality, the place has the hardness, the institutional malignity such places evoke. Here, we are as blinded to the truth as the blindness of justice itself. Behind those bars are men who are truly as earnest and friendly as the face they've just shown us.

Or there are men who are brutal and cowardly in their determination to resolve a case at whatever cost. No answers seem to peer from those windows.

Back at the hotel, I'm phoning staff at the hospital. Caroline Ionescu is happy to chat, but she says she can't be interviewed. Kathryn Lyons reveals herself as one of the women we tried to chat to in the hospital canteen. These two women are the first to give their off-the-record condemnation of Lucy and Debbie. Guilty, they say — without doubt. Caroline bases her belief in their guilt on her memories of the week she spent with Lucy and Debbie after the murder. Kathryn didn't know either of the accused women closely, but she has heard plenty from the other staff.

I'm shocked. All along, I've assumed the innocence of the two British nurses. Clearly, I've thought, Frank Gilford is a simple man prepared to believe that anybody charged with a crime must be guilty. Now, I'm slapped in the face by my own brittle assumptions.

Though Caroline Ionescu is on a list of people at the hospital Michael Dark has suggested I call, she is certainly no character witness for his clients. And Kathryn Lyons, though she seems as friendly as any Australian abroad, is grim in her desire to see her former colleagues executed. Even though she has seen the reality of the executioner's sword in the chop-chop square down in Al Khobar.

I've had enough of cauliflowering my ear on the hotel-room phone and call the crew to go shopping. We're lured, just like the hospital expats, to the carpet *soukhs* with their cheap carpets from all over the Middle East. An Afghani gives us good prices as we chat about his homeland. He's happy that the fundamentalist Moslem Taliban have taken over his country, he says. At least they don't loot his family's houses.

Outside in the heat, I stumble across a woman I'd met at the British Trade Office. She points to the clock and the fountain out in the main road. 'Chop-chop square,' she confides. There had been an execution there two weeks ago. I cast around for Paul, our reporter. We decide to film a piece to camera in the place where Debbie and Lucy would most likely face the sword, should they be found guilty. He's not dressed for the occasion, so Alex and Greg make cracks and take happy snaps as Paul and I swap shirts on the pedestrian overpass which stands astride this ghoulish place. In the late-afternoon sun and with the filters in Greg's camera, the water in the fountain looks bloody, ominous. But this execution site is otherwise unremarkable. Taxi drivers call for trade nearby, people catch buses. The sharp edge of justice is humdrum here. Back in 1990, a driver had taken us to another execution square in Riyadh. There, all we saw was a carpark. No scaffold, no bloodstains to mark the demise of hundreds. Here, in Al Khobar, the grisly scene described by Kathryn Lyons is nowhere in evidence, dusted over by the drowsy tedium of diurnal life.

Like the Saudis around us, we return to our shopping. In a fluoro-lit modern white showroom, a woman clad all in black looks at the expensive white ceramic porcelain of imported bathroom furniture. A lone black figure among the brilliant white sterility of toilet bowls and vanities, she's a living symbol of medieval ways coexisting with twentieth-century consumerism. This country, more than most, is caught between the two.

At the hotel, we have dinner with a very different kind of Saudi woman. She's a journalist, half-Egyptian; her father is a wealthy medical specialist. This is the privileged modern woman of Saudi Arabia. She wears the *abaya* and a scarf, though not a veil, in public and at her workplace. She is educated, knows the relative freedoms of Cairo, and yet is outraged by what she sees as Western presumption in reportage of the Saudi kingdom. Her paper, the *Arab News*, covered the disastrous fire which killed many pilgrims at the annual *Haj* in Mecca, yet she's read reports in the Western press that the event was ignored by the Saudi media. She has been covering the Gilford case for her paper and was arrested, briefly, one day outside the court in Al Khobar, trying to get a glimpse of the British nurses. Yet she defends the justice system and doesn't doubt their guilt.

Until our visit, both the English-language and Arabic press had covered reports of the case. Soon after, as the international heat grew fierce, the coverage stopped. Saudi television never mentions the case.

Next morning, we head for Riyadh in the van. With us comes our minder, Hamad, who will hand us over to a colleague in the capital. When the old man at the mosque in Al Khobar challenged us to embrace Islam, I'd challenged Hamad in turn. Surely the *Koran* tells me to respect the wishes of my mother and father. Yet if I were to reject their Christian religion and turn to Islam, would I not be dishonouring them and therefore disobeying the *Koran*?

Now, Hamad has brought along a copy of the *Koran* with an English translation. As we drive through the desert he intones verses in Arabic, then reads them to us in English. He finds his answer to the conundrum of filial duty versus acceptance of the prophet's teaching: one must follow the teachings of Islam, if one has the good fortune to be exposed to them, even though this may invite the displeasure of one's parents.

In gaol in Taif, claims Irishwoman Monica Hall, she was forced to study the *Koran*. In gaol in Dammam, Debbie has been looking at it out of curiosity and trying to learn Arabic.

The outskirts of the oil towns, Al Khobar, Dammam and Dhahran, are cluttered with the paraphernalia of the oil industry. Rusted piles of pipes, obscure-looking pieces of metal and machinery, like so many junkyards stretching out into the desert. It's a relief when the freeway takes us out to a more featureless, timeless waste, brown, then pink, then finally the classic red of the desert of the European imagination. Dunes, tall and graced with delicate curves, the wind sifting their peaks.

Occasionally, across the freeway, are bridges, leading from desert to desert. These are for the camels, tended out here by Bedouin, as for centuries past. We scan the horizons either side of the modern tarmac, looking for the best pictures. Suddenly, ahead but quickly behind is a camel bridge with a herd of camels about to cross. Greg and I call to the driver to stop and we trudge out into the heat, hopeful of filming a sequence of classic desert images. The metal fence either side of the bridge turns out to be tall and unbroken. We find ourselves at the top of the sandy rise with the camels on one side of the fence and us on the other. No trouble, I suggest — we'll jump over.

Hoisting myself up on the hot-to-touch barrier, my head appears just in time to spook the buck camel on the other side. As I drop to the ground 20 metres away, I realise I've just soured half an hour of work by the cameleer nearby. He's been trying to shoo the buck ahead across the bridge so that the rest of the herd will follow. Now the big male camel turns, looking back to the refuge of the great desert beyond. The cameleer wields his stick firmly, whacking that camel in fury as his mate in a brand-new Landcruiser roars up to help. Between them they manoeuvre the scared but defiant beast back to the start of the bridge and the rest of the herd. The buck starts often, fear in its eyes, and almost falls twice, its pads slipping on the tar of the bridge.

Finally, the cameleers turn the buck, ready to use him as a lure to the others. I skulk beside the fence as the crew with the camera sneak up behind me to film. Chastened by my earlier foolishness, we try to melt into the sand, discreet as a couple of Italians and an Irishman on the set of *Lawrence of Arabia* can be. All looks to be going well, the cameleer on foot, wielding his stick with gusto.

Then the disciplined herd breaks into a melee as two Taiwanese businessmen in their own Landcruiser rumble up the sidetrack to the end of the bridge, dispersing the camels in all directions. The two men jump out to take photographs, heedless of the chaos they've caused. We film, too, as the herd makes for the open desert. It will be hours before the Bedouin can round them up again. Somehow, Western film crews and Asian tourists don't seem to belong here. Our editor, back in Sydney, uses the footage as a metaphor for discipline in Saudi society. Out of context, the beating of the camel looks brutal.

Riyadh looms as a patchy bunch of Bedouin encampments and dusty concrete huts out of the desert. Closer in to the city, enormous modern buildings rear up, testament to the wealth of the kingdom. Between elaborate and lavish villas are areas of wasteland, untended by landscape gardeners. This is a desert city.

We're late for our first meeting with Salah Al-Hejailan. He's promised us lunch but, perhaps too politely, told us to take our time. We drop our gear at the Intercontinental Hotel, just around the corner from the spaceship-like edifice of the Interior Ministry. As well as his words of considered wisdom and Koranic verses, Hamad hands over a large box of dates. A gift. Then he says he hopes I'll do the right thing with our troublesome vision of Saudi women in the street. I don't mention it's already gone to air in Australia and Britain. He mentions that the dates have small, maggot-like creatures inside them. They're not harmful, but we should wait for them to crawl out of the dates before eating them. I express warm gratitude for his help and for his gift — even though the Australian immigration authorities will never allow the dates into the country. Hamad makes a sad figure as he leaves us, still praying he won't get into trouble for allowing us to take forbidden pictures.

Salah has sent cars and drivers for us and we turn up at his villa around three, still dusty from the road. We meet a large man in the standard white *thobe* of everyday Saudi male dress. He has a black moustache, short dark hair, and the imperious manner of both the desert *sheikh* and the modern business lawyer. We feel we should have dressed, as we're ushered into a palace. This man has 14 domestic staff, and each of his many entertaining rooms is as big as my whole apartment. As we're shown into the dining room where a feast of Arabic food is laid out, it's clear we've kept everyone waiting. Michael Dark is there, as well as four or five other staff from the law firm. No one complains about our lack of punctuality as we settle down to eat. The food has been prepared by — or under the direction of — Salah's wife, who has written a cookbook. Neither she nor Salah's daughter is in evidence. This is a business occasion. Salah seats me on his right side, a place of honour, and mindful of the warnings of his lack of patience with dullards I fight the desert drowsiness to chat. He's still promising we'll be able to see his clients.

After lunch we adjourn to the vast games room, with snooker table, hubbly bubbly and cigars. We talk about the other big case the firm is handling: an ex-Finance Minister, a lawyer, who is alleged to have stripped his dying client's estate of millions. We consider changing stories. Salah holds court but is impatient to have his say on camera. We cast around for the right room in which to film an interview. We settle on his office, decorated in the style of an English club.

Fiddling with his red coral worry beads, Salah holds forth for the camera. His demeanour suggests impatience with the foolishness that's dogged the nurses' case so far.

'It is my expectation that the judge will not see enough evidence and will therefore, hopefully, dismiss the case on the basis of inadequate evidence.'

'Dismiss it altogether, just like that?' asks Paul.

'Yes, yes.'

'How do you deal with the fact that Lucille McLauchlan at least appears to have been caught withdrawing from Yvonne's bank account using her ATM card?'

'She denies that totally and I have to see evidence that she has done it. She said she has never seen that card at all. She found it in her ... handbag when she was visiting the bank. She's suggesting that it was planted in her bag.'

'Do Saudi police do things like that?'

'No, it is not likely at all. This matter will have to be investigated.'

This is a fudged answer. Salah is still wary of directly criticising the Saudi justice system and the investigating police. But he exudes a confidence that the court will not accept confessions which have been withdrawn and that there is no other evidence of guilt.

'Ordinary people would say innocent people don't confess.'

'Oh, but they do in circumstances like these.'

None of the Saudis we've spoken to have expressed anything like this level of scepticism about the ways of their system of law. In this country, the judges expect police to have a watertight case before any accused person is brought before them.

'It's been suggested that once a case gets to court, people are generally found guilty. Is that so?' Paul asks Salah.

'That's why I think this case is a good opportunity to demonstrate to the world that that is not the case, and I think the authorities here are quite conscious about that. One signal of their consciousness is your own visit here.'

After the interview I prevail upon Salah and his expatriate lawyers to chat about the case so that we can film some extra footage. Bob Thoms, the brash New Yorker, and Michael Dark, the austere Englishman, gather on a peach satin couch in a room decorated in Louis Quatorze style. It's Salah who notices that the miniatures on the wall in the background are in somewhat poor taste given the topic of conversation. Guillotine victims Louis XVI and Marie Antoinette sit in delicate porcelain over his shoulder. We assure him the little reminders of grandeur decapitated won't show up on camera.

There follows an extraordinary display of national temperament as the three lawyers discuss the women's claims of sexual harassment/abuse during their interrogation. Michael Dark, as is his wont, chooses to say nothing, as he clutches a satin-cloaked cushion as close as a teddy bear. Bob Thoms, all garrulous outrage, insists that Salah has underplayed the seriousness of the women's claims.

Salah, in his urbane, man-of-the-world way, makes less of his clients' alleged suffering, saying that sexual harassment is open to cultural interpretation. Finally, Salah pushes Michael, the discreet Britisher, into a few noncommittal words. He agrees that Salah may have underplayed the police harassment in our interview.

Filming over, the gathering lapses into Australianesque informality as we sip tonic water and laugh at Paul Barry as he tries on Salah's gold-threaded sheikh's robes. He and Salah pose on the grand Scarlet O'Hara-style staircase for snapshots, El Lawrence of Arabia and the sheikh. For a moment I wonder what Frank Gilford would make of this scene. Playing with the enemy.

As we sip tonic water and lemonades the chat turns to the Saudi ban on alcohol. Someone has briefed Salah that Australians like a drink. On my last visit, I mention, it wasn't hard to get a drink at one of the embassies. Someone asks what I'd do if caught with a bottle of illegal plonk. Get Salah to represent me, of course, I laugh. Salah says, quick as a flash, he'd blame it all on the Filipino servant who'd given me the bottle. We all laugh at his lawyerish alacrity in shifting blame. Privately I wonder if his avowals of the nurses' innocence are as glib.

Salah has asked for suggestions of who might act as an intermediary between his side and Frank. I give him a number for Sue Taylor, Yvonne's best friend. We talk about Yvonne and Frank. We tell them Frank's a nice man, not the brutal buffoon he's been painted. And Yvonne, by all accounts we say, was a lovely woman, generous to a fault, far from the moneylending loan shark one Scottish paper has claimed her as. I mention that Sue Taylor has told me Yvonne has left most of her money and assets to the children of her friends in South Africa. Little do I realise, Salah is making mental notes behind his genial hospitality.

We make moves to leave, reluctant to end an unusual afternoon and evening. Salah asks what else we'll do in Riyadh and scoffs at our intentions to visit The International Law Firm. The diplomatic Michael Dark reminds him it's the task of journalists to objectively address both sides. We make our goodbyes with promises for more lunches/dinners.

On the phone back at the hotel is Khaled Al-Ateeg, our new minder. He'll meet us in the lobby next morning. Khaled turns out to be a bit more fun than Hamad, his Eastern Province predecessor. He smokes and laughs and doesn't pray so often. He obviously enjoys hanging out with Western crews. Although he went to the Islamic University in Riyadh, he's travelled a bit and knows the world outside the kingdom.

He takes us in the van, provided by the Information Ministry, to the offices of The International Law Firm. These are somewhat less ostentatious than the villa of Sheikh Salah Al-Hejailan. A suite of offices that could have served lawyers anywhere in the world.

We're met by Jim Phipps and the other American, Yusuf Giansyracusa. The Saudi sponsor of the firm, Hassan Al-Awaji, is there for a moment but makes polite apologies and leaves. It's a Friday. Everyone else is on their weekend.

We choose Al-Awaji's office for the interview and the Italian boys, Babyface and Big Al, set up the lights. Under the oil portrait of Al-Awaji's father, a former deputy minister, Jim Phipps is telling war stories. An interpreter with US forces in Operation Desert

Storm, he'd been there in the desert to accept the surrender of demoralised Iraqis as they came in over the dunes. His face lights up as he enthuses over the heavy artillery 'melting' Iraqi defences. If you have seen the Hollywood version, *Courage Under Fire*, you'll know that in many American eyes, Iraqis had no faces. An enemy of cyphers. A Mormon with a Fulbright scholarship in *Sharia* law, Jim Phipps believes in that law. 'They'll get a fair trial,' he says of Lucy and Debbie. But his mind is made up. He has seen their faces. 'I've had an opportunity to look these women in the eye and to size them up and they don't appear to me to be incapable of doing a crime like this,' he says on camera.

Paul Barry, asking the questions, is shocked by this blithe claim of seeing evil in the eyes of the accused. 'That's a bit of a judgment, isn't it?' Jim backs off, trying to make it seem he was referring to the women's ability to commit the crime in terms of physical strength, rather than their innate evil.

'Well, I've been in the room with them and I don't believe that it takes incredible manly force to do this and the suggestion that women are somehow less capable of committing crimes like this than men has been disproved by too many tragic incidents in history.'

'It's a bit much to say, though, you're looking them in the eye and feel that they're capable of guilt?'

'I'm saying that, simply that I have looked them in the eye and my estimation is that they're not a great deal smaller or less strong or less able than the person who they're accused of killing.'

Jim Phipps is squirming as he parries a line of questioning more aggressive than he expected from friends of Frank Gilford.

'The defence say there is no evidence apart from the confessions. What do you say to that?'

'I say that it's true the only evidence reviewed in the trial to date has been the confessions, but it's not true that that's the only evidence. And they can say that for the newspapers, but as a matter of course they're going to be facing the other evidence in court.'

Despite Jim's assertion, no such evidence was ever presented in court. Its existence can still only be assumed.

'Frank Gilford has said he's seen other evidence that convinces them the two girls are guilty. What is that evidence?'

'Well, let me give you an example. We've been receiving over ... I don't call all of this evidence per se, because what is evidence is what the court admits as evidence. But we've been receiving letters from the colleagues and co-workers of Parry and McLauchlan indicating that they believe that they're guilty and providing details. The way we get this evidence is they send the letters to Frank and Frank sends them back to us.'

'Providing details of what?'

'Oh, details of the behaviour of Miss Parry and Miss McLauchlan following the murder — what they did in the morning just after the murder.'

'Such as?'

'I don't think it would be appropriate for me to say publicly what these nurses are saying in these letters, because the information could be perceived as my trying to pursue this trial outside this court and we're certainly interested in seeing the case tried by the court.'

'This sounds like trial by hearsay, doesn't it?'

'Well, what we're telling our client is the only evidence that is evidence is the evidence that's taken by the court. So you know this is evidence that you have to put in brackets and you have to wait and see what the court says about it .'

As he utters these words, the gelatin film over one of our lights falls on Jim's face. Perhaps this is a message from the Lord; perhaps it's just another in the series of technical accidents which have dogged this shoot. Perhaps the interruption provided by the light incident gives Jim the chance to remind himself of the standard of evidence required in American, British and Australian courts. When we resume, he backtracks:

'I might explain at this juncture that our role is not an evidence-gathering role; our role is to speak for Mr Gilford to the court, and the court is the body that evaluates the evidence and the state has gathered the evidence, so our role is simply to speak the mind of the Gilford family. So whether or not I have seen evidence in one way or the other is immaterial. Frankly, I haven't seen evidence disproving their guilt. I've seen the autopsy [report] and I've in court now heard the confessions and have my own opinions about the correlation of the confessions to the autopsy report, but my opinions don't matter on that point — it's the court's opinion.'

This is a mess. Jim, a newcomer to practising law in Saudi Arabia, is just as much a newcomer to the game of playing the international media. On the one hand, he's trying to plant in the media the idea that there is evidence which damns the nurses. On the other, he's playing scrupulous Western lawyer who won't consider evidence not seen in court. It's a game Salah Al-Hejailan plays better, though even less scrupulously. Jim looks like what he is: an earnest Mormon swot who is taken in by the claims of Saudi justice and is trying to put a spin on a big international story.

Paul has another go.

'Let me put it to you again. The defence say there is no evidence apart from the confessions. Can you gainsay them?'

'I'm not going to play the game that they're playing. They know there is other evidence and what they're, I think, trying to do is establish in the media, certainly not in the court, that this case is somehow weak.'

Rightly or wrongly, that is certainly what the defence was doing then and would do in the ensuing months. Jim is out of his league. But he's the man in the hot seat. Under Saudi law, a member of the victim's family or a representative of the family must attend the execution of a convicted murderer. Jim says he'll be there, as a representative of the family, if it comes to that.

Over in the corner our lights have over-taxed the office circuits. The fax machine is giving off smoke. The heat of the interview seems to have an echo in yet another technical hitch. Babyface Barbera wonders if we should sneak out without mentioning the fax, but I point out the trouble to Jim, offering to pay for the damage.

Chapter 14

Dead letters

The families' greatest chagrin in Al Khobar was reserved for the mailman. Following the advice of their own lawyers, they sent their personal letters appealing to Frank Gilford to Jim Phipps. Jim Phipps declined to pass them on. The modest first-floor premises of The International Law Firm in Riyadh became their Dead Letter Office.

After our interview with Jim we badgered him about the families' distress. Why not pass on their heartfelt appeals to Frank? Phipps and his colleague Yusuf Giansyracusa, already back-footed by the harsh exchange over Phipps' 'see it in their eyes' comments, looked for a way out. They claimed they'd held back the letters for fear the content might further antagonise Frank Gilford, pushing him even more firmly into a hardline position.

Months later, an examination of the letters sent by Deborah Parry's sister and brother-in-law revealed little that could be viewed by Frank as potentially antagonising. To the contrary, they are almost obsequious in tone.

29 April 1997

Dear Mr Gilford,

May I begin by offering my sincere condolences to you and your family for the terrible loss you have suffered ... No, please don't discard this letter — we share so much in this horrendous situation and I hear from our UK lawyers that you have been kept almost bereft of information ...

Jonathan Ashbee's letter goes on to give biographical details for Debbie and her family, and he distances himself from the ill-fated Rationale for an Early Waiver of the Death Penalty:

> ...can I please apologise if the 'Rationale' document produced by our Saudi lawyers offended you. I had serious misgivings about the document as apart from the fact it appeared to suggest the guilt of the two girls, from a Western point of view, I felt if our roles were reversed, the last thing I'd want to receive would be such a document. Our Saudi lawyers, however, were adamant that it should be done as it is common practice in Saudi etiquette and it was necessary to address the process in a Saudi way. I'm sorry if it upset you, but we are so frightened of doing anything wrong from a Saudi point of view as we're in the hands of a system that we don't understand and which historically has a far from glowing reputation.

Far from attacking Frank Gilford, this would seem to be a diplomatic attempt by Jonathan to place himself in Frank's shoes. Perhaps a little ingratiating, the letter attempts at once to distance the Ashbee family from the antics of the Saudi lawyers and also to encourage Frank to doubt Saudi justice. This was the first clear indication of rifts in the defence camp.

Jonathan's letter tells Frank of the tragedies in the Ashbee family and paints Debbie as a compassionate person, without malice and with 'a deep respect for life, with Debbie carrying that respect to incredible levels, not allowing us to even kill a wasp!'

> ...what I have seen is a quiet and unassuming lady, dedicated to her calling of nursing, and whilst yearning for a husband, pouring endless love and affection over our children. Her hobbies are indicative of her personality and include gardening, reading and sewing, and Debbie has an enormous love for all animals, especially cats. Wherever she works, she quickly earns the respect and friendship of her new colleagues, and such is the disbelief in this country about the accusations against Debbie, that most of the hospitals where she has worked have indicated that they would love to have her back working for them. Do you think they would this willingly employ a

> suspected murderess unless they knew beyond any doubt that she is innocent? ...

The letter offers to put Frank in touch with nurses in Australia who could vouch for Debbie's character. In another attempt to encourage a sense of common ground between the families of the victim and the accused, Jonathan expresses outrage about negative reporting of Yvonne Gilford in the Scottish press.

> ...you will recall the horrible article that appeared in the papers about Yvonne which was so against everything we had heard about her up to that point. For her part, Debbie was absolutely incensed that Yvonne's name was being dragged through the mud and told us that it was all lies ... right from the beginning, Debbie has wanted to write to you to share her grief at Yvonne's demise, but she has been advised that this would be imprudent in the circumstances.

Jonathan argues against the guilt of his sister-in-law, reasoning that because he and his family '*know* that Debbie isn't a lesbian, Lucy was to be married in February and you have been reported as saying that Yvonne was not a lesbian', then the alleged motive for the crime was suspect.

Because his lawyers kept this letter and didn't encourage him to read it, Frank Gilford was denied early knowledge of the women's claims to have been forced into their confessions.

> Debbie made her 'confession' after 6 days of interrogation where she was kept awake for 16 hours a day, in the nude and in the presence of a dozen Saudi policemen who systematically assaulted her both physically and sexually, promised her that she would be sent home if she 'confessed' and told her that she would not be permitted to see any British official until she had complied. In the end, the threat of rape was what caused her to give in, but even this was not enough for the Saudis — she then had to make a reconstruction video. As she had no idea what to do as she hadn't committed the crime she was threatened with having to have oral sex with a policeman if she didn't act out the part as she was told.

> It makes you wonder doesn't it? Why does a confession have to be obtained in such a way if a crime such as this could be more than proven using some basic forensic techniques?
>
> ...I feel so much sympathy for you, but I must put forward that the punishment of two innocent girls will do nothing to alleviate your pain, and will multiply that pain through several other families who are no more deserving of it than you are.
>
> We are in your hands, please write back.
> Yours Sincerely
> Jon Ashbee

Characteristically, Jon's letter is computer-typed and carefully reasoned, while his wife Sandra's is handwritten and more nakedly desperate.

> Dear Mr Gilford,
>
> This is one of the most difficult letters I have ever had to write but firstly please let me say how sorry my family and I are feeling for you.

Sandra writes of the hundreds of letters she has received in support of Debbie, one former patient whom Debbie 'nursed back from death' describing Debbie as 'An Angel Saint'. Sandra asks, 'Do you really believe a girl like this could have committed such a dreadful crime?' Telling Frank of the loss of four close members of their family, Sandra asks, 'Why is life so cruel? We are very ordinary girls, very law-abiding — neither of us would hurt a fly. Life just isn't fair but that doesn't make us hateful towards life — anything but, it makes you love everything — life is precious, very precious.' After the loss of Sandra's first husband, she writes, 'Debbie immediately gave up her job and came down to Hampshire to live with me, to give me support, to help me rebuild my life. That's the type of girl she is — no thought for herself.'

> I wish we had the chance to meet you face to face. I know it would be so hard for all of us but we know so much that we want to tell you and I think it would wipe all the doubts from your mind.

...Mr Gilford, please believe me, Debbie is innocent. She is a loving, caring, well-liked human being. She used to have a brilliant sense of humour (I don't know if she'll ever get that back). She has spent nearly five months in a Saudi prison for a crime she didn't commit. Her health is failing her. She's frightened. She's totally bewildered and can't believe that anyone in the world would think that she was capable of such a dreadful thing.

...What I'm asking Mr Gilford, from the bottom of my heart, is that you reconsider your feelings about the death penalty.

...Thank you for taking the time to read this letter. I hope it hasn't offended you in any way. It wasn't meant to. I'm just trying desperately to make things right...

Our thoughts are with you all.
Yours Sincerely
Sandra B. Ashbee

Frank Gilford never read these words of appeal. Perhaps his lawyers did. They lay in a filing cabinet in an office in Riyadh, mute tokens of the love of a family far away, as silent as the love letters that went down with the *Titanic*. As secret as the feelings in Frank Gilford's own heart.

Chapter 15

Kayf

Interviews filmed, it was time to send our reporter home with the tapes. The Italian boys and I stayed on, still hoping for a chance to see the accused women. Salah promised to talk to the acting Interior Minister, Prince Sultan, on our behalf.

With minder Khaled in tow, we played tourists in a land that doesn't really have tourists. Plenty of businesspeople come here and millions come for the *Haj* pilgrimage to Mecca. You can feel like an old-time traveller here, despite the city's bustling modernity. We wandered about the *soukhs* clustered around Riyadh's remodelled chop-chop square, an attractive series of courtyards near the old town clock which has witnessed the scything of many prisoners' heads. Riyadh is still centred on its old central fort, Al Masmak. This is a deeply symbolic place, now restored to its mud-brick 1930s' glory. The first modern king of Saudi Arabia, Abdul Aziz, stole in here in the dead of night with a band of 40 men, to win back control of the central desert region from his rivals for his clan. There, in the centre of modern Riyadh, is the same old wooden door that Abdul Aziz and his men climbed through to take the fort and the town. Even the metal head of his comrade's spear is still embedded in that door.

During our listless days of waiting in Riyadh we filmed that door and its old iron knocker-ring. A symbol of all the fortresses and all the gaols in fortress Saudi. The historic fort itself was made a gaol when Abdul Aziz moved on to grander things. Here, the man who united the Arabian peninsula in the twentieth century received his first motor car, his first British and American visitors.

As we waited, in hope, Big Al and Babyface and I would sit around in the courtyard of the fort at dusk, or in the courtyards of the nearby *soukh* as the evening calls to prayer from three or four mosques competed for ascendancy. We relaxed into the *kayf* that Richard Burton describes, a lazy acceptance of our fate.

Later, we would retire to the air-conditioned marble of our hotel foyer, there to smoke cigars and drink tea among groups of Saudi men drinking, not beer, but tea. Still waiting for permission to see Lucy and Debbie, we tried one morning to play golf on the hotel course, only to be told it was women's day and we wouldn't be welcome among the black-shrouded players. So we moved to the hotel's ten-pin bowling alley, the only players through lazy days.

One evening, we make our way into the suburbs, to another well-appointed villa. It's not quite as ostentatious as Salah's. This is the home of another lawyer, this time an academic — Dr Saleh Al-Malik. He's a member of the Shura Council, the 60-member body which advises the king. This group of distinguished subjects, appointed by the king and with a purely consultant role, is the closest thing the kingdom has to democracy. Dr Al-Malik is very concerned that I get down all the details of his various degrees. Masters in Geography, PhD in Sociology, author of a book on Saudi law and the West. He ushers us to an over-lit room, papered in blue, with at least a dozen chairs around the walls. We opt to do the interview in the hall. It's a very big hall. On camera, this well-educated man defends executions and rejects the argument that capital punishment hasn't saved America from a dreadful homicide rate. 'Other factors,' he claims, such as the social disintegration in American life. 'And in Saudi Arabia homicide is, if not the lowest, it's one of the lowest all over the globe.' Dr Al-Malik quotes, extensively, from the *Koran*. 'He who forgives will come closer to God.' So, under *Sharia* law, I ask, which is given more weight, mercy or justice? 'Mercy is more, because there is a statement by the Prophet Mohammed, peace be upon him, saying if somebody settles for mercy instead of justice God will bestow on him a higher position. As a matter of fact, even in the holy *Koran* there is a very explicit statement saying if you refer to forgiveness this is making you closer to becoming pious.'

Dr Al-Malik is at pains to point out that Saudi society does its best to avoid executions. 'We just don't come and employ capital punishment like this,' he says, clicking his fingers. 'As a matter of fact, we employ all resources to try and prevent capital punishment and if the heirs settle for other options we will go for it.'

Is it likely that the court will accept an accused person's withdrawal of a confession? 'A mere withdrawal just because he withdraws does not really mean that the court has to change his decision; but if he can provide some factual evidence, very convincing, that he did not do it, then withdrawal would be warranted. But it would not be warranted if he is saying that he did not do it after it has been proved in front of the judge that he or she is the murderer.' This doesn't sound as reassuring as Salah's confident assertions that the case against Lucy and Debbie will be thrown out.

We turn to the question of Frank Gilford's powers. I point out that Yvonne's mother, Muriel, is the closest relative still living. Frank has spoken for her because Mrs Gilford has Alzheimer's disease. Dr Al-Malik says his comments are general, not to be taken as a pronouncement on Yvonne's case. 'In the case of any sick heir, if he is mentally sick or if he cannot make a decision because he is mentally sick or mentally retarded, they have to wait until they are cured.'

This could be good news for Lucy and Debbie. Although Mrs Gilford is in her eighties and has the memory loss associated with the disease, she may live for years yet. 'If their illness is not curable, then this is a very delicate issue. We either have to wait until they are cured or until they are passed away.'

Saleh Al-Malik calls in his young son, who wants to have his picture taken. We film them reading the *Koran* together.

The doctor offers cranberry juice. As I take a glass, its bottom, cracked, gives way and the red juice soaks the carpet. Dr Al-Malik, the ultimate in Saudi politeness, obviously believes it's my clumsiness but jokes that the colour is appropriate for our bloody subject. Two Filipina housemaids scurry and kneel to mop up the bloody cranberry. The doctor snaps at them to hurry. We discuss the efficacy of salt in removing stains from carpet. He heads back to his study to watch the football as we step into the balmy Riyadh night.

Each day on the phone in the Intercontinental Hotel, I'm calling the hospital back in Dhahran. Chasing staff who knew Yvonne, who know Lucy and Debbie. Two people give heart to one who still believes in the women's probable innocence. Joe Robinson, a middle-aged Brit, is a friend of Debbie. He scoffs at his colleagues' gullibility in believing the women's confessions. Yet he doesn't want to be interviewed.

Neither does Catherine Wall, an American dietitian, who also knows Debbie well. Something in her voice inspires trust. She says she can't talk of her feelings about the case, it's all too personal. I assume she means she's upset that her friend has been falsely accused. I mark her down on the side of the angels, those who are prepared to at least consider innocence.

No one at the hospital is prepared to put their hand up for an interview. They fear for their jobs, or simply fear the opprobrium of their colleagues.

Waiting. From Glasgow comes news that the British families, now back in Britain, had appeared at a press conference. They didn't get to say much. Their British lawyers made statements questioning the evidence before the Saudi court, especially the confessions.

'The confessions are each inconsistent with each other and there are many discrepancies. They also don't match up with the post-mortem report we have seen,' said Glaswegian Peter Watson.

The human rights lawyer, Rodger Pannone, used Yvonne's fitness and strength as a reason why the murder must have been committed by a strong man or men: 'Looking at the forensic evidence and demonstrating whether or not the two women, one a very frail woman, could have committed that murder and then saying we would have expected to find the following pieces of information if they did it, which was lacking.'

Jim Phipps, in Riyadh, scoffed. 'I don't believe that argument for one minute. They're not a great deal smaller or less strong or less able than the person who they're accused of killing.'

The British lawyers were attempting to discredit the Saudi investigation, albeit in a respectful, British lawyer way. They told the Glasgow press conference that they would offer to the Saudi court expert analysis that would suggest the confessions were not written by the women. They said three unnamed British experts had volunteered to travel to Saudi Arabia to testify.

Rodger Pannone told our London researcher, Sue Quinn, of the expert evidence: 'They have analysed over 1000 similar cases. It's the words that are used in relation to the confessions, the evidence contained within those confessions. It's the differences within those confessions and then it is the forensic evidence we have obtained to date, which is limited.'

The anonymity of these 'experts' didn't stop the British newspapers, which wheeled out their own experts to back up the claims that the confessions were not in the words of the accused women. The trouble with this argument is that the confessions can indeed have been forced and yet still be true. Or parts of them may be true.

One thing all the experts didn't do was look at the retractions of Debbie and Lucy and compare them for possible contamination. A close reading can easily lead to a suspicion that Debbie's may have been heavily inspired by Lucy's. Michael Dark told me as much when we met in Al Khobar. He said Debbie had come up with a pathetically sketchy single page when he'd asked her to write her account of the interrogation ordeal. After that, he'd asked Lucy to help her.

One night in the lobby of the Riyadh Intercontinental we are playing our tenth round of Machiavelli, surrounded by tea-drinking Saudis. There is no wagering over these card games; gambling is as illegal as alcohol in the kingdom. Salah Al-Hejailan comes on the mobile phone. He says he will be talking to Prince Sultan and the minister is well-disposed to our request to see the accused nurses. We drink more and more tea for three hours, on tenterhooks. At midnight, the bad news. The prince has decided he can't give preference to the British women's case. If he allowed a television crew in to see them, prisoners of all the other foreign nationalities would want the same.

We drown our sorrows in tea and make bookings to fly home.

The next day, I doze despondently by the pool, waiting for the night plane. The mobile phone rings. It is Caroline Ionescu, ringing in outrage. Her mother in Australia had seen the on-air promotion for this week's *Witness* program. The promo claimed the accused nurses were innocent, she said. I am sure this wasn't the case and that our story, as well as the promo, was much more even-handed. Surely Caroline's mother had caught only half the voiceover. Caroline takes some placating. 'How could you do this when you know all of us at the hospital think they're guilty?' she asks. All of us? I promise to ring home and check that we weren't making unbalanced claims of innocence. Left alone in the noon heat of Riyadh, I am shaken out of the complacent *kayf* into thinking hard about this woman's claim. They all think they're guilty? How could that be? Did the hospital staff know more than had emerged so far, or was this a case of group hysteria, a pack ganging up on their former friends and colleagues?

These thoughts crowd in over the in-flight movies as we head home.

Chapter 16

Frank at home

Frank Gilford is laughing, like he hasn't since I've known him. He's laughing because I've just told him what some Saudis in his position have done. Like the boy who was under-age when his father was killed. When he reached legal maturity, sixteen, in 1995, he was able to call for the murderer to be publicly executed. At the last moment, even as the executioner raised the sword, the boy called for clemency. He'd wanted the guilty man to feel what his father must have felt at the time of the murder. Is Frank laughing with the thought of vengeance, or is he only laughing at the idea of telling the world that a journalist has suggested such a fiendish revenge?

We're standing in Frank's backyard, kicking at the dust as we chat. Above is the tin cut-out of the magpie on the radio mast, silently listening to my careful nudges at Frank's conscience. In the drive, my seven-year-old son, Liam, is kicking a soccer ball with Frank's younger grandson. Frank shouts sternly when the ball hits the side of the house.

Jet-lag is dogging my thoughts. We've driven up here from Adelaide, just a few days after the flight home from Saudi. I've brought Liam because I've been away from home too long. My wife, Annette, wonders why I have to fly off again so soon, but I've promised the British families I will see Frank as soon as I can. Liam and I have brought Frank's mail: tapes of the interviews with the nurses' families. I hope this will edge Frank towards, maybe not forgiveness, but anyway mercy. By now, he's already had phone conversations with Therese Feeney. He tells me they have much in common. Not, of course, a common view on the death penalty.

Debbie and Lucy's families have asked me to talk to Frank on their behalf. A tricky business. I don't want to cruel our relationship with Frank by seeming too partisan to the other side. And yet I can see their anguished faces, hear their pleas, as I'm talking to him now.

Gently, I suggest that what I've seen in Saudi Arabia doesn't give me confidence that the women will have a fair trial. Frank says little. In his head, I don't realise yet, are the words of staff at the hospital: 'They're guilty and should get what's coming to them.' We're not invited to stay for lunch. Liam and I head south through the wheat fields, my son telling me he now wants to be a producer when he grows up. It looks like a doddle to him, I guess, flying around, chatting with people.

I hope the tapes I've left might plant some seeds of doubt in Frank's determined mind. But that's a field now well-ploughed by the likes of Caroline Ionescu and Kathryn Lyons.

Chapter 17

Doubts?

One way to test our witnesses is to examine their level of gullibility and scepticism. Two of the central women interviewed for this book show a remarkable willingness to believe in the Saudi way, despite personal experiences which might cause doubt in more questioning minds.

One woman, who asked that she not be identified in this context, has married a Saudi. He is a modern man, she says, who has lived abroad. He doesn't ask her to wear the traditional cover-all, the *abaya* and veil, which many Saudi women are still expected to walk the streets in. He doesn't want her to stop working as a nurse. He has travelled to her homeland and met her family, which is trying hard to accept the unusual cross-cultural relationship.

The couple plan to live in another Arabic country — where the social mores are not as strict as in the Saudi kingdom. Here, a problem has emerged. The Saudi husband's father hasn't sanctioned the marriage and, according to this expatriate wife, has refused to endorse the husband's passport so that they can take up their new life in the third country. Despite the consequent frustration, the nurse involved has put her faith in Saudi legal justice: if the Saudi court found Lucy and Debbie guilty, she said, then she would go along with that.

Another expatriate nurse from the King Fahd Military Medical Complex, also a central witness on the character and behaviour of the two accused, places a similar blind faith in the Saudi legal system. This despite the fact that her own boyfriend, an American, was last year arrested and imprisoned for a month on what she claims were trumped-up charges of hashish possession. The man was allowed no legal or consular contact and was held in harsh prison conditions, unsure of his future, until he was released and deported with as little warning as he'd been arrested.

Such tales of expats' encounters with the arbitrary nature of Saudi officialdom abound.

In 1979, another British nurse working in Saudi Arabia, Helen Smith, a 23-year-old from Leeds, fell off a balcony in Jeddah during a drinks party. Such gatherings, though common in the expatriate community, are ostensibly illegal, because of both the consumption of alcohol and the mixing of women with men. Helen's body was found, gruesomely impaled on a railing, next to the body of her Dutch boyfriend, beneath the apartment of a British surgeon. Penny and Richard Arnot were gaoled for several months for hosting the party but escaped the feared sentence of a caning. At the time, Helen's death was accepted by the British Foreign Office to have been an accident; that she'd fallen while making love with her boyfriend.

Helen's father Ron, an ex-policeman, refused to believe this was the truth. His agitation finally led to an inquest in Leeds in 1983, which found that Helen had been raped. The inquest also heard evidence that her injuries didn't seem to tally with a fall from the balcony and that a head injury could be interpreted as having come from a blow. Suspicion of Foreign Office complicity in a Saudi cover-up grew when the inquest heard that these details had originally been suppressed by a British coroner. The inquest returned an open finding. Eighteen years after Helen's death, Ron Smith won't release her body for burial; he's still waiting for justice.

After hearing of Debbie and Lucy's arrest he told the British *Sunday Mirror*: 'The Foreign Office is again going all out to prevent embarrassment to the Saudis. Natural justice and democratic rights are forgotten because of the multi-billion-pound oil and arms contracts. I am convinced to this day that Helen was murdered.'

In 1996, the BBC's television current affairs program, *Panorama*, reported on the case of Neil Tubbo, a young Filipino. Tubbo was beheaded for the 1988 murder of two maids of the same nationality. He, too, claimed that he'd been tortured into making false confessions.

Panorama's reporter John Ware, who called his report *Death of a Principle*, described executions like Tubbo's as 'like a public circus, with people jostling for a grandstand view'.

The biggest international response to the perceived roughness of Saudi justice came in 1980. The documentary filmmaker Antony

Thomas caused a period of diplomatic tension between Britain and Saudi Arabia when his film *Death of a Princess* was broadcast on ATV in Britain. This was a dramatised version of the 1977 case of Princess Misha'il, granddaughter of Prince Muhammed ibn Abdul Aziz, who was executed in a carpark next to the Queen's Building in Jeddah. The princess — who was married young to a much older relative — was shot for having eloped with her young lover, Khalid Muhalhal.

After witnessing her execution in the carpark, Khalid was beheaded, their fate the simple outcome of enthusiastic dispensation of Koranic law.

Robert Lacey, in *The Kingdom*, describes the hurt which this film and the public furore which accompanied it caused the Saudis. On the one hand, says Lacey, younger, more modern members of the Saudi royal family resented a depiction which suggested that 'the murderous anger of one powerful old man should be taken by outsiders as representative of the general flow of life in their country'. On the other, the film had re-exposed the family of the princess to the shame of her promiscuity. Many Saudis Lacey spoke to during the four years he researched his book — including members of the Al Sa'ud, the royal family — defended the execution of the princess and her lover as the just application of Islamic law. '"What this proves," they would say, "is that princesses must submit to Islamic law like everybody else",' writes Lacey. Yet Lacey describes the huge resentment of Westernised princes and educated Saudis when the government ordered, in the wake of the executions, that women must travel accompanied by a male member of their family. Clearly, feelings about such issues among the Saudi population are not monolithic. While most would surely endorse the application of the *Sharia*, many smart under the yoke of the more rigidly enforced aspects of Islamic tradition. Lacey points out that the king's brother, Muhammed, grandfather of the princess, could have intervened to save her life if he'd wanted to but that, 'for all the talk of Islamic justice, the law which truly did the princess to death was the unwritten and ancient law of the tribe, which places the purity of the woman, the heart of the family, at the heart of family honour'.

Writing in *The Independent* in January 1997, the Saudi ambassador to Britain, Dr Ghazi Algosaibi, chastised what he saw as British misreporting of Saudi legal tenets in the wake of the Gilford case. He pointed to women's divorce rights in *Sharia* law as being more progressive than those applied in the West. He said that reports of hand-chopping for crimes of theft were exaggerated.

> Nobody in the media bothers to point out that this punishment is applied only in very specific kinds of theft and under most stringent conditions. No one, for example, would lose his hand for embezzlement, forgery, stealing public money, or helping himself to items not properly protected.

Dr Algosaibi also claimed that the crime and punishment of adultery was misreported.

> According to the Sharia, adultery cannot be established unless four witnesses convince the court that they saw with their own eyes 'the whole thing'. During the early period of Islam, a man appeared in front of a judge to testify in an adultery case. He told the judge that he saw the man on top of the woman, saw the movements, and heard the grunts. The judge asked if he saw 'actual entry'. The witness grumbled that he would have to be a part of the woman's vagina to witness such an occurrence. Despite the grumblings, the accused were set free and the man was lashed for bearing false testimony. As some acute observers noted, this stringent requirement makes adultery a crime only if practised during an orgy.

An amusing tale, but this is the argument of an urbane and erudite modern Saudi. In the *Death of a Princess* case, there was no question of four adult male witnesses observing sexual congress between the princess and her lover. She had eloped, she confessed. Case closed.

John Ware's *Death of a Principle* continued the tradition of liberal British criticism of Saudi ways and re-screened the dramatised beheading from *Death of a Princess*. His program also showed two secretly filmed 1995 beheadings of foreign workers, as well as interviews with workers from Britain, Egypt and the Philippines said to be falsely accused of crimes. The BBC screened the program at home and on its Arabic service.

The point of the title of the program is the suggested lack of principle of the British government and business in failing to use their diplomatic and financial clout to pressure Saudi Arabia on human rights.

This is the point also made in *The House of Saud*, by Said Aburish, who reported the case of British engineer Neville Norton, gaoled for three years in 1989 over a contract dispute. Aburish claims that no foreign government is challenging the Saudi system because of fears that to do so would encourage the even more extreme Islamic fundamentalists in Saudi society which have occasionally challenged the Al Sa'ud.

In 1979, extremist guerrillas took over the Grand Mosque in Mecca in protest over what they saw as the corruption of Saudi Arabia by the West. These men were in the tradition of the *Wahhabbi* and *Ikhwan*, hardline Islamic groups which had alternately underpinned and challenged the legitimacy of the Al Sa'ud family in its dominance of the Arabic peninsula in the nineteenth and early twentieth centuries. According to Robert Lacey, the 1979 rebels were inspired by the success of the Ayatollah Khomeini in his Islamic Revolution in Iran the same year. But they followed the teachings of Muhammad ibn Abdul Wahhab, the eighteenth-century desert leader and *quadi* (judge) who organised purges of shrines and superstition which stood between man and God. As such, they abhorred what they saw as the superstition of Iran's Shi'ite revolutionaries. They wore long beards, clipped their moustaches, and cut their *thobes* short above the ankles in the tradition of their predecessors. It took a week for government troops to subdue the 200–300 rebels in the mosque, with the death of more than 200 rebels and soldiers and worshippers caught in the crossfire.

Independent of the rising in Mecca, Shi'ite Moslems at Qatef in the Eastern Province rioted that same November 1979. Their uprising, too, was ruthlessly put down by the Saudi government. But the rulers of the kingdom had learnt a lesson. Straying too close to the ways of the West invited internal dissent. This would be a modern kingdom which would maintain strict observance of many of its traditional ways. While the privileged, who could travel, holiday and educate themselves and their children overseas, might stray from literal observance of the *Koran*, publicly at least the face of the Islamic state would be preserved.

Saudi people are not mad, bad, stupid or unquestioning — or no more so than many in the Western world. But they live with what is, more than what could be. To the east is Iran, slavering for power in the Arab world. To the north, Iraq, whose Saddam Hussein sees himself as a new Nasser, or even Saladin, uniter of the Arab peoples. Also Syria, with Hafez al Assad looking in the mirror and seeing something similar. To the west is Israel, a nation in fear for its life and perceived as the major threat to the Arab place in the world. Everywhere, throughout this century, is the West, powerful, greedy, duplicitous. Talking in grand words of democracy and freedom but always with a forked tongue.

What is, for the average Saudi, is more of the same. Religious certainty allied to political absolutism. Questioning is not recommended.

What about a modern Saudi talking about Arabian ways? In *Arab News*, the English-language Saudi newspaper, in 1996, Abdul Rahman Al-Rashid wrote with high dudgeon of what he saw as a 'rape of truth and attack on the honour' of his people. He cited the story of Sara Balabagan, a Filipina domestic servant in the United Arab Emirates, who was condemned to death for killing her employer two years before. Sara claimed the man had tried to rape her. After she was pardoned she was released and returned to the Philippines, to a hero's welcome. Her story was being made into a film and Sara became a celebrity in the Filipino media.

Al-Rashid maintains that Sara was treated by most Arabs without bias, even though the dead man was an Arab citizen of the Emirates. In a commentary that perhaps confirms Robert Lacey's analysis of Saudi male attitudes to the law, Al-Rashid says that Sara was pardoned

> ...because no one can take a stand against a woman defending her honour, especially in the Arab world where the honour of a girl is considered much more important than the life of a man. That the assailant was an Arab doesn't make any difference. Therefore, no one resented her release.

In a disgust that was to be echoed in the later British outcry against the Saudi treatment of Debbie and Lucy, Al-Rashid complains that the Filipinos made Sara's case 'a national issue'.

> They behaved as though they were defending the honour of their entire nation from a foreign rapist. The prisons of the Philippines, as those of any other country, are full of criminals convicted of crimes such as rape and murder.

> So one single crime, involving one individual, didn't deserve to be treated as an issue of national honour. If the event had taken place in the Philippines, Sara would still be behind bars, that is, if she had not been sent to the electric chair.

Al-Rashid has a point — up to a point. Exercises in cultural relativism can be fraught with pitfalls for the accuser. In Australia, there is liberal intellectual support for tribal law to apply to outback Aboriginal people. Such law can, and still sometimes does, provide for the spearing of murderers and other miscreants by the family of their victims. Such practice is claimed as culturally appropriate by some Aboriginal leaders and some white commentators. Yet Aboriginal tradition also has allowed for the binding of very young women, often with violence, to the old men of a tribe. Whose human rights are protected in that instance?

When we in the West point fingers at Saudi Arabia and other Arabic and Islamic states, it is wise to keep in mind the shortcomings of our own systems. Saudis have truth on their side when they point to a very low murder rate in their country. That this is due to the deterrent effect of the death penalty may be less arguable. Doubters point to the patchy examples offered by the United States. There, states which use the death penalty often have higher murder rates than states which don't. Of course, a complex array of social and economic factors determine those rates. But that doesn't discredit an alternative argument that the murder rate in Saudi Arabia is low because of the country's homogeneity and social cohesion, rather than capital punishment itself.

Anyway, rape is rape under whatever system and is everywhere a violation of human rights.

In one of Debbie's gaol letters, she wrote:

> Called on again for my midwifery skills. Midnight last night.
> I said the girl should go to hospital, as in labour. Thank goodness, she did. She had a little boy.

Debbie says the gaol guards ask for her advice because some of the women prisoners who have been raped are expecting babies. She has to do internal examinations and say how much the women in labour are dilated and whether they should go to hospital.

Raped? Writing for Reuters in 1995, William Maclean reported on the suspected high incidence of rape of Asian domestic servants in the Arab Gulf countries, including Saudi Arabia. These women are in the lowest of low positions, without power in a strange and often hostile social hierarchy.

'The maids, mostly from Sri Lanka, Bangladesh, India and the Philippines, encounter more misery at work in the Gulf than in any of the other regions they go to, Asian diplomats say,' wrote Maclean. He quoted the Philippines' ambassador to the United Arab Emirates, Roy Seneres: 'It is a highly hazardous occupation that can be life-threatening. I am for the phasing out of Filipina maids working abroad.'

The maids are desperate for the work, often being responsible for the survival of family back home. In Saudi Arabia, their passports and *iqama*, work permits, are controlled by their employers. Maclean quotes figures from Philippine embassies in the Gulf suggesting that by far the main problems are with non-payment and overwork, followed by verbal abuse. Physical abuse and sexual harassment make up about 20 per cent of cases, with rape a smaller percentage.

This is, of course, a very difficult problem to measure, although it can be assumed that such frightened, powerless employees would under-report rather than shout about their troubles. In defence of the Saudis and other Gulf countries, the West has no great record on domestic violence, another notoriously under-reported phenomenon.

It is in truth very difficult to compare our different systems, with the real figures, facts and their meaning obscured. What is clear is that both Western and Arab pots need to be wary in calling the other kettle black. Which doesn't remove the fact that Lucy McLauchlan and Debbie Parry cannot be said to have had a fair and open trial in the Saudi system. And just as it is reasonable for the Arabic press to criticise race relations, the incidence of crime and breakdown of values in Australia, Britain or especially the United States, so it is reasonable for the Western press to point to the Arabic emperor's lack of new clothes.

In December 1996, commenting on the fate of Lucy and Debbie within this system, the London *Daily Telegraph* was pessimistic about their prospects. The paper published the cautionary tales of foreigners living in Saudi:

> Several offenders have been flogged publicly for selling alcohol. Expats tell newcomers about the Briton in Dhahran who was burned when his illegal still exploded

and suffered a quieter but more sinister fate. He was not allowed to be flown home for hospital treatment and subsequently died — an outcome the Saudis regarded as just punishment.

Frank Gilford, sitting with us in his loungeroom in Jamestown when we spoke to him in January, knew little of all this. Nor did he seem to want to know. We offered to fly him to Saudi Arabia to see the system for himself. He declined. Later, he told me his family had forbidden him to go. Theirs may have been a small-town fear of the strange wide world, but, given that one of their own had just died in grievous circumstances in that far-off kingdom, surely understandable.

What's more sure is that, given Frank's ignorance of and unwillingness to be educated on the shortcomings of Saudi justice, the onus was on his advisers to inform him. Many expatriates living in Saudi are blithely unaware of the abuses existing in the system around them. Some of those who rang and wrote to Frank were almost wilfully uninformed about what goes on in the country they described to him. When they asserted the guilt of the accused women and the reliability of the system about to judge them, they did Frank a disservice. Yet their failing is also understandable, given that they were the shocked colleagues of an Australian woman who had been murdered. Even more reason why Frank's legal representatives in Saudi Arabia ought to have been especially vigilant in advising him of the risks of relying on a closed legal system.

Chapter 18

The grasshopper in gaol

While Frank Gilford hides from the world's acrimony in fortress Jamestown, in Dammam Central Prison, Deborah Parry sits with her cross-stitch, a very English domestic pursuit in very strange surroundings. Some days, she and the other women prisoners will sit in boiling heat in the rough schoolroom, doing craft. Some weeks, Debbie has only an hour a day to work on her cross-stitch. In her twelve-person cell the fluorescent lighting isn't strong enough and she is only allowed scissors in the schoolroom. Sometimes she and the other prisoners are only allowed out of their cells for an hour a day. This is because Ratma, one of the Saudi women, is rampaging. Ratma is schizophrenic, happily admits to the murder she's accused of, and terrifies both inmates and keepers. She has flourished fluorescent tubes as a weapon. Debbie, in particular, lives in fear of her. So the warders keep the women in their cells. The scissors for handiwork are locked up in the craft room. When the wardress can't be bothered, she won't open it up for a week. There is a small square off the cell for hanging out washing but no room to sit without it all dripping on you. So, mostly, Debbie sits in her cell and reads.

She reads romantic novels by women authors. Some of it is more literary, some of it not. Her recent list includes Charlotte Bingham's *Grand Affair*, Eileen Townsend's *In Love and War*, Joanna Trollope's *A Spanish Lover*, Helen Fielding's *Bridget Jones's Diary*, Maeve Binchy's *The Glass Lake* and Rosie Thomas's *Every Woman Knows a Secret*. (It's tempting to dwell on the last — but unfair, really.) The list tells something of what Debbie would like life to be. Romantic, dramatic, yes — but ultimately life-affirming. Happy endings.

Maeve Binchy conveys a sense of the wholesomeness of rural family life. Something Debbie once had but now feels she didn't appreciate enough. In prison now, she writes poems in which she chastises herself for this neglect: why did she pursue adventure at the expense of the love she had at home?

Sometimes, Debbie writes poems, shiftless daydreams, often a mix of meter-less banality not far beyond the British clink lament of mad Freddie Krahe's 'Often, when I'm lying in my sleep/I wish I was free/Like the sheep.' But with the occasional moment of insight:

> *March 17*
> My spirits are raised because of you all.
> If I didn't have you I'd have nothing at all.
> You fill my mind both day and night.
> You're the only things I have in my sight.
> Heathrow Airport means only one thing to me,
> To see you all waiting for me.
> Never again will I go across the sea.
> When losing your freedom ever happens to you,
> You stop, think and appreciate all that you have.
> That is why it has happened to me.
> No more a grasshopper will I be.
> This prison is to me
> A thinking place to be.
> Never take for granted your freedom.
> Make sure each day of your life has reason.
> Never look for things which cannot be.
> To me, this is what I see.

Each day the prisoners eat rice with beef or chicken on top. Fish one day a week. They're entitled to one piece of fruit a day. Debbie eats mainly Arabic bread because she suffers from diarrhoea.

Debbie and Lucy help the mothers in the gaol look after their kids. Through the British consular pressure, they have been able to get disinfectant in to clean the area around the two holes-in-the-ground which serve as toilets and drains for showering and washing. To gain privacy in the rough toilets, the women jam wet paper, smelling of urine, into the door. Debbie and Lucy, the nurse coming out in them, organise the other prisoners into cleaning the courtyard and cells. The others are amazed; they expect Westerners to have servants. Debbie and her family call the prison 'Bedrock', in reference to its prehistoric likeness to *The Flintstones*.

A friend from the outside, Paul Thomas, tried to send Debbie a teddy bear, dressed as Santa Claus, to cheer her up. It's been disallowed because the gaol kids aren't allowed toys for fear of contraband. So Debbie can't have a toy either.

Early in her gaol time, Debbie writes to Rosemary Kidman to organise the packing and shipping of her belongings at the hospital. She says she's missing Purdy, the cat they discussed on the night of the murder. Debbie says to tell the hairdresser her hair is going white. 'No mirrors allowed, maybe a good thing.'

Debbie writes that she is spending her days doing puzzles, eating and sleeping. 'Hard to sleep as obviously lights on all night.' There is some consolation, with 'so much support from UK. Many, many letters and faxes' from strangers, friends, even old school chums. But there is too much time to think. 'We have clear consciences,' she claims. 'I keep on saying, why us? No answer, well not that I can speak of!'

Rosemary writes back, a stern letter that puts a halt to their correspondence: 'You are right in saying "justice will prevail" Debbie, so long as the *truth* is told — only then will "justice prevail". Don't try to kid yourself otherwise, we don't. We must face reality that is for sure. Purdy is well and safe,' she writes, slipping from lecture back to chatty letter and back to lecture again:

> It is difficult to know what else to say Debbie and you are right in saying this is all a "total nightmare". We *never* lose sight of the fact that Yvonne is dead and under such horrific circumstances! No one deserves that. This is the absolute reality and what is important. This is the *focus* of all this mess. What you are having to suffer and what we are having to suffer is far less important and is a mere consequence of the fact that she was murdered. We are alive and what if it had been any one of us?... Yvonne went home dead. You will go home alive.

And later, 'I think we all deserve to know the truth here, no holds barred.' This from a woman Debbie thought of as her friend.

In May, Debbie finds a pigeon in the yard with a broken wing. She gathers a shoebox and cloth and tries to nurse it. Someone chides her. A bird must be free. Debbie sets the pigeon loose in the yard.

Later, she looks for this small friend. She finds it, dead. Someone has wrung its neck. Birds again; this one a symbol of what? The death of hope? The death of reconciliation?

The eight cells accommodate twelve people each, but often there are only six in Debbie and Lucy's as other prisoners come and go. The two share a cell generally occupied by non-Saudis. Nationalities are grouped together, so they fall into the group of sundries in what's known as the International House. There's a Saudi cell, a Filipina cell, a Somali cell and so on.

Lucy seems to be the stalwart, holding the two women together, as other cellmates come and go. One of her mid-year letters to a Scots friend shows her grit:

> There is so much evidence to prove my innocence Freda. Any fair and just court will hand out an innocent verdict.
>
> As I have said before she was my pal. I have not even grieved for her properly yet because of where I am — pisses me off that I am still here.
>
> Anyway thanks for your latest letter and cards. I'm fine. Court delayed again. Things don't look good now — unbelievable considering all the evidence our lawyers have. The only evidence the boys in blue have is our 'confessions'. No fingerprints, no forensic evidence etc etc. This place is so f— corrupt it is mind boggling.
>
> Anyway you know me Freda. I won't go quietly. The authorities here don't know how vocal I can be. Debs is OK. Getting angry now like me which is great. She's not frightened anymore. Jail continues to be hell on earth. What more can I say. That's about it. Take care of yourself and be careful. The [NHS] Trust are so ruthless Freda. I will have my say when I come home. Hopefully before I'm wrinkled and bloody bald.

Chapter 19

Complicity

Back in Sydney, it's clear that The Law Firm of Salah Al-Hejailan now sees its new friends from the *Witness* program as allies in the women's cause. A fax arrives from Salah.

> Dear Mick,
> I hope you arrived home safely.
> Could I ask to arrange to have Frank Gilford see the enclosed Press Release before Sunday.
> Best Regards.

Salah seems to have given up all hope of a soft approach to Frank. The press release is a tirade.

> Frank Gilford has no business insisting repeatedly and emphatically — in the face of contrary evidence — that the two nurses are guilty of murdering Yvonne Gilford. His representative has even gone so far as to say on television that he can see the capacity for killing in the nurses' eyes. Indeed, the wife of Frank Gilford has been quoted as saying to the press that darts should be thrown through the nurses' hearts, then their lungs, livers and kidneys, if they are convicted.

Laurel claims she never said such a thing. I wonder. She is certainly capable of shooting her mouth off when her blood's up.

Now, in the press release, Salah is making capital of things I'd mentioned to him back in Riyadh.

> ... we intend to request the Saudi Arabian court to verify whether Frank Gilford, beyond being a blood relation of the victim, is also, as required under Islamic law, an heir under the Will of his sister Yvonne Gilford. Evidence has come to light *indicating he is not* — and that his representative has known this fact for some time.

In Riyadh I'd been speaking in defence of Yvonne Gilford. To demonstrate her generosity, I mentioned she'd given much of her estate, money and an apartment, to the children of her friends in South Africa. Sue Taylor's son Matthew, in particular, had benefited. Now, Salah's lawyers were on the phone wanting to know where they could get Yvonne's will, so they could show that Frank had been written out. Technically, they reasoned, this could mean Frank was not an heir and therefore had no right to demand the death penalty for his sister's death.

I hadn't seen Yvonne's will, but Frank told me that he and his mother had benefited from Yvonne's insurance policies. Sounded like they were heirs to me. And surely a Saudi court would make its own decisions on the rights of heirs in a criminal trial, regardless of where Yvonne's assets were disbursed in foreign jurisdictions.

But Salah had stepped up the pace of the game. His lawyers tracked down Yvonne's will in South Africa and found that she had, in fact, given most of her money and property to the children.

As well as pushing this line in the court, Salah was using it to turn up the public heat on Frank:

> If Mr Gilford is not at all an heir under his sister's Will, he has no right under Islamic law to demand before the court the imposition of the death penalty ... How ironic that Mr Gilford may be keeping himself before the spotlight condemning the nurses, when he seems to have no right under Islamic law to assume this role.

I feel the sting of complicity, knowing that Frank's enemies are using information I've passed on. I'd not foreseen how the talk of Yvonne's munificence might be used against her brother. While it was good to see that the accused women might now have new arms against their accuser, and maybe a way to escape the sword, there was the creeping feeling of guilt at having helped them attack Frank again.

Chapter 20

Doing time

While two women sit in the Dammam gaol, the number of people around the world doing the time with them is growing. Frank's piles of letters for and against his position are growing — among them, assuming Jim Phipps actually passed them on, formal letters from Lucy and Debbie explaining their positions. Too formal, too late. These are lawyer letters, without a hint of the personalities of the accused. Dead letters. They ask Frank to grant clemency but still maintain their innocence. Catch-22. How can he forgive if they won't say there's anything they've done to be forgiven for?

Michael Dark rings from Riyadh to ask the denomination of Frank's church. 'We are simply thinking that whichever church he belongs to, we might approach them to talk to Frank about the death penalty.'

Frank is not a churchgoer, though he tells me he has had a visit from the local minister in Jamestown to offer support during his ordeal. Frank says you don't have to go to church to be a Christian.

Visiting his daughter in Dammam, Stan McLauchlan is growing desperate. From the British Trade Consulate one day, he calls me at home in Sydney. It's late Australian time, but I'm glad to hear from him. He wants me to talk to Frank, to plead for his understanding. Stan has always insisted Frank must see that if he doesn't accept the claims of lesbianism, then he should reject the rest of the story against the women as well.

Sandra Ashbee calls too, her grief palpable on the international line. Debbie isn't doing well. Sandra says she doesn't think her sister will survive the year if the pressure keeps up. Jonathan Ashbee sends an eight-page dossier he's put together, bits of gossip really, and claims from Lucy and Debbie about why they can't be guilty. It's very patchy, not entirely convincing, though he's convinced himself it's all true.

I call Frank, determined to be more strident with him than I've risked before. He should go to Saudi, I urge him. The more I hear from over there, the less convinced I am of the truth of Yvonne's death coming out in court. Frank says his family have voted and forbidden him to go over.

He talks about the claims the women are suffering hellish conditions in gaol. Susan Supple, an American woman who has spent some time in the prison with them, has spoken to the press in Britain and talks about holes in the ground for toilets. Frank is unsympathetic. He talks about the luxury prisoners have in Australia and Britain. Televisions in their cells. This is an old right-wing line. Is he just the redneck he's portrayed as by some?

Later, I mention to him I'm working on a story about death threats against the right-wing politician Pauline Hanson. 'You can understand 'em doing it against her,' he says. So he's not a Hanson supporter, I think. But then he adds it seems like Pauline's heart is in the right place. Frank is not a redneck. Just an average conservative rural Australian.

I go on for some time about my doubts in the case against the women. He listens, saying nothing. In the end I apologise for soap-boxing. 'I'll catch you,' he says at the end, giving nothing of his thoughts away. This doesn't look good. I phone the British families to tell them I've tried but that Frank is now saying he needs to wait for a verdict before doing anything more.

A month of quiet follows. Frank doesn't answer my calls. I suspect he's insulted by the impudence of my last call.

The same thing happens to Therese Feeney. After she badgers Frank in a phone call from Ireland to push him to give up on the death penalty, he stops calling her. She sends a note saying she'd like a call on her birthday. A gent, he rings, apologises and they're friends again.

No apology comes from Saudi Arabia. How can you apologise for a murder if you're innocent?

Salah Al-Hejailan is confident. He tells Lucy and Debbie, and anyone else who will listen, that the judges will not recognise the confessions. Even his friend, the Saudi ambassador in London, Dr Ghazi Algosaibi, tells the press the withdrawn confessions will not be accepted as evidence. Salah is so confident he lets the two women know they will be released after the court hearing on June 15. In gaol, the two give away their sugar and coffee, their toothpaste. They won't be needing it.

False hope. The Sunday hearing comes. The lawyers for Frank tell the court there has been no progress towards reconciliation. According to Salah Al-Hejailan, the court rejects a memo from Frank's lawyers, demanding the death penalty, for 'lack of clarity, accuracy and appropriateness'.

June 23 and the court sits again. Another impasse. Now the lawyers for the women are pushing the court to have Frank's lawyers prove that Frank has the right to ask for the death penalty on his mother's behalf. It seems Salah is again using information I gave him back in Riyadh.

After my interview with the member of the Shura Council, Saleh Al-Malik, I'd mentioned his thoughts to Salah Al-Hejailan. Al-Malik theorised, hypothetically, that the death penalty might have to wait until the death of a relative deemed not mentally competent to demand it. While he wouldn't speak specifically about Yvonne's mother, Muriel Gilford, he agreed that the memory-sapping Alzheimer's disease could cause such a concern for the court. Now, Salah Al-Hejailan was using this possibility as a tactic against Frank. According to a June 24 press release from Salah's firm, 'although pressed by the court Gilford's lawyers said they were not aware that Mrs Gilford is suffering from Alzheimer's disease and therefore is not competent to make a valid decision'.

The court again asks Frank's lawyers to consider reconciliation. Instead, they make a submission, demanding the return of the money allegedly stolen by Lucy and Debbie with Yvonne's ATM card. They want SR8000 from Lucy and SR7000 from Debbie.

Frank's Saudi lawyers, Hassan Al-Awaji and Osama Al-Solaim, repeat the demand for *Qisas*, the death penalty.

Salah Al-Hejailan fires off a press release about the demand for the SR15 000:

> This seems a strangely mercenary request for Frank Gilford to make when he has stated publicly on more than one occasion that he is not interested in receiving any financial recompense following his sister's death.

Back in gaol, this argument is small comfort. The British women ask for new toothpaste.

It's up to Lucy to keep their spirits up:

> I'm staying strong and being a real pain which makes me feel happy. You know me — not one to shut my gob easily. Debs my pal is as mad as usual but she's OK.
> I'm still waiting on the bloody verdict. I have eternal hope I will be home soon but am prepared for the worst ...

And later:

> I'm fine. Looking after myself and learning the [Arabic] girls' fun words as in dickhead etc etc ...
> Debs is not so good. She has not coped as well in here as me but she has crazy Lucy to look after her so I'm on a mission just now to keep her sane. It's hard going though. Jail is hell on earth but bearable.

In South Australia, Frank Gilford is saying he can't give forgiveness if the women won't acknowledge their guilt.

Chapter 21

Tactics

Salah Al-Hejailan takes the fight to Frank. In August in Adelaide, he hires Michael Burnett from the law firm Minter Ellison to attack Frank in the Supreme Court. Although the case against the women is in another jurisdiction in another country, the Supreme Court of South Australia grants a temporary injunction against Frank making any move in the case, including pushing for the death penalty. The court ordered Frank Gilford not to make further comments on behalf of his family until his mother's mental state had been assessed. In his judgment, Mr Justice Len King declared 'until further orders, the defendant be restrained ... from further advising the Saudi Arabian court that it is the unanimous view of the heirs that the death penalty be inflicted ...' Frank was also required to tell the Saudi court of this ruling and to hand over Muriel Gilford's health records to the British nurses' lawyers.

The idea of the defence lawyers was to have the Australian court declare Frank to be biased and prejudicial in the case. Then, they hoped, they could have the Public Advocate appointed as Muriel Gilford's guardian. As South Australia now outlaws the death penalty, the Public Advocate would be bound to ask the Saudi court to rule for clemency. That was the theory, anyway.

Flushed with the success of the temporary injunction, the nurses' lawyers now sued Frank for damages. Again in the South Australian Supreme Court, they sought an unspecified amount of compensation from Frank for anxiety, stress and loss of income suffered during their months in prison.

All this seemed dangerously aggressive to anyone who knew Frank. Surely this would push him further into a corner. But now chance threw a new player into the game. The prominent Adelaide Queen's Counsel, Michael Abbott, happened to catch the same plane as Alexander Downer, the Australian Foreign Minister. Downer is an Adelaide-based Liberal politician and knew Abbott well. Sitting together on the plane, they got to chatting about the Gilford case. Downer had been to see Frank in Jamestown but had scrupled at pressuring him on the death penalty.

Michael Abbott is a man who fancies himself as a performer in the courtroom. He had played to the press gallery during his prominent role in the Hindmarsh Island case, representing Aboriginal land claimants who disputed the claim of other Aborigines that a proposed bridge would damage a sacred site. He stood as an independent republican candidate for the Australian Constitutional Convention. Now he prepared to jump in front of the spotlight again. He offered his services to Frank Gilford.

On September 12, 1997, Michael Abbott stood up in the Supreme Court in Adelaide and declared, 'These proceedings are to a very great extent a charade.' He added: 'The Saudi justice system is under attack in these proceedings.'

The quixotically named barrister for Debbie and Lucy, Dick Whitington, had told the court that Saudi law was 'abhorrent to the common law of Australia' in allowing an individual to impose such 'a cruel, unjust and inhumane punishment' as public beheading, and to do it without due process.

Michael Abbott challenged the right of the British nurses to use an Australian court and called for the injunction against Frank to be thrown out. 'How can non-citizens and non-residents derive any benefit from South Australian laws when they are being tried in another country?' he asked.

While the public knew only of the court hearings, there were secret moves beginning behind the scenes. Alexander Downer met British Foreign Secretary Robin Cook at the Hong Kong handover ceremonies and checked that there was no in-principle opposition to a deal. Now Abbott's junior, John Keen, put out careful feelers to see if there might be some chance of a negotiated settlement. Would the lawyers for the nurses consider making Frank an offer? According to Jonathan Ashbee, it took some time for the reply — in the positive — to get through. A breakdown in communications between the diplomats led to a second approach and reply being made. Yes, there could be negotiations.

Until then, Frank had always maintained he would not consider compensation through the Saudi court, the so-called blood money in return for clemency. Now reality crept in, largely due to the pragmatic efforts of two men, Salah Al-Hejailan and Michael Abbott.

Had Salah not taken the aggressive course and chased Frank around the South Australian Supreme Court, Frank may never have felt the financial pressure which tipped him towards considering a money offer. And Michael Abbott would not have entered the picture.

I later met Abbott in the bar of the Adelaide Hilton, an establishment on whose board he sits. I described the Saudi lawyers to him, especially the tough and flamboyant Salah. I lamented the lack of lawyers on the other side equipped to stand up to him. 'I'm a match for him,' said Abbott, relishing the contest.

But at this time, mid-September, I knew no more about the private shenanigans and deal-making than the rest of the world. The hard men were discussing deals, while the rest of us still hoped for reconciliation.

Chapter 22

Breaking news

Tuesday, September 23, 1997. The weekly deadline comes around again. I should get back to chasing the Saudi story, but there's little time in weekly journalism. In the edit suite we're finishing a story on Mickey Mouse and Walt Disney monstering an Australian small-businessman. Out the door at 4 pm to rush to the airport. Just time to make a 6.30 dinner with the new Saudi ambassador in Canberra, Mohammed Al-Hejailan. It's the usual ridiculous scramble through airports but, I hope, a chance to lobby the brother of the man who helped us in Saudi last time.

Canberra's evening shouts a pink western sky after weeks of Sydney rain. In Canberra you can dodge the queue for taxis at the airport if you jump into a white chauffeured car. It costs more, but Kerry Stokes, network chairman, can afford it.

At the hotel, ironing a shirt as they turn down the bed; the news on the telly screams about politicians' travel rorts. Nothing on Frank Gilford.

Searching for the Hyatt ballroom, I feel in my pocket for the two invitations: one to the opening of the 'exhibition of industrial factories in the Kingdom of Saudi Arabia'. A pity I've missed it. The other, for dinner, gives the option of lounge suit or national dress. In the event even Tim Fischer, special guest as Deputy Prime Minister, forswears the usual Akubra bush hat and only the Saudis and fellow Arab diplomats go folkloric.

The intimate dinner with the new ambassador is attended by about 150. His first major function. He shakes hands; the waiters cut lots of lamb. The Saudi information video — on a very big screen — dominates conversation but I can just hear the Maltese High

Commissioner, sitting on my right. It's affable conversation, about windsurfing and the Maltese catacombs, between people who are here for other reasons.

During my snatched few minutes with Mohamad Al-Hejailan he smiles when I tell him his brother and nephews, the other Al-Hejailans, were very hospitable back in Riyadh. He gives no hint of having the faintest idea what I'm talking about. He looks just like his elder brother in a brown, gold-edged robe. He says nothing about the murder case. Abdullah, his offsider, says they've sent off our visa application to return to Saudi. We must wait for Riyadh to respond. Nobody makes a speech, and guests are invited to load up with Saudi industry and history pamphlets as we file out the door. At the Saudi ambassador's first big bash there's been no hint that the first big news in the Gilford case for months is about to break.

Back in my room; dozing in front of CNN, switching to the ABC for the late news. Suddenly, I'm awake. They say Lucy has been given eight years and will face 500 lashes. For Deborah the death penalty.

I'd vaguely thought of making Saudi calls tonight; now I'm chained to the phone. Lonely hours until 2 am, trying to raise someone in one of these three countries who knows what's going on. I fall asleep before the TV announces Salah Al-Hejailan's next ploy. At 3 am Australian time he claims, speaking in Washington, a deal's been done. Frank Gilford, he says, will waive the death penalty.

In Al Khobar, the court sits to pronounce Lucy's sentence. She's taken to the court, but to the wrong room. By the time this is realised, she's missed her own case and is taken back to the Dammam gaol.

There, the Scot and the Englishwoman sit by their cheap transistor radio, listening to the BBC World Service. Today, they are the lead item: 'Reports from Saudi Arabia say British nurse Deborah Parry has been convicted of the murder of an Australian colleague and has been sentenced to death ... Lucille McLauchlan ... 500 lashes ... eight years in prison ...' Debbie collapses in shock. Lucille continues listening long enough to hear her father condemning the news. 'These two nurses' human rights have been completely violated ... not one shred of evidence against them has been heard in court,' he thundered.

The other 10 women in the cell bang on the steel doors, calling for a doctor, as Lucy holds Debbie. The guards come, and Debbie is taken to hospital for treatment. Michael Dark rushes to see both women to reassure them. There'll be an appeal for Lucy, and for Debbie it's a false alarm. As she recovers the next day, Debbie writes home:

> *September 24* [Day of the press release from The International Law Firm claiming Lucy faced eight years and five hundred lashes, and Debbie faced execution]
> I was astounded by what I heard on the world news. I'm not going to feel sorry for myself as I did last night. The inner strength comes from knowing you are there. Please help us. Stupid thing to say as I know you will. Lucy desperately upset but, as she says, we can't feel sorry for ourselves. The fighting Debbie will come out, so please don't worry. I will be home one day, just longer than I thought. Please don't get upset about this as we have to help each other.
> PS: I'm OK.
>
> *September 24, 7.07 am*
> I thought that I'd write a bit more to say hopefully others get involved now in some way. You still have to carry on with your lives as before all of this. I hope that Willow is doing well and has not eaten the goldfish or Georgina.
> I miss you all so, so much. Life in the prison carries on as unchanged. Comings and goings all the time. I'm afraid that I've started smoking again. They have no right in doing what they've done. Hopefully we'll see someone today. I need to see you. Love you all lots and lots and lots.
> PS: If I die, I'll die innocent. I will fight.
> PPS: Lucy is on hunger strike.

Lucy's hunger strike was over in a few days, when her mother, Ann, sent a fax to her saying the family had enough to worry about without that.

Michael Dark rings Scotland and finds Ann McLauchlan at home by the phone. He confirms the news that Lucy has been found guilty, the charge not yet clear. But his news for the shocked household in Alton, Hampshire, is different. There has been no confirmation of a conviction or sentencing for Debbie, he says.

In Britain and Australia, a press storm worthy of a princess breaks loose. One radio voice from London claims people's hearts are still raw from Princess Diana's death; that's why 'the people', newly defined after the princess's funeral as a quasi-revolutionary, crypto-Republican, sobbing congregation, are so upset about Lucy's lashes. The tabloids, never shy of baying for blood, have become human rights campaigners. If politics and selling newspapers are all about defining the other, it's surely been defined. Forget Saddam Hussein; now we have Frank Gilford and the Saudi justice system.

In Dundee, Alton and Jamestown, there's pain and panic. Jon Ashbee, sounding rushed but efficient, won't quite say it but they're angry with Salah. Jon admits there have been secret negotiations between lawyers for the two sides. Now they're upset that the flamboyant sheikh has made his splash announcement — without consulting the families — before Frank has quite been brought to the water of conciliation and made to drink. In Jamestown, dozens of media types swarm the Gilfords' front lawn. They want to know if it's all true: have the women been found guilty, and is Frank calling off the sword? Instead, Frank calls off an expected press conference. Actually, the local copper does it for him, telling the assembled press corps there'll be no announcement today. Laurel comes home to 'feed the chooks', Bjelke-Petersen style, and mutters that 'Frank hasn't made his mind up yet.' Later, she steps out to take photos of her roses, ignoring the crowd, as if it were normal for two dozen adult men and women to be camped on her footpath, calling her name. The photographers snap away and she turns to take a photo of them. The next day the world will see a photograph of Laurel Gilford, wife of the notorious Frank, snubbing her camera at the cameras.

Frank finds it harder to make light of the pressure. As he comes out next morning to begin his courier rounds at 5 am, two photographers swarm his car, heckling for a reaction. He scrabbles at their cameras through the car windows. He's lost his cool. Maybe that's what they wanted.

Frank is a worrier. He worries all day about what he's done, striking out at the press. That night, he calls a couple of friendly reporters staying at the Railway Hotel. He asks, redundantly, if they'll be in the bar. He goes over to buy them a drink and talk with the photographers involved in the morning incident. He's nervous and hesitant but apologises for hitting out. The two snappers, from *The Sydney Morning Herald* and *The Adelaide Advertiser*, say they won't run pictures of Frank striking at them. The *Herald* sticks by the promise. The *Advertiser*, cunningly, runs their aggro pic only in the city edition. So Frank, up in Jamestown, doesn't see it.

Beyond his South Australian redoubt, Frank has stirred greater passions. Here in his small town, he has neighbours, fellow Jamestowners, who watch out for him. The pub rings as soon as any of the journalists book in. Frank, with old-world stoicism, refuses to allow the fuss to deter him from continuing daily life. Each morning he's in the car for a three-hour drive to Port Pirie and back, collecting the day's courier load. Elsewhere, the hounds of righteousness are now baying for *his* blood.

Nineteen ninety-seven became the year Britain stood up for its English — and Scottish — roses as they were mistreated at the hands of foreign brutes. The French paparazzi were self-evidently to blame for Diana's death, just as the American legal system could not do justice to nanny Louise Woodward, found guilty by an American jury of murdering the boy in her charge. Likewise, the Saudi legal system and Frank Gilford were in tandem to torment the innocent nurses in Dammam.

Amid headlines that scream that Frank had done a deal for 'blood money', all is confusion as the press in Britain and Australia try to work out the truth of the reports. The Saudi legal system is as impenetrable as ever; no official pronouncements come from the courts on guilt, innocence or sentence. In this vacuum, it is open to the rival Saudi-based lawyers — Salah Al-Hejailan and Jim Phipps — to make rival claims, which the other inevitably rebuts. The lawyers elsewhere, for the families in Britain and Australia, squirm at the damage done to delicate negotiations.

The announcements of the claimed convictions and the claim of a deal are yet another case of tit-for-tat press-releasing by the law firms in Saudi Arabia. The International Law Firm has sparked the storm by issuing a press release claiming that both women have been convicted and that Lucy faces lashes and gaol while Debbie faces death.

In Washington, Salah is incensed by this premature announcement. He knows the court has not yet made its decision on Debbie. Hearing of Debbie's collapse, he rushes into press release himself. 'In the court hearing today in Al Khobar, Lucille McLauchlan was found to be not guilty of intentional murder,' his release of November 23 declares, and 'we shall immediately lodge an appeal against the court decision convicting Lucille McLauchlan of a lesser charge.'

The release doesn't say what the lesser charge is. Only months later do I have it confirmed that it's theft and concealing a major crime.

Salah's release lambastes The International Law Firm for making false claims about Debbie's conviction. 'In fact, the name of Deborah Parry was not mentioned once during the hearing today in Al Khobar.'

It was probably a fair assumption on the part of The International Law Firm that if Lucy was facing a conviction for a lesser charge, then Debbie must have been convicted of something. It was irresponsible, though, to rush to print with an assertion as fact that she would be beheaded for murder.

Deborah Parry suffered deeply from that announcement, but elsewhere it was the news of a deal that was shaking the tree. The negotiations were supposed to be secret. Announcing the deal in Washington, Salah hadn't consulted the other lawyers involved.

In Adelaide, the lawyers for both Frank and the women put out an unprecedented joint press release: 'Both parties confirmed,' it said, 'that the comments attributed to Mr Salah Al-Hejailan that Mr Gilford had in any way waived his rights as an heir under Saudi Arabian law were wrong.' Far from the bombast of Salah, holed up in his Washington house, the lawyers he had hired to run the women's case in Australia publicly defied him. Dick Whitington, QC, and Michael Burnett, from the firm Minter Ellison, put their names to the press release. In language much less colourful than Salah's too. The joint statement added that 'discussions are continuing' in bland acknowledgment that there had, in fact, been secret negotiations between themselves and Frank's lawyers.

The press release also has a kick in the teeth for Frank's lawyers in Saudi. It had been The International Law Firm in Riyadh which announced that both women had been found guilty. Now, the Adelaide Queen's Counsel Michael Abbott and his junior counsel John Keen were cutting the Riyadh lawyers out of the picture. 'Both parties acknowledge that the only representatives of Mr Gilford who are authorised to say anything on his behalf in relation to his rights are his lawyers in Adelaide ...' ran the joint press release. At last, Jim Phipps and Salah Al-Hejailan were sidelined. Their personal animosity had held up conciliation for months. Now it was time to deal.

The next day, Thursday, the Adelaide defence lawyer Michael Burnett finally accepts my call. Originally hired by Salah, a man he's never met, he had asked us for a copy of our stories so that he can study the men who hired him — Al-Hejailan and his team, Bob Thoms and Michael Dark. Today, he grunts when I mention the bull in his china shop. He's beginning to sound like Michael Dark, long-suffering and incredulous at his master's antics. Michael intimates that discussions are continuing with Frank's lawyers. And sure enough, later in the day comes a fax, also dumping on Salah: 'Mr Al-Hejailan did not take any part in our discussions.' Quite. But how extraordinary that there are such discussions. Frank may have hung up on me two weeks ago, but it seems he's taking advice from somebody. After nine months of Mahathir-like recalcitrance, he's finally talking to the other side.

Meanwhile, in Washington, what is Salah's game? He's clearly not concerned about upsetting the delicate Adelaide tea party. This time he's playing to the Saudi gallery. If Frank has even begun to talk about money, he claims, he has by inference already waived his right to the death penalty.

And meanwhile, the rest of the world has the jump on what I've come to see as my story. How to get back in the game?

Late-night phone calls. Perhaps one in ten yields a real voice. Night voices in Arabic and English declare the lines are congested; you may wish to try again later. Dial again.

The hospital. A list of names and numbers; people not spoken to for months. Will they still be there? Will they still talk? The hospital switchboard finally yields and I'm put through to Caroline Ionescu. I've woken her after a night shift but she's cheerful, as ever, and happy to hear a voice from home.

Caroline says she is still waiting for justice to take its course but she finds the ordeal, the waiting for a verdict, 'horrific'. It was Caroline, when we spoke by phone in Saudi in June, who first claimed that nearly everyone at the hospital had the same view of the case against Lucy and Debbie. Now she repeated her claim: 'We all believe they're guilty.'

Caroline had been closest to Lucy. She has just received a letter from her, dated September 15. In the letter, says Caroline, Lucy sounds like she's unsure of what is happening in the courts; worried that the judges will believe the confessions. It sounds as though Lucy is unaware that her friend has turned on her. 'I can't take it any more,' says Caroline. She says, not for the first time, that she wants to get away from the drama of the hospital. 'But if it's like this for me, imagine what it's like for them?' On the line in Australia, I imagine what it will be like for Lucy and Debbie to have their former friends condemn them.

Caroline says she's still not prepared to be quoted or to appear publicly. 'One day, many of us will get together and give our version,' she says. I wonder, silently, venally, why this couldn't happen now — and on our program. So, would anyone be prepared to talk now? 'I think Rosemary would do something like that,' says Caroline. Rosemary is Caroline's Australian friend, another nurse at King Fahd, who has returned home.

For a television producer, this is the glimmer of hope. The person you're talking to won't go on the record; they know someone who might. It's a chain of relationships over which you have no control. In this case, Caroline says she won't give Rosemary's number in Australia but she will ring her and encourage her to get in touch. A nebulous link with someone who just might talk.

Before we say goodbye, Caroline offers some slight equivocation in her dreadful certainty of guilt: 'If they haven't done it, God help us with the murderer still around.'

Sandra Ashbee has been to collect her children from school. As she twists into her steep drive from the street, reporters and photographers swoop, pointing cameras in the windows. This is her first inkling of the news: Debbie has been convicted and will be executed. Distraught, Sandra ushers her children inside, seeking refuge.

Similar scenes continue over the next month in Alton, Dundee and Jamestown. In the South Australian small town helicopters land in fields, and photographers with long lenses camp in Laurel's chook runs. Even before the latest announcements the mood had been set, with the death of Princess Diana in France and the nanny murder case in the United States. In Alton, reporters and photographers had bailed Jon and Sandra one day as they came home from shopping. Did they know the Saudis were going to use the distraction of Princess Diana's funeral to quickly chop their Debbie's head off? Now, with their aunty so often in the news, the Ashbee children are suffering, says Sandra. 'The young ones are bed-wetting, having bursts of crying. Our six-year-old can read. He saw a banner at the newsagent. He said, "They're going to kill my Aunty Debbie".'

On the families' next visit to Dammam, Debbie is in a bad way. Sandra describes her sister, 'looking at Michael Dark and saying, "Does this mean I've been found guilty of intentional murder?" He said, "We don't know for sure; can presume it." She just burst into tears. She's very thin, her face drawn, she's often on drips.'

The flogging part of Lucy's sentence seemed to create some of the greatest outrage. In Dublin, Monica Hall described floggings she'd witnessed in gaol in Taif.

> *You don't know the name of the person to be flogged until the police actually arrive in the compound. The name of the person to be flogged is called out and all of the rest of the inmates have to dress appropriately and sit and watch this flogging as it takes place. The sentence is read out to the person that's to be flogged. She hunches down facing the wall and one of the police with a very long bamboo cane which thins towards the end begins to flog her, usually on the shoulders and on the buttocks while one of the police counts and the other police person looks on. It's a very demeaning exercise. It is grossly humiliating and it is brutally painful for those that have got it. The lashes would be delivered in bunches of 50 over maybe a two-to-three week period. It was just awful to sit and watch that kind of brutality and that's all it was — it was brutality.*

The coverage in Britain especially ran heavily in favour of the two women expected to suffer that brutality. While some reports still mentioned the fact that Lucy faced questions of criminality back in Dundee, most were very favourable towards the two accused. My own sympathy still ran the same way, though the story was about to lead us in the opposite direction.

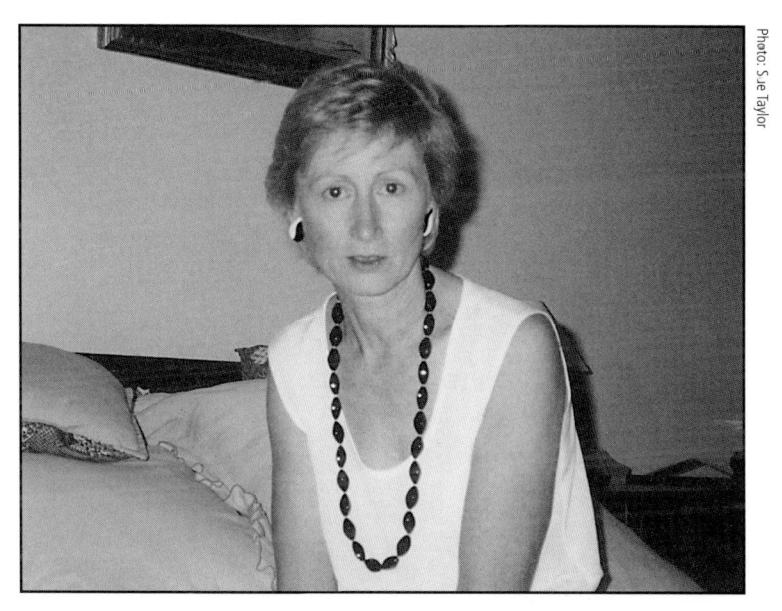

The last photo taken of Yvonne Gilford before she left South Africa in 1996, the year of her murder.

Yvonne (left) with best friend Sue Taylor on holiday in Tunisia, 1976.

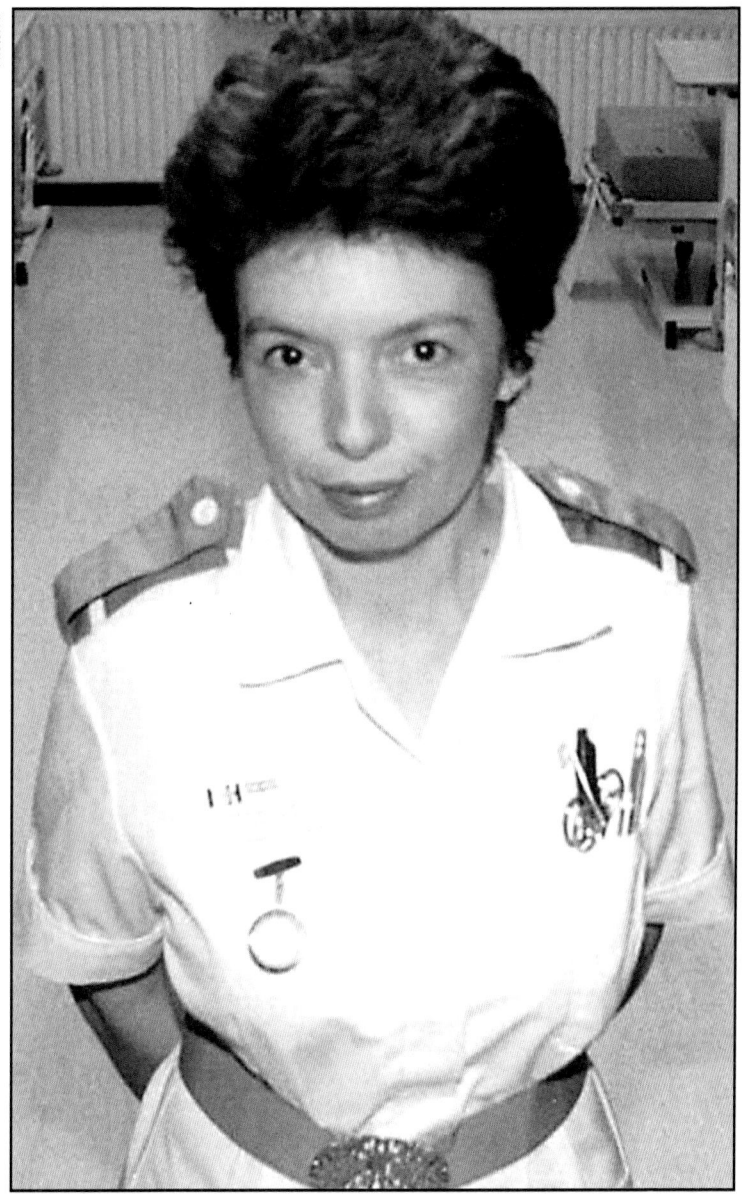

Emotionally affected by a series of deaths in her own family, Deborah Parry fled to Saudi Arabia to start over again. After Yvonne's murder, Debbie behaved strangely in the company of her nursing colleagues and failed to corroborate alibis for mysterious bruises, scratches and missing hair on her person.

Photo: AP

Lucille McLauchlan. A woman with an alleged shady past in credit card theft and fraud, Lucy was reportedly arrested carrying Yvonne's ATM card but denied having any knowledge of it. Debbie's sister and brother-in-law now claim they have strong proof that Lucy possessed, and used, Yvonne's ATM card after the murder. Her visits to ATM machines corresponded with police claims of when money had been removed from Yvonne's account, and the amounts involved corresponded to money otherwise unaccounted for in Lucy's accounts.

Lucy's parents, Stan and Ann McLauchlan, arriving at their hotel in Dammam, Saudi Arabia, on 12 January 1997.

Yvonne's brother, Jamestown courier Frank Gilford, became 'the lightning rod for Australian public opinion on the death penalty'. Widely painted as an ogre, Frank was a quiet, gentle man to journalists who came to know him.

The Witness *crew in the Saudi desert.* From left to right: *Sound recordist Alex Garipoli, reporter Paul Barry, interpreter/minder Hamad Al-Madhi, the author, cameraman Greg Barbera.*

Lawyer for the two accused British nurses, Salah Al-Hejailan, entertaining Paul Barry at his opulent Riyadh villa.

Saudi police accosting the Witness *crew in the* soukh *of Dammam. The police responded to a complaint from a local who objected to the crew filming women on the street.*

The author by the highway in the Saudi desert.

Friends and colleagues of Yvonne holding a wake in the Meceda Recreation Compound. Lucy and Debbie had asked for the ceremony to be delayed until the murder was solved. Rosemary Kidman is fourth from left; Kathryn Lyons is front row, eighth from left; Catherine Wall is fourth from right; Caroline Ionescu is back row, fifth from right.

Frank at his press conference donating the bulk of his 'blood money' to the Adelaide Women's and Children's Hospital.

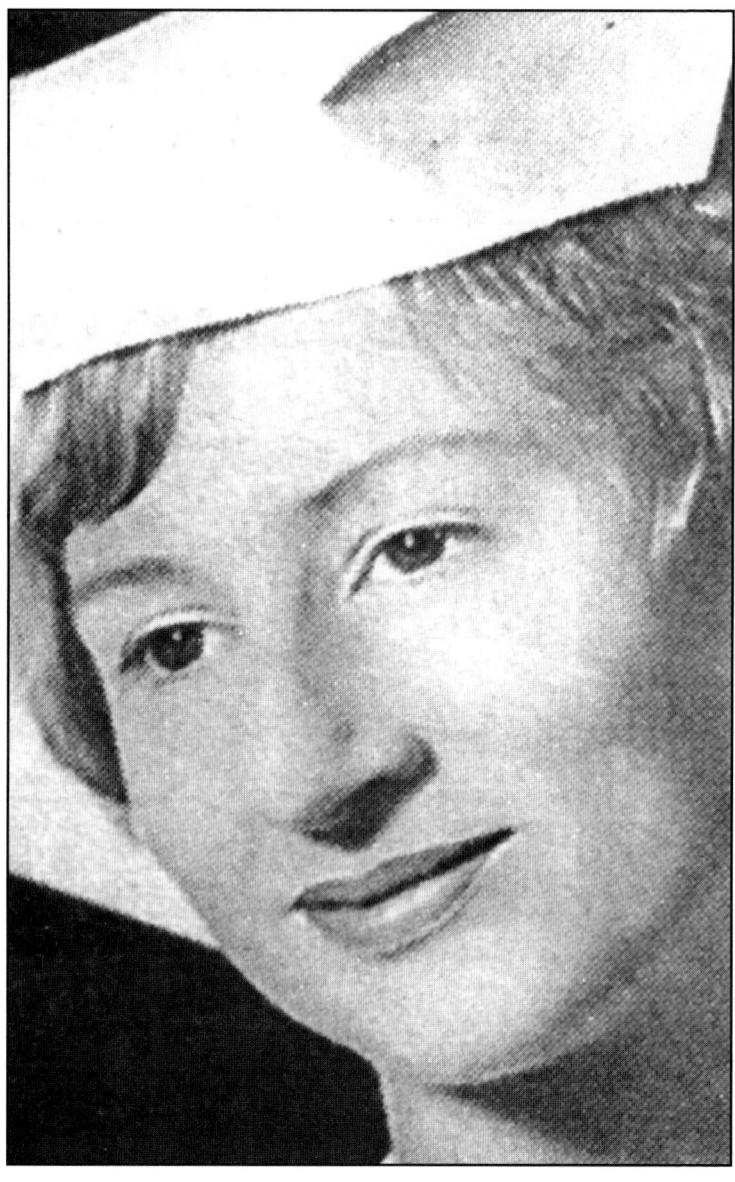

Photo: Courtesy of the Gifford Family

A young and hopeful Yvonne in the infamous 'Florence Nightingale'-style photograph that was beamed around the world when news broke of her violent murder. This is the image Yvonne's family wanted the world's press to publish. Thirty years old, it shows a much more formal woman than the friend Sue Taylor knew.

Chapter 23

Betrayal

Betrayal. It's a nasty word. Rosemary Kidman didn't want to face it. In September 1997, she grasped the nettle.

Back in June, Rosemary had rung us at the *Witness* program to talk. She hadn't wanted to be interviewed, only to pass on her impressions. This was the day before we went to air with an account of the lack of public evidence against Lucille and Deborah. Rosemary spoke to the *Witness* reporter, Paul Barry. I was still in Saudi Arabia with the camera and sound crew. Rosemary, like all the hospital staff we'd spoken to at that stage, was too nervous to go public.

Now, in September, she had decided it was time. In Sydney, working casually at nursing jobs and staying with her adult daughter, she called me. She had been back in Australia for three months, coming to Sydney via Adelaide, where she'd visited Yvonne's grave. She had sent photos of herself at the headstone back to a friend in Saudi and urged others to contact the Gilfords with what they knew. She struck up a telephone friendship with Frank and Laurel. She felt Yvonne and her family had been forgotten in the furore over the British women.

'Talent' is another nasty word. Journalists working in current affairs use it to refer to their interviewees. It's a cynical, dismissive word, left over from production-line vaudeville but, like social workers, police, nurses and others who work close to life and death, journalists talk in an argot of black humour. So we call the people who bare their souls in our reports, *the talent*. The bravado in such talk hides an emotional tussle in the heart of every journalist, good or bad. How far should you push an individual to reveal themselves on national television? Do you have any responsibility to protect the vulnerable from the unpredictable consequences of television exposure?

Journalists don't like their friends or family to listen while they're working the phone, simpering, wheedling, used-car-selling their talent into talking. We look up to see our husbands, girlfriends or mothers raising eyebrows. Can this be the person they know, speaking into the mouthpiece in a — to them — mawkish display of flattery, finessing and flirtation. In one infamous example, a Sydney journalist told her talent she had cancer in an effort to gain an interview. She got the interview. And she did have cancer. Others say they'll be sacked if they fail. Others, myself included, use a reverse psychology, discussing with interviewees the reasons why they should *not* appear. Often the talent just wants to be persuaded.

In the end, it's our job. Our job to push, to flirt, cajole, encourage, badger, ease our talent into saying 'yes'. To agree to be interviewed, to say their piece, to show their face. Now, in September 1997, it was my job to persuade Rosemary Kidman to betray her friend on national — and ultimately international — television.

It began in that first phone call. Rosemary came on the line, uncertain. She was calling, she said, because one of her friends back in Saudi had told her I was looking for people to talk to about the murder. Someone who might be able to explain why Frank Gilford was so convinced Deborah and Lucille had done it. There is a moment in all such conversations when the journalist has heart in mouth, looking for the opening to pop the question. Sometimes it's best to delay that moment to a face-to-face meeting. After a few minutes' chat, much of it pleasantry rather than substance, I suggested to Rosemary that we meet in person. She agreed and set a time for the next day. Like many nervous people in her situation, she didn't want to give a phone number or an address. She chose a pizza joint near where she was living. The Red Centre in Sydney's Crows Nest, 6 pm.

The best-laid plans of producers and researchers are stymied by traffic and too many stories to work on at once. With my head in the files of another story I jumped late into a cab to reach the meeting with Rosemary. Traffic forbade punctuality, so I rang ahead to make sure she wouldn't leave the restaurant before I arrived. She wasn't yet there, so I left a message with the waitress — now my only contact with a nervous witness, potential interviewee, who could easily walk away if I failed to show up.

Thank you to that waitress. Pulling up, 40 minutes late, I found nobody, Rosemary or otherwise. The waitress spotted my worried frown and said the lady had come and slipped home but would be back. Relief.

As I sipped a beer, I looked about. By chance, Rosemary had chosen a favourite lunching spot of the Sydney television crowd. Normally a hubbub of gourmet pizzas and gossip, the place tonight was thankfully deserted.

Rosemary stepped through the glass doors. It had to be her. A woman alone, looking for someone. She looked younger than I expected, honey-brown hair worn down over her shoulders. We greeted, she sat, I delivered the opening pleasantries to put her at ease. She began to talk.

Of all the King Fahd hospital staff I'd spoken to, this was the first time I'd come face to face with someone who could answer at least some of the questions which had nagged for months. Nursing a desire to believe the story of Lucille and Deborah, I'd long tried to discount the claims of their fellow staff. If you don't want someone to be executed, it's tempting to believe in their innocence, even in the face of mounting persuasive assertions to the contrary.

As Rosemary talked, she represented not only herself but many others from the hospital; people I'd suspected of working themselves into a dread, a collusion, a community of suspicion. How credible were they? How credible was Rosemary?

At first, not very. She was nervous; she was almost girlishly flighty. Rosemary is in her forties. She has two adult daughters. She told me this in our first conversation. Her words came in a rush. It was as if she needed, at last, to talk to someone outside the circle of nurses and other hospital staff who had lived for months in that hothouse of suspicion and fear. She, like most who have a story to tell, wanted vindication. She wanted me, representing the rest of the reasonable world, to believe that she wasn't turning on Debbie, her friend, for callous or questionable motives. She talked at length of how she had gone out of her way to pack Debbie's clothes and belongings at the hospital dormitory; of how Debbie's sister had questioned items on the inventory as if she suspected Rosemary of nicking things. As if she would. She wanted me to feel outraged along with her.

These conversations with potential talent are intense. It's not normal to hear so much of a stranger's life in so short a space. Soon, I know that Rosemary is giving up nursing; she plans to move to the

New South Wales north coast to work as a manicurist. Her conversation is peppered with personal anecdote, much of it centred on hairdressing. The trivial and banal mixes with the macabre. It becomes clear that hairdressing is central to Rosemary's belief in Deborah's guilt.

A week before Yvonne's death, Rosemary had introduced Debbie to a hairdresser in Al Khobar, Susanne, and had made an appointment for her. What followed later played on Rosemary's mind as an indication of Debbie's mental state. Impulsive, was her dominant description of her friend. Debbie had, on impulse, gone to a fellow nurse for the cut, because she just couldn't wait for the appointment with Susanne. 'She wouldn't wait the two days to go to the hairdresser. She went and got a Filipino to cut it and came back to me and she didn't like it at all. She was most unhappy. I said, "Debbie, we had an appointment in two days." She said, "That's me, I'm impulsive." She was like that.'

Rosemary's stories came tumbling out. At times they seemed wafer-thin as evidence of her friend's imputed murderous nature, like one tale of petty jealousies among friends. Not long before she was murdered, Yvonne had caught a bus to town with Rosemary. As Rosemary said, the Westerners stuck together, so on a bus full of Filipinas they found themselves talking. Rosemary told Yvonne of her plans to change career on returning to Australia. Later, said Rosemary, Debbie had been very upset hearing Yvonne talk of Rosemary's plans. Debbie hadn't liked Yvonne presuming to know more about her friend than she did. (Debbie has claimed to her family that it was the other way around: Yvonne was the one jealous of friends.)

The upshot, as had been clear on the phone, was that Rosemary, one of those closest to Debbie at the compound, was now firmly convinced that her colleague, neighbour and friend was guilty of the brutal murder of one of their own.

'Deb was my friend. I knew Lucy. But I've had to come to accept that they're guilty and you know you can't always spend your life in a fairyland pretending that it's not true,' she said, though it was clear it cost her much to put it so baldly: 'They're very much guilty, and everyone at the hospital feels that also and we did a lot to come to that.'

Once again, those words: 'everyone' felt they were guilty. It was now clear, having met Rosemary and having held many midnight conversations on the phone with her friends back in Saudi, that there was indeed a consensus on the guilt of the two accused among their former workmates. Yet there was no sense of this in the media coverage up to that point. In Western judicial systems, with open courts, it would be a contempt to publish the speculations and assertions of witnesses which had not been given in court. Here, though, there was no question of legal openness. Was this enough to justify publishing damning comment on Lucy and Debbie, even before their convictions had been confirmed? As I finished beer and pizza bread with Rosemary, it seemed wise to leave the ethical angst to later. For now, it was time to put the question. Would she appear on camera?

Despite Rosemary's earlier telephone agreement in principle, the reality of the demand was now a jolt. She baulked. Yes — but. Rosemary didn't want to appear as her recognisable self. She didn't want to cop the kind of flak that Frank had been getting. We talked around potential disguising techniques. Electronic pixels, filming the interview in silhouette. I promised we'd bring a television monitor so that Rosemary could check how she'd look.

The second 'but' was more problematic. Rosemary had spoken to another journalist, a British freelancer who had befriended the Gilfords. She felt loyalty to him, though he didn't know when his interview with her might be published. We agreed that we could perhaps stick to the general, to avoid treading on the exclusive elements she'd given the other guy. In truth, I knew that when it came to the pent-up emotion of an interview, it would be a rare person who could resist spilling everything. It's a rare journalist who will scruple about stealing someone else's talent. This looked like our exclusive now.

We made an arrangement for Rosemary to be filmed — at a Sydney hotel away from her present address — in two days' time. Such a long period between the pre-interview and actually rolling tape is always risky. Prospective interviewees have disturbing tendencies to consult solicitors, mothers, neighbours — all sorts of noble interventionists who will talk them out of appearing on the telly. Would Rosemary stay solid? This time, she had at least given her phone number. I could smooth her through the next two days.

In the meantime, there was now time to talk. To colleagues and witnesses. Was this OK? Would this not be trial by media, with the women themselves unable to answer the claims of Rosemary and her fellows? In the office we talked ourselves out of worrying about prejudicing their trial. Whatever we published would have no influence on the Saudi judges; no question of a jury to be swayed. There was no jury.

The bigger question was the wider court of public opinion. In Britain the tide was running heavily in favour of Lucy and Debbie. Frank Gilford was being pilloried in Britain and at home. A bit of balance, in the form of informed supporters of Frank Gilford, wouldn't go astray. Rosemary and her friends were, in fact, the women behind Frank; those who had written to him and phoned from early on to support his tough stance on the death penalty and to convince him he was right to think the accused were guilty. Surely it was right to illuminate the pressures behind the scenes that had confirmed Frank in his stride towards punitive justice?

Yet how reliable were Rosemary's claims? Back in Saudi in June, I'd talked on the phone to two members of the hospital staff, friends of Debbie, who had refused to condemn the British nurse. Their reluctance had bolstered my own inclination to give the accused the benefit of the doubt. Catherine Wall was a quiet dietitian. She had impressed especially by contrast to the loquacious gossiping of Caroline Ionescu. It was possible to believe that Caroline had been carried away by fear and suspicion, as long as someone who sounded as responsible as Catherine Wall refused to endorse Caroline's claims that 'everyone' at the hospital believed the British women guilty.

'I feel too deeply about it,' she'd said in June. Her feelings, she said, were too private to discuss. I took this to mean she refused to join in the chorus of innuendo. I'd taken it to mean she doubted their guilt. Now, this plank in my own certainty of the women's innocence gave way.

On the phone, Catherine was very friendly. She remembered my earlier call and seemed not at all to resent my persistence. Would she now be prepared to talk? Not publicly, she said, but for background. Even as background, what she said shocked. She said, 'There are some people very dedicated to the idea of innocence until proven guilty.' I knew who she meant. Joe Robinson was the other hospital staffer who had shored up confidence in the women's innocence back in June. He'd used that very line of holding judgment until proof of guilt emerged. Tonight, Jonathan Ashbee had told me Joe Robinson had actually made a statement to the lawyers, supporting Debbie's innocence. But now, said Catherine, there were 'only a couple of people talking like that. Most of us are pretty certain that Debbie did it.'

You, a reader of newspapers, may have presumed from the first report of Yvonne's murder that the accused were guilty as charged. Until now, I had not. Now, with the telephoned words of Catherine Wall, a woman I had never met in person, my confidence dwindled. Of all the hospital staff, Catherine sounded the most reasonable. Now, in reasonable, reluctant tones, she too was condemning her friend. 'I think she was and is very unstable,' she said of Debbie. 'I doubt she has any mind left... she was so fragile when I knew her.' How alarming that these women, these friends of Debbie, spoke of her in the past tense. 'She *was* labile,' Catherine went on, remembering Debbie's panic when her pay was late. Catherine believed Debbie had had a terrible life, with both parents alcoholic. I reminded her of Jon and Sandra's assertion that a woman who had so much tragic loss in her family could never willingly take life herself. Catherine said she had met Jon Ashbee in Saudi but that it was 'psychologically not sound reasoning to point to the deaths in Debbie's family as a reason why she wouldn't resort to violence'.

'Some people here are very angry with Debbie and Lucy and have called Frank.' Catherine said she hadn't contacted the Gilfords. 'I didn't want to influence anything; just let it develop according to the authorities.' Again, the blithe assumption that the Saudi police, any police, would always do the right thing. 'I just worry about Frank in a few years, when he may not be so angry. I respect whatever he decides.'

Catherine said she believed Debbie was so unstable 'she could do it again'. So why would she have done it? 'Simple explanation, loss of control of temper.' These words seem very cold, reading them back, but Catherine herself seemed a warm person. Could she be part of some group hysteria, some festering of suspicion which had blown circumstantial facts out of proportion? If so, she was one of a growing crowd.

I tried again, to test the assertions. What was the motive? Catherine seemed to go on the money. She said Yvonne was the kind of person who would help out. Yvonne had said, 'Girls, I haven't had to spend a dime of my money,' to her group. 'I have enough to cover everybody', when the perennial worries of late pay came up.

What about the claims of lesbian affairs? 'It certainly shocked me,' was Catherine's response. 'I never suspected anything like that going on. I've had many gay friends. Some of them I wouldn't have known unless I was told.'

I mentioned the claim that after the murder Debbie had been obsessed with having developed photographs of a man she'd recently been out with. Perhaps this had been an attempt to seek an alibi if the lesbian claims were true? 'Debbie was obsessed when she had a project,' claimed Catherine. 'Obsessive-compulsive.' On the idea of alibi-concocting, she said, 'That's very possible, too. With me she tried to establish an alibi to explain how she got a bruise on her thigh. After the murder, she asked me did I remember when she fell when we were taking a hike in Scrivener's Canyon.' But Catherine said this hike had been 10 or 11 days prior to the murder and she didn't recall Debbie falling.

Through Catherine, Debbie's wished-for boyfriends in Saudi, Paul and Jeremy, declined to be interviewed. 'Neither one will say a word,' she says.

From her own experience with the Saudi authorities, Catherine said she believed the system was fair. During her four or five hours of questioning by police, they'd done a psychologically sophisticated job, she said. On the claims of police harassment she asked, 'Where else in the world do you get tea on a silver platter while being interrogated?' She recounted Saudi police interrogation humour: after writing 'everything I said into a book, at the end the policeman asked me to sign. It was in Arabic, so I didn't know what it said. The interpreter said it was OK. I signed. Then the policeman said "OK, you've signed this and now I will arrest you."' Maybe you had to be there.

This conversation with Catherine was enough to kill any doubts about running a story with Rosemary. It isn't hard for journalists to rationalise to themselves what they do. While most will not do *anything* for a story, we will surely do quite a lot. Now, on the one hand, I had a story. A world exclusive, as the hyperbole of the promo department would shout. Yet memories of night-time voices from Britain kept nagging. How could I tell Sandra Ashbee I'd found someone to tell the world her sister was guilty?

I phoned Alton, the Hampshire township where Jonathan and Sandra Ashbee live. Where Debbie Parry had lived with them until she'd gone to Saudi. Time and again came the British Telecom voice, claiming they were busy or out. They were, in fact, very busy.

This was the September week which painted the case back on to the front pages. The week The International Law Firm put out a press release claiming that both women had been found guilty. Reports claimed that Lucy faced eight years' gaol and 500 lashes.

The tabloids were outdoing each other in condemnation of perceived Saudi barbarism. Experts were quoted and spoke on the radio about just how painful and long-term would be the effects of caning. We all recalled our sixes of the best on cold school mornings and shivered at the prospect. Ladies and gents of the press gathered on the doorsteps of the British and Australian families for comment.

Finally, Jonathan came on the line. He was at least able to shed a little light on the claims of conviction and sentence. There had been a court hearing in Al Khobar on the Tuesday. The judges heard what Jon called a technicality. Lucy's case had been passed back from the Court of Cassation — the first line of review — because Lucy hadn't been given the chance to oppose the sentence of gaol and lashes. This was, of course, the first the world knew that there'd been any such sentence. And there was, apparently, no mention of a conviction in the day's court hearing. Both sides had presumed that Lucy, at least, had been convicted, given that she had been sentenced. In a not too far-fetched leap of logic, The International Law Firm had seized on this to presume that Debbie, too, had been found guilty, given that the known evidence against her — the confessions — was the same as that against Lucy. And, as there'd been no discussion in the court of lashes or time for Debbie, it could be presumed she'd been sentenced to death.

Jonathan, of course, was outraged by such logic. My news gave no comfort. I told him we'd been approached by a friend of Debbie who now asserted Debbie's guilt. He was shocked. He had met Rosemary, back in Saudi, when she'd packed up Debbie's things. At the time, Rosemary had appeared supportive of her friend and had mentioned nothing of her fears. To his credit, Jon didn't disparage Rosemary. He said she'd seemed sincere when they'd met and he didn't doubt that she was now acting sincerely. I told him we didn't want to go to air with Rosemary's claims unchallenged. He said he could give a blow-by-blow rebuttal to what he saw as a collation of rumour and happenstance. I apologised that we wouldn't be able to come to him in person for an interview, arranging instead for a freelance crew in London to drive out to his home, to film him talking by phone to our reporter in Australia. Jonathan said the families had decided to do no more media for now, but that Rosemary's claims certainly warranted challenge. His lawyer, Rodger Pannone, was on his way back from holiday on a Turkish island and knew nothing of the recent claims of Debbie's conviction, let alone the news of Rosemary. Jon said he would like to do the interview but would need to check with Rodger. We agreed to aim for the interview on the Saturday night.

So, tentatively, we had both sides for the next Tuesday's piece. The only trouble was we didn't have Frank Gilford. He was the man of the moment. With convictions presumed and Debbie presumed to be facing death, the power of life did, in fact, lie in his hands. Frank was still not talking to me.

I phoned Sue Taylor in New Zealand. She agreed that Rosemary's story would be good for Frank. She had seen the mass of media against him and hoped that sentiment might change if the world knew he had good reason for thinking the worst of Debbie and Lucy. I told Sue that Frank had not responded to my calls — had in fact hung up on me once — since I'd lectured him on his need to go to Saudi Arabia. For weeks now, Sue had been standing by in case the Saudis agreed to allow her to come to the kingdom with us as a kind of stand-in for Frank. This seemed unlikely if there had in fact been verdicts and sentences for both of the women. Now I put another suggestion to Sue. Would she come to Australia to meet Rosemary? She offered better: she would come and be filmed meeting this other nurse who knew her dead friend; she would also come with us to Adelaide to repair relations with Frank. This was Friday. The interview with Rosemary was set for that afternoon. Sue, who'd travelled the world with Yvonne, made no hesitation. If she could bring her eleven-year-old son Matthew, she would be with us on Saturday. Rosemary, reassuringly at home when I called, was excited at the prospect of meeting Sue. It looked like we had a story, no matter what.

Producers are not permitted to exhibit exhaustion. Despite all-night international phone calls, you have to answer the reasonable queries of freelance camera crews when they want to know how you'd like the interview shot. And you have to brief the reporter. Paul Barry was filming in Western Australia, so now Virginia Haussegger came on to report Rosemary's story. Like many who had vaguely followed the Gilford case, Virginia had plumped for an early presumption. In her case, for the presumption that Frank Gilford was an ogre; the women innocent. She was given the story on the Thursday. Somehow, by Friday, despite the incoherence of my sleep-deprived mumblings, she seemed to know all about the case. She'd reviewed our earlier stories.

Now I had the bad news. Our talent wanted to appear on the telly as a black blob or a silhouette and she wanted to be nice to some other absent journalist and talk only in vague generalities. At the hotel in North Sydney we set up, awaiting Rosemary. Someone else turned up in her place. The soft-looking woman in her mid-forties had turned into a severe, anxious-looking person with her hair pulled back in a tight bun. Rosemary had dressed and done her hair for television or to bolster her confidence. Or something. Some producers may have asked her to return to her earlier, softer self. I was worried about her nervousness. We went with her pulled-back hair.

We bumbled about with various versions of identity-disguise, but Rosemary felt she could still be recognised. Virginia soon realised that here was a woman who wanted to be persuaded. With much discussion, Rosemary came around to persuading herself that she would look like she was hiding and not standing up for her convictions if she didn't show her full face. She'd worn scarves over her hair, *abayas* covering her body during her years in Saudi Arabia, but she went unveiled for Australian television.

It was Virginia, too, who helped cast aside the remaining veil: Rosemary's reluctance to relate the detail she'd given to the other journo. Slowly, it all came, as Virginia gently pushed. A few days after the murder, Rosemary had gone to the hairdresser. Debbie had come along:

> Rosemary: *I just feel like I'm opening up so much. She came to the hairdresser's with me. She didn't have an appointment that day ... and she'd just had her hair cut the week before that. I don't know how far I can talk here. I'm really exposing.*
> Virginia: *What was it about the issue of the hairdresser's that helped confirm in your mind ... ?*
> Rosemary: *Well, Debbie had two chunks of hair missing out of the top of her head here. I did tell the Ashbees. They were lovely people. There were things I didn't tell them, I just didn't want to. I thought they must be worried enough. It was almost a protective thing.*

It was the hairdresser at the British Aerospace compound, Ann Fitzpatrick, who had noticed the missing hair: 'It was enough to give her an asthma attack,' said Rosemary.

When the story screened, four nights later, we cut in Jonathan Ashbee's responses to Rosemary's points. His response to the claims of scratch marks on Debbie's wrists was as loyal as ever.

> *The scratches — yes, indeed, Debbie did have scratches. Apparently, however, they were scratches from Purdy the cat. Debbie is pretty daft when it comes to cats and she likes to cuddle them and sometimes won't let them go when perhaps she should. The cats sometimes react to that and scratch, so I can well see that happening.*
>
> *The autopsy didn't show evidence of anything whatsoever underneath Yvonne's fingernails and, secondly, when the girls complained about the treatment they'd received while the confessions were being extracted from them, a doctor was asked to report on their physical well-being and he wrote a report stating there was not a mark on her. Now this was only a few days after the murder.*

In fact, this was more than a week after.

Regarding the missing hair on Debbie's scalp, Jon explained that Debbie was the kind of person who could be dissatisfied with a haircut and have another one soon after. He also pointed out that the hair found in Yvonne's hand was medium length and blonde. 'Debbie has very short dark-coloured hair and Lucy has very long curly black hair.'

On the matter of the bruise on Debbie's thigh, Jon explains:

> *Apparently whilst in the desert on one of these expeditions she slipped and fell quite heavily on a rock ... We have written evidence from one of the other employees at the hospital confirming this fact.*

I try to confirm this with the employee he's mentioned — Debbie's friend, Joe Robinson. But Joe is away from Saudi on holiday in Thailand. I don't get the chance to question him until months afterwards.

The bulk of our story centres on Rosemary, the first hospital staffer to speak publicly about the murder. We film long, long interviews sometimes to elicit the skerricks you eventually see on the screen. The interview with Rosemary was a long exchange revolving around one, central, veiled point. Rosemary was turning on her friend but didn't want to face it. Finally, Virginia put the question directly:

> Virginia: *Why has it taken you so long to actually speak out and say you really believe that the women are guilty?*
> Rosemary: *Because I didn't, you know, you don't want exposure yourself but then you get very frustrated that the public don't know a lot of the facts ... I just feel the public need to have a more open mind, not believe everything they read in the papers about this. To have feeling for Frank and Laurel. They've lost a loved one ... I've wanted to speak up, I don't want to speak up too much because I get fearful of the weight it puts on my shoulders.*
> Virginia: *But what you're saying effectively is condemning both the women despite their pleas of innocence.*
> Rosemary: *And that's hard. That's hard, too. I don't even like to face that publicly because it's something we came to grips with over there. I miss the support of everyone else at KFMMC [the hospital] in that regard, but it's been a traumatic event. I don't want to be seen to be negative towards them because that's not really how, you know, that part fights inside me to say that because I mean Debbie was a friend.*

Past tense.

We eased Rosemary out of the interview. She was jumpy and upset, wanted to be told she'd done the right thing. I gave her the advice I'd given before the interview: remember why you're doing it. She'd said her reason was to support the Gilfords. The interview would certainly do that. That night Rosemary, with all of her anxieties, went off to tend premature babies in her casual job at a Sydney hospital. I went to an outdoor show in Centennial Park with my wife and my seven-year-old son. As we settled among the crowd, the lightning and thunder exploded and heaven dropped buckets. Just like Rosemary had been doing all day in a Sydney hotel room.

Chapter 24

Deal done

Rosemary's story is shown in Britain as well as Australia. It prompts Kathryn Lyons to give an interview to *The Australian* newspaper and Caroline Ionescu to tell her story to the British press, anonymously. Their treachery is quickly reported on the accused nurses' daily information source, the BBC World Service. They are shocked and enraged. Debbie writes home:

> Unbelievable about Rosemary Kidman and Caroline [Ionescu]. No wonder they've gone into hiding. I still wish our other friend could be spoken to.

Debbie is referring to her claims of suspecting Karolyne Palowska, another staff member and a friend of Yvonne's.

For weeks, there's denial on Frank's side that he's done a deal. Salah keeps hammering. On October 6, his press release declares:

> Mr Frank Gilford has personally signed the Deed of Settlement by his hand on 19 September 1997 under which he is legally obligated to waive any death penalty which may be imposed in this case. Pursuant to this agreement, the settlement sum of US$1.2 million has been deposited in full into the trust account in Australia and will be disbursed to Mr Gilford when he performs his part of the bargain.
>
> Under the Islamic *Sharia* law of Saudi Arabia, Mr Gilford has effectively waived the death penalty already by the very act of engaging in serious negotiations over

> money in exchange for waiving the death penalty. Mr Gilford went far beyond that by signing a formal and binding agreement ...

On the radio I hear Bob Thoms being interviewed, revving Frank up even more. This is dangerous brinkmanship if that deal isn't watertight. Scary for the accused and their families.

> Originally there was a sum of a million US dollars proposed that would go to charity. At the last moment Mr Gilford asked in addition for two hundred thousand dollars for legal fees. Then closer to the final settlement he said that the million dollars was not US dollars but was Australian dollars, meaning it was the equivalent of seven hundred thousand US dollars, leaving not two hundred thousand dollars for his so called legal fees, but five hundred thousand dollars.

So much for the confidentiality clause. Thoms is having a bet each way here. Suggesting that Frank is after more than the relatively small amount the later announcement gives him and at the same time having a go at the law firms. In Riyadh, Jim Phipps at The International Law Firm had told us they were doing the job for nothing.

Over the following days, the denials by Frank and his lawyers look increasingly unconvincing. The deal is out there; Frank has signed something; does he have any way of getting out of it now that Salah has blown their cover?

I fly to South Australia to see Frank. Laurel shows me to his cramped office at the front of his home. I eat humble pie and apologise in person for my pushiness on the phone weeks earlier. Frank had known more than I did, from the staff at the hospital, I agree. But I manage to point out that I still have to consider the women's lack of a fair trial. Frank starts being nice to me again. He's expecting to be in Adelaide soon if the deal comes off. I offer him a way of avoiding the media crowds: make his announcement on our program. That's up to his lawyer, he says, and gives me complicated directions back south through the purple and vivid yellow of the crop flowers.

I meet Michael Abbott in Adelaide at the Hyatt bar. He tries to maintain that Frank has never asked for money. The other side has insisted he specify an amount. I try to talk about other stories we've done, with Frank and others, like Stuart Diver (the sole survivor of the Thredbo landslide in 1997), who have been in the public glare. Abbott wants to talk about how much money we'll give his client. I say it may be possible for us to give a donation to the trust which will disburse the money to a charity in memory of Yvonne. 'How much?' Abbott asks, as I try to talk about our sensitive approach to the story. I'll have to talk to the boss, I relent, giving up on the sensitivity stuff. This man only wants to talk about money.

In the end, Abbott goes for a press conference the next day, October 15. It's a curious affair, 'invitation only'. The only people locked out seem to be an ITV television crew from Britain and a British press reporter. Abbott looks ridiculous as he tries to tell different branches of the ABC that one or other of them has or hasn't been invited. Osama Al-Solaim, from The International Law Firm, makes a statement in Arabic. There are no Arabic speakers there and he declines to deliver it in his reasonable English.

Frank, wearing a knitted maroon jumper, smiles nervously under the lights and strokes his beard. He reads a prepared statement.

> From the outset I have only kept open the option of the death penalty, pending the determination of the British nurses' guilt. This was required because under Saudi Arabian law once any of the family of the victim waives their rights, then all of the family's rights are foregone.

This is true and not true. Frank could have kept his rights without saying publicly that he wanted these particular individuals beheaded. He and Laurel need never have made all the inflammatory comments they did in the press.

> I now believe that the time has come to make a final decision, as Lucille McLauchlan has been convicted as an accessory of the murder of my sister and it is therefore highly likely that Deborah Parry will be found guilty of the murder of my sister.

Frank says he has been in

> ...an unenviable position given that the prison sentences for murder in Saudi Arabia, namely five to ten years, are quite insignificant compared to the prison sentences which

we normally expect for murder in Australia. There is also a possibility that Parry could be released now that I have waived my rights to *Qisas*.

The settlement details are revealed. Frank waives the death penalty for A$1.7 million. One million of that is to go to the Adelaide Women's and Children's Hospital to build the Yvonne Gilford Children's Day Surgery. Frank says he will receive

> ...only a nominal sum of $50,000 from the settlement monies, which I think that you will all agree is only reasonable considering the pain and suffering that I have had to endure over the last ten months. My mother will receive a payment of approximately $9,000 being the specified payment of *diya* under Saudi Arabian law. I would like to make clear that I have not accepted any blood money as that is a specified sum under Saudi Arabian law of approximately $19,000, but have accepted compensation, which is an alternative to blood money under Saudi Arabian law.

There seems to be some confusion here about whether the blood money is $9000 or $19 000 but, at any rate, the rest of the dough, A$630 000, is to go to the lawyers. Nice little earner.

Frank finishes by saying he hopes that now he and his family can resume their normal lives. A journalist from *The Australian* snaps that Frank has been deceiving him in denying the deal.

Abbott, schoolmasterly, ushers everyone out and Vern Cassin, principal of The International Law Firm, says he hasn't time to talk to me.

The press release from Salah that day is true to form. He's now signing them 'Salah Al-Hejailan Pro Bono', to make the point that he's doing this brief for nothing, while the opposition is milking it.

Already, Salah is equivocating about the deal. 'One thing is now clear and that is the amount to be paid to Frank Gilford must be adjusted, by the Saudi Arabian court if necessary, in view of the fact that Lucille McLauchlan's conviction is for a lesser crime than intentional murder.' Frank has been promised payment for two, when only one person's conviction puts her at risk of the death penalty. Salah only wants to pay half of the agreed settlement.

He also has a go at Frank for trying to paint his receipts as 'compensation' rather than 'blood money':

> There is however no substance to this distinction which he has fashioned. In truth, Frank Gilford is receiving a very large amount of 'blood money'.

Michael Abbott's claim to be equal to Salah's wiles is disappearing in the sands of the South Australian and Saudi Arabian deserts. At best, Frank, his mum, the lawyers and the hospital might get half of the promised amount. And when it's paid is up to Salah.

The other point in this vibrantly assertive press release is that the whole deal could have been settled back in March. Nothing had in fact changed to make this settlement more morally attractive now. Frank might claim he'd been waiting for the court's verdict but there was still no verdict for Debbie, the only one he now had potential right to condemn.

Frank had put himself, his family, the accused and their families, and all the rest of us who had agonised along with them in this process through an extra six months of uncertainty. For what? For a principle which he was not now upholding. If he was truly waiting for the court to have its say on Debbie's guilt or innocence, then he must wait for a verdict and wait for the three tiers of review of the Saudi legal system.

From my point of view this was a case of lawyers — on both sides — standing in the way of a sensible settlement. While Salah might claim he had tried for a settlement all along, his aggressive stance towards Frank precluded any conciliation, any negotiation for months. It was not until the result-driven Michael Abbott joined the loop, effectively shouldering out the useless antipathies of The International Law Firm on Frank's side of the equation, that sense could be talked by both sides.

If a woman, Deborah Parry, were not to die by the sword, a deal had to be done, sometime. All those who rang or wrote to Frank urging him to stick to his guns and hold out for the death penalty did him no good service. If he was eventually going to follow the principles of Australian-style humanity, he had to strike a deal sooner or later. Anyone who urged him to hold off, simply put him through more pain. Fortunately for all, the realists, Salah Al-Hejailan and Michael Abbott, finally prevailed. Unfortunately for Abbott, Salah still held the purse strings.

Chapter 25

We go again

One phone call in November and I'm heading back to Saudi Arabia. Salah Al-Hejailan takes the call and sounds genuinely pleased. Come back? No problem. He will write to the Saudi ambassador in Canberra and have them issue me a visa. Fortunately, his brother is the ambassador.

I will come as a 'consultant' to The Law Firm of Salah Al-Hejailan. Exactly what I'm to consult on isn't clear. What about visiting the nurses? No problem. You can go as part of our legal team, with Michael Dark. For that, I'd be happy to consult on just about anything.

In practice, the visa's not quite so easy. Many calls to the embassy later and finally Abdullah al-Rashoud has a secretary call to say they need a further letter from Salah's law firm, confirming the request for a visa, addressed to the ambassador. Wasn't this what the first letter did? Calls to Riyadh; they agree to fax the new letter. Next day, Abdullah can't be found. The next day, Friday, he calls me. Send your passport. Entertaining hopes of going to Britain before Saudi, so that I can cement relationships with the nurses' families, I ask if the visa can be issued in London. My flight, booked in premature confidence, leaves Sunday, so there's no time to get my passport to Canberra for the visa stamp. Not possible, he says; send the passport to Canberra. I rebook for Tuesday, wait impatiently over the weekend and fly to Canberra on Monday, to make sure of the visa. Just as well. Abdullah is surprised to see me. I thought you were in London, he says; the ambassador has signed your letter and we've sent it to the consul there. Some self-control is required to betray no hint of amazement at this turn of events.

Now, the ambassador is out. He needs to sign the visa. Won't be back until tomorrow. Evidently, I look sufficiently forlorn. Abdullah says he'll get the passport to his boss this afternoon, if I fill in the form. The visa officials aren't quite so benign. It's now 3.20 pm. The office closes at four. You need a photo and a money order for $75. Cash OK? No. Outside, it's 35°C in a Canberra scorcher; a cab takes ten minutes to arrive; I rush to the Woden plaza, looking for a photo booth and the post office. There's a queue for the money order. The photo booth is broken down. I find a chemist that does passport photos. They take 10 minutes to dry. I run to the cab, waving the wet Polaroid in the hot wind. We arrive back at the embassy in O'Malley at ten to four. As I jump from the cab, I slam my finger in the door. At least the photo is dry. They take my passport, the letter from Riyadh, the photo and the money order and I'm left in the antechamber, chatting with the Australian staff. One of them admits his bosses aren't the easiest. Ten minutes later, one of the Saudi visa officials — possibly the Mr Algamdi I've sometimes spoken to on the phone — bursts through the door with my passport; inside it a visa. You can have five days. I'd asked for a week. Five days is enough, he says; send me a copy of your report. Certainly, I say, wondering what report he's talking about. Just what did that letter from Riyadh say? I guess that's what consultants do, write reports. [In a strange irony, Mr Algamdi was found brutally murdered in his Canberra flat in October 1998.]

Outside, waiting in the shade for a cab, there's the chance to farewell all the embassy staff as they leave for the weekend. Some seem like old friends, we've spoken so often on the phone. The white sword on the green flag of Saudi flutters overhead as the cab arrives in the heat. Good training for a Saudi holiday.

That night, back on the phone. The King Fahd hospital switch at last gets me through to Catherine Wall. Yes, she'll see me when I come over; just call and we'll meet. She says staff like her want their story told. They feel the world has heard and believed only Lucy and Debbie's version. Her words are reassuring; even if I never get to see the accused nurses, I'll be the only journalist to meet their closest friends at the hospital, as well as those close to Yvonne.

The day of departure brings its usual thousand things to be done in not enough time. I practise using the tiny video camera which Alex, the sound recordist, has lent me. Would it be possible to carry this into a Saudi prison or police station unnoticed? Not likely.

Off to swimming lessons with my son. He says he likes the fact that I travel and meet interesting people and tell him about it, but he misses me too much. I resolve to change careers and leave for the airport.

This flight is funded by Rupert Murdoch, whose publishing firm has furnished a travelling budget. Economy, not business class. A cheapie on Gulf Air. The plane is arriving from Bahrain, bound for Melbourne before it bounces back to the Gulf. Arabic is being spoken in the Sydney waiting lounge. The transit passengers look bleary-eyed and grumpy. No one is being nice to anyone else as we file on. My seat is taken by a teenage girl, whose mother, holding a tiny baby, is arguing with the hostess. Two women from Nottingham are sitting in the Arabic woman's seat; she needs the bulkhead where they can hang a bassinette. The English girls are refusing to budge; their seats were stuffed up too, back in Singapore. Surely they'll move for a woman with a baby? No. Old World contempt for the Arab prevails. The Nottingham girls won't shift. Ten minutes elapse before another seat is found for the mother; then teenage daughter is shunted from my seat. We fly, uselessly, to Melbourne to hang around for another hour in a transit lounge among more grumpy travellers. It's after midnight, but the boy behind the bar serves last (alcoholic) drinks for those heading to lands of prohibition.

The club lounges are out of bounds; they refuse my cards because I'm on an economy ticket. Phone calls from phone boxes. In Riyadh there's no one but a secretary in Salah's office. Michael Dark has gone to London. Who's going to take me to the gaol to see the nurses? Has luck gone on another holiday? On the plane I read Peter Carey's reworking of Dickens, *Jack Maggs*. His pre-Victorian English journalist is busily stealing the secrets and soul of a runaway Australian convict, in order to write a book on the mind of a criminal. The journalist is exploiting the tragic life of the thief and murderer for his own fame and fortune. Half asleep, chewing bad plane food, there seems to be a maudlin parallel here. I switch to the Lonely Planet guide to the Gulf States. Maybe I'll have to stay in Bahrain until Michael Dark gets back, biding my time for a chance to plunder the lives of alleged thieves and murderers.

Chapter 26

Fishmongers

Back in Al Khobar, jet-lagged in the hotel room, watching CNN at 4 am. Winnie Mandela is defying demands for her to seek forgiveness at the Truth and Reconciliation Commission in South Africa.

Joe Robinson comes around to the hotel for a chat. He still, like almost no one else from the King Fahd Military Medical Complex, believes in the innocence of the accused; finding alternative explanations for the claims about Lucy and Debbie. He says that when the Australian consul came to talk to the Australian staff at the hospital, they were calling for blood. Ready to string up Lucy and Debbie themselves. He tells of his habit of winding up friends at the hospital who were all for the death penalty. 'You know they do the beheading at the mosque closest to the scene of the crime,' he tells them. There is a mosque in the grounds of the hospital. 'You can be there to watch it, if you want.' That silenced them, he says.

But Kathryn Lyons isn't silenced. Kathryn is an Australian medical scientist who's been working at the hospital for three years. She's a likeable, phlegmatic rugby player. We meet at the Al Shola Mall, the place where Lucy and Debbie were arrested a week after the murder.

Kathryn, like several of the hospital staff I've been talking with, is disappointed that Frank Gilford has gone for a money settlement. Many of them rang or wrote to the Gilfords to urge them to stick to their guns and refuse clemency.

It's perplexing to meet Kathryn and Joe on the same day, here in Saudi. Both people I warm to, both determined in their stance. Kathryn tells how she invited Yvonne to join her running club, the

Hash House Harriers. Joe tells of desert trips with Debbie, in their social group, known as the Travelling Naturalists. These everyday, down-to-earth people seem far from the drama of murder, accusation and guilt. Joe says he's been ribbing Kathryn about Frank's settlement. Both he and Kathryn say people at the hospital don't talk much about the murder any more, everyone retiring into their private convictions. But today, to an outsider, they talk a lot.

The Thursday Debbie was arrested, she was at the Al Shola Mall looking for a cat scratching-board. Joe had told her where to find one. The night before, he and Debbie had driven out for a desert barbecue with some of their friends from the Travelling Naturalists. They wondered why there seemed to be a lot of police cars about. The previous night, the Tuesday, they'd gone to one of the group's monthly lectures. Debbie had been tense during the meeting, seeming to drift off as a guest lecturer talked about the Jewish history of Jerusalem. The speaker was a last-minute fill-in. They'd actually come to hear a scheduled talk about desert falcons. Everyone was a little embarrassed because four young Saudis from the medical school had come along — Moslems, of course — and were shifting uneasily in their seats as they heard of the Jewish view of things.

Afterwards, Joe and Debbie had gone to a popular Italian restaurant in Al Khobar, The Gondolas. Debbie had brightened up and they'd had a good laugh, blithely unaware of what was to happen. Police had followed them to the meeting from the hospital. Afterwards a police car had followed some of the others back to the hospital. Deslyn Marks, the nursing coordinator, chided Debbie for not saying where she was going, in case the police wanted to talk to her. Joe stood up for his friend, saying the police could find her when they needed to.

Some colleagues have suggested that Joe was a bit sweet on Debbie. He says she didn't seem interested in anything serious with the men she met in Saudi. She'd had dates with a couple of guys in the Naturalists, Jeremy and Paul, but still seemed upset about breaking up with two previous boyfriends. She'd been engaged to one man in England, Roger, for ten years and was upset that, as the godfather to her niece and nephew, Roger was visiting her sister's family with his new wife. This had led to a falling out with her sister, Sandra Ashbee. Joe had advised her, 'Don't be stupid; your sister's your sister.' Joe had been exchanging letters with Debbie in prison. After her arrest, when Sandra called the British consul wanting to speak to Debbie, Debbie had said she couldn't believe Sandra would care to talk to her now that she was in gaol. But Joe says people like Sandra, Paul Thomas and himself have stuck by Debbie.

Joe says it seems Debbie and Lucy have had relatively good treatment in the gaol. When they complained of the broken-down air-conditioning in 40°C summer heat, the British consul had spoken to the prison governor. It was fixed within days.

Joe describes Debbie's demeanour in her letters. At first, her writing was disjointed; she'd repeat things. In recent months they've been better. She says she's been seeing an Egyptian psychiatrist in the gaol and he's helped her. Joe says there are claims that Debbie was on Lithium. Did she behave erratically before the murder? Not that he saw. There was the day she'd been left behind by her lift when the Naturalists went to Scrivener's Canyon. She always cooked for the whole group on these trips and when she saw her lift driving off without her she'd dropped her hamper on the ground in a fury.

The Scrivener's Canyon trip was two weeks before the murder. Debbie had come along after Paul had gone back to get her. Joe was there. Debbie later claimed she bruised her thigh when she fell on this trip. Joe says he was unaware of her falling. Joe can't recall the hair missing from her head, but he remembers Debbie showing him her arms, in the week after the murder, saying her cat had scratched her. He can't remember what they looked like. Kathryn remembers many scratches down Debbie's forearms, raised and infected. Joe remembers Debbie asking whether she should tell the police about Yvonne lending money, SR3000, to one of the Filipinas. 'I said, "Listen to their questions. Don't go off on a tangent, telling them things they haven't asked about. Let them finish their questions".' Debbie had a habit of cutting you off in mid-question, he says.

At work, Debbie had seemed confident and in control. She would start at 7 on a 7.30 shift. She'd always said she might be a bit dizzy elsewhere, but she knew what she was doing as a nurse. Joe says she doesn't want to nurse any more, when she's released. She wants to work with animals. Sandra has been telling Debbie that the kids, her nieces and nephew, are going to get her a cat when she gets home.

Joe is upset by the behaviour of his colleagues. 'My fish is bigger than yours,' he says, was the attitude of the rumourmongers as staff tried to one-up each other with news after the murder. It started on the first day. As word of Yvonne's death filtered out, the gossip flew. At lunch in the cafeteria that day, one man had walked up to Joe's group with a big smile on his face. 'You know the South African's been stabbed.' Joe had snapped at him that Yvonne was Australian and, anyway, nobody knew anything yet. There are rumours about the behaviour of Debbie and Lucy. That Debbie had been phoning Casualty to ask about Yvonne even before the body was found. That the security chief, Captain Asiri, had refused to open Yvonne's door when she didn't answer knocks. He wanted to wait for the police because he'd been in trouble when he disturbed the scene when Liberty da Gusma was murdered two years before, leaving prints all over the place. One rumour said Lucy had been there screaming at Asiri to open the door to see if Yvonne was OK.

One man, a Scot from the Medical School called Colin Campbell, had started many rumours. He'd told the police that the South African mafia had done it, because a former hospital staffer had been murdered when he moved to South Africa. The same man had loudly announced in the cafeteria that a hospital security guard had gone to Yvonne's room with a bowl of fruit, killed her when she resisted his advances, and gone back to clean up the mess with other security guards. In his favour, says Joe, is that Colin Campbell was the one who rang the British consul after Debbie and Lucy were locked up.

The night Yvonne died, Joe had seen her, at around 7 pm, in the courtyard talking to somebody about videos. He'd heard that both Brangwen Davies (name changed by request) and Lucy were in Yvonne's room later, planning Yvonne's birthday. The rumours said Brangwen left first.

Both Joe and Kathryn talk of rumours that the night-shift security who were on when Yvonne died were badly treated afterwards. Kathryn says six of them were seen in leg-irons at the Dhahran Police Station. Joe says two of them were seen back at the hospital, looking badly beaten. All have left after the disgrace of having failed to prevent the murder.

The Friday after the murder, all the women off-duty and the men from Building 79 — not far from the women's quarters — are assembled in the recreation centre auditorium. They're addressed by the police chief and the army colonel in charge of the hospital. Everyone is told they're to be physically examined, their hands inspected, on the way out and some are to have fingerprints taken. Debbie is absent, on shift. An American pharmacist calls out in protest: 'Does this mean we're all suspects?' The colonel says everyone is, for the moment, and this is how it's done, in Saudi. 'Mary, a Canadian girl, laid into him,' says Joe, complaining that the colonel hadn't even told them what had happened in the Liberty da Gusma case. The colonel replies that the police haven't told him, so he can't tell the staff. Then Mary complains they weren't told their pay would be delayed. The meeting breaks up in anger, but all have their hands checked and have to lift their T-shirts or pull collars down to show their necks as they file out.

Joe remembers the day of Debbie's arrest. He'd rung her room at six in the evening. Somebody else had answered before hanging up. Joe had been worried the murderer was there, striking again, and rang Catherine Wall to say, 'There's something going on in Debbie's flat.' When they got there, there were police cars around. Nursing supervisor Deslyn Marks had said, 'It's OK, they're safe. That's all I'm allowed to say.'

The next time Joe saw Debbie was Christmas Day. He and Catherine Wall were greeting each other in the carpark when he saw Debbie being led from a police car towards Yvonne's block. She and Lucy were there for the video re-enactment. When Joe and Catherine had waved, one of the police nudged Debbie to show her. Debbie's wave in response was despondent. Joe hasn't seen her since. Early into her incarceration he'd been refused permission to see her. Now, back from a month's holiday in Thailand, he's been putting off writing to her, embarrassed that he's been having a good time while she's in gaol.

As we say goodnight in the lobby of Le Gulf Meridien, Joe seems despondent. He repeats for the fifth time his dismay at his colleagues' behaviour.

The meeting with Kathryn Lyons is in the Al Shola Mall, scene of Debbie's arrest. We talk in a fast-food bar, empty but for us. The non-Moslem staff allow us to stay, drinking thickshakes, during the noon prayer.

Kathryn, from Australia, has been here since 1994, just after Liberty da Gusma's murder. Before our meeting, she's been buying blue T-shirts, newly monogrammed with a little fox and the name of her Rugby team, the Al Khobar Foxes. A desert fox used to skulk around their training ground.

Kathryn is a senior scientist in the hospital's haematology department. She hadn't been especially close to Yvonne, Lucy or Debbie. 'I've been to a few social functions with Debbie; been out in the desert with her and the Travelling Naturalists.' Lucy had seemed to keep to herself. 'We thought afterwards she'd always been closed-in; hadn't let anybody close to her.'

Were they having a lesbian relationship? 'I don't know. Whether there was relationships or not, to me that's not an issue.'

Tension? 'No, not at all, but again I would only see them at mealtimes or on the bus, or Debbie when a group of us go out in the desert.'

Friendship between Yvonne and Debbie? 'Because they worked on the same ward at one stage; it was only recently that Debbie moved over to the renal unit. Debbie and Lucy arrived at the same time and Yvonne was already there. It's like when new people come, everybody looks after each other. So every time I saw them, virtually, Lucy and Yvonne and stuff were together, like at meal breaks and stuff like that. I considered them as a group of people that were friends. Debbie moved to renal and the other two girls worked on Male Specialty One. There's another girl, Brangwen, that was friends with them as well. '

The night. 'I was working a 12-hour shift. It was my fourth 12-hour shift ... I didn't have any contact with anyone. There were people like Bodil that saw Lucy doing the washing at some strange hour in the morning. It was in the hallway; Bodil was in the hallway, doing her washing as well.' Bodil Valle was a Dutch nurse who lived in Lucy's building. Other hospital staff, though not Bodil herself, have confirmed she reported this sighting of Lucy.

Loans: 'Because we weren't getting paid again, everyone lends people money — like, for example, I've lent my workers money. At one stage we didn't get paid for three months, so you sort of gave them rice and food. If these guys don't have food, how can they work for me? A hundred riyals here or there; people do it all the time.'

Kathryn said pay had been intermittent for some time. 'It could have been a real reason for the whole situation. We don't know what everybody else's personal circumstances are. At some stage earlier, money was stolen out of people's purses and so on [in Male Specialty Ward].'

On the Thursday morning after the murder, Kathryn had found it difficult to believe the news of Yvonne's death.

> *I went downstairs to my lab and my Australian colleague, Linda, told me. Then another friend came in with worse news. Murder. What had happened is that one of the Casualty doctors had got there [to Casualty] and told the girls there were three stab wounds, so it proved it wasn't*

> *natural causes and it probably wasn't suicide. So immediately we started thinking, was she sexually molested? So I got on the phone to Lucy and said, 'Listen to Bev and she'll tell you what has happened to Yvonne.' She was in her room, someone else was with her. I went up to Brangwen's ward. She was at tea and so I went up and told her. And then Brangwen went and told Debbie what I'd just told her, because Debbie was working. Debbie was also ringing Casualty before anyone knew that it had happened. Beverley [Reeve] was acting as charge nurse in Casualty. She was taking those phone calls. This was probably 8.30 in the morning or 7.30, or whatever. Debbie was ringing up and asking whether Yvonne was in Casualty and that was before anybody knew what had happened to her.*

Beverley Reeve, now in England, later confirmed this account. Kathryn talks of suspicions mounting among the staff.

> *There was an inkling that it was one of us. The seeds were being planted and it was a matter of: what's going to happen next? I had three girls from Yvonne's block all staying in my room. One of my friends lives across from Yvonne's room, Gail. She wasn't in her room the night Yvonne died, she'd stayed out somewhere. She was going through 'Maybe if I'd been there I could have done something.'*

So Kathryn had asked Gail and two other women in Yvonne's building, Judy and Karolyne Palowska, if they wanted to stay in her room in another building.

Unbeknown to the other hospital staff, after her arrest Debbie began to point to Karolyne Palowska as an alternative suspect for the murder. According to Kathryn, Karolyne 'was really good friends with Yvonne. Like she'd only been there for six weeks, but they used to do things like go bike-riding and stuff like that; spent a lot of time together.' Karolyne's cats had often visited Yvonne in her room.

In the days before her arrest, Kathryn says Debbie had made much of what she called the 'Filipino moneylending gang'. Kathryn scoffs.

> *This isn't relevant, you know. But Debbie was adamant, 'I'll tell them about this.' The Filipinos have their various things they do. They probably do lend each other money, I don't know at what interest. She was grasping at this, saying she was going to tell the police. She was very adamant about that.*

The staff had all been called to the meeting in the auditorium on the Friday.

> *Debbie, Joe and I went to the Travelling Naturalists together on the Saturday evening, to a meeting in a compound. Debbie was chatting away and stuff; we were trying to calm her down. She was very sort of hyper. I saw the scratches on her forearms; she showed them to me and said, 'I was so lucky that I wasn't at the meeting [when staff had their arms examined by security in the auditorium] because the cat got me.' It looked like there were heaps of scratches along her forearms. They looked like physical scratch marks, from whatever source; crisscrossing on both arms. They looked like they were welted as well; they were a little inflamed.*

Kathryn says that on the Tuesday after the murder, when the Travelling Naturalists went on their desert trip, Debbie had attached herself to a man called Charles Horton. 'Charles was the one that told me Debbie tried to latch on to him.' Was this another example of Debbie trying to distance herself from any assertion of a relationship with Yvonne gone wrong?

> *Lucy was jittery as well; like when she was waiting to be taken down to the police station; people making tea or coffee for them. As the week went on, everybody else was getting better and they were getting worse.*

When had Kathryn become so sure of their guilt?

> *After they'd been arrested. We had a counselling session and there were just certain things that had happened, when we related it all out. It made sense; a combination of things like the arms, like Debbie saying to Catherine Wall*

> 'You've got to be careful who you let in your apartment'; Bodil's comments about Lucy doing the washing so early in the morning. Things like that. I'd said to Debbie, 'If they find out who's done it, I'll go to the beheading.' She said, 'I will be at the beheading.'

Kathryn remembers Rosemary Kidman being quite disruptive at the counselling session. 'I think there was about eight of us there at the time and Rosemary wasn't believing [in the nurses' guilt] at all and she was really upsetting everyone else. It would have been far better if she'd not been there at the time.' Only later had Rosemary become convinced of their guilt.

> And then it got to the stage: we want them to be punished. We don't want them to walk free. We don't want them to be able to, after their time in gaol, go back to England and make a fortune out of a book or anything like that.

Kathryn had wanted to organise a staff service for Yvonne in the week after the murder. Debbie and Lucy had insisted on putting it off, saying not until the murder was sorted out. 'Perhaps they knew they were going to get caught.'

The service was held after the arrests.

> We just got together as a group of people at Meceda [the staff recreation area a kilometre from the hospital] and had a service for her. Wesley [a staff member] read 'The Lord is My Shepherd'. I found a few poems. Karolyne [Palowska] had written a few words about Yvonne, so we read them out. Andrew Cathela [a doctor] did some poems. We sent them to Frank. One of them was off a card, something about friendship; one was about autumn. I got some white carnations, so everybody held a flower. We got a card and we sent it away to Frank. It was a picture of a little boy or girl holding a rose with a luggage bag, sort of saying goodbye.

As the noon prayer drones in the background, a Filipino waiter brings chips, gratis, to our booth. I question why Kathryn is so prepared to accept the death penalty.

> *British Aerospace and other British businesses that gave the money, how wrong is that? Why should somebody give money for somebody that's committed a crime? It's like I can kill anybody and get away with it.*
>
> *I don't blame Frank for accepting the money. The thing that got us most was all this rubbish in the British press [accusations of Yvonne running a moneylending racket]; now, we know anything you read is dubious. Why do that? She's dead and buried; she hasn't hurt anyone.*

Kathryn likes living in the kingdom because of all the sporting opportunities she's had. Unlike more timid women on the hospital staff, Kathryn refuses to walk around in the *abaya*. 'The contract says you should always wear it, but I don't.' During our meeting she's wearing jeans and a short-sleeve shirt. Her hair is cropped short. Clearly an independent-spirited person.

Is Kathryn aware of the claims of arbitrary justice in the kingdom? Yes: 'Westerners can't leave the country if someone's killed in a car accident.' But this doesn't diminish her belief that the Saudi authorities are correct in their accusations against the two British nurses.

I find her friendly and genuine, like Joe Robinson. Yet their views are far apart. We say goodbye and I ask Kathryn for directions to the nearest bank with an ATM. Of course, around the corner is the bank where Lucy was arrested. I leave the mall, scene of Debbie's arrest, and walk towards the bank, imagining the police closing in.

Arriving late last night and rushing off to meet Kathryn this morning, I've had no time to change money. So the visit to the automatic teller machine is urgent.

Last time I was here we filmed a re-enactment of a woman using the ATM. Laura, the American woman I dragged in to volunteer as Lucy's stand-in, told us she'd been living in Saudi on one of the American compounds for six years. It was a secure place to raise kids, not like the crime and trouble of the United States. During our filming she got chatting with Hamad, our minder. Later, she said this was the first conversation she'd had with a real live Saudi man since she'd been here. That's compound living.

For the re-enactment we used my Visa card to go through the button-pushing motions for the camera. Everyone laughed when the message came up: Insufficient Funds to Process Transaction. This time, I'm in a hurry, bladder stretched after the coffee and the long chat with Kathryn. It's difficult to concentrate on the ATM buttons. The message: Insufficient Funds. Great. My publisher back in Sydney hasn't managed to get my expenses into the account on time. Hopping from one foot to the other in the bank's automatic teller vestibule, scene of my own (and, allegedly, Lucy's) earlier embarrassment, I consider the options. There are none. Thursday afternoon, the banks and shops are closed. I scurry around a carpark looking for a corner to find relief. That'd be just great, to be arrested in Al Khobar for indecent exposure. But Allah be praised, there's no one around as I leave a puddle in the dust of the carpark. Relief is too mild a word for how I feel as I jump a cab to Le Gulf Meridien where the cashier spots me 10 Riyals to pay the cabbie.

Now, expensive time passes in a hotel I can't afford. The man who has sponsored this visit isn't answering my phone calls. I need to stay in the most costly place in town because that's where the lawyers lob when they're here. When are they coming? No one in Riyadh can tell me. With little time, I make frantic calls to the hospital to set up further meetings with staff. And dream of a meeting with Lucy and Debbie. Salah Al-Hejailan made it sound so easy when I was on the phone from Sydney.

The hotel is full of business and engineering types. No tourists. Looking for some sort of reality, I head out into the mild winter evening. On the corniche, stretching along the waters of the Gulf, families gather, picnicking, watching the kids play. The kids look like kids anywhere, the women are black sacks. Three young women pass me on the path, leaving behind the frozen instant of huge dark eyes with the flash of white. Perhaps if you're shrouded head to foot you feel freer to look about you, make eye contact. Like mask-wearing revellers at a Rio Mardi Gras. Not quite. In the seaside cafes, there are only men.

Chapter 27

False accusation

It's Friday. All offices are closed. Today, the families are arriving from Britain to visit Lucy and Debbie and *Insha'allah*, God willing, Michael Dark will return from London so that he can set up my meeting with the accused. Killing time now, I phone the hospital. No one I need to talk to is home. I scan the *Arab News* over an expensive hotel breakfast. Being Friday, there are commentaries on passages in the *Koran*. Today's is headed: 'False Accusation and Irrefutable Testimony'. It concerns the servant Joseph and his attempted seduction by his master's wife. He runs away from her advances, to the door; she tears his shirt just as the husband arrives home. The wife accuses Joseph of trying to violate her, but Joseph says he's falsely accused. One of the household says to check the evidence: if Joseph's shirt is torn at the front the wife is speaking the truth. But Joseph's shirt is torn at the back. He is vindicated. The husband says to his wife: 'This is indeed [an instance] of the guile of women. Your guile is awesome indeed! You, woman, ask forgiveness for your sin. You have been seriously at fault.'

I turn to my notes of interviews with hospital staff, scanning for irrefutable testimony. Nothing seems quite certain, though there are some damning assertions. Will I be able to put them to the women themselves? How to test the 'guile of women', both accusers and accused?

The claims so far:
- Debbie was ringing Casualty to ask after Yvonne before the body was discovered.
- Lucy was spotted (by Bodil Valle) in the early hours of the morning after the murder, washing clothes at the communal laundry.

- The hairdresser at British Aerospace, Ann Stevenson spotted clumps of hair missing from Debbie's scalp after the murder.
- Debbie had a bruised thigh after the murder, alleged in the confessions to have come from her falling over a table in the struggle with Yvonne. Two close friends, Catherine Wall and Joe Robinson, can't vouch for Debbie's alibi that she received the bruise in a fall during a desert walk before the murder.
- Several people, especially Kathryn Lyons, recall scratches on Debbie's forearms in the days after the murder.
- Debbie especially, and sometimes Lucy, behaved strangely after the murder.

Does this all add up to guilt on the balance of probabilities?

This morning, Al Khobar reveals its jumble of concrete buildings on haunches in the mudflats. Some imposing white concrete villas. Low and white-grey, these are Lego jumbles of towns stretching around the bays of the Gulf. With the necklace of the causeway reaching off to Bahrain. Shopping malls, closed to the world outside them, just as in the suburban Safeways of Britain or the Westfield Plazas of Australia. Inside, there is life. There the expats find the order they know from home, the order of modern commerce, tinged with a little of the exotic. All the brands are here — Chanel, Sony. But there's also the *abaya* shop, a boutique of black. Some of the dark robes beaded, some laced, some shirred, but all, ultimately, long bags of black.

Back at the hotel I ring Salah's home in Riyadh, hoping he's out of bed. A night owl, he's a late riser. 'How are you?' he says, as always booming the 'you', rolling the 'rrr'. He hopes to be over here on Saturday, for a family wedding. We can meet then. I'm in his hands. In the meantime, there's the chance to talk to more staff at the hospital.

Karolyne Palowska sets bones. When I get through to her in the plaster room, there are cries in the background; she's setting a child's leg. But Karolyne has the voice of a professional. She doesn't sound flustered, not even surprised to hear from me, as she asks if I can call back at another time. You bet.

I finally catch her in her apartment at the hospital. A warm voice with a soft Yorkshire accent. When I say that many people describe her as the person closest to Yvonne before her death, she's surprised. 'I only knew her eight weeks.'

Karolyne's name is on the list. Jonathan Ashbee's hit list of people crucial to the defence, outlined in the dossier he'd sent to me earlier in the year. Debbie has been suggesting to her family that Karolyne is an alternative suspect for the murder. There seems to be no evidence for this assertion, aside from Karolyne's reported distress after the killing. Mind you, many were distressed, and if Karolyne had become Yvonne's friend at the hospital, during the short period of their acquaintance, then distress would be only natural. Once again, one person's grief can look like guilt to another.

'I don't understand why Debbie has been saying this about me,' Karolyne says. And, adamantly, 'They did it,' she says of Lucy and Debbie. When did Karolyne make up her mind they were guilty?

> *Not till weeks after, when we started hearing things from the interpreters. They were there in the police station while Lucy and Debbie were being questioned. I'll just say to you one thing. We were all there together at the police station. The Saudi police treated us very well. They were really good.*

Jonathan's dossier on Karolyne is frightening in its demonstration of the way the simple actions of our lives can be made to look suspicious.

The page of allegations about her is headed 'Carolyn (alias Sandra Pawlowska)'. This really upsets Karolyne. Her name is misspelled. The suggestion that she has an alias she finds laughable. 'I'm a single woman. "Pawlowska" is my father's name. It's Polish. Do you want to see my passport?' Karolyne hates the mention of 'Sandra', her middle name. She doesn't like it and doesn't want everyone at the hospital to know of it.

The dossier goes on:

> All the things we've found out about this lady match what Deb has been accused of. Have the Saudis arrested the wrong girl and then forced the confession?? Brangwen [name changed] could well have some information here.

Brangwen has volunteered no such information.

The dossier describes Karolyne as:

> An English nurse working as an orthopaedic technician on Male Specialty 1, who went by the name of Carolyn despite her real name (is it a middle name?). Came to Saudi from Jeddah.

In fact, Karolyne works in the plaster room. And she uses her middle name because she doesn't like 'Sandra'. My own sister uses her middle name instead of her first name. She hasn't murdered anyone, as far as I know.

> Had blonde, bob style hair — similar to that mentioned in the autopsy.

Yvonne had blonde, medium-length hair. The one hair mentioned in the medical report as being found in her hand may have been her own. The police have never said.

In response to this part of the dossier, Karolyne says, 'I have a good alibi. I was on call that night. I can't remember if I were called in.' Karolyne says she could check her book to see if she was called that night, but she doesn't see this as necessary and she doesn't think she was called. She says she was told by the nursing supervisor, Deslyn Marks, that the police had checked her out thoroughly.

Of Yvonne, Lucy and Debbie, she says, 'I don't understand. How can three people fall out so badly in such a short time together? How could that happen in a couple of months?'

> Owned a bike — bicycle torch found on Yvonne's bed.

Karolyne says the torch that was found belonged on the bike Lucy and Yvonne bought together and shared. Yvonne had taken it off to fit a mirror on. 'She was using it as a torch. My torch is still on my bicycle. Where else would it be?' She laughs, finding it strange that the simple facts of her life are under scrutiny.

> Being treated for tuberculosis — police were very interested in which drugs Deb was taking and kept asking her if she was diabetic. Would the treatment for TB give a similar result in a blood test to diabetes?

Karolyne is puzzled by this. 'When we arrived, me and another girl reacted positive to the heave test [for TB]. I think it was a fluke. I had no symptoms. I was on strong antibiotics.'

> She never mentioned boyfriends.

This really makes Karolyne laugh. 'Should I? Should I tell everybody my life, when I just started working here? I'm 46 years old. I know better than that.'

> Yvonne's closest friend at time of murder, but she was making a new 'friend', and Yvonne always got very upset when her friends made new friends — it was as if she wished to 'own' people.

Karolyne says she wasn't close to Yvonne. She had just started working at the hospital before the murder. At first, she and Yvonne had been on the same floor of Yvonne's building. 'There were very few people in the building. Yvonne was showing me where everything was. That was quite normal. I was friendly with everybody. You do meet people. It's strange that something so innocent could be made to look evil.'

> Wore thick cardigan following murder. Why, in temperatures of 30 degrees+? What was she hiding?

'It wasn't hot. It gets very cold here in December. We were all wearing cardigans. We were all checked by a doctor in the auditorium. We had to show arms, legs and neck. The nursing director was there, a woman. We all filed into a room. Debbie didn't. She was working.'

> Always carried a hammer to protect herself.

Karolyne laughs again. Can you imagine me coming to work with a hammer? I don't possess a hammer.

> Lived in Yvonne's building (No. 44).
> Known to have returned to Yvonne's apartment later the night of the murder.

That's where she lived, so it's not surprising Karolyne returned to the building that night. Karolyne had moved upstairs from Yvonne's floor because her ground-floor flat had been plagued by big cockroaches. 'Maybe it wouldn't have happened if I hadn't moved.'

> Wore dangling earrings etc of the same ilk as the chain that was found (only Carolyn [sic] seemed to know that the earring had been found).

Karolyne says, 'I never wear dangling earrings. I've still got on the same studs I was wearing then. Emeralds and aquamarine.' Karolyne says that when she and a group of other hospital staffers were at the police station, 'Police came in with a brown envelope. We were all waiting. I can't remember who was there. They said, "Do you recognise this?" It was part of the chain that had been found. It could have been from a bracelet or a necklace. One of the girls said Yvonne was wearing it before she was murdered. I said, "No, it couldn't be Yvonne's, it's not gold."' The police had asked Karolyne to pick up the piece of chain. 'It weighed like costume jewellery to me, not real gold.' Karolyne, who understands Arabic, heard the police say that earrings which matched the chain had been found in Yvonne's room. So maybe the jewellery *was* Yvonne's. Karolyne had seen Yvonne as a person of taste who wouldn't have cheap costume jewellery. 'It's possible it was hers. I only knew her eight weeks. I thought she never would wear it. She was a very nice lady. Would have worn it if someone had given it to her as a present.'

> Brangwen [name changed] was cross at Carolyn's 'over' reaction to Yvonne's death. Said it was as if she was her only friend.

'I was very, very distressed,' says Karolyne. 'You would be. It was the Thursday morning, I was getting ready for work. Deslyn rang me because Yvonne hadn't come to work. She asked me to go down and knock on Yvonne's door. I was ringing the bell and calling. I went back up to my room and called Deslyn. I was convinced she'd overslept and then I'd just missed her. Deslyn said, "No, Yvonne's never late for work." So Deslyn called security. It was horrific. I'd never ever experienced anything like this. Didn't know where I was, it was like being in a nightmare. I wasn't the only one. We had a counsellor called in to help us.'

I mention that Rosemary Kidman had loudly expressed disbelief at Lucy and Debbie's guilt at a meeting with the counsellor. 'I was the same at that point. I couldn't believe it was Debbie. That one of ourselves could do something like that. I really don't know how Lucy couldn't go for help.'

> Police accused Deb of being there at the 1994 murder [of Liberty da Gusma] under an alias and Interpol had a file on her (far fetched but better fits Carolyn?)
> Nobody ever convicted of this murder.

Karolyne had been in Jeddah for three years before she came to Dhahran. But that could not put her anywhere near Liberty's murder.

'Alternative suspect, my God. Why would I work in Jeddah for three-and-a half years, go home for three months, then come here and murder Yvonne, who's supposed to be my best friend? Why would I? I hardly knew Yvonne.'

Karolyne remembers Yvonne as 'very gentle, very kind. She'd help anyone. She was very motherly. Motherly towards the Filipino girls.'

On the claims of police abuse of Lucy and Debbie during the interrogations, she asks: 'Why did they make statements like that? The police were not like that, sexually abusing them. If I'd been accused of something and didn't do it, if I were innocent, nothing would make me confess.'

Karolyne still has regrets about December 11–12, 1996. 'If Yvonne had rung me that night, it wouldn't have happened.'

What about lesbian affairs? 'Who knows? From what I knew of Yvonne, nothing was ever mentioned. Yvonne talked about men. Owen Joyce. From what I can remember, there'd been some trouble between him and her, he'd crashed a car or something. She'd left him. She cared about him, but it wasn't a good relationship. She was still hoping to get married and settle down with someone. Never talked about being fairy or anything.' She pronounces this 'feery' and I have to get her to explain that she means 'gay'. 'You wouldn't tell somebody you'd only known for such a short time.'

Then Karolyne tells an odd story. 'I have two cats, Maureen and Buffy. I brought them from Jeddah. They used to go to Yvonne. She liked cats. Each night I would get up at two, three, four o'clock, leave my door wide open, and take them downstairs and outside. An hour later I'd have to bring them in. They'd make a terrible noise. Except that one night. I didn't have to take them out. That Wednesday evening they didn't make a sound. I find that very weird. I told that to the police.'

After the murder, Karolyne and the two other women still living in Yvonne's building were given a three-room apartment in another building. 'We made it an open house. People could drop in for coffee any time. That's where we had the meetings with the counsellor. The only two people who didn't come to that apartment were Debbie and Lucy. We all thought that was weird.'

Much of the mishmash of supposition in Jonathan's dossier has obviously come from Debbie. How sad if this fingerpointing at Karolyne is the desperate act of a guilty woman seeking to shift the blame from herself. How much more sad if it's the desperate act of an innocent woman. Or could there be something in this smearing of a character by putting a spin on circumstantial details? Try looking at what you did yesterday, then ask yourself how your actions of the day would look if your new best friend had been killed.

No other staff member I talk to has any suspicion of Karolyne Palowska. Caroline Ionescu had dinner with her at the Oasis restaurant on the Thursday night, the evening after the murder. 'She was devastated, needed someone to sit and talk to,' says Caroline. 'She was hyperactive, vague, dizzy, looked at you blankly.'

I tell Karolyne of Debbie and Lucy's intentions to publish their stories, for cash. She's shocked, particularly at the prospect of being mentioned in their versions. 'You can't say my name's an alias, make up lies about me.'

Chapter 28

Brangwen

Brangwen hasn't called my room. Maybe she's downstairs, waiting in the lobby. Taking the lift and scanning the vast hall, full of Western business suits and Saudi *thobes*, there's only one woman in sight. In a chair near the door, looking a bit nervous and out of place on her own. She's in an *abaya*, nothing on her long dark hair.

She looks relieved as I say hello and we move up the marble staircase to the coffee shop. I get a sense of what it's like to be a single woman here. We both feel exposed, the centre of attention. Only a couple of customers in the coffee shop. In her Celtic lilt, Brangwen says she feels she must point out that she's not like the others, not convinced absolutely of Lucy and Debbie's guilt. I say that's good to hear; that it's never seemed cut-and-dried to me. We discuss not using her real name, but she agrees to me taping the chat. We warm up and she talks freely. Sometimes I interrupt, but she needs little prompting:

'The point is, because I'm sceptical about so many things, I cannot speak out like some people speak out.' God, what must it have been like to be a dissenting voice among the lynch mob at the hospital all these months?

I mention the circumstantial evidence: the bruise, the scratches, Lucy doing washing at three o'clock in the morning, Debbie making phone calls to Casualty. 'I know all about that [the calls to Casualty] because I was the one, she was ringing Casualty, ringing me.' She was at work.

> *First of all I got a phone call, 7.20 am, from MS1 [Male Specialty One, where Yvonne worked], asking me did I know where Yvonne was because she hadn't turned up for*

> work. I mean if you knew Yvonne, Yvonne would turn up
> for work whatever. And if she didn't, she'd call and let
> them know. So I knew she was going to be unconscious. I
> thought she'd had a heart attack. She was so reliable, so
> hardworking. If she hadn't called in, not turned up for
> work, there had to be something very seriously wrong.

That fitted with everybody's picture of Yvonne. The hardworking saint.

'So anyway, I think it was about twenty to eight when Debbie rang me and said, "Have you heard, they're looking for Yvonne; Yvonne's not turned up for work?"' Each promised to call the other if they heard anything. 'I went over there [to Casualty] and said, "What's going on?" They said they'd sent somebody over [to Yvonne's room] to knock on the door.' So Brangwen waited back at her own work.

Next thing,

> Debbie rang me, saying Yvonne was in Casualty. That
> would be nine o'clock. All the staff would tell her was that
> it wasn't very good. So I rushed down to Casualty and
> Deslyn was there and Karolyne [Palowska] was there in
> tears; they told me she's dead. Karolyne and I went to the
> dining room for an hour; we just started crying. I went up
> to the renal unit after an hour to tell Debbie; she came to
> the door, she was very calm and composed. Before I said
> anything, she said: 'I know. I know. I rang Casualty back.'
> She said, 'I had to find out, I had to know what was
> happening.'

I suggest that you could put various constructions on Debbie's actions and words. Brangwen agrees. 'The MS1 staff probably rang her as well, asking: 'Do you know where Yvonne is?' She, thinking the same as me, maybe ended up phoning Casualty. There's nothing incriminating in that itself.'

But would there be any reason for Casualty to ring Debbie, given that she and Yvonne hadn't been around together in recent weeks?

> Well, they might not have known that in MS1, because
> Debbie was no longer working there [as she had been,
> with Yvonne, when she first arrived]. And I actually asked
> the MS1 staff, some time after they [Debbie and Lucy]

*were arrested, 'Did you ring Debbie that morning. After
you rang me, did you ring Debbie?' And the night staff,
can't remember his name, said he probably did ring
Debbie as well.*

Why ring Debbie, as opposed to say, Karolyne?

*Deslyn rang Karolyne and asked her to go down and
knock on [Yvonne's] door. They knew Debbie; they knew
me. They knew [Yvonne] and I were very close friends;
they knew that Debbie and she had been close. So I don't
see why not.*

So what was the friendship between Yvonne and Debbie?

*It was very complicated; they had a strange relationship
from the start, really. I remember, I had this impression.
Debbie was very highly strung. One of the first things
Yvonne said to me about her was, 'I'm going to be looking
out a lot for her because she's got problems.' She [Debbie]
told her [Yvonne] all about her psychological counselling,
the loss of members of her family and so on. And she could
be very hysterical, a highly strung person, which we saw
for ourselves right from the start.*

Yvonne was the same rank as Debbie and Brangwen — 'She was
an RN1, like the rest of us' — but made a point of keeping an eye
on Debbie.

*Initially they spent a lot of time together, because Debbie
was new; she had no other friends. Yvonne didn't really
make friends easily. And Yvonne tended to impose herself
on people, not that she was ... she found it difficult. She
wanted to make friends, but she had a manner which was
quite off-putting, you know?*

Blessed relief. At last someone who was close to Yvonne and
doesn't find it necessary to paint her as a saint.

*If you met her, if you talked to her, you'd think her very
school-marmish. As you got to know her she was fine, you*

> know, but she had a way of talking, a way of walking, the way she said things, that didn't make you immediately want to be her friend. So I don't think she made friends that easily. And when she did make a friend, she became very possessive. And she tended to go a little bit too far. You just had to distance yourself to give yourself a little bit more space, you know?

Brangwen says that part of Yvonne's practice of lending money was 'a way of buying friends'.

So, given this rather unpolished view of Yvonne, why were Brangwen and Yvonne friends?

> We both like to swim; we used to go swimming a lot. We both were great shoppers, window-shoppers. We used to go into town [Al Khobar] every day off. We'd be downtown exploring different parts of town.

Brangwen was in Yvonne's room on the Tuesday night (the night before the night of the murder).

> I'd just come back from holiday for three weeks and Debbie had been telling me that she hadn't been to see Yvonne for over a month. And Yvonne just said, 'I've obviously outlived my purpose; she has no more use for me.' That was the only thing she said. It sounded very strange to me. I was quite taken aback. They were both friends and I didn't want to get caught between, listening to one saying things about the other and vice versa. So, instead of asking her, 'What do you mean?', I was quite taken aback and speechless and she changed the subject. But she did say that. But then again, it could be because two friends had grown apart.

Brangwen had realised the two were no longer getting on. 'I'd known for a long time that Yvonne was getting on Debbie's nerves. There *had* been one or two scenes, really. But nothing that would make you think Debbie was capable of killing.'

One incident had occurred on an outing with the Travelling Naturalists.

> *There was one day-trip we went on, to Al Uqayr, [an ancient coastal town near the Al Hasa oasis] about 70 miles south of where we live. And we went out, about seven or eight four-wheel-drives. Of course, women can't drive, so we're in different cars. What happened was, Yvonne and Debbie were put in the car with Jeremy. Debbie had an on-off thing with Jeremy. I was put in another one with two men. We got to Al Uqayr. Debbie comes storming, 'I've had enough, I've had enough. I'm coming with you. I'm not travelling with her anymore.' She was really worked up, she really was. She said, 'That woman, she's done nothing but ...' Apparently all she'd done was — Yvonne was very intelligent, a very clever woman, and Jeremy is also. So they'd been talking all the way. Debbie threw a tantrum. That was Debbie's way, very childish, throwing tantrums. She felt left out. He's supposed to be her boyfriend, and Yvonne was monopolising him. She sulked and threw a tantrum in the car and she insisted on going to sit in the back.*

After Debbie's outburst at Al Uqayr, Yvonne had come storming up. 'She could be very school-marmish. It drove Debbie mad. She's saying, "Don't be silly, don't be silly. You're coming with me, and that's it."'

Our conversation among the bland, vast marble interior of the hotel is coming to an end. Brangwen is nervous again as she asks if the tape has stopped. She says she wants me to know, but for the Saudis not to know it's come from her: at 10.30 on the morning Lucy was arrested at the Arab National Bank — two hours after the arrest — one of the hospital officials rang Brangwen to find out which bank Yvonne belonged to. 'I'm not saying it means anything,' says Brangwen. 'But why would they need to ring me if they'd just picked up Lucy with Yvonne's card in her bag?' Curious. 'That's why I'm not prepared to say they're guilty.'

We part. She seems a little flustered now it's over. Has she said too much?

Chapter 29

Consultant

Saturday and suddenly, that rich baritone voice is on the phone. It's Salah and he's here in the hotel. Would I like to join him in his suite for lunch? You bet, as the Americans say. I check in the mirror; I'm sporting several days' growth in honour of Michael Hutchence's sad demise. If it's good enough for Yasser Arafat, who's on the screen on CNN with his Parkinsons' quivering lip, it's good enough for me. Up I go to the top floor, smoothing my rumpled shirt.

As the door opens, the Filipina maid is there. I'm saying hello, effusively, before I check myself and turn my attention to the big man, Sheikh Salah Al-Hejailan, who's over there on the couch. He rises for a handshake and pleasantries. I hear my voice deepening to keep up. Now I'm to discover what's expected; what he wants in return for his sponsorship of this foreign journalist as a consultant to the case.

Behind me, Bob Thoms arrives — the New Yorker who works with the law firm in Riyadh. They're both in mufti: Salah in a long white house *thobe* with short sleeves; Bob Thoms in an open-necked, collarless shirt and weekend slacks. They've come down to Al Khobar on the Hejailan family bus for an engagement party. Salah's nephew. This is a rare venture to the Eastern Province, generally seen as a more relaxed, less formal place than the administrative centre and capital of Riyadh. Salah is making the most of the trip — he'll fit in some negotiations between his client, Raytheon, and the oil giant Aramco while he's here. That's his regular line of work. And, more interestingly, he says he'll pay a visit to the judge in the nurses' case tomorrow. My eyebrows shoot up. Is that how it's done? You pop in for a word in the judge's ear?

So much for the Saudi Information Ministry officials' assurances of the solemn and religious independence of the *Sharia* court. As Salah steps into the adjoining room to attend to some family concern, Bob whispers to me that this private meeting with the judge will be *ex parte*. The other side, The International Law Firm, acting for Frank Gilford, won't be there. And, Bob adds, Salah's voice will be one among several influences on the judge. Extra-judicial influences. Meaning political, I suggest. Exactly.

The other news they have is that the cassation court in Riyadh has referred the nurses' case back to the Al Khobar judge with comment and direction. In other words, higher forces are telling the judge where he's erred in his sentencing of Lucy — eight years and 500 lashes — and his presumed finding of guilt against Debbie.

Salah Al-Hejailan has a constantly shifting focus. Bob warns that he's unlikely to sit down with me for an extended, detailed interview on the case; he hasn't the patience. I'll need to pick up the pieces as we go. One moment Salah is harassing his staff to get the hotel waiters up here and take our lunch order; the next, he's ordering his secretary to get on the phone to Australia to check the latest court developments there.

In the next breath, he's asking me which Australian newspaper would be the best for him to 'place' an article he's written on the case. They want me to run through it for an opinion on how it will run in Australia. I'll be shown it tomorrow, after they've redrafted it. From the snippets of conversation, I gather it's a diatribe against Frank Gilford and his lawyers. This is all to do with the elaborate thrust and parry over Frank's waiver of the death penalty and the money to be paid. Salah informs me the money hasn't yet been released.

When is a deal a deal? Apparently not until a fat lady in purdah has sung. Bob and Salah gloat that Frank's Australian and Saudi-based lawyers have insisted on a very legalistic settlement. Bob suggests that the defence side has got Frank on toast, in a way they would not have if the whole deal had been more informal. Salah maintains that Frank lost his rights over the death penalty as soon as he began to negotiate money. The defence lawyers have early negotiation documents which they're now prepared to release to show how long Frank's side has been in negotiation. In an informal deal, Bob says, Frank would have had deniability (as the Americans say). Is there not a confidentiality clause on the Australian contract, I ask? Salah suggests this no longer holds, for reasons that are unclear to a boy from the Australian suburbs.

Salah is very interested in my claim that The International Law Firm told us in Riyadh, in June, that they were working for nothing on Frank's case. Part of the Adelaide deal involves hundreds of thousands of dollars for that firm. Salah is wondering if this is a way of getting more money to Frank, beyond his announced $50 000.

For several minutes, Bob works himself up into Manhattan outrage about the duplicity of the other side. To an outsider, this all seems an arcane display of lawyer-on-lawyer moral violence. Where do the nurses — where does Yvonne — fit into all this?

The subcontinental waiter arrives, nervous, to be shouted at. 'Speak up,' snaps Salah, demanding lunch in haste, all the while solicitously asking about my needs and whether I'd like some 7-Up or tea. In the midst of this, he's asking about my 'program' here. Would I care to join him and his family on the bus back to Riyadh tomorrow? I point out that my major concern is to meet the nurses, here in the East. What is there to talk about with them, he wonders, jaw-droppingly unaware of their centrality in the human interest aspect of the story. He assures me I can visit them with Michael Dark, the British lawyer, when he's here on Monday.

Bob rings London to talk to Michael. Michael's out, visiting his son's school. What day is he back, wonders Salah. No one is sure. Don't worry, they assure me, all will be well; I'll get my meeting. Salah wonders aloud how to describe my consultancy. I'm here representing the Australian lawyers, he decides. We move to the dining table and Salah motions Bob to move to his left, myself to his right. Over lunch there's discussion of the Australian newspapers. I mention I know an editor at *The Sydney Morning Herald*. They're looking for the equivalent of *The New York Times*, Bob says, to place the article. I find myself wondering what Frank Gilford would make of me supping with the enemy as they plot their next salvo against him. Bob asks if Frank is as bad in the flesh as he appears in the press. I trot out the old line that Frank's a simple man caught in difficult circumstances, the salt of the earth and, in my view, badly advised by his American lawyers in Saudi.

A fax arrives from Michael Burnett, the Adelaide lawyer from Minter Ellison, working in the South Australian Supreme Court for Salah. The court there has adjourned its latest hearing, which had considered the latest news from Saudi. The court has been informed of the Saudi cassation court's developments. Frank may have waived a death penalty which now doesn't exist as a threat if, as expected, the Al Khobar court is directed to reconsider its verdicts and sentences.

Salah mentions that his sister is about to arrive and I offer to leave. Instead, it's the tea arriving at the door and I'm motioned to the armchairs for a few more minutes. As the tea is poured, Salah now harangues the waiter about the Arabic sweets on the coffee table. 'They've been in the air uncovered too long,' he says. 'Get me some more.' The waiter stutters that he's just replaced them, only just removed the covering of cling-wrap. Unsatisfied, Salah demands another plate be brought. 'This time, leave them covered.' A sense of impatient *droit de seigneur* hangs in the air. To Salah we are all — waiters, foreign lawyers, foreign journalists — more-or-less at his beck and call. I wonder how the British and American lawyers can stomach this, year after year. While I'm here, and presumably useful in some way that remains obscure, I have a certain latitude. It's with a tolerated cheek that I mention the press release, months ago, in which the Minter Ellison lawyers had contradicted Salah over his claims about the negotiations with Frank. 'That was later retracted,' he claims, though I know this isn't so. Fishing for material to round out a portrait of the big lawyer, I joke about Salah's enthusiasm for Egyptian films of the 1940s and 1950s. His sons have told me their father is a big fan. Salah looks a little shocked that I should know something about his personal life. 'This is not relevant to the case,' he protests, but agrees that he feels the old films are better than today's. 'The actors are nicely dressed and clean-cut,' he says. 'Today, they look greasy.' I feel the stubble on my chin. I ask after the family and wish him well in the evening's festivities. I suggest he might be singing or reciting poems. As I've read in the guidebooks, Saudis don't like an outsider's scrutiny of their personal affairs. Bob seems delighted that a blundering visitor has crossed the line. Fortunately, Salah is prepared to tolerate my transgressions — for now. This is the pleasure of being a non-aligned Australian in such an intercultural affair. The Saudis, the Brits, the Americans — none of them are quite used to Australian disdain for form; a small compensation for the creeping feeling of being drawn into one of the partisan cliques of the case. What will they say when I write what I really think of all the machinations?

Thanking Salah for the offer of the bus ride, I take my leave with Bob Thoms. Downstairs we sit for a chat. He says this trip to the Eastern Province is unprecedented for him. For a non-family man to be on the bus with the Hejailan women was somewhat beyond the norm. There'd been much rushing to get into veils as Bob boarded. I look forward to the return trip.

Bob jokes about the Americans and their use of Salah as a conduit to the Saudi system. Heads of American universities, Columbia and Georgetown, use him to ask for funding for their schools of Arabic and Islamic studies. 'Salah tolerates them,' says Bob. I think back to my urgings to Frank Gilford to come to the kingdom and see things for himself. What would he have made of all this?

We chat about how the case has played in the press in the three countries. Bob says the two British women have come through remarkably unscathed in coverage in their home country. When they're released, they should be able to live their lives without shame. It's true that the UK reportage has been remarkably sympathetic to Debbie and Lucy. Bob suggests that if they'd been Americans, there would have been outrage from minority lobby groups about the assertions of lesbianism, meaning that sexuality should never have been an issue. I'm more surprised by the minimal coverage of Lucy's alleged lifting of a patient's credit card in her Dundee hospital. Bob suggests it's media concern about defamation. I think it's more to do with the outrage over the death penalty and the British *hauteur* when a foreign — perceived to be medieval — nation does wrong to two Britons. Of course, if all this had happened at home, the British tabloids would have had the nurses for breakfast. They don't mind doing it to their own, but they don't like someone from outside the family laying their heavy hands on daughters of the British Crown. Remarkably like the Saudis, really.

In Saudi, The International Law Firm trashed Salah in the local press for his reference to the Pope in the 'Rationale for Early Waiver of the Death Penalty'. A cheap shot to play to Saudi prejudice. A couple of months later, says Bob, Prince Sultan (Defence Minister) visited the Pope in the Vatican, the first member of the house of Al Sa'ud to do so. Salah had brimmed with vindication and kept a photograph of the Saudi prince sitting in deferential pose with the pontiff.

Shamelessly self-seeking, I compliment Bob on the eloquence of the Rationale, which had received short shrift from the other side. Bob says it was written jointly by himself, Salah and Michael Dark. They'd drawn on sources from all their associated law firms. The head of the capital punishment section of the US Bar Association had helped. The British law firm Clifford Chance had contributed the South African reference to a decision overturning the death penalty there. I said I was impressed by the quotations from the French author Albert Camus. 'My sister sent me that from New York,' said Bob. They'd wanted to include a quote from Victor Hugo's *Les Miserables*, but the bookshop in Riyadh was out of stock.

Elevated by this discussion of literature, I retire to my room to dip into Dominick Dunne. *A Season in Purgatory*, the author's account of an Irish-Catholic journalist wading through privilege and power in 1960s' New England, is a touchstone of cautionary sentiment in my present circumstances. Adopted by a powerful Irish–American dynasty, the book's protagonist finds himself being drawn into becoming the resident hagiographer for the family. An eternal outsider, he craves to belong and be approved of by his powerful friends. But at what cost?

Next morning, Bob Thoms calls my room to talk about the Australian newspapers and the negotiation to place Salah's diatribe against Frank Gilford. Bob mentions that he's seen an interview on *BBC World* this morning with a British pilot the Iraqis shot down during the Gulf War. The experience led to two bestsellers and changed the guy's life. Maybe that's what Lucy and Grant are hoping for. Good luck to them, I guess — as long as she is, in fact, innocent.

Sunday and I'm ready at midday for Salah's bus. In the foyer I spot him striding towards the exit, followed by two tall women in full black garb. I make to speak to him, then realise this isn't done as he is escorting the women of the family to the bus.

I meekly follow the family entourage of a dozen or so and we hit the road. Bob Thoms and I are the only non-family aboard. I sit close behind Salah, hoping for some scraps of interview on the four-hour journey to Riyadh.

He dispenses 'finger sandwiches', chips and salad to all on board. His brother and sister are there, a sister-in-law, plenty of kids and Salah's lawyer son, Hassan.

Bob Thoms, thrilled to be included in the family circle, joins me up close to the boss. Salah is in expansive spirits, and asks me why I'm not taking notes. I take notes. He fills us in on his private visit to the Chief Judge of the Al Khobar court on Friday. Judge Lehedran, a man in his seventies, has told Salah and Hassan that Debbie has been convicted of murder but that he has accepted Frank's waiver of the death penalty. Now her sentence is up to the Interior Ministry and, ultimately, the king. Theoretically, she could be released tomorrow, even though her crime is more serious than Lucy's.

The judge has confirmed that Lucy has been convicted of theft and concealing a major crime. He has referred her sentence, eight years' gaol and 500 lashes, to the Court of Cassation in Riyadh, which has the power to reduce the penalty.

Salah says he told the judge he objected to paying all the money, now that only one of the women had been convicted of murder. The judge has told him he should pay half and come back to the court if the women's side objects.

We talk about the lack of objective evidence. Salah claims he's seen the video re-enactments taken at the hospital. I suspect he hasn't but doesn't want to admit his lack of access to the court. I ask if the women look guilty in the video. 'I am emotionally tied to their innocence,' he says. 'Maybe some time in the future I can be objective.'

Bob Thoms is like an enthusiastic puppy trying to get his master's attention. He's amused by my Lonely Planet guidebook, which suggests good restaurants to visit. He's delighted to find that he had eaten at an Italian place described as the best in Al Khobar, the night before. He laughs when I tell him this is where Debbie ate, with Joe Robinson, the night before her arrest. It's a popular place with hospital staff. Bob tells the whole bus, 'We were eating in a place that may have been full of murdering nurses.'

Al Khobar recedes as the bus roars down the expressway. Until now, I haven't addressed Salah's adult female relatives, not being sure of the etiquette. In the privacy of the bus they've abandoned the *abaya* and veil. Now they address me, asking about the case. They're both well-educated women; one lives in London. They believe in their country's system of justice. The family makes jokes about the murdering nurses. The incongruity of their position in relation to Salah's doesn't seem to occur to them. Salah's young sister-in-law defends the death penalty. All her educated young friends feel the same, she says.

These women don't seem oppressed by the place of women in Islam. But then they're in privileged, affluent families, exposed to the culture and ideas of the West. All the same, their loyalty to Saudi ways is strong.

Hassan sits down for a chat. He wonders whether I've read the Robert Lacey book, *The Kingdom*, which he gave me the last time we had lunch in Riyadh. It's a wonderful book, I tell him, which it is. So it surprises me when Hassan launches into some conspiracy theory stuff about American Jews chasing Nazi gold in Swiss banks, the mysterious demise of Michael Hutchence and the death of Princess Diana. Not very sophisticated thinking for a Western-educated lawyer. Uncomfortable with his anti-Semitism, I pop downstairs to the on-board loo.

Back in my seat, Salah launches into an address on the ways this case suggests the Saudi legal system could be improved. He's careful to phrase this as the system needing to adhere more closely to the true principles of *Sharia* law, not as a criticism of the *Sharia* itself.

One, there should be a member of the *Muttawa*, the religious law enforcers, accompanying investigators, especially during a confession. This had not been the case with Lucy and Debbie.

Two, defence lawyers should be present at confessions.

Three, the judge who asks the accused to confirm a confession — a requirement soon after police obtain the confession — should not be the same judge who eventually tries the case. Lucy and Debbie had the same judges for both phases.

Four, there should be a defined mechanism for retraction of a confession.

Five, judges should be prepared to accept prosecutions where there is no confession. The present practice of requiring a confession before a judge will even look at a case places undue pressure on investigating police to come up with a confession, no matter what.

Six, defence lawyers should be able to take an active role in court and to examine the evidence.

Although these ideas reflect what is an openness taken for granted in Western courts, they are radical here. The implied criticisms of the existing system are rare from a Saudi. Only someone as well-placed as Salah Al-Hejailan could make them with impunity.

As we drive into Riyadh, Salah and his family chat about shops along the route, good places to shop for shoes.

The unusual roadshow ends as we pull up to Salah's villa in the early darkness. The family scatters inside and into cars and a veil lifted briefly on upper-class Saudi family life closes again. The guests, Bob and myself, are provided with a car and driver to take us to his home and my hotel, outsiders again.

Chapter 30

Hotel blues

It seems like every hotel I stay in on working trips around the world. The Marriott is under renovation. This evening the food in the restaurant could do with some renovation, too. The football team down the corridor is raucous into the night.

Next morning, on *BBC World* television, the citizens of Mexico City are marching to protest against crime. The middle-class-looking woman in the parade is demanding the death penalty be introduced to deal with the problem. A simple solution to her problems; she already has walls and alarms around her home. The reporter says there are 600 acts of violence in the city each day.

Hours pass, spent nervously reading Dominick Dunne and waiting for the return of Michael Dark. Now the office is saying he's straight off to Bahrain this afternoon and won't be back until Tuesday. My visa expires tomorrow. To get into the gaol to see the women, I need Michael Dark. Bob Thoms, well past his holiday mood of yesterday's bus trip, is impatient on the phone, busy with some other case. I trouble him with my visa problems. He says it'll take more than a day to get my passport restamped; I'd better come into the office this evening.

Calling the British Trade Office in Al Khobar, I miss the consul. He's already gone off to the prison with the family. There are rumours that Grant Ferrie is marrying Lucy this weekend. A Reuters journalist in Dubai has been calling the Trade Office. I'm in Riyadh, far from an interview with the nurses, far from the wonderful tabloid tale of a gaolbird's wedding. Running out of cash, unsure of my prospects. For escape, I dive back into the seamy world of the big New England Bradley family in Dominick Dunne's bleak description of a modern American business–political dynasty. The journalist at the heart of the story has been drawn deeper and deeper into complicity with the rich and corrupt. As my own spirits sink along with his, I consider heading for the airport and home, giving up journalism altogether, spending time with my wife and sons. Loneliness and the cabin fever of too long in hotel rooms. Impatient, sending faxes downstairs, I buy some cigarettes. Back in my room I smoke three in quick succession, then throw the pack away. Dunne's flawed hero faces the quandary of hurting people he loves by revealing the grisly truth that his best friend murdered a young woman 20 years ago.

The British Trade Office calls; my heart leaps. False alarm. It's only one of the officials calling to say they've missed a page of my faxed letter to Lucy and Debbie. I rush downstairs to send it off again. Returning to my cell, no one has called. I make another desultory round of calls, looking for Michael Dark so that I can get back on the merry-go-round to Dhahran.

I call Michael Dark's home. His wife answers for the first time in the dozens of calls I must have made over the months. Yes, he's back from visiting their son in Britain. But now he's off to Al Khobar. You might catch him at the airport.

I do. Michael peers through the vastness of the King Fahd airport terminal and finally recognises me as I stride towards him. He's surprised, but friendly. The message hadn't got through from Salah's office that I was here and chasing him.

Hello. Yes, he's heading to Al Khobar to see the families. Yes, I can come with him if they agree. Yes, I can come and be a consultant at the prison. Maybe, maybe, I'm back in the game again. All the way to Al Khobar he briefs me on the case. We both describe the phenomenon of being asked by others whether Debbie and Lucy are innocent, trotting out the innocent-till-proven-guilty platitudes and going through a personal rollercoaster between belief of innocence and guilt.

I tell him about the bus ride with Salah, that Salah has told me he's seen the video of the re-enactment. I tell him that when I ask for his reaction to the video, Salah says he has an emotional commitment to the women's innocence and that he can't be objective.

This interests Michael because of his own discussions with Salah about their guilt or innocence. He describes attempts, early on, to get Lucy and Debbie to face the difficult question of the allegedly stolen ATM card. Was there not an innocent explanation they could put forward, Michael had suggested to them. A way to show it was reasonable they were in possession of the card. Such as that Yvonne had given it to Lucy before the murder to get some money out for her, something like that. Lucy had cottoned on quickly that they were being invited to construct a scenario to explain away the card. It had taken Debbie a while to see Michael's point. Both, however, had declined the temptation to take this possible easy way out. They wanted to tell the truth, they said, and the truth was that they didn't have the card.

Salah, hearing reports back from Michael, had been perplexed by the women's unwillingness to clean up their story. Finally, he travelled to the Eastern Province to meet them. The only time he did so the whole year. They were impressed by him; the big man with the deep voice, the imposing manner, the confidence that he knew what was what in this system and he would get them out of this mess. But surely, he suggested, there was some reason why they might have had the card? Both stood up to him. They didn't care if it meant being convicted, they said; they wanted to tell the truth. Salah was taken aback. As he left with Michael Dark, he muttered that now he believed the women were innocent.

Michael and I discuss the witnesses we've spoken to — the staff at the hospital, the bank manager. We're both impressed by Brangwen who, though a close friend of Yvonne, is not so prepared to convict as some of her colleagues. We laugh about her description of her fellows as having criminal and mental troubles.

We bemoan the fact that the Australian government hasn't intervened in the case earlier. I suggest the government was being careful not to be seen to lean on a citizen — Frank Gilford. Why shouldn't they lean on a citizen, in a case like this, asks Michael.

He suggests that, despite Salah's quibbles, all the money will be paid to Frank. He thinks Michael Abbott will get into the Supreme Court in South Australia this week and demand that the contract be fulfilled.

The rest of the trip is taken up with discussion of missing our families — his children are in Britain and his wife stays only some of the time in Riyadh. And Michael's perplexity with the lack of formal structure in the Saudi court hearings. He has no objection to *Sharia* law in itself, he suggests. But the court should be open so that the people can see the process for themselves. And there should be a procedure in the court, not the formless jumble he's observed; the participants apparently speaking up at whim.

We're met at Dhahran airport by Sunil, a driver from the British Trade Office. He takes us to Le Gulf Meridien, where the hammering continues in the foyer. But, they're pleased to announce at the desk, tonight is the first night of the new Royal Club rooms. I blanch at the price but pay up, to be close to Michael Dark and the holy grail. On the eighth floor we agree to meet again in five minutes, after he's rung the families to check it's okay that I come along to see them tonight.

Heart in mouth, I slip into my new-smelling room and over-tip the porter. I'm waiting at the floor-concierge's desk when he gets back. 'Bad news, I'm sorry. They don't want you to come. Not the Ashbees, the McLauchlans.' He's spoken to Sandra. She and Jonathan would be happy to see me; it's the others who object. Grant Ferrie — who married Lucy only yesterday — and Lucy's brother and his wife. Michael suspects Lucy and Grant have cooked up their own publishing deal and see themselves in competition with me. What? Lucy's actually thinking of making money out of the murder of her supposed friend? I guess she doesn't see it that way.

Grasping at straws, I suggest to Michael that he and I could meet the women — or maybe just Debbie — for an hour before or after the family visit. The trouble with that, he says, is that the families naturally want to spend as much time with Lucy and Debbie as they can while they're here. Michael can see I'm crestfallen. He looks a bit sad for me, too. He promises to see what he can do at tonight's meeting.

I ring Salah in Riyadh and explain Grant and Lucy's resistance. 'That son of a gun,' he says of Grant. 'I'm paying for his visit. I'll talk to them.'

I wake early, chasing the Australian papers by frighteningly expensive hotel phone to see if they're interested in Salah's commentary on the dispute over paying the blood money. They'll look at it, they say. I suggest some toning down to its co-author, Bob Thoms. Accusing Frank Gilford of fraud may not be very productive. Defamatory, too, by the way. I wonder what Frank would think of this conversation with the authors of yet another tirade against him. I hope he'd appreciate my wan attempts at tempering the Hejailan tempest.

At 6 am I go down and iron shirt and trousers. Dress to impress.

Breakfast with Michael Dark: the families aren't at all keen for me to come. Could he not, please, talk to Salah to have him persuade them? First of all, Salah is probably not out of bed yet and anyway, says Michael, he's not optimistic about getting around the McLauchlans.

I mention Salah's keenness to press Frank Gilford to abide by a clause of the Deed of Settlement which binds him to asking the Saudi courts to release the evidence in the case. Between you and me and well, everybody, says Michael, the women and their families don't want the evidence released now. Now that they have a result — the death penalty waived in Deborah's case, and the likelihood of shorter gaol terms for both — any further aggravation in the courts in Saudi or Australia is unwelcome. Why stir up trouble? The Saudis are hardly going to release any evidence which suggests the women aren't guilty. All that might show up is questionable evidence — say, fingerprints possibly dubiously obtained — which would only confirm the Gilfords in their already firm view of the women's guilt. Not much I can say to that. I'd feel the same if I were them. Keep their heads down and hope the king will dispense an early release.

I can't imagine Michael pushing the families very hard, not with the lugubrious manner he's wearing as we discuss my chances. He offers to seek separate permission for he and I to visit the prison on, say, Saturday. He wasn't going to be here then, but will if it will help. Generous. Trouble is, my visa runs out tonight. Should I try to get it renewed and waste time and money sitting here in Saudi, or should I go to London in the hope of a new one for my return?

Chapter 31

Wedding bells

When Lucy and Grant married, the Saudi police taunted Debbie: 'We'll find someone for you now.' She said, 'No way. There's no way I'm getting married here. I'll wait till I get back to England.' The guards laughed. 'You haven't got anybody.'

'Don't be so sure,' she retorted, thinking of Stuart and the love she left behind. Sandra, Debbie's sister, keeps tabs on Stuart through their mutual friends. 'I think he's still holding a light for Deb. So I think when she does come back, there might be a small chance. I'd love it if they got together. She really fitted him well, and the children absolutely adored him.'

Sandra and her husband, Jon, believe in the redeeming powers of the right match. Their own marriage is their evidence. Sandra's first husband had died of a brain haemmorhage. Six months later, 'my first wife had disappeared with another fella, leaving me with our two-year-old daughter,' says Jon. Sandra and Jon were working in the bank together and became close, talking each other through their troubles. Eventually they realised there could be more to it. Now their family has become the replacement for what they each, as well as Debbie, had lost.

Grant Ferrie returns to Scotland, leaving his new wife behind. The press around the world is trumpeting the story of the gaol bride. A cynic might wonder if the union is a move calculated to boost the saleability of their tale, but a letter from Lucy to a friend suggests her passion is real enough. She says that during Grant's visits she wanted to rip his boxer shorts off 'but holding hands and a few kisses had to suffice meantime. I'll sort that out when I get home if you know what I mean.' Sometimes, during the family visits every couple of months, she's been able to see Grant on her own. She writes of one occasion 'which was brilliant. There was a policeman there also but he gave us 10 minutes on our own at the end of each visit for kisses and feelies, etc. I'm easy pleased now Freda — we were like a couple of teenagers.' Later, they're to be allowed conjugal visits.

Chapter 32

White lady from Louisiana

With hope of meeting the accused women diminishing, I turn back to the sources closer to hand. Lucy and Debbie will tell their own story. What seems more useful now is to test it against that of the friends who believe Lucy and Debbie are guilty. I'd like to have tested this on the women themselves, but Lucy and Grant's commercial instincts have removed the opportunity.

I use the last day of my five-day visa to see another couple of hospital staff.

When Catherine Wall steps into the lobby of Le Gulf Meridien, with her husband by her side, she's a vision in white. A long skirt and a long-sleeved blouse, all loose-fitting. White shoes. This was a medical woman who wore white off-duty as well as on. Her voice was as warm and gracious as on the phone, though a little tense at this first meeting, with that Southern sense of how do you do, the polite end of the South. Her handshake is warm, not too firm, just like her voice. Her husband, Andrew, makes his apologies and, having performed the requisite handover, leaves. For an outsider it takes some getting used to, this social form of not leaving a lady alone in public. I gesture to the marble stairs, worthy of Scarlett O'Hara, and we ascend to the tea shop, with a nervous sense of being on show.

This is my third meeting with a King Fahd staff member among the potted palms and tea in as many days. A very public confessional, though we choose the table furthest from the few men in *thobes* in the large, open cafe. As we meander through politenesses and settle to business, I have a slightly uneasy awareness of why this woman has seemed always the most dependable of those on the phone from the King Fahd compound. She seems caring, together, sensible, very polite and concerned. Very middle-class. I find myself attempting to gird my more gullible, trusting impulses in a filter of disbelief, of scepticism. It wouldn't do to hang the reputations of Lucy and Debbie on the simple prejudice of class. Just because a nice woman says they're guilty doesn't make it so.

As we order tea and cookies from a softly spoken Sri Lankan waiter, Catherine begins to unburden herself to an outsider for the first time. She can't understand Lucy's involvement in the murder, but she's convinced that Debbie did it. Why?

> *Because of all of the conversations that we had that week after the murder. Every night, almost every night after the murder, Debbie and I were together. She would come over to visit. So I saw her every day between the murder and when she was arrested, or spoke to her on the phone. I kept having this uncomfortable feeling about a lot of the things that she was saying. Like, I thought that she wanted to tell me something. Unconsciously I thought, well, maybe she knows more about it than she's telling me.*

There is a modicum of tension and suspense in the way Catherine is speaking. The man with the cake trolley interrupts. There are no cookies. Would we like Black Forest cake? 'I'm a dietitian, you know,' cracks Catherine, but orders something sinful anyway and an eclair for me. There is now absurdity in our situation, as tea cups and silver tinkle and we fiddle with sweet cakes while Catherine gets to the point.

> *I kept having this feeling that she was trying to tell me something, but I wouldn't ask her directly because I thought that it might get her in trouble if she told somebody what she knew. That maybe in the course of the investigation, all the times that she'd been called down there, perhaps she had seen or heard something that revealed to her who had murdered Yvonne. And maybe she'd been directed not to tell anybody. So I wouldn't ask her.*

Catherine stops herself, collecting her thoughts, not wanting to get it wrong. At first after the murder she and her friends had thought it must have been one of the security guards. 'I couldn't imagine a woman committing this violent a crime. And I said this to Debbie. She seemed to take some comfort in the fact that I was so absolutely sure that a female couldn't commit this crime.'

The next night, Debbie had told Catherine the police thought a woman had committed the crime because a woman's hair was found in Yvonne's hand. 'Then she told me that it was a long dark hair, so perhaps a Filipina woman had done it. So I just kept insisting, "No, no, a woman couldn't do this." She said, "Well, I think a woman could do it."' Throughout this there is the clinking of knives and spoons as we cut our cakes and stir our tea. Catherine speaks very softly.

Catherine had told Debbie she couldn't believe a Western woman would commit such a crime. Debbie had said she agreed with the police. 'And so then I thought she maybe knows who did this, but I wouldn't ask her. She said, "I think whichever one of us did it, we just need to have our heads chopped and be done with it."'

Another incident which disturbed Catherine occurred when she was at home sculpting in her room.

> *The sculpting clay is sort of a reddish brown and I had spread a sheet out and I had the sculpture in the middle of the sheet and, putting water on it — you know, it was a mess. It was just this reddish-brown splash everywhere. And Debs had called and said she was coming over, so I left my door open.*

At that time, Catherine hadn't yet married and was living in the single-women's quarters in a building not far from Debbie's. In Islamic culture, it is considered blasphemous to make likenesses of the human form, so Catherine would rather not mention just what it was she was sculpting.

Debbie had walked into the room without knocking.

> *She was taken aback, she looked very startled, she sucked in her breath because it looked like blood. And it really, really upset her. So I sort of quickly folded all that up and put it in the corner. She came in and she looked at the sculpture and she said, 'Oh, aren't you clever?' And she really calmed down. So we started talking and then she showed me all of these claw-marks on her hand.*

Another scratch-mark witness. Let's hope Catherine has a clearer memory than Joe Robinson of these marks.

'She had on an *abaya* so I could only see up to a couple of inches above her wrist, but there were these crescent-shaped marks all over both her hands.' Catherine gestures with her own nails above her hand, making clear exactly what she thinks made those marks.

'She said, "Look what Purdy's done." Purdy was the cat that she had. She said, "I could just choke Purdy for doing this. Now I look guilty. Isn't this terrible?"' Catherine hadn't consciously thought about the strangeness of the scratch-marks at the time.

> *I completely repressed any evil thoughts. But later on in the conversation I said something about the fact that I had cut all my fingernails off so I could do the sculpting. And I didn't relate that to anything we were saying. I just remember that as being a rather strange non sequitur that just kind of came out of my mouth. And I remember she just looked down at me, like this, over her glasses and she went, 'Oh really?' She made the association, I believe. So, I very quickly moved on to another subject, but not really consciously being aware of what I had just said.*

Catherine had picked up that the marks were crescent-shaped, rather than cat-like. 'Yeah, obviously, in my mind I thought they were like fingernail marks.' Catherine gestures to show the marks were on the topside of Debbie's hands. Joe had mimed scratches on the underside of her wrists. Maybe that's why their accounts are different.

Debbie had told Catherine she'd been putting sterile wash from her ward on the scratches and that some of the redness had gone and the wounds were healing quickly.

> *She was very, very concerned about it. But, again, that wasn't unlike her to focus on something small like that and just go on and on about it. She seemed to me to be, you know, sort of obsessive-compulsive and often she would get on to some small detail of her life and go on about it.*

Catherine had been among the majority of staff who attended a large meeting on the Friday, the day after the murder, at which staff-members' hands had been inspected. Debbie, at work at the time, had missed the meeting.

> *She called me to find out what had gone on at the meeting. What was said, what was done. They actually let all the men go and they asked the women to file one-by-one through the back and there were a couple of policemen sitting there who asked us to show our arms and our necks.*

I tell Catherine about my earlier scepticism, the fear that a group of people, frightened, had convinced themselves of Debbie and Lucy's guilt simply because the two had been arrested. I tell her of my concern on meeting Rosemary Kidman that, should we broadcast her claims, we would be destroying what remained of the two women's reputations with assertions based on hearsay and conjecture. That I'd been very shocked by what Catherine had to say on the phone back then and that I was even more shocked now. 'Because obviously you were friends,' I say.

Catherine is crying. I've been talking away and suddenly realise this. I want to reach and grasp her arm. I feel I can't do this, in public, in Saudi and blunder apologies. Through tears, Catherine continues, talking about Debbie, someone she clearly still sees as a friend.

> *I really think Debbie is just like this innocent sort of person; has some sort of chemical imbalance or something and she just got over here and she was scared. Lots of times she was very scared. You know, I can't really figure out what happened between her and Yvonne, but she was so easily upset and everything was so frightening to her because, with that obsessive-compulsive nature of hers, when she got something on her mind she just simply couldn't let go of it. She couldn't sleep, she couldn't eat, she couldn't think of anything else. But I never saw her as someone cruel, or anything like that. And I just think that maybe a lot of bad things happened to her in her life. And that it just really weakened her and she just lost control on the night and did this terrible thing that's ruined her life and ended somebody else's life. And then how Lucy got involved is pretty much a mystery to me, but now her life is pretty much beyond repair and it's just a really sad thing.*

There's an announcement in Arabic over the public address system as this all comes in a rush. Catherine recovers. 'I can't ever get really mad at Debbie because I understand her too well.'

Before coming to Saudi, Catherine has spent 14 years working in Louisiana psychiatric hospitals. Hence, no doubt, her willingness to see what she's sure is Debbie's guilt as coming from pathology rather than criminal intent. My thinning veil of resistance draws around again as I wonder just how knowledgeable Catherine is about psychiatric illness, or whether this is an amateur's enthusiasm. We move back to the safer ground of her direct knowledge of Debbie's relationship with Yvonne.

'I knew that Debbie was mad at Yvonne.' The two women had come to know each other because Debbie worked on Yvonne's ward when she first arrived. They'd become friends, but had then fallen out.

> *Debbie at some point finally said, 'Yvonne really bothers me. She drives me crazy, she's so controlling. She controls the conversation and I just can't be around her any more.' You know, that sort of thing, which seemed perfectly reasonable to me.*

So, had Catherine witnessed Debbie's outburst on the Travelling Naturalists' trip to Al Uqayr?

> *I don't recall any specific outburst. I know that Debs and Yvonne were in the same car together. Later on, Debbie complained to me that she couldn't get a word in edgewise and Yvonne drove her crazy all day and she just hated her. That's what she said.*

After this, Debbie and Yvonne hadn't spent time together, for maybe six weeks leading up to the murder. 'And Debbie hadn't really discussed Yvonne during that time. She really didn't talk about her.'

So, any indication of a lesbian relationship?

> *I never saw any signs of that, but I'm not the most observant person. I often find out that people are gay and it's always a surprise to me. Also, because it doesn't matter to me, I'm not really looking for it.*

What about the claims of missing clumps in Debbie's hair?

I didn't really see that, but one night she was over and she said she had an appointment with the hairdresser the next day. I said, 'What? You just got your hair done last week.' She'd just had it cut and coloured the week before.

On that occasion, prior to the murder, Debbie had gone with Catherine to Ann Stevenson, the hairdresser at the British Aerospace compound. Now, after the murder, she was going back.

I questioned her about it. She sort of put her hand to the top of her head, to the front here, and she said, 'Yeah, but it's sticking up kind of strangely right here and I want her to fix it.' Well again, that's Debbie, because I know that every night she would examine her face, look at each wrinkle. She was very, very critical about her appearance and everything had to be just so. That was her personality. If she found one hair out of place, she would go back and have it fixed, you see. So I didn't really think that much of it.

What of the story that Debbie was ringing Casualty early on the Thursday morning, before everybody knew that Yvonne was dead? 'Around 9.30 or 10 am, Debs called down to the office where I was and said, "Have you heard? Yvonne's been murdered." Joe was with me.'

Did Joe seem to have a bit of a soft spot for Debbie? 'Very much so.' Other boyfriends? Jeremy and Paul Thomas.

Jeremy had driven Debbie to Al Uqayr, the day of the falling-out with Yvonne. Paul had driven her to Scrivener's Canyon, two weeks before the murder.

Were they dating? 'I think they would have. They were talking on the phone a lot.'

On the day of the Scrivener's Canyon trip, Debbie had accidentally been left behind. Because of the ostensible ban on single women travelling with men, arrangements for the Travelling Naturalists' forays were elaborate. Cars would assemble by the side of the road leading out to the King Fahd compound. The single women would have to catch taxis or rides with married couples to leave the compound and meet up with the group. Catherine laughs at the memory.

> *We had forgotten her. Getting out of the compound sometimes is such a scene, such a confusing scene, such a circus. We had gone, and I think she was late because she was bringing some food and couldn't get it all together. Paul volunteered to go back and pick her up.*

Due to the gender-mixing regulations, he couldn't drive into the compound to collect her but had to wait for her to catch a taxi to meet him outside.

'Then they turned up later at Scrivener's Canyon.' This place has mounds of boulders taller than human-height. Paul, who'd been in Saudi for years, knew a way through from the top, to meet up with the rest of the party. 'The rest of us had started at the bottom and worked up, so I didn't see her for some time.'

Was there any mention of Debbie having fallen and bruised her thigh? Not, says Catherine, until after the murder, when Debbie had tried to draw her into corroborating her alibi for the bruise on her thigh.

'She said, "You know, it's really awful, I've just discovered this huge bruise on my hip and thigh. It happened that day at Scrivener's Canyon, do you remember?" I said, "no" and then I said, "You're just now noticing it?"' Two weeks had elapsed since the canyon trip.

> *I just remember I registered that as a falsehood, because I couldn't imagine having a bruise that big, with somebody who's so particular and notices every little hair out of place, I couldn't imagine having a bruise that big and not seeing it.*

I mention that the Ashbee family are depending on Joe Robinson to corroborate Debbie's story about the bruise and that, to me, he's said he has no recollection of it and had never made the statement Jonathan Ashbee claimed he had, verifying Debbie's version.

'More tea?' asks Catherine, with the charm, though not the decay, of a Tennessee Williams character. 'I think Joe wants to remain neutral in his opinions. He liked Debbie and he would have liked to have dated her, but she wasn't interested in anyone in particular.'

Catherine offers to treat me as the bill arrives.

'Are you going to consult any psychologist or psychiatrist in your quest?' she asks, turning the conversation back to Debbie's state of mind.

> She told me that she'd been on Lithium before and that she'd been diagnosed as a manic-depressive. She said that had been a couple of years before she came here. And then she said that she went to another therapist who said, 'Nah, you're not manic-depressive' and told her she didn't have to take the Lithium. I don't know how much of that is true, but I can't imagine she would make up having been on Lithium before.

We turn to Debbie's previous experience in Saudi, when she'd worked at a hospital in Riyadh two years before. Catherine says that Debbie often threatened she was going to give up and go home, as she had done on her first Saudi stint. 'I'm just leaving, I'm going home,' Debbie would say, if the pay was late or one of her friends annoyed her.

> So I asked her, 'Have you ever made any rash decisions like this before and followed through on them?' And she said, well, yes, actually, she had. She'd been in Riyadh and she was almost at the end of her contract. I think she'd been there ten months, or something like that. And she got mad at some of the nurses on the unit and she said she was fed up and she just went home. But she said it was the wrong thing to do and she regretted it.

Was this anger with some of the nurses directed to the Filipinas in particular? 'Yes, she did say that.' Catherine laughs at this attitude Debbie had to the Filipina nurses.

> She felt that they would set her up sometimes, make it look like she had made mistakes in her nursing care. There was a drug interaction one time. She said they tried to set it up to look like she had done it. That was here. But she had this view of Filipinos before she came. Other people were a lot more aware of that than I was, because I think she knew that I wasn't comfortable with prejudice. Some of the other people told me later on that she was quite unpleasant towards them, just openly hostile sometimes.

I remind Catherine of our first conversation, back in June, when she had agreed there'd been some harassment from guards at the compound. 'Yeah. There was this one little guy, my son's age, who'd decided — well, they do this, you know — that they love you. They've never met you, you know, and, "Would you like to go for a ride in my car?", and things like this.' Catherine is laughing as she tells the story, an older woman amused by a young man's attentions.

> *When I first came here I didn't know how to handle this, so I would try to be nice and polite. I was so afraid of offending somebody and I didn't know what that would cause. So he started phoning me at six o'clock in the morning sometimes.*

How would a guard have her number? Once Catherine had locked herself out of her apartment. The guard had come to let her in. Under regulations, he had to call in to the security office to say he was leaving, to show he wasn't in the room for more than 30 seconds.

'They have to give the extension number they're calling from.' After that, armed with the number, the guard would often call.

> *He would ask me if I wanted him to pick up food for my cats, or did I want him to bring some doughnuts for breakfast. But the phone calls became quite annoying. Sometimes he would call late at night, that sort of thing. So I thought the best thing to do would be just to get out of his sight. I had an apartment at that time close to the guards' little shelter. So I moved to an apartment at the back of the compound, where I didn't have to walk by him to go to work.*

This was in Building 42, just across the carpark from where Yvonne lived but before Yvonne had arrived.

Had Catherine spent any time with Yvonne? 'She came on one of our Monday-night picnics with us one time. She cooked for us.' Was it one of Yvonne's famous cakes? No. 'Some sort of lamb dish, lamb lasagne.' Catherine laughs at the memory.

> *It was really good. We spent some time with her that night, and she went on the Al Uqayr trip with us. She worked on Male Specialty, which is my unit that I cover in the*

> hospital. I would just say hello to her. I had noticed that she was really upset, I guess about a week before the murder.

There is a lull in the high singing of the call to prayer, now replaced by a deep, reverential and amplified male voice: *'Allah U Akhbar.'* Catherine continues, not noticing a five-times-a-day ritual which has become routine to her. 'I remember I said to her, "Are you OK?" and she said, "I just can't talk about it right now, I can't talk about it." And she was on the verge of tears and she just sort of did this to me.' Catherine is holding up both hands, palms outwards. 'Yvonne gave no indication of what the trouble was.' Catherine felt Yvonne hadn't wanted to confide in her because Catherine was a friend of Debbie.

Did anybody else seem to know what was wrong?

> *I mentioned it to Debbie and she said, 'Oh, Yvonne doesn't like being in charge.' Every night there's one nurse who's what they call the Charge Nurse and she's responsible for seeing that all the charting gets done and all the procedures go smoothly.*

Is that what really troubled Yvonne? Who knows?

I mention the Australian consul's assertion that people who came to work in Saudi must have some reason other than the money for being there. 'A lot of people think that,' Catherine acknowledges, but she maintains the money is good when you don't have to pay taxes and have no overheads like rent and utilities. 'It's quite nice,' she says. 'I think people who come here, maybe some come just for the money, maybe some people are trying to get away from something personal, or it may be professional problems. Maybe they have problems getting jobs in other places. Sometimes I think that,' she laughs, 'about some of the management people.'

> *A lot of people come here just for the adventure and experience, but many times — I'm speaking as somebody who's worked in psychiatric hospitals for about 12 years, OK — people who like adventures sometimes, like, can have sociopathic tendencies. That's a feature of the sociopath, they say. Because they have no feelings, they have no ties to anything, so they're constantly off and they*

don't feel any pain when they leave something behind. I've met a lot of people here who are in a lot of debt and so maybe we have a lot of impulsive people.

Sweeping statements from someone whose own motivation for coming to work in Saudi seems to be adventure. She'd wanted to live somewhere exotic for years but had waited until her son grew up.

Was it strange that Lucy was seen washing in the very early hours of the morning? 'No. Hospitals run 24 hours a day. People are working day shift or night shift.'

But Lucy wasn't working nights. She'd been at Yvonne's flat, by her own acknowledgment, earlier in the evening, before the murder.

If she were working days, that would be an odd time to be up. But the first day when you shift from day to night you're still on your previous schedule. But they usually get two or three days to make that adjustment.

Inconclusive.

As someone who'd seen a lot of Debbie, had Catherine seen much of Lucy and Debbie together?

I never saw those two together. Debbie would tell me, 'Oh, I've gotten to know this lovely girl, Lucy, do you know her?' She also worked on the Male Specialty Ward, so of course I've seen her, but I've never talked to her. Debbie would say, 'What do you think of her?' I said, 'I don't know her.' Debs seemed to like her quite well. They had become friends a few weeks before the murder, closer friends. A lot of people have said, 'How did those two ever find each other?' But Debbie was really vulnerable and if that stuff about Lucy was true, if she were being investigated for using the credit card of dying patients or dead patients, then this would be a repeat of a familiar thing to her. And also she may have seen in Debbie an opportunity, someone who could be manipulated. And, you know, these people here, the Saudis, are very sensitive to that sort of thing, so a lot of people say, 'Gee, Debbie's been given clemency and she may be going home when she's the one who actually did the stabbing.' But, if you ask

> me, I think the punishment is appropriate. These people here [the Saudis] would see what Debbie did and they would abhor it, of course, but they would understand losing one's temper. But someone who would stand there and watch it and then take advantage of it, they wouldn't understand.

Catherine was among those at the hospital who initially thought the murder was committed by someone in the security staff. The security on shift the night of the murder have been dealt with severely since.

> That security guard, Mohammed, the one who bugged me, he was gone. They fired him because they heard his name too many times. I also heard, when I was questioned later on, that the ones who were on duty close to Yvonne's apartment, they beat them; tied their hands up above their heads and beat them. When I was questioned, he [the police officer, a Major Abdulrahman] told me, 'Do you know that something you said caused us to strongly suspect the guards?' What I had told Debbie, and she went back and told the police, was that Lars Larssen — he's a friend of ours — had seen a guard. He'd watched Yvonne go home, and when she went around the corner of her building the guard had left his post and walked down the back of the building. Because I had told Debbie that, she told the police and the police got Lars in the next day to hear the story from him. He [the officer] told me, 'Because you said this, we strongly suspected the guards and they were harshly dealt with.'

This piece of scuttlebutt, though it had serious consequences for the guards unlucky enough to be working the night of the murder, proved less reliable when I checked it out later. Apparently, Lars had remembered the incident from another night, weeks before, not the night of the murder.

Catherine explained the initial fear of the guards following the murder:

> Many of the girls complained about them peeping in, and Yvonne was on the ground floor but I doubt if she had her

> *curtains open. Another thing, too, is the guards don't have a restroom and they often walk that way to go to the bathroom [that is, in the bushes].*

Given her own knowledge of the mistreatment of the guards by the police, does Catherine not give credence to the accused women's claims of having been harassed by the investigators? 'They may have been. They may have been forced into a confession, but it doesn't mean they didn't do it.'

'I'm glad you said that,' I say to Catherine, 'because now *I* won't have to say it.' Catherine laughs for a moment, but it fades as she adds: 'It doesn't make them any less guilty if the confession was beaten out of them. If they did it, they did it.'

So, what did it for Catherine? What finally convinced her they did do it? 'It was probably the use of the ATM card.' That allegation, though, remains unproved in a Western sense. It's a police claim, untested by cross-examination or the tendering of supporting physical evidence in an open court. Catherine reflects that she made up her mind immediately after the women were arrested.

> *As soon as I was told that Debbie had confessed, I believed it. Because all of the things I hadn't let myself think about, these things that she was saying to me, everything that that meant; suddenly I could think about it. The fingernail thing, the sculpting thing, the 'We should have our heads chopped off' — all of it. Also, one night, as she was leaving, right at the door, she told me, 'You know, Catherine, you should be more careful who you let into your apartment.' And I said, 'Well, there's no one here but you and me.' And she said, 'Yeah, I know, but somebody could plant some evidence on you.' So, I just said, 'Debbie!'*

Chilling, if in fact Debbie was — is — guilty.

Listening back to our interview, I can hear the reserve drop in my own voice, the scepticism. Whether it's Catherine's quiet, even tone or her responsible demeanour, it's very difficult to believe this woman in white isn't wearing a white hat. At that moment, in that conversation, I believe her. Her friend is guilty. Yet, even at that moment, I'm worrying, thinking forward to the next meeting with Debbie's family. How can I say this to them?

I mention Debbie's preoccupation with Karolyne Palowska, as an alternative suspect. The woman who had spent most time with Yvonne in the weeks just prior to the murder. 'Oh,' says Catherine, 'I wondered why Debs wanted so badly to get in touch with her. That's too bad.'

Though the conversation is compelling, I'm glancing at my watch. There's just time to get in one more interview — with someone close to the nursing supervisors — before a rush to the airport and before my visa expires. This is investigation on the run. But Catherine is not quite finished. Our chat turns to the nursing supervisors and their role after the murder.

'Debbie would tell me that Deslyn Marks [one of the two supervisors under the nursing director] was keeping very close tabs on her. One night we went to a meeting and Debbie went with us.' This was the Travelling Naturalists' Jerusalem lecture, after which Debbie had gone to dinner with Joe Robinson.

> *When she got back, she called me and said Deslyn had just chewed her out for leaving the compound without telling her. I remember I was very defensive and I said, 'Well, tell her to give you a bloody bleeper if she wants to know where you are all the time.' I was very protective of her. Joe and Charles both believe that we were followed by the police that night. Because on the way back, Debs went out to dinner with Joe, so Charles, who she'd ridden there with, had another female ride back with him. So they must have thought that was Debbie. They followed Charles on the bumper all the way back.*

This close police scrutiny of the Westerners' activities must have raised a few official eyebrows. Even travelling in men's cars was against the expats' regulations. Catherine laughs at this thought, too. And she laughs at what must be the Saudis' reaction to the marriage of Grant Ferrie and Lucy, two days before my talk with Catherine.

> *Just when the Saudis thought they'd seen everything, some Scot crosses the ocean and marries a murderer. Not long after Debbie and Lucy had been arrested, Rosemary and Caroline Ionescu and I tried to go see them in the gaol. The police were just astounded. They said, 'Why you care?*

> *These are cold-blooded murderers. Why you care? Forget them.' You know, they're very cut-and-dried and practical people.*

'Will you [forget them]?' I ask. 'Oh, never,' responds Catherine, without pause. 'If Debbie wanted to see me, I would go visit her. But my feeling is that she doesn't want to see me. I did write her a letter, and I did tell her I thought that she did it.'

Had she written it as clearly as that? 'Yeah. I told her, we think the worst, but we still care about you. Well, I couldn't deceive her and I couldn't deceive her family.' Catherine is now crying. 'I don't think it's good if she has to live with this without getting help.'

I mention that there is an Egyptian psychiatrist seeing Debbie in the gaol. The tears turn to a soft laugh.

> *I imagine he does provide some comfort and some support for her, but if she's telling him that she didn't do it, it's not doing her any good. I think she needs to deal with the fact that she did it. Otherwise, I think it's going to destroy her. Everybody who has to participate in this lie. Can you imagine the energy? It takes a lot of energy to support a total fabrication.*
>
> *The last time she was over at my apartment before she was arrested, which would make it two days before, as she was leaving, she told me: 'I want you to prepare yourself for the worst, Catherine, because I think you're gonna be very, very shocked.' And I think she was concerned.*

'About you?' I ask. Catherine nods as she continues crying, softly.

> *It's just hard, you know. I look back on it and she had this nervous eye and that week it never stopped jumping. I mean, you know, it was just constantly going. I know she must have been frightened out of her mind. I think, sick with guilt.*
>
> *She's got to stay under someone's care. She's got to be properly medicated. I hope nobody's expecting her to just go back to England and have a few weeks off and then go back to work in one of these jobs that's been offered to her.*

These are not the words of a disinterested party. They are genuine words of friendship. That's what I carry with me from this meeting, along with a jumble of bags, notebooks and a tape-recorder, as we now both rush for taxis. I want to hug this woman I've just met, to comfort her, as we part. But this is Saudi Arabia — unrelated men and women don't do that, not in public. I promise to keep in touch as Catherine takes the first cab, then the lady in a white taxi is gone.

It's been raining and my driver dodges puddles as he heads for a nearby villa in Al Khobar. He's had a quiet night and happily agrees to collect me in an hour for the trip to the airport.

In yet another compound are the neat, white villas of expatriates. Anonymous and bland as any American condominium. At the address I've been given, I step inside to a warm, Irish welcome. There's Christmas cake on the table, coffee; I can have Irish whiskey if I want it. These are friends of the woman I've come to meet. She, in turn, is a friend of the nursing supervisor, Deslyn Marks. Deslyn herself, a vivacious, shortish West Indian from London, has refused to be interviewed. The woman I'm meeting, Deslyn's friend, doesn't want to be identified.

She confirms the descriptions others have given of the morning of Yvonne's death. She remembers Deslyn calling Karolyne Palowska. Karolyne had been surprised Yvonne was late for work. She and Yvonne had arranged to have lunch. Deslyn had told Karolyne to get over to Yvonne's flat to check on her. The friend does a good version of Deslyn's West Indian Londonese: 'Come back lickety-split' — without the Ts — had been Deslyn's words to Karolyne.

Deslyn had spoken to a manager who confirmed that Yvonne had been with Lucy McLauchlan the night before. So Deslyn spoke to Lucy, who confirmed she'd seen Yvonne between 9.30 and 10 pm. Lucy had said she'd held a spare key for Yvonne and had gone around to the flat when Yvonne locked herself out that night. Yvonne had shown Lucy the food she was preparing for her birthday dinner two nights later, as well as videos she'd rented for the occasion.

On the morning of Yvonne's failure to arrive at work Deslyn had told Lucy to wait while she and others went to Yvonne's room, but Lucy had arrived there before her. An ambulance and security jeeps were gathered outside Yvonne's block. It was now about 8 am. When Deslyn and her friend went inside, the corridor was very clean, except for a cigarette butt outside Yvonne's door. They had with them sanitary gloves and resuscitation gear. The Military

Police major had gone in with the hospital security boss. The nurses were kept out. The security police immediately asked for a doctor. 'The look on his face was of shock, mixed with disgust — everything.'

Lucy had said, 'Is she dead, Deslyn? Did somebody murder her?' The police hadn't said anything about murder.

Deslyn's friend described Lucy that morning as very uptight, smoking a lot. Although her friend had just died, Lucy didn't break down.

The friend describes Deslyn as a woman who believes she has 'senses beyond normal people'. Deslyn had warned Caroline Ionescu to take care when she was spending time with Debbie and Lucy in the week after the murder. Deslyn had actually said to Caroline, 'We don't know who did it. You could be in the company of killers. Even our own friends.' When Caroline had repeated this to Lucy and Debbie, Lucy had vomited immediately. [According to Caroline Ionescu, who was there at the time, Lucy's reaction was actually to feel sick and have an attack of diarrhoea. Many of the facts surrounding the events before and after the murder have been distorted by the rumour mill of the hospital. Hence Deslyn's friend recounts this story as Lucy having vomited in front of Caroline.]

Deslyn's friend discounted the security men as alternative suspects. 'Whoever killed her must have felt very comfortable being there. I thought it had to be somebody who knew her.'

Deslyn and her friend had been to the police station with Lucy soon after the murder. She described the investigator, Major Hamed, as 'very professional, astute, clever'.

That night, Lucy had phoned Deslyn to say, 'You know, Debbie and Yvonne weren't getting on.' Deslyn had later felt Lucy was using her as a pawn, through whom she could cast suspicion on Debbie. Lucy had described a conversation with Yvonne two weeks before, in which Yvonne had said Debbie was 'a nutter' and that was why she didn't want to remain friends with her. Deslyn's friend mimics Lucy's accent. Lucy had said, "You know what I mean by 'nu'er', Deslyn? It means she's crazy."

In his dossier of suspicions about other staff and so-called evidence of Debbie's innocence, Jonathan Ashbee had suggested that Deslyn Marks was in cahoots with the police, helping them to keep an eye on Lucy and Debbie. But Deslyn's friend says the nursing supervisor wasn't told of their arrest. She had been mothering Lucy and Debbie, with Lucy telling her every time she went anywhere.

On the morning of the arrests, Deslyn had gone to town with her friend. Deslyn had got 'one of her feelings' and wanted to return to the hospital to see if anything was happening. When they'd arrived, the news was out that the women had been arrested, that 'one of them was already singing and blaming the other'.

The taxi driver disturbs us before this conversation is done, but I have to rush to the last flight before my visa expires. As I wait blearily with the rest of the motley crowd in the airport, the contradictions of the Arabic world pass by. A drunken but wealthy-looking Saudi businessman tries to befriend me, talking about Australia and his friends there. Hordes of Filipinos line up, ant-like, for the Philippine Airlines flight home. The air in Dhahran airport is close with many bodies. It's a relief to climb on to the flight for London, though I'm leaving with many questions unanswered. Maybe there'll be answers in the hometowns of the two British women sleeping tonight in the Dammam gaol.

Chapter 33

Dundee

I drive through the Edinburgh rush hour, across the Clyde Bridge and on down the freeway to the town by the Tay. Dundee. A beautiful old industrial town, this, with even some hope springing through the tarred footpath cracks of unemployment and 1990s' despair. Now there are the technology parks, the expanding universities and the blue, futuristic Wellcome research establishment. Progress, though not many jobs for the old Tayside workforce of 'jam, jute and journalism'. These were the mainstays of industrial-era Dundee. Processing the fruit and textiles from elsewhere in the British Commonwealth, with a hearty local dash of print scandal to leaven the grey winters. The old certainties are gone now. A strong union man, Stan McLauchlan has lost his job as an industrial engineer. Union sympathies don't fit well with the new post-Thatcherite ways of contracts and enterprise negotiation. The journalism's still going strong, with the scandalous rumours from Michael Hutchence's death screaming from newsagent and cornershop doorways. Strangely, though, the local press, the *Dundee Courier* and Glasgow's *Daily Record*, have mostly left Lucy alone. The coverage here, of Lucy McLauchlan's plight, has been friendly, mostly. There's mention, sure, of the allegations of card-lifting at the hospice. But these papers have gone along with the British media outrage that two of Britain's own could be subject to the Dark Ages' justice of the hated Arab. Their latest is sympathetically sentimental stuff about Lucy's marriage to Grant Ferrie, tyre-fitter. Lucy's brother John gave her away in a 20-minute ceremony before the Saudi judge, they report, and Lawson Ross, the consul, brought along a cake from the British Trade Office.

The *Courier* waxes on about Lucy and Grant's 'Arabian Night of Love', rushing to print before the reality: in fact, the Saudis kyboshed the couple's 'contact visit' because of their annoyance over international publicity surrounding the nuptials. The closest Lucy and Grant have been to such a romantic notion would be picking up a post-pub bite from the curry, kebab and pizza stop in Dundee's Hilltown called, quaintly, Arabian Nights.

After checking into a three-storey Victorian hotel, the manager offers me 'the room at the top' to overlook the Tay but I'm blind in the early dark and have to take the river on promise. From the room I phone Grant Ferrie and Ann McLauchlan. Recorded messages, as usual. 'Sorry, I'm out just now,' says Grant in his very Scots Scots. Something's afoot. Nobody answering. Not the warm welcome Ann promised me before I left Australia. Getting out my much-practised weary sigh, I head out for the Dundee pubs to check out the local 'crack'. In a pub by the art school it's cheery and loud, though this wouldn't be Lucy's scene. But these streets are where Lucy lived and laughed, like the others sharing a laugh and a drink. The words in her letters come to life, as you hear the accents of other young Dundee women roundabout, cocky, defiant: 'I will have the last say in this matter be assured of that. Not to those gits at the *Daily Record* I might add. I found out about one article — total bollocks.'

Up the road is Speedwells, all fine old ales and spirits. Old Vatted Demerara is the favoured local drop, a black rum. You could see Lucy's dad, Stan, in this one. Not tonight. Where are they, these McLauchlans? I step up to their red door on Blackness Road. No answer from the battered intercom. One of six or so in a three-storey stone block of flats. 'A dump,' Ann had called it. But close to the heart of things. It's hard not to warm to these streets, even in their cold and darkness. There are people about. The school across the road is lit up in its fine Georgian form as late students file out. But where are the people of Lucy's life? Two middle-aged women throw hearty smiles and flirt as we arrive at a small Italian restaurant together. Seems a friendly town, though I feel shut out from those I know here.

Through the evening I call occasionally, pouring 20-pence coins into the slots of pay phones. Recorded voices. Despairing, I climb the hotel stairs to bed and a bit of John Grisham. His fictional journalist, 'Mole' Moeller, seems to have no trouble getting people to talk. The reality's not so easy, as my phone records from various hotels would testify.

Morning and it's true. There's a beautiful river where last night there was only blackness. The Tay, over there from my window, is a grand sheet of silver and grey, the iron necklace of the Tay Bridge girding it with grace. There is sun, glinting on the morning water, and breakfast downstairs is warming and plentiful. The hotelier is keen for a chat.

Armed with this friendly woman's admonitions, I step out to explore Lucy's former haunts. Kings Cross and Ninewells hospitals, Dundee's pride thanks to the NHS Trust. I slip into the Nursing College library to look for old records or photos of Lucy. Dozens of chirpy young women, a few men, hang around the corridors, waiting for the next class. The assistant director, smiling, does the polite fob-off. They don't have any annual journal, and anyway the trust wouldn't really want them to cooperate. The PR woman from the trust isn't much more help. The chairman and CEO are away; in any case, the hospitals' official response is 'No comment'. The card-theft allegations have been referred to the Procurator Fiscal. The Tayside Police say the investigation of the allegations is still current, able to be reactivated should Lucy be released from Saudi. The kids filing in and out of the schools are as rosy-cheeked as she must have been at that age. Still is, for that matter. Or was, before her incarceration.

She, like all Dundonians, was born and bred under the Law. Not the law of Britain, nor of Scotland, but the Dundee Law, the remains of a volcano, stretching above the Tay, they say, like Pompeii over the Bay of Naples. But Tay and Law need no comparisons. Generations have climbed the Law, site of prehistoric, Roman, Pict and Scots forts, to look across to where the river reaches out from the Dundee port to the Firth and the sea beyond. From here, you can almost see the hopes and sense the aspirations of all the young Dundonians who have stood up here and looked out towards their futures. It's not hard to imagine Lucy and Grant up here, walking, bringing their kids up here one day. The monument remembers the Great War boys who looked out from this height and then went off to meet their fate. Why did Lucy go? Was she merely going off to save for her future with Grant, or was she fleeing?

I call Freda Garty, Lucy's best friend at the Kings Cross Hospital, scene of Lucy's alleged credit-card crime. Freda says she'd be happy to give me the human background of the woman in the headlines. But when I ring to arrange a time to meet on Freda's day off, everything has changed. She's spoken to Grant, who has told all friends and family to keep their mouths shut.

Others at the hospitals and the NHS Trust have been silenced by their employer, though Lucy clearly holds grudges against some: 'Can you believe I got letters from Jessie and Wilma the two faced cows,' she wrote to Freda from gaol. 'I felt like writing back and saying fuck off but since my face is splashed all over the bloody place just now I thought I had better not.'

The NHS Trust now wants nothing to do with its former staffer. Lucy wrote to Freda of this with great bitterness: 'I can't believe those tossers at the trust Freda. Be careful. They are a bunch of bastards. I know. Don't worry though, when I come home a lot of people will want my story if you know what I mean.' One woman, writes Lucy, 'will wish she had never ever heard the name Lucy McLauchlan. There is nothing she can do to me so if it makes you feel any better she will get whats [sic] coming to her.'

On the phone in Dundee, Freda says of her younger friend, 'She is very much a fighter. The past year speaks for itself.' Freda says that in her latest fax, Lucy is still on a high 'with the marriage'.

If Freda's friend is guilty, Freda has had the wool pulled over her eyes. She has no doubts about Lucy, who writes to her, 'You're like a second mum to me. I hope you know that. I just wanted to tell you.'

I head back down to the pubs of Lucy's neighbourhood, this time to a corner place across the road from the McLauchlans'. With a dozen pound coins I ring Salah in Riyadh. He's written to the governor of the Eastern Province on my behalf. He won't hear back until after Sunday. If ever, I think to myself. He sends his regards to Ann McLauchlan. Among all the family members, he likes her. Stan has yelled at him; the Ashbees quibble about his antics. Ann is the easiest to get on with. She's been to his Riyadh villa, a long way — in style and resources, as well as distance — from the flat I can see over the road. The soccer on the telly above the phone makes it hard to hear, but the thrust of what Ann's saying, when I get through at last, is clear enough. She has to check with Grant, she says, before she sees me. 'He's the main man now,' she says of her new son-in-law. I suggest that since the marriage, Stan and Ann have been sidelined. Ann is more polite about it. 'We're not pushed into the background, but he's at the centre.' Call back in an hour. She's been saying that for three days, since I arrived in Britain. Of course she's not there when I call back. I leave this place, with regret, and head back to Edinburgh with a pub hamburger and not much else under my belt. Dwindling finances dictate it's time to get down to see the

Ashbees and then fly home. If Lucy and Grant have drawn the shutters, that's up to them.

The tone of her letters to her friend Freda suggests that Lucy can look after herself. 'I have learnt [sic] the girls a song, "If you hate Saudi Arabia clap your hands." Childish eh? Makes me feel a wee bit better though. The song is always met with thunderous applause. I wonder why?'

As I drive into the dark on the motorway to Edinburgh I wonder about Lucy's future here. A woman cloaked in the veil of her denials and her Saudi conviction — not an easy prospect in the close-knit Dundee community. I'm sure she'll be back soon, armed with her publishing deal. In one of her letters she has told a friend she will give up nursing. 'I'm going to be a young trendy housewife when I get home — sounds good eh?'

Chapter 34

Pride and prejudice

From Heathrow to Alton doesn't take long, though on a dark night, with no one to navigate in the rented car, it's easy to miss motorway turn-offs. A couple of missed turns and I'm down the A3 and the A31 to Jane Austen country. She lived here near Alton for a time and the signposts in the dark point to her former home. On the car radio, pop singers are saying what an honour it will be to play in the Christmas tribute to Princess Diana. They sound pathetically grateful for the recognition. Breathless earnestness. Like a Jane Austen heroine. Deborah Parry would indeed be at home here, herself the product, like so many modern English girls, of that melange of romantic novels and the public sentiment of the Diana press.

Much less reminiscent of old England is the Travelodge at Four Marks, a soulless convenience stop for business travellers. Booking from Edinburgh, it was a place on the map which could be found in the dark. I dive into John Grisham for distraction, his modern heroine disparaging journalists for their thoughtlessly prying ways. The sleep of exhaustion is welcome.

Morning, and what *is* revoltingly English is the excuse for a croissant they serve up in the bacon-smelling Little Chef attached to the hotel. The little cerise rented car is dusted in frost and has to be scraped with the key ring. The crystals on the windscreen are lovely in a surprisingly bright morning sun as I drive the few miles to Alton.

The woman in the tourist information shop in downtown Alton is as crisp and bright as the morning, with directions and local lore. This was always a brewing town and the Bass brewery is still pouring out Carling Dark. I promise to have one later, in honour.

She draws arrows in Day-Glo green on the photocopied map and sends me easily towards the Ashbees' home. Near the brewery and their corner is Sainsbury's. I skate on the frosted carpark, nipping in for some shortbread to take around for morning tea. The Christmas buzz in the supermarket is all so normal. This is where Debbie did her shopping, before she ran off to Saudi. It should be *her* queuing amid the muzak of 'Hark the Herald Angels Sing' and a medley of the last 10 years of Britpop Christmas songs.

I'm nervous as I pull up outside the Ashbees' two-storey home. After the brick walls of Dundee, I'm depending on Sandra and Jon's continued goodwill to continue my access to Debbie's side of the story. But as Jon answers the doorbell, it's instantly clear that nothing has changed. His greeting is warm and friendly as ever, and Sandra, in the kitchen, gives me a kiss on the cheek. It's also obvious, on stepping inside, that this is a home of children. A room by the hall, the boys' room I'm told, is full of toys. There are children's drawings on the walls in there and in the kitchen. Photos of Debbie, smiling, with the kids. The children are off at school and kindy, which is why we've agreed on this time to talk. Jonathan, local bank manager, is home on two months' leave to recover from the fatigue of the long battle to save Debbie.

Sandra is distracted, a bit tense. She's been crying through the night. I enthuse about the latest news in Saudi, Salah's discussions with the judge suggesting that all will be well. Sandra isn't so sure. She pulls out a fax they've received overnight. It's a letter from Salah's office to Michael Burnett, the lawyer in Adelaide. One line suggests there may be some doubt over the waiver of Debbie's death penalty, given the continuing dispute over the settlement money. I try to reassure Sandra that these are simply lawyers' machinations, that Debbie is safe. She isn't convinced, having lived through too many shocks and disappointments in the past eleven months. She makes tea, and Jon and I settle in the loungeroom, a large space, tidy but with scattered reminders of the resident kids.

Light streams in through French doors from the garden. It's cheery in here, away from the frost. Jon, ever positive, agrees happily to me switching on the tape. He says Debbie will write her own account, once she's released, as a way of funding expensive counselling. A post-trauma expert who has counselled hostages released after many months from kidnapping in Beirut has agreed to work with her. Jon speculates on the gaol time Debbie faces. Two to four years is the guess.

Perhaps it's shamelessly self-seeking, but I go back over my efforts on Debbie's behalf during the long wait for Frank Gilford's decision. We discuss Frank's reluctance to go to Saudi and see for himself. Simple fear, I suggest. Jon chuckles as he points out the parallel fear of Mutlaq, one of the Saudi lawyers. When it seemed that a settlement with Frank was in the offing, it was suggested Mutlaq should go to Australia to help seal the deal. He kept making excuses until eventually he revealed that his mother wouldn't allow him to go to that strange land. A place which nurtured a man such as Frank Gilford, a man who would seek to use the penalties belonging to a culture not his own, must be a fearsome, uncivilised place.

We discover other parallels with Frank's experience. Like the phalanxes of media at the door. On the day of Princess Diana's death, the British press were turning up here in Alton, claiming the Saudis would use the distraction of the Diana story to go ahead with Debbie's death penalty. Jon and Sandra arrived home from Sainsbury's with the shopping in the car, only to meet the reporters and photographers in the drive. Sandra nearly fainted at their suggestion that Debbie would be killed within 48 hours. Jon, ever-phlegmatic, tried to maintain his outward calm. 'What will you do now?' one reporter asked him. 'Get the shopping out of the car,' Jon had replied.

I mention that I've seen Catherine Wall and that she has written to Debbie, saying she believes in her guilt. Jon and Sandra hadn't known this and worry about the impact on Deb. They're perplexed by the actions of Debbie's friends, like Rosemary Kidman, in turning against her. 'Rosemary was a great supporter of Debbie's,' says Jon, who had met her on his first visit to Saudi in January. He'd also met Joe Robinson, Catherine Wall and Caroline Ionescu.

> *They all spoke favourably, except for Catherine Wall. Catherine was the one who talked about the hair, talked about Deb in the desert, acting strangely after the murder. The other three were 100 per cent in favour of the girls. Caroline Ionescu, the express purpose of her coming down to the [British] Trade Office, was to put down in writing the truth. She said to us that the Saudis had been putting her under extreme pressure, flicking her eyes and all this sort of stuff.*

This was during Caroline's 12-hour interrogation on the day Debbie and Lucy were arrested. 'And she felt that she was going to break, so she wanted to tell the truth to somebody before she was forced to say something else.'

After we broadcast Rosemary Kidman's claims, Caroline Ionescu gave a press interview claiming she hadn't been harassed during her time with the police in the Al Khobar police station. Her earlier account to Michael Dark in the British Trade Office was clearly at odds with what she was now claiming, 10 or so months down the track. No wonder Jon was nonplussed.

'It appears to be a complete turnaround from Caroline,' he says. 'They must have been subjected to such a degree of gossip in the hospital, it's actually convinced them.'

Joe Robinson had always been distressed by the gossip among his colleagues. Jon seemed to respect Catherine Wall, that despite her views she was genuinely concerned for Debbie. 'Precisely. She was the one who was saying, "I'm sorry I've got to say this but I must say it", when she told us about the hair and all this sort of thing.'

During Jon's January meetings with the four hospital staff, Debbie's uncle, Terrie Knight, a solicitor from Alton, had taken notes. They seem to reflect an over-rosy version of Catherine's comments: 'Catherine Wall seemed to think Debbie innocent but felt the hair and scratches might implicate her ... Debbie's anxiety might lead her to pull her own hair ... did not discount the cat had done the scratches.'

When I'd spoken to Catherine in Al Khobar, her recollection of the meeting with Jon Ashbee and Terrie Knight was very much at odds with Terrie's notes. According to Catherine, Terrie had said, 'I must say you've caused me to have some doubts.'

Perhaps Catherine had been at pains to protect their feelings. Perhaps Jon and Terrie had subsequently slipped into believing what they wanted to believe. Whatever the case, Jon had now built up a sturdy resistance in his own mind to any thought that Catherine may be right in her belief in Debbie's guilt.

Today, in the winter sun in Alton, Jon is able to laugh. 'You take what we heard in January and everybody's changed sides,' he says. Rosemary had volunteered to collect together and list all of Debbie's things. 'She was extremely concerned; she was 100 per cent in support of Deb. She didn't say any of the things that she said in your program.'

Jon is still firmly of the belief that Catherine and Rosemary's claims are 'flawed and we can prove they're flawed'. He points to Rosemary's stumbling over the confessions' assertions of lesbianism. 'She said something like, "I don't know why they put that in there,"' Jon splutters. 'Who put it in there?' Jon relies on this logical inconsistency on the part of those who maintain the guilt of the accused women. He overlooks his own flawed syllogism, which goes along the lines: The confessions say they're lesbians. They're not lesbians. Therefore, they didn't murder Yvonne. To Jon this is one plus one equals two. He chooses to banish from his mind the possibility that even if the Saudi police forced the inclusion of lesbianism in the confessions, that didn't make the whole of the confessions false. And as Catherine Wall pointed out back in Saudi, even if the two were physically and verbally threatened into making the confessions, that didn't necessarily mean they were innocent. Yet Jon talks of a 60:40 balance in favour of Debbie and her claims of innocence. Just back from Saudi, he's flush with new facts to add to his dossier. He and Debbie have been collecting documented evidence of what she bought in the week after the murder, to try to discount her association with the use of Yvonne's ATM card. 'In the confessions, Deb was forced to write about things she'd bought with her share of the proceeds,' he says.

> With every item we have proof that it was purchased before the first withdrawal from the bank account. She mentioned a watch, for instance, and we have a receipt showing she bought the watch on the first of December. She mentions a duvet set. She actually bought that duvet set with Joe before the murder took place. She mentions a necklace which we actually gave her as a present before she went to Riyadh in 1993. Deb was actually being clever when she put that in to tell us that she'd been forced to tell lies. So we've got cast-iron proof of something like that.

Of course, the first rule of good lying is to mix truth with the untruth.

'You've got the logical progression,' says Jon, quoting Rosemary Kidman's account of sharing a chat with Debbie on the night before the murder.

> Coming home from work, whacked out, sharing a cup of coffee with Rosemary; coming back to read the letter and Deb's already in her nightgown. That seems to be

> *somewhere between nine and ten o'clock in the evening. Yvonne's apartment was in a separate block. There's no way anybody would wander across that compound in anything but full attire. We're asked to believe she gets dressed, she goes round to Yvonne's, she has enough time to have a steaming row, Yvonne calls Lucy down. The time of the murder's a bit sketchy but I think it's around four o'clock in the morning. They're then able to conclusively clean the place up so there's no forensic evidence whatsoever. One imagines there'd be a huge forensic footprint, but these two amateur girls were able to totally clean the place up, except a fingerprint on the door. She cleans it all up, she washes her clothes, she goes back with Lucy to Lucy's flat for a cup of tea and a chat about it; then she goes back to her apartment, showers, gets changed and she's at work at seven o'clock.*

Jon is peppering this account with derisive laughs. 'She's only murdered Yvonne at four o'clock in the morning, so it's three hours.'

We turn to the allegedly missing clumps of hair on Debbie's head. Sandra pipes up and laughs that it would be nothing unusual for Debbie to want to change her hair even the day after a haircut. Jon says that when he went to see Debbie at the police cells in January he went over her hair 'with a fine-tooth comb, as it were' and found nothing unusual. Still, Jon arrived in Saudi on January 13, a month after the murder. Time enough for whatever hair trouble there'd been to have abated.

We bemoan the lack of conclusive scientific evidence from the Saudis. Jon's knowledge of what they have is sketchy. Both Lucy and Debbie had to provide samples of their own hair, including pubic hair. This suggests some attempt on the part of the Saudi police to match samples they've collected in Yvonne's room. The official medical report has mentioned a medium-length, light-brown hair in Yvonne's hand. Neither Lucy's nor Debbie's hair (in any of its incarnations) would match. Jon says the Saudis eventually suggested that the hair in Yvonne's dead hand may have been her own. Why all the frustrating maybes in an affluent country, well-equipped with sophisticated medical science?

We discuss the widely noted animosity between Yvonne and Debbie before the murder. Sandra remembers Debbie saying of

Yvonne, even before the murder, 'She's older than me but I can't keep up with her.' Yvonne had always been suggesting places to go: to town, the beach. 'I just haven't got the energy,' Debbie had said. Yvonne would get cross. Sandra mimicked Debbie mimicking Yvonne's voice, stern: 'Come on,' she'd insist.

I wondered how to introduce the question of Debbie's flightiness and alleged mental instability. Sandra and Jon talked freely of Debbie's previous visit to Saudi in 1993. Debbie had been nursing at a Riyadh hospital but hated it. She'd left a month before her year's contract was up. 'Every day or every other day she'd be sobbing on the phone,' says Sandra. 'So I'd say, "Come home." She'd say, "I can't afford it." I said, "I'll send you the money."'

So Sandra had been worried when Debbie went off again to Saudi in 1996. 'Oddly enough, she was really enjoying it. She'd got in with a nice crowd — or so she thought. She was really enjoying the desert trips. She still talks about it now.'

According to Sandra, Debbie was liking this stint so well that she was putting off coming back to England. 'Next thing she was saying, "Maybe I'll apply for another year."'

Sandra says that since the series of deaths in their family, both she and Debbie have had medication for depression. 'We've both been troubled by anxiety attacks, finding it difficult going down to the shops. We've both "had help". I mean we were both quite nervy children. She hasn't got a psychological problem. Her problem is the loss of her family.' In quick succession their brother, their mother and father, and Sandra's first husband had died. 'We've both been on medication for *that* reason. I've had the odd pill because there are times when I just can't cope anymore. It's all anxiety. She's not mentally deranged.' Sandra is at pains to make this clear. She seems simply unaware of the Lithium use and the diagnosis of manic-depression which Debbie confided to Catherine Wall. 'If you're saying to me she's capable of murder, you're saying I am too. If you're trying to say she's got a mental problem, then I must have the same problem.'

Jon, who has shared this house with his sister-in-law on and off for six years, feels he knows her well. 'I can see Deb's reaction [to death] being rather deeper than most people's' because of the loss in her own family, he says. 'The other thing,' he says that her family trauma has caused, 'is that she can't stand confrontation. If there's any kind of argument, Deb will just disappear. If San has a stern word with the kids, Deb goes out for a walk. She just will not stay anywhere where there's any kind of confrontation.' Jon seems inured to another way his words could be interpreted. How would a person unable to deal with confrontation react if she felt trapped?

Despite his conscious or unconscious blindness to what facts may implicate her, it's impossible not to admire Jon Ashbee for his tenacious defence of his sister-in-law. She couldn't have had a better, more concerned advocate. Much of the weight of the English and Scottish families' campaign for Debbie and Lucy has fallen on his shoulders. The press, the lawyers, the British government, all direct their approaches through him. 'They know if they ring Dundee they'll get shouted at,' he laughs. Debbie has told him that as she's not able to make decisions from her cell, she'll trust him to do it for her.

Jon first met Debbie as her bank manager. She'd been nervous and he'd tried to put her at ease. When she later met him in jeans and pullover, by then dating her sister, Debbie had asked, 'Are you the same bloke from the bank? You don't seem at all threatening any more.' Jon laughs as he remembers. Sharing a home, they've had their disagreements with each other over the years.

> *But in a way, that being totally open with each other, that's been a great help to us in this, hasn't it San? Deb looks to me to be the one that just gives it to her as it is. She trusts me. And the number of times she's said to me in there, 'Look, I'm not in a position to make any kind of sensible decision. Whatever you tell me to do, I'll do.'*

It crosses my mind that, one day, it may be Jon who has to prevail upon Debbie to do the hardest thing of all: admit what she's done.

Debbie is a couple of years older than Jon but accepts the fatherly role he's had for her since he married Sandra. Sitting with him, in his home in Alton, it's easy to see why. He smokes too much and could lose a little weight and is obviously unfit with the stress of the defence campaign. But he exudes a confidence, a reassurance that must have been a rock in Debbie's troubled seas, before and since her arrest. Receding hair, black beard, gentle eyes and a frown. He laughs his full, throaty smoker's laugh as I joke that he's in that league of respected community men: priest, lawyer, bank manager. For Debbie, he's been a bit of each. I like this man very much and can't help the pangs of guilt, knowing that my own beliefs in the case have tipped against his.

Perhaps he senses this. 'I've always wanted to ask you,' he says. 'Where do you stand on this question of Debbie's guilt or innocence?' He asks it like that, formally, as if he's been preparing. I gulp but quickly slip into professional, reasonable, weighing-all-claims mode. I talk about having to weigh the inconsistencies in people's logic. I say my own motivation has always been opposition to the death penalty. I've fudged the answer and I think he knows it. But that doesn't stop him from helping. He also knows I sincerely want his and Sandra's sympathetic view of Debbie. They devote the whole day to giving it to me.

Sandra says she and Debbie have a thing about the moon. They both watch its progress, knowing it's one thing they have in common, the same moon in the same phase in their different parts of the world. They each look up, in their very different yards, as a way of thinking of the other and willing each other closer.

Much of their communion concerns the children. Debbie writes weekly to all of them. Jon answers the phone as Sandra talks about the effect of Debbie's imprisonment on the kids. Alex, the eldest, is like her father: laidback and trying to look after everybody else. If stories about Debbie come on the telly, she'll switch if off before the other kids see. Young Jon and Ben seem worst hit. Seeing his much-loved aunt on the newspaper banners has traumatised Ben. 'They're going to kill my Aunty Debbie,' he sobbed one day in September. There's been bed-wetting. Maddie, the sweetest little preschooler you could hope to meet, thinks her aunt is on holiday. Months later, Sandra will take three of the children to Saudi to see their aunt.

I want to be honest with these people. I like them and they have welcomed me into their home. Again I raise my own doubts about Debbie, through the questions of others: 'I had a very upsetting conversation the other day,' I start, 'with Catherine Wall in Al Khobar.'

As if we're discussing the weather, Jon comes back, 'Oh, yes.' He's so adept now, at being unflappable on his sister-in-law's behalf, I wonder if it's taking a toll inside. What was upsetting, I tell them, is that Catherine was obviously still very concerned about Debbie, even though she felt her friend was guilty.

'Catherine Wall,' says Jonathan, 'delves into sort of amateur psychiatry. She and Deb got on well because she was sort of being a counsellor for Deb from the deaths that Deb had experienced. She was the one very much who was hanging on the way Deb was behaving on one of the desert trips. She used the phrase to me that

Deb was "curled up in the coital position" next to the campfire.' I'm sure Jon means 'foetal', as Sandra mimes pulling in her head to her chest and wrapping arms around knees. Jon says Catherine was using her amateur knowledge of psychiatry to interpret Deb's behaviour. 'Since we spoke to her in January, her [Catherine's] opinion has been able to grow and grow and grow.'

We discuss the Saudi system of conciliation between those affected by a murder. How could there be conciliation when the accused wouldn't admit guilt and apologise and when the brother of the victim needed acknowledgment and apology before he could forgive? 'We've had to work very hard on Deb,' says Jon, 'because when she started to get a picture of how Saudi justice works, when we explained the need for us to pay blood money in return for Mr Gilford waiving the death penalty, her initial reaction to that was, "Don't. No way are we paying money to Mr Gilford to get me clemency. I don't want clemency, no way."' It's difficult to get past first base in this conversation. There is simply no acknowledgment of any possible conclusion other than outraged innocence. When it comes to Lucille, though, there's a slight shift in attitude. Sandra's voice drops as she speaks of Lucy making her confession early in the interrogation and then dragging Debbie into the admission of guilt. Jon, too, almost whispers as he allows himself a brief lapse in the corporate two-family defence. He mutters that he wonders about Lucy's alleged history with terminal patients' credit cards. Here is the ultimate closing of ranks. Jon and Sandra resent the fact that Lucy's past might taint their own family member.

If Catherine Wall is right, this family is trapped in Debbie's lie. Perhaps Debbie has even fooled herself. How could the soft, gentle person she knows as herself be guilty of such a grievous crime? A couple of times during the day both Jon and Sandra, repeating their almost mantra-like protestations of Debbie's innocence, start a sentence. It's a part-sentence I've heard from them before. It goes, 'If I felt Debbie was guilty ...' But they never complete it. The import of it is that they're saying they wouldn't be supporting Debbie like this if she was in fact the murderer. The funny thing is, I'm sure that's not so. Their support has been so constant and loyal, it's difficult to imagine them dumping her had they been convinced of her guilt.

Sandra goes off to the local kindy to collect their youngest, Madison. A three-year-old with a shy, sweet smile, Maddie hides her face in her father's chest as she's introduced. The little girl plays with a long-suffering tortoise-shell cat. Not much more than a kitten, the cat is obviously used to the rough play of kids. 'This is Willow,' Jon explains. They've bought her for Debbie. She had said, 'Give me something to look forward to', so Jon, who doesn't much like cats, relented and they gave Willow a home, in preparation for Debbie's return. Debbie thought of the name. Soon, Maddie's diverted by *Postman Pat* on the telly as Jon and I turn to his ever-thickening file of correspondence. There are many letters from Debbie. Each is headed 'Dear Sandra, Jon, Ben, Jonathan, Alex, Maddie and [in the more recent ones] Willow'. Even the hamster, Georgina, often gets a mention.

After a while, Maddie tires of her video and comes to sit on her father's lap and talk to the stranger. Jon reads lines from Debbie's letters, one at a time, and Maddie repeats them in her jumbled, little-girl voice. A sweet, bitter-sweet time, as some of the words this father and daughter recite are sad indeed.

> A poem on March 17:
> One day I'll be home with you
> But in years not days afew
> Memories of home linger,
> They fill my mind every minute of the day.
> Why could I not stay instead of searching here
> For the family I have lost?
> You are my life, my family.
> If I was told how long I'd stay
> There would not be a day
> I'd wish to be home and not alone
> Counting every day in every way.

Jon: 'She says herself, she lives in the past.'

> Even if you found the real killer, I don't think I want to know.
> They want to blame us and they don't like Westerners. I'm trying hard to imagine being here for years but I cannot. ...I miss you all so much. I'm so desperate to come home and yet I know that as everyone has said it will not be soon. I could cry and cry about this awful nightmare.

August 10
Still frightened about the death penalty. I wish I'd stayed at home. How awful to think if we're found guilty, when we've had lawyers, we have not even defended ourselves. And yet the case is closed for a verdict.

Have received an interesting magazine called Prisoners Abroad. Sounds awful. That's me.

August 20
Who knows when we'll be home. I know that I have so much to face. I could cry and cry. Imagine what shame this has brought to our families.

I want to hear the verdict but I don't, if you know what I mean.

Why did this happen to us? For life it will be there. I cannot deal with that. I think that I will need to talk to someone. At present I can never imagine coming home. It seems like a past life and this is now my life. The feeling is hard to explain. You know that I care and believe what other people think.

Called on again for my midwifery skills. Midnight last night. I said the girl should go to hospital, as in labour. Thank goodness, she did. She had a little boy.

I miss you all so, so much. It's awful. I could cry and cry. I hope you are all OK and recovering from the awful news about Lady [sic] Di and Dodi Al Fayed. It is tragic. I still cannot believe it. Please. I just want to come home. I should not say this as I know that you are doing what you can.

September 3
Unconfirmed report on BBC World that we have been found guilty. Is this so? (It said no more except that Salah had denied these reports and papers were up in a higher court awaiting a decision.)

September 3
Lucy's just heard on BBC World that we've been found guilty and we've been gaoled for an unspecified period of time. This is unconfirmed and denied by Salah. I cannot handle the above and nor can Lucy. Oh, why didn't I go in

1989? [Debbie had been almost fatally injured in a car crash in that year and spent months in recuperation at her sister's home in Alton.] I don't want to go on. There's no point. All I keep thinking of is all of you. Will I ever come home and see you all again? Remember, I love you all as always.

PS. Salah has to help us.

Later, she's cheered up enough to laugh at her situation.

I can handle a couple of years of being here. (Only joking).

Just re-read Earl Spencer's speech and Elton John's words to his song. [Debbie's sister Sandra had stayed up late one night transcribing them into a fax to her.] Brings tears to your eyes.

September 21
If I were a bird I'd fly away
Across the sea and through the sky
To my family's home,
Where I'd feel safe and build a nest,
And look after all the rest.

PS. I won't give up until I find the right person (ie the real killer).

September 21
Worked myself up talking about work. Suddenly feel frightened. Will have no money and no job when I come home. How am I going to start again? Who will really want to employ me again? From reality, the situation is horrendous. I'm very, very frightened. Will try and make something of my life if possible. You will all give me the strength to carry on.

5.19 am: Life is like a gem-stone, it sparkles and then gets chipped away.

September 28 [This is after the shock news about Lucy's actual and Debbie's claimed sentencing.]
Hope you're both well and so are the children. This must be my worst fax to try and write as I still don't know what to say. I'm stunned. Please, if there's any chance of you

coming one or two weeks earlier, please will you come. I will understand if you are not able to. I'm just having a bad time at present; up and down like a yo-yo. I heard on the BBC World that it was unconfirmed as yet that I would receive the death penalty.

Lucy is upset about her eight years but not the lashes. I had to go to hospital to have an injection of valium. I was smoking heavily but have stopped again. Every time I'm upset your audio helps me so much. [The Ashbee family had put together a tape of the kids singing and reading to her.] Every time I listen to Michael Jackson's music I get upset as I think of Princess Diana and Dodi. Life is so unfair. I hope that Jon's interview [for a new job] went well. Maybe you have some news by now. Don't let this affect your career. It's my problem. Maybe you should become a diplomat or a lawyer. Is Sandra doing nights again at the school? [Sandra works at a school for developmentally disabled children.] I should think that you'll need to rest after all this.

You can imagine how I felt when I heard the headlines in the newspapers: 'Don't Let Debbie Be Beheaded'. I could not believe what I was hearing. It was about me. Not someone else. To hear 'Debbie Parry' on the radio is like your worst nightmare coming true. I feel so ashamed to be accused of such an awful thing. I could not hurt anyone. When you come across please could you just bring a box of Thornton's chocolates for Dr Assam? He's so kind to me and when I eventually get my money back I will buy him something to keep for when and if I leave here. He always has time to see me, even if he is busy. I've had to have a few drugs recently, due to stress, dehydration and not enough food. The blood pressure drops. Still not allowed food but the menu system that was meant to start has not started. Not eating well because we are still in the boiling hot school in the mornings, sometimes for six hours. No air conditioning. Horrendous. Lunch is left in the sun for two hours before we get to eat it. And so I won't eat it as I don't want to end up with food poisoning too. One of the managers brought me an English–Arabic book from home and told me that I could keep it. Trying to switch off to everything but finding it so hard not to worry. Hope that Willow's behaving herself and

> not eating Georgina. Phipps has a lot to answer for. One day maybe he'll know how it feels to do what he has done to us. I will never, never take life for granted again.
> I CANNOT BELIEVE THAT WE'VE BEEN FOUND GUILTY. How can we be? Can we be found innocent when we eventually come home?
> I got dressed for the first time in ages. I'm trying to fight my depression and just feel glad I will not get the death penalty. We've done nothing wrong, except being frightened of Dhahran Police. Please bring hairdressing scissors to trim the bottom of my hair.

Debbie likes to have her hair cut short. Her old boyfriend Stuart likes it that way. The prison authorities have insisted the women grow their hair long.

> *October 6*
> Fancy Rosemary doing a thing like that [her interview with *Witness*]. Dad was always right: you don't have friends, only acquaintances. And to think that I'd started to feel differently to this.

Sandra mentions times when Debbie has been very low. Lawson Ross, the British consular officer in Al Khobar, has let them know. Then, by the time Sandra and Jon arrive in Saudi on their next visit, Debbie's spirits will have recovered. Lawson visits Lucy and Debbie every ten days and has come to know Debbie well. So if he tells Sandra Debbie is down, she knows it's serious. Sometimes, Debbie is suicidal. A few days ago, when Sandra last saw her in Dammam, her sister was distraught. Debbie had knitted Christmas presents for all the family. They'd been stolen just before she saw Jon and Sandra on the last day of their visit. The last straw. Sandra is worried about her sister's survival.

She leaves to collect the children from school. I offer to leave but she and Jon urge me to stay and continue reading Debbie's letters.

> *November 3* [The families are undecided whether to agree to the BBC airing its *Panorama* program looking at the women's lack of a fair trial.]
> Jon, I've been thinking, really, and I want you to do something for me. I know what I'm doing and I want you to

ask JW [John Ware, the *Panorama* reporter] to carry on with the work that he's doing and to go ahead as soon as possible. I am the one who will take full responsibility. You have it in writing. I believe that it has to be done and I've discussed the pros and cons with Lucy who also agrees and will tell Grant. To keep our sanity, please do as I ask.

I keep on listening to Elton John and the hymn after Earl Spencer's speech. I love that hymn. I do not think it will really sink in that Diana is dead until we come home. I am so angry at what was done to you at the airport.

Jon explains: 'That's when a couple of passport officers, as we were going through they started singing a song in Arabic and the word "Sandra" came up and they giggled and pointed at San — you know, everybody in the airport have a look at these two. They really took the mickey out of us all the time as we were going through the Customs. I think there must be something in the visas that says who we are because they pull them out and you can see them all pointing and looking. One of the most horrible experiences I've ever had going through that airport on the way home. It's not so bad going in. It's on the way home. Because we're not allowed to have any officials with us, you see. Once you go beyond the exit barrier you're on your own, so you're at the mercy of the Saudis. I mean, they do believe the girls have done it. So, from their way of seeing it, we're murderers' kith and kin.'

They should do it to me, not to you. They've succeeded in making me really angry at what is being done. It's what I needed to make me fight. I will never give up until the truth comes out.

I still cannot believe that I'm in prison. Innocent, with a destroyed life and reputation. I must be jinxed or something. I lie here and wonder what is lying around the next corner. Still, no point in feeling sorry for myself.

I'm so frightened of the thought what the people in Britain will think of me when I come home.

October 31
I nearly ended up delivering a baby girl here. The lady was eight centimetres dilated. Lucy woke me up. This lady was in the guards' room. Thank God we managed to get her to

hospital. She should have gone earlier as her waters had started to leak. It was her fifth baby.

I've decided I might get married and settle down now.

October 31
[Letter to the British Prime Minister, Mr Tony Blair]
I am writing to express concern over the way the Saudi Arabian authorities have been allowed to keep us in prison for ten and a half months for a crime we did not commit. My name is Deborah Parry. I live in Alton in Hampshire. I've been a nurse all my working life. My friend and I were made, under duress, to write statements. We can be proved innocent but nobody wishes to listen. We're deteriorating both mentally and physically and need your help. Please, please help us. Hopefully you will receive this letter. [No reply had been received by late December.]

November 3
Dear SAS,
Please, please, please, can you help us to get out of gaol as we are innocent. Just lower a rope from a helicopter and we'll catch hold of it. If help is needed, send for the A-Team. We are desperate. Please help us.

Maddie sits at the table with us, counting out her M&Ms. 'Here, Poppet, why don't you go and sit and watch the telly?' says Jon, while telling of a visit to the gaol cancelled because of rain. 'Because there's no drainage on the roads in Saudi, when you go through the underpasses the roads dip down. They all filled up with four or five feet of water, so nobody could go anywhere. So they had to call off the visit.'

November 10
It's raining so much. We've had thundering and lightning. The only walk I get is across to the doctor's. Great isn't it? I will not be home this year. I think we've been forgotten about over here.

[To the children] I hope you gave Mummy a happy birthday.

I've decided not to return to England unless people are aware of what really happened. Even then I might not come home. I've had enough now. I may even sack Salah if the money's not been released. I thank Michael Dark and Jon but still don't understand why everyone doesn't want to upset the Saudis. Everyone will wonder why nothing was said in all this time. All I hear is that it won't be long and everyone knows the truth. Well they don't do they? People have not been told anything. I'm not sure if I can cope with any more visits. It's too distressing for everyone and too expensive. Why have people let us be in prison for so long without saying anything to the public? Everyone is frightened to upset the Saudi–British relationships. And of course we're not important people. Just leave them in gaol, it doesn't matter, for a while longer. Well it does. It's destroyed my life. I want no more faxes etc. Thank you for what you have done but now it is time for me to take over and get us out of here. Get on with your own lives. I assure you that once I have told the press we will not be here for much longer. Lots and lots of love, Debbie.

Jon wrote back on November 17:

Incidentally I was delighted to read your last fax and whilst I was initially quite hurt that you were sacking me, that soon gave way to pleasure that you were still angry and fighting. Forgive me but I've asked Lawson not to pass on your letters to Salah and Michael just yet. The time is almost right to take that sort of action but to do it now would only produce unnecessary complication which might further delay things for you. The sentiments are spot on but let me try to explain why we have not done it yet. The Sharia court is shortly to issue an official document to the ILF confirming the waiver of the death penalty. It will provide a copy to Salah, who will arrange to release the monies in Australia. If we sack Salah now we lose the ability to tie the release of the monies with tidying up legally in Saudi as quickly as possible. Although as a last resort we do of course have your direct authorities to the Australian lawyer [Michael Burnett, ostensibly working to the directions of Salah Al-Hejailan]. Also, if the sentencing hearing is to arrive as quickly as we think it will, we won't have enough time to arrange for an alternative lawyer to

> attend the court on your behalf. Such a lawyer would need to have a working knowledge of the situation in case the opportunity does arise to negotiate your sentence downwards. Hope you can understand this and believe me, as with everything else that we do, we are doing this in what we believe are your best interests ...

I ask Jon if there's no problem getting some of the sensitive material in these letters through the censors: 'We just don't care now. If they chop a bit out, they chop a bit out. I don't care now either. Couldn't give a monkey's. This thing's sorted now as far as they're concerned.' I suspect this response is a little disingenuous and there is a secure route for sensitive correspondence.

Jon continues reading his letter:

> We believe that things should start to move along quickly now and provided they do and the outcome is acceptable you're probably best to continue along in the same way as we are at the moment. With the proviso that we shall probably dispense with Salah's services as soon as the legal process is concluded.
>
> *November 10*
> I hope you've had a good day. Happy birthday [Sandra's]. I should be admitted to hospital if I'm not out of here soon. I can't take much more. I meant everything I said in the first three pages. John Ware must do his thing. Weather here is bad. Rain, thunder and lightning. Smell of damp is awful. Please help us to get out of here. I may write to the press myself for help. At least the nanny [Louise Woodward] is having better coverage than we are. The Foreign Office has just left us here so as not to upset anyone. Don't be upset by what I've written. I'm just writing what I feel, as you said to do. I feel as if I'm going to go crazy. Please help us.
>
> *November 17*
> I've not heard what happened at my hearing today but one Saudi said Mr Gilford had forgiven us on the seven-thirty news. Forgiven us for what? The truth will come out, I'm sure about that. I feel so frustrated being here for nothing.

And for the fact that I cannot just walk out. My handbag was returned, minus the money. Except fifty Saudi Riyals which I must have put in with my sunglasses. How can they take all my money and my salary and $US1.2 Million?

Sometimes I think I can't take much more. I hate my life now. I don't know how I'll cope in England. I'm so frightened that I won't cope. By the way it's been a full moon the last few nights.

Sandra arrives home with the other three children. All have a drink and a snack waiting for them. Alex, the oldest, goes upstairs to practise her euphonium. The others watch telly as Jon continues reading letters.

Where I will go to and what I will do when released, it doesn't bear thinking about. I just feel I'm going to be so alone. I can't write in here how I really feel, as it is read. I'm feeling sorry for myself. I cannot deal with any more tragedy. My life ... I don't want to come home, I want to go elsewhere, alone for a while to re-think everything. I cannot listen to the radio and hear my name or watch a television with me on it. It would mortify me. I know you're having a hard time and I'm sorry for it. It's so unfair. It's not long till Christmas. Why has all of this happened to us?

'Oh, here we are,' says Jon, 'We change around now', and he reads an example of how Debbie's mood and intent will swing wildly, even in one letter:

I so want to come home. But only to see all of you. No radio, no TV, no newspapers. I cannot handle it yet. Hope that Maddie's better now. I hope and pray this doesn't affect the children. Did Jon get the job? It helps me if you tell me of your bad days as it stops me from thinking of just myself as you do in here. I love you all so much I want to come home.

'And yet, earlier on, she says she can't face coming home,' says Jon. 'Strange how it'... But Jon won't allow himself to see a darker side to Debbie's erratic nature. I suggest this is something they'll have to think about when Debbie does come home. How she'll deal with the attention.

'We'll have a combination of sorting Deb out and dealing with the media side of things as well,' he says. 'We've got it fairly well sorted,' he says, ever optimistic, and turns back to the letters.

Debbie has received her diary along with her handbag and is able to put a date to the visit of the Travelling Naturalists to Scrivener's Canyon.

> *That's where she got the bruise on her thigh. We've got a statement from Joe saying, I think he saw her do it. At least he knows of her having done it and she showed him the bruise before the murder, so that bruise was already there before Yvonne's murder. That's another one of the evidentiary things if you like.*

Yet, on Joe Robinson's account, this is just not true. He says he never gave a statement about the bruise and was not aware she'd had a bruise. So much for the 'so much evidence' that Sandra has talked about, convincing the family their girl is innocent. To be fair, it's Jon who really relies on his mass of papers. He draws them about him as a kind of intellectual comforter, heedless of the inconsistencies in its cross-stitch.

Upstairs, Alex blasts out practice scales on her euphonium. Jon and I chat about the romantic stories of simple and fulfilled country life in a Maeve Binchy book Deb has been reading. 'She'd like her life to be like that. When she hasn't got it, she reads it in books and that's a sort of good compromise.'

He returns to Debbie's early letters:

March 10
Have you ever been in gaol?
Your answer will be no.
You know I came here for a reason,
To gain strength and to appreciate what I already have.
No more wandering from place to place.
I have the love of my family,
I need no more.
Searching the world was no answer.
This was done to make me settle
And to stop me looking for what doesn't exist any more.

> My mum, dad and brother,
> They're in my heart.
> My living family is in England, where I belong.
> I will stop this looking and searching now.
> My life has just begun.

Maddie and Ben come to the table, looking for the shortbread I've brought from Sainsbury's. 'Daddy, can I have one of them biscuits?' They're sweet children, ask before taking. This polite English living room seems so far from the dusty concrete reality of Saudi institutional buildings.

> *April 7*
> I was watching a Sri Lankan girl who was making some lovely children's dresses with no pins or pattern, just needles and cotton. I will try this when I come home.
> Watch some small birds that have made a couple of nests in the building. They eat the rice. One learning to fly tonight. No moon.
> The new sister reminds me of a nun in The Sound of Music.
> Air conditioning not working. Thank goodness the fan in the centre of the room is working. First day of summer today. Haj holiday soon.

Debbie's life is drifting into the lunar rhythm of the Saudi year.

Jon rehearses his old theme of frustration with what he sees as the illogicality of Frank Gilford's approach to the case. 'Laurel says something about these foul-mouthed people daring to call Yvonne a lesbian. And we say, "Well, we agree. Doesn't it seem a little odd to you that this is the prime motive and you're saying it's rubbish, we're saying it's rubbish and yet you're saying they're guilty?"' Jon has argued this out with Frank Gilford in his head many times.

> *It's something I've never been able to get past. He says he has other things that have convinced them of their guilt. I just want to say, 'What are they?' Are they things like Rosemary Kidman and Caroline Ionescu talking to them? If so, we know that's rubbish. It must be something pretty solid, if he's willing to say no way was Yvonne a lesbian.*

I know Deb isn't a lesbian and we've got pretty firm evidence that Lucy isn't because of Grant's existence. We all seem to agree the lesbianism doesn't exist and if that's the basis of their guilt, he must have something pretty mega to override that and consider they are guilty.

So what is it that he's got? I can go a certain way to condoning Frank Gilford. I can understand that he's not equipped to deal with the media pressure. He's lived in a small town. He's never had to deal with places like Saudi Arabia before and probably never had to deal with instances like this before and he's totally fazed. And certain people around him are advising him a certain way. And yet deep down inside him somewhere, if he's got any feeling for his sister whatsoever, he must actually want to know what's happened. And unless he is blinkered enough to actually believe what we've got on the table at the moment, that nagging doubt must still be going on inside him. So has he cast it aside in the interests of making life as easy as possible from his point of view? I can't think that, because he's been through hell and back. If he really is that convinced, an alternative idea shouldn't affect him, shouldn't make any difference to him.

How hard it is to walk in another man's shoes. In some ways, the trials of Jon and Frank have not been so different. Frank has lost his sister, cruelly. Jon has had his much-loved sister-in-law ripped from safety and family. They've both been through ordeal by media. Yet Jon is stuck in a one-sided imaginary conversation with a man he will never meet. And that man wants only an end to the pain of everyone telling him what to do.

I try to explain to Jon Frank's determination to maintain his own dignity, not to change his life, to go on as before despite the media and the rage of the world.

But what I don't understand about that is, if he did just want to ignore it and make it go away as fast as possible, if he'd waived the death penalty in January, that'd have been it. No one would have been interested. But he didn't. He stuck resolutely to his path. Against all criticism, he stuck to it. He created the environment that he didn't want. So he must be so firm in his belief to do that.

Who does this description remind me of? Jon doesn't see that in some ways he's painting himself. 'I just can't conceive of anybody being that gullible.' Scared, I suggest. 'If he's scared, why stand by something everybody's telling him he's a horrible man to do?' I remind Jon that Frank had hundreds of people telling him he was doing the right thing. 'I suppose I'm thinking about me and how I'd behave,' Jon concedes.

I've not met the man; I've got no conception of what he's like. Well, I started off hating him. I thought the man, he's just out for publicity. It's a game. He's going to up the ante as much as he possibly can and make as much money out of this as possible. Then everyone was coming back to us and saying, 'We don't think he's like that. He's not interested in money.' We said, 'Oh yeah, yeah. What other motive has he got?' And then, over a period, I think hearing what he was doing and what was happening, we thought nobody would put up with this just for money. Whatever sort of man he is. There must be more to it. And we started to think, maybe he just believes that they've done it; maybe that's his motivation. That he's doing the right thing by his sister. And we started thinking, we need to talk to him, we need to let him know the information we've got. If it doesn't change his mind overnight, it would certainly make him doubt his stance. And then we went beyond that and I personally established a middle ground between the two, in that I've got a great sympathy for him because we've been through hell and back. He's lost his sister in a pretty dastardly crime, a horrible way to go. We've got Deb living in terrible circumstances in Saudi. So there's a lot of similarities between us and him. So, I have a great sympathy for him. But I can't get beyond the 'Why didn't he investigate more?' Why did he just believe what people were telling him? If it'd been my relation, I would leave no stone unturned to find out the truth.

Somebody said to me, 'Go to Saudi.' I was absolutely terrified of going to Saudi. I actually made arrangements here before that trip in January thinking that I wasn't going to come back. Because I thought if Deb can be arrested when she's going to buy some cat food, they'll stick some drugs in my pocket, they'll do this, they'll do that, but one way or another I won't be coming back. They won't let me out of that country again. And as Deb told me more and more about what had happened to her I was more and more convinced I wasn't coming home. I thought, they won't let me out of the country with this information. So I was petrified of going to Saudi. But I went all the same, because Deb was there. And if Deb had been murdered in Saudi, I'd have gone over to Saudi to find out the truth. And done it without hesitation, even though I was terrified. But he just says, 'No, I'm not going.' And how can he live the rest of his life not knowing? The only way is to convince himself that he does know.

But to actually execute two girls, how could he do that? And he was willing to. My ability to condone his behaviour stopped right there. He can be blind, he can salve his own conscience, I can understand that. You can't execute people on something you've created to make yourself OK. We were trying to say to him, 'Hear it now before it's too late.' I give him as much rope as I can, but I can't forgive him that. Never, ever could I forgive him that. I could forgive him for burying his head in the sand, but for condemning them to death without at least checking up ... makes my blood run cold, I tell you.

We hug as we say goodbye. I tell Jon and Sandra that Debbie is lucky to have them. Sandra says she hopes I'll meet Debbie one day. Then I'll know, she says, that her sister is innocent. I don't tell them which way I'm now leaning. So that's both of us keeping things from them.

Driving into London, trying to think of alternatives to the guilt of two ordinary women. The story on the radio news is of a stolen baby. We hear the grief-choked words of the parents, appealing for the kidnapper to return their child. Who could do such a thing?

The story is in the papers next morning, when the culprit is found, baby safe. The experts are wheeled out to explain: ordinary women do these extraordinarily awful things.

Chapter 35

Who guards the guard?

Home to Australia for Christmas. It's a lonely one for Debbie. Her family had planned to visit, children included, but a car accident puts Sandra out of action.

I meet Caroline Ionescu, Lucy's Australian friend, to chat about what I've learnt on my travels and to explore any remaining doubts about the women's guilt.

What about the hospital guards? Caroline remembers the suspicion about them in the days after the murder:

> *The day that Major Hamed came to the hospital with Colonel Solafir and the women were taken into the auditorium for our arms to be checked, that day the six guards or five guards that were on night shift the night the murder happened also were in the auditorium. And we never saw them after that. And I actually asked one of the security guards what had happened to the guys because he was friendly with one of them and he told me they were taken in there [to Dhahran Police Station]. He told me that they were shackled, they were questioned for about three days, they were beaten and that sort of thing.*

Caroline says she had been shocked to see one of the guards back at the hospital when she ran into him with Kathryn Lyons in the week after the murder.

> *I never actually suspected them. One of those security guards [on duty on the murder night] that had harassed*

> Catherine Wall and had harassed me was one of the guards that was taken in for questioning. When I saw him, because he'd harassed me to the point where he'd knocked on my door one night, I opened the door and he'd pushed the way in, wanting to come into my room. So I looked at him and I thought, oh my God, could this be a man that's done this?

That incident had occurred about eight months before the murder. The guard was a young man, around 25 years of age.

> He was always friendly. He was always ringing up, very gentle, always wanting to give you something, trying to confess his undying love for you, all this sort of stuff. It got to the point where he became more obsessive in his behaviour, to the point where I went and saw one of the nursing supervisors — who was a Moslem — to ask advice.

As usual, Caroline talks all in a rush, words running together.

> I was getting really concerned, especially after he knocked on my door and pushed it in. I said, 'I'll give you to the count of three to get out, otherwise I'll start screaming' and then he left. So I went and I reported it and said, 'What can I do about this?' And she said you can either take him to Religious Affairs and get one of the Muttawa to talk to him, or just leave it. And I thought, I didn't want any recall from any of his relatives and you just don't know how Saudi Arabia at that stage works. So I used to leave my answering machine on and let him say what he wants on my machine. But I kept the tapes.

What did he say on the tapes? 'I confess my undying love to you. Is there anything you want? I want to be with you forever and ever.'

Caroline knows enough to be sceptical about some of the rumours surrounding the murder. Many claimed the guards on duty on the night of the murder had 'disappeared'. Caroline says one of them, Mohammed, was leaving anyway. He'd spoken to her before the murder and said he'd been offered another job and was leaving the hospital in December, the month of the murder.

> *If it was security, you tell me where they're gonna go and have a shower, change their bloodied clothes if Yvonne was stabbed 27 times or however many. Being away from their box. It doesn't make sense.*

Chapter 36

Moon

A bushfire moon rises over Bondi, huge as it launches from the horizon and reaches into a starlit but smoke-filtered sky. It's blood-red. The bushfire smoke does this, in summer, slipping a colour lens across the beam of the moon, giving that belly-fat ball its big, meaty colour. One summer, four or five years ago, fires ringed Sydney and cloaked the bowl of the sprawling city in smoke. The sun refracted through this smoke lens in the late afternoon and turned the whole bay of Bondi blood-red. Swimming out, all around you was red. Singed leaves and twigs came on the afternoon breeze from inland. In the bush suburbs, people's lives went up in smoke. Some died, many lost homes. At Bondi, we carried on in hot, summer, carefree ways. Somebody said it was like swimming in other people's dreams as the embers came down into the red, lapping waves.

Today, I swim out, at dusk, leaving behind the cares of the shore. My eight-month-old son splashes, sitting in the sand of the shallows, watched by his mother. I pull myself out into the bay in long, slow strokes. Under the moon. A sensible father of two, on holiday in the Sydney summer, would be thinking only of Christmas coming, presents for the kids and the large extended family. And what's for dinner. I'm thinking of Debbie Parry. She's watching this moon, I'm sure, over there in the squalid yard of Dammam gaol. She looks up at that moon, knowing her sister, Sandra, is doing the same, standing at night in her yard in frosty Hampshire. The moon unites hearts and hopes across miles. So why should I have tangled my own hopes, my summer, in the sad life of Debbie, forgotten by most, in Saudi Arabia? I'm not sure we'd even like each other, if we met, but even enemies can sometimes recognise each other's suffering. She's always said she feels for Frank in his loss, under the same moon.

As the lunar month slips by, I read Debbie's letters. It's the closest I can get, for now. Sandra wants me to meet her. Then I will know, she says. Know that Debbie cannot be guilty of this blood-red crime. In Saudi Arabia, the devout scan the sky for the first glimpse of the new moon, signalling the start of Ramadan. Like Britons writing to *The Times* of the first cuckoo of summer, Moslems are exhorted by their newspapers and *imams* to rush immediately to the *Sharia* court if they glimpse the new moon. The moon runs the *Hejira* calendar in the Islamic world, not some digital clock. While Christian festivals and holy days often coincide with pre-Christian pagan feasts, the Moslem calendar abhors such ungodliness and uses the lunar cycle to dodge unwelcome coincidence with the pagan, pre-Mohammed past.

Back in Dammam, Debbie can't cope with the disappointment of her family's cancelled visit and threatens suicide. For a time, she's locked up in the hospital for her own safety. Along with the Saudis, Debbie and Lucy begin the 30-day dawn-to-dusk fast of Ramadan, the fast of penitence that is as alien to them as their surroundings and their predicament.

Here in Bondi, the streets are full of revellers, heading out to celebrate New Year's Eve by the Julian calendar. I kiss my wife goodbye at the door as she heads off to watch the harbour fireworks on a friend's boat. The baby sleeps in the back room. I sit at the laptop, thinking of Debbie, a woman my own age with little to look forward to and much grief in her past. What would I say to her if we met, there in Dammam Central Prison? I would say what her friends want to say to her: 'Tell the truth, Debbie. It's your own, your only, salvation. Don't carry that bloody secret in your heart through the rest of your life. Now you have a life. It's been given back to you; Frank Gilford gave it back. Friends and strangers have offered you work on your release. Your family has offered you a sweet return to that safe life you lived before you went searching for, what? Adventure? Escape? The answer, Debbie,' I would say, 'is in your own letters.'

> I love you all so much.
> My world would come to an end
> If I did not have you all
> To take the pain away.

> One day the pain will go away
> And the sun will shine again.
> Until then the rain will pour
> And no one will open the door.

Her friend Rosemary Kidman wrote to her in gaol, 'You'll fly home alive. Yvonne's dead.'

Confess, repent, start again. Redeem yourself.

Redeem. This morning I half-jokingly used the word to my seven-year-old son. He'd been mean to his step-cousin, a few years younger. We talked of something nice he could do to make up. Let him have first go of the Super Soaker, a water gun for squeals and cold splashes in the heat. Young boys don't like to be in the bad books; he readily agreed. Not so easy for a woman, now 38, who has committed a terrible deed in the heat of the moment and hidden her crime from all who love her. Take these gaol days of penance to look into your heart. I hope you can, Debbie — redeem yourself, for your own sake.

It's New Year's Eve. Everybody's out but me, home with the computer and the telly. Earlier, I glanced at the media-satirising *Good News Week*, sending up the labours of people like me and the foolish collections of words we throw at a weary, bemused, but still buying public. My wife, out partying, has rung to send a hogmanay kiss. Now, as the Old Vatted Demerara sinks in, I'm growing misty with TV sentiment on Bette Midler doing a live show in Las Vegas. Outside I can hear the drifting sounds of a New Year's concert at the Bondi Pavilion. The hip young audience is seeing the year out with Beck, while I'm here with Bette. As an encore she's doing Yvonne's favourite song. 'The Wind Beneath My Wings', by Bobby Lyle. He's there too, playing the piano. It's a middle-of-the-road song, like all of Bette's, but moving, when you're in the mood and don't have too low a schmaltz threshold. *Did you ever know you're my hero?/You are the wind beneath my wings.* A woman sings to her lifetime friend, acknowledging how central this woman has been to her confidence, her sense of her self, allowing her to soar. All the while the friend has been in her shadow. Every time Sue Taylor hears it, she cracks up. This was the song she shared with Yvonne. Sometimes, when Sue is just driving in the car, she finds tears on her face. She hasn't been thinking of Yvonne, not consciously.

Yvonne Gilford is the woman in the shadow of this story. The true story of her passing has not been told, lost in the struggle for two other women's lives. Let them live. But let the truth of Yvonne's death be known.

Our lives go on, as those of Debbie and her gaol companion do not. As the months pass, with no resolution, I return occasionally to their story. One moonless night, flying over Dammam from Abu Dhabi on the way to the conflict in Iraq, I look down and see the gaol, a golden bracelet of lights, a compound among other compounds. Over there I can make out the hospital, snug in its own golden ring. They're pretty, from up here, those lights, two bracelets manacling Debbie to her fate. I think of her, down there, still scribbling in her cell:

> Watch some small birds that have made a couple of nests in the building. They eat the rice. One learning to fly tonight. No moon.

Chapter 37

After

The first months of 1998 drift by, with occasional hints that the women will soon be released. I'm in the jungles of Papua New Guinea one morning in April, standing in the middle of a stream to get the satellite phone to work through the tree canopy. That's when I hear the news: release is imminent.

Weeks pass, but this time it's true. On May 21, Deborah Parry and Lucille McLauchlan are released, pardoned by King Fahd. The press report that the two have written to the king, thanking him for his mercy. While many prisoners released in the kingdom have their head shaven, Lucy and Debbie are spared this last ignominy. They're driven to Dhahran airport and flown home to Britain. There is a furious press scrum at Heathrow to meet them, but both women have deals with the tabloids. Their stories have been sold for hundreds of thousands of pounds each.

Reporters note the lack of warmth between the women during their momentary appearance at Heathrow. The two stand well apart.

'Goodbye,' says Deborah.

'See you again sometime,' says Lucy. One newspaper account notes that both clearly hope they never will.

Lucy flies off in a helicopter chartered by the *Mirror*, to spend a night in a luxury hotel in Surrey with her new husband, Grant Ferrie. Debbie is driven off to join her family at a hideaway in Bath.

Despite the large sums paid, the *Mirror* and the *Express* get little more than elaborate reiterations of the women's descriptions of police abuse which had already been published months earlier. There are no startling revelations to prove the women's innocence.

Saudi ambassador Dr Ghazi Algosaibi laughed at the women's claims of their innocence and police mistreatment. 'If you go around any prison in the world and ask the inmates whether they committed the crime of which they are convicted, I suspect the vast majority of them will deny the charges,' he said. 'Human nature works that way.'

The BBC's *Panorama* airs its much-delayed program on the women. Again, there is little that's new. The program ignores the claims of hospital staff who believe the two are guilty, although it does question Lucy's denial about the ATM card. Reporter John Ware interviews Deborah Parry, sympathetically. She is not challenged about any of the staff claims which conflict with her story. Debbie looks tired, harried. The impressions of viewers vary. She's Lady Macbeth or Princess Di, depending on your point of view.

I ring Hampshire to congratulate the Ashbees on the end of their ordeal but the family is in hiding, taking a break from the media attention.

At the end of June, it feels like the dust has settled. Time to ring Britain again. Debbie answers. Odd, it seems so matter of fact after all this time. She knows who I am; Sandra and Jon have told her. She's friendly in our brief conversation before she passes the phone to Sandra. The voices of the two sisters are very similar.

Sandra sounds happy, much lighter than ever before, as she fills me in on what's happened. The children are 'thrilled to bits', she says, that their aunty is home. On the day the news came through that Debbie was to be released, Sandra asked young Ben what could be the best possible thing to happen. 'Aunty Debbie coming home,' was his instant reply. When he learnt it was really happening, he ran out into the backyard and jumped up and down. Now he and Debbie have lived out the dream of revisiting their local Alton milk bar for a doughnut and milkshake. Although some people would gawk when they recognised Debbie in the street, life was returning to a kind of normal. Debbie was 'up and down like a yo-yo', says Sandra, but trying to face up to the reality of public reaction at home. Most people had been friendly, but Sandra and Jon were having to spend a couple of hours talking Debbie back up each time she went out. Debbie had bought a small car and was having sessions with Gordon Turnbull, who'd counselled Terry Waite after his release from his Beirut kidnapping.

The Ashbees and Debbie spent a few days in Bath after Debbie's return, far from the media and the crowds. Since their release, the two convicted women have had no contact. Debbie and the Ashbees are now frank in their dislike for and suspicion of Lucy. 'We know Lucy had the card,' says Sandra. 'She can't account for her money, and the times she used her bank account tie up with what the police claim.'

The rift between the two women is deep. Salah Al-Hejailan had tried to arrange a meeting with both women in London, but Debbie had refused to be there with Lucy. 'She blames her for having to spend 17 months in hell,' Sandra says.

Salah Al-Hejailan has been quoted as saying he's shocked that the women have sold their stories. Sandra says he claims to have been misquoted.

What shocks me is that Debbie is considering a request from Australian media to come to Australia to meet Frank Gilford. Sandra says the Australian *60 Minutes* has told them Frank is thinking about the meeting.

Sandra and Debbie want Yvonne's body to be exhumed, to seek DNA of the attackers on the corpse. The British lawyer Rodger Pannone has told the family there would be particles still retrievable. Ghoulish. I suggest this should not be the first thing to say to Frank Gilford.

Sandra says Jim Phipps has said publicly that the Gilford team would always have gone for the money settlement — if this hadn't been taken out of his hands by the lawyers in Adelaide — but they would have waited until the sword was raised. I feel a pang of guilt hearing this, remembering how Frank Gilford laughed when I told him of cases where this had happened.

Sandra is very cynical about Grant and Lucy. 'I know why Grant married her,' she says. 'They were always talking about how much money they could make out of this.'

I suggest I still need to talk to Debbie about the claims of her former hospital colleagues. Sandra says this may be possible after Debbie has had another couple of weeks of counselling. She is very disparaging about the staff who have made claims against Debbie. She says the statements Rosemary Kidman and Catherine Wall made to Michael Dark soon after Debbie's arrest were vastly different to the allegations against her they've made since. Debbie claims Catherine, who's made much of Debbie's mental problems, has a psychiatric history herself and is 'in debt up to her ears'. It's no wonder there is venom for Rosemary and Catherine. Debbie now realises the extent to which her former friends have betrayed her.

I call Catherine Wall in Dhahran to tell her what Debbie's been saying about her. She is sad but not shocked that Debbie is bitter about the comments she made to British parliamentarian George Galloway. 'I still say that she was a good friend. I still want what's best for her, but I know she can't see it,' says Catherine. 'I can't get angry with her for being defensive.'

To Debbie's claim that Catherine had a history of mental illness (and was therefore, presumably, unreliable), Catherine happily admits, 'I do have a history of depression. I told Debbie because I was encouraging her to get help. I never hide the fact that I take antidepressants. I'm always straight with employers and people I work with, so it will be no surprise to people around here if they hear what Debbie's been saying.'

Meg Smith, an Australian psychiatrist who herself has suffered manic depression, urges caution in accepting Catherine's assertions about Debbie's condition. Meg, who teaches a course on psychiatric illness and crime, says people with manic-depression are often the first suspects when a crime occurs. 'They get over-involved in what is going on.'

It's difficult for a psychiatrist to pass any sort of diagnosis on somebody she hasn't met. On Catherine's claims that Debbie had stopped taking her treatment, Meg says, 'If someone wasn't getting proper treatment, I'd be surprised if she could continue working. It would be very disabling and difficult to hold down a job.' Caroline Ionescu described having to prevent Debbie going to work because she was so manic.

'Yet,' says Meg, 'people often go into high gear when they're in high stress. If Yvonne Gilford was a close friend of Debbie and the nurses were terrified that the same thing could happen to them, that could trigger an episode for Debbie. If she had a manic-depressive illness, the stress of the death of her friend could have set it off. That doesn't mean she was the murderer. If people have a history of psychiatric illness, they do become suspects. One wonders why Deborah Parry in particular was picked out as a potential murderer.'

Meg describes the case of a friend of hers who had a manic episode when another friend suicided. The woman with manic-depression became convinced she had killed her friend, running her over in a car. She went as far as reporting herself in a police station and describing the blood on her car windscreen. Only when the police had the sense to check the car and found no blood did they realise the woman was suffering from manic-depression triggered by the stress of her friend's death.

Meg's words of warning are a reminder that guilt should not be assumed because of the stigma of mental illness. Yet colleagues like Catherine Wall are not relying only on their knowledge of Debbie's illness. They have seen the scratches and observed Debbie's behaviour and the inconsistencies in her story.

Catherine says staff at the hospital saw the *Panorama* program after Debbie's release. 'We laughed at it,' she says. In the *Panorama* interview Debbie had claimed she hadn't known of the murder until seven in the evening of December 12. Catherine recalls that Debbie had rung her at ten in the morning that day, telling her not only of the murder but also details of Yvonne's wounds.

Is Debbie not aware of the slip-ups in her story? Is she putting on a brave front when she wants to see Frank Gilford? Catherine Wall believes she is simply trapped in her lie and is trapping her family there with her.

I phone Frank, who says he doesn't think his family will want him to meet Deborah. He's well aware of what she said to *Panorama* and the claims of other staff that Debbie knew all about the murder on the morning of the twelfth. He seems philosophical about the remaining questions and wants the controversy to die down for the families on both sides of the tragedy. 'None of us will ever really know exactly what happened,' he says, unless one of the women confesses. He's not holding his breath for that.

Frank has had letters from the parents of kids using the Adelaide Women's and Children's Hospital. He's quietly glad that Yvonne's death will lead to some good in the new kids' ward being built with his money. He has no regrets about how he handled the case and thinks that if he'd relented earlier on clemency the women would have served even less time in gaol.

Another call to the Ashbee household in Alton. We discuss Frank's reluctance to deal with Debbie and Lucy. Jon Ashbee says they're considering various arenas to demonstrate Debbie's innocence. The first had been aborted on the day after Debbie's return to Britain. They'd arranged with GMTV in London to conduct a public lie-detector test on that day. Then came the news from the United States of the state trooper who arrested one of nanny Louise Woodward's lawyers. The trooper claimed that the lawyer, stopped for drink-driving, had said she no longer believed in her client's innocence of the killing of the young boy in her charge.

Louise Woodward had had two lie-detector tests which confirmed her claim of innocence. Now the story of her lawyer's doubts, true or not, might cast doubt on the reliability of lie detectors in the mind of the British public. Debbie's team abandoned the idea.

Debbie's counsellor had advised that Debbie's determination to establish her innocence was central to her recovery. So her lawyers and family were exploring tribunals such as the European or International Courts of Human Rights. While the Saudis had signed international human rights treaties, they would not accept an international court ruling which differed from their own. And they would take no notice of the European court.

So Jon was interested in finding ways for Debbie to show her innocence through the media. I suggested Sue Taylor had always been eager to meet the accused women and might be persuaded to suspend her belief in guilt to take an objective look at Debbie's claims. Or there might be a way to construct a television version of a commission of inquiry which would have wider rules of evidence than a conventional criminal court. In this way, the assertions of Debbie's former colleagues could be tested against her version. Although Jon was intrigued by this idea, I pointed out that perhaps it would be better for Debbie to let the whole business lie. There would never be a truly objective tribunal with access to all the relevant witnesses and evidence in the case, so doubts would always remain.

The Ashbees now believe they have strong proof that Lucy had, and used, Yvonne's ATM card. Her visits to ATM machines corresponded with the police claims of when money had been removed from Yvonne's account, and the amounts involved corresponded to money otherwise unaccounted for in Lucy's accounts.

The bitterness of the Ashbees and Debbie against Lucy McLauchlan stems from Lucy's pressing of Debbie to sign her original confession. There is still no chink of doubt in the armour of Jon and Sandra's belief in Debbie's story. This is despite the gathering of further contradictions in her claims by the British MP George Galloway.

Galloway visited Saudi Arabia in June 1998 to speak to many of the witnesses I'd interviewed earlier. Catherine Wall, who had resisted all other media, gave him her account of Debbie's behaviour. Two hospital interpreters who were present at the Dhahran Police Station during the days of Lucy and Debbie's interrogation had rejected the women's claims of police harassment.

Abdallah Moh'd Al-Zahrani told Galloway that Lucy had been given tea and even McDonald's hamburgers during her interrogation. She had written her confession 'in her own words and the police did not interfere at all'.

Debbie has been 'quite upset' about the interpreters' claims. 'They clearly lied,' says Jon Ashbee. He had reassured Debbie that the men had no option but to go along with the police version of events. Debbie claims one of the interpreters witnessed at least some physical abuse by the police, was present when Debbie was forced to copy Lucy's confession and had advised Debbie that Lucy was blaming the murder on her.

The investigating police officer, Lieutenant Colonel Hamed, promoted since we'd seen him a year before, was more forthcoming in his interview with George Galloway. Hamed said his attention had been drawn to Lucy and Debbie because 'it was our good luck these two nurses were among those going to town every time money was withdrawn' from Yvonne's account.

In Galloway's account, published in the British *Sunday Mail*, Hamed said he had evidence other than the confessions. He said that a kettle with a broken handle was found in Yvonne's flat, confirming the part of Debbie's confession which said she hit Yvonne in the face with a kettle. 'No one could tell you this unless they were there,' Hamed told Galloway. As well, 'there were bruises on Deborah's bottom which the doctor said could be dated to the same day' of the murder. This had corresponded to the confession, in which Debbie said she'd fallen on to a table when Yvonne pushed her.

As Galloway pointed out in his article, although Hamed denied he'd coerced the confessions from the women, 'He would, wouldn't he?' In the absence of proper cross-examination, no one's claims can be accepted at face value, be they Debbie and Lucy's denials or the conflicting accounts by the many others involved in the story who believe they are guilty.

Whenever I speak again with Debbie's family, I want to believe, as I once did, that she is innocent. Lucy is still mired in legal troubles in the Scottish Sheriff's Court over the theft of money from one of her patients' accounts.

As this book goes to press, Lucy has already done so herself, publishing *Trial by Ordeal: One Nurse's Hell in a Saudi Jail*. And as Debbie and her family have done privately, Lucy now attacks her fellow-accused publicly, saying she is not sure of Debbie's innocence. The launch of Lucy's book is accompanied by media reports of her plea to Frank Gilford to meet with her. Frank believes Lucy is just hungry for publicity for the book. He says he still believes she is guilty and he has no intention of meeting someone who has made nasty comments about him in the press. He also pledges to begin legal proceedings against Lucy to seize all profits from the sale of the book and have them donated to the Adelaide Women's and Children's Hospital.

Lucy's success in making money out of what is actually the story of her friend's death causes some outcry in Britain. Debbie's employment by Holy Cross hospital in Haslemere, Surrey, also stirs a fuss but the governing body of nursing in the UK, the Central Council, says it has no grounds to act on a complaint which seeks to have her struck off the nursing register.

Both women have difficulty in dealing with the public scrutiny of their day to day lives. Lucy gives up on the idea of attending university. Debbie avoids being seen in public in Alton. Both continue to maintain their innocence.

Debbie tells *The Times* newspaper, 'When you feel that other people suspect or might feel badly toward you, it does something to you inside ... how do you prove your innocence 100 per cent? It's not possible. It's something that I have to learn to live with but I still find it hard to accept.'

Yvonne's friends reply that at least Debbie has a life to live.

Australia's Channel Seven gives up on quality current affairs after its bruising three-year experiment with *Witness*. So it falls to Channel Nine's *60 Minutes* to interview Debbie and Lucy, from an Australian perspective, in November 1998. Lucy agrees to the interview with reporter Richard Carleton as part of the publicity for her book. Debbie comes on to counter her former cellmate's comments.

In Carleton's story both reiterate their claims of innocence, though Lucy says that when she confessed and pointed the finger at Debbie back in the Dhahran police station she believed Debbie was guilty of the murder. The scratches on Debbie's hands and her missing hair had led Lucy to this belief.

Now, at long last, a journalist asks Lucy the heavy questions, although he fails to do the same with Debbie. Instead, Carleton invites Debbie to comment on Lucy's failure to tell her crucial things during their long months together in prison. Such as that Lucy had been in Yvonne's flat the night of the murder.

'I was amazed,' says Debbie, pausing to look to her advisors off-camera. Smiling nervously, she adds, 'It does make me a little bit suspicious.' This is the first time Debbie has publicly pointed the finger at her co-accused. Not for the murder but for the raiding of Yvonne's account with the stolen bank card.

'The only thing I will say is, yes, I believe she had the card and it doesn't make her guilty of murder but I do say to Lucy, "Lucy just tell us how you got the card and then we can work together. But please just tell us how you got the card."'

She says she can't understand why Lucy told the Saudi police that Debbie was guilty. 'OK, she feared rape. But to me that still isn't enough to accuse someone of murder. I still don't understand her motives.' Yet Debbie has told the world her own fears of rape induced her to confess to a crime she says she didn't commit.

Lucy tells Carleton she'd spent the night of December 11, 1996, watching a video with Yvonne in Yvonne's apartment and had left at 10.30 pm. 'She was fine, absolutely fine. That's the last time I actually saw Yvonne.' Lucy says there are phone records to show her fiancé, Grant Ferrie, called her in her flat that night, after she'd left Yvonne. This, of course, would prove that she — or someone else — answered Grant's call. It would not prove that she was absent from Yvonne's room at the time of the murder.

Debbie tells *60 Minutes* Lucy had also neglected to tell her of the charges against her back in Scotland, until, 'when we were in prison, we managed to get hold of an *Arab News* one day. And in it it said that one of the two British nurses faced a fraud charge and I looked at it and said, "What's this fraud charge? I haven't done anything." And then Lucy said, "Oh, that must be me. I faced a charge in Scotland," but didn't enlighten me as to what it was.' Debbie agrees that this makes her suspicious.

Carleton provides some compelling televisual theatre, grilling Lucy over the charges of stealing money from an elderly patient in Scotland. 'If I get found guilty of stealing money off a patient then it's a very, very serious offence.'

Did you do it? asks Carleton.

'You'll find out in December, won't you,' she replies, referring to the hearing date for the charges against her. Under the harsh gaze of the camera and Carleton, she certainly looks harried. 'I'm not going to say if I'm innocent or guilty. I pleaded not guilty.'

Carleton points out that it's difficult to understand Lucy going to the bank four days in a row after the murder. 'Who says I went four times in a row?' retorts Lucy, perhaps unaware that Caroline Ionescu has given elaborate detail of Lucy's banking. Lucy claims again that it's the Saudi police who've concocted the whole story of the thefts from Yvonne's account. 'Somebody would have to be completely mad to go and use Yvonne's bank card' after the murder, she says.

Lucy points out that the charges of credit card theft in Scotland are 'something completely different from murder, you know what I mean? Yvonne was stabbed 14 times. This wasn't an accident. Whoever murdered her certainly intended for her to die. And to have her bank card no matter by what means you got it, why go and use it? I mean it's just sheer madness. I wish somebody would give us some commonsense for not being so bloody stupid.'

Carleton puts to her a 'guilty' scenario: 'You were found by Yvonne in her room stealing. You had a key to her room, you acknowledge that. A fight followed. You killed her. Then you concocted the story that has your colleague doing the actual stabbing.'

Lucy's response: 'It's absolute nonsense.'

Strangely, Carleton puts no 'guilty' scenario to Debbie, instead inviting her to agree with his conjecture on how Lucy may have come to murder their colleague. 'She did it and then accused you,' he suggests. But Debbie declines to comment: 'I want you to wait for me and my investigators and everyone else to be able to show the world and everyone who did it.' She adds, mysteriously, 'I think I know who did it.' Debbie appears to be leaving the way open to blame the guards or Karolyne Palowska for the murder, and Lucy for the bank theft.

Lucy, on the other hand, now says she doesn't believe Debbie is guilty. 'No. I don't know who murdered Yvonne.'

Meanwhile, Jon Ashbee continues to claim in the press that the evidence establishing Debbie's innocence is mounting and will be published in her book. Negotiations also begin with three television production companies to film a drama centred around Jon and Sandra Ashbee's fight to secure her release from gaol. Both Debbie and Jon claim the drama will contain new evidence that clears Debbie's name.

But in another development, Debbie's hairdresser from Saudi Arabia goes on Britain's Channel Four to repeat her claims about the clumps of hair missing from Debbie's scalp after the murder.

'Scissors couldn't have done it like that. It was definitely a pull.' More and more alleged detail, which adds to the patina of a murky tale but never finally resolves the question of guilt.

Sadly, it looks as though Frank Gilford was right. We'll never really know quite what happened that night in December 1996. So I'm left with opinion. And I know too well that opinion can sting the likes of Jon and Sandra Ashbee in their family home in Alton.

I believe the two women are guilty. This is an opinion based on hearsay. It is untested in court. The opinions and accounts I have heard from others have not been subject to rigorous cross-examination. My knowledge is not based on pub gossip; it is the gleanings of many interviews with individuals whose claims I've cross-checked with others. Too many of Debbie and Lucy's 'facts' don't stack up. All is never quite as it seems.

Even Lucy's co-accused now claims the brash Scot used Yvonne's ATM card. Debbie herself has failed to establish corroborated alibis for her bruises, her scratches and her missing hair. Many staff question the behaviour and statements of both women after the murder. This is not conclusive evidence but sufficient for deep suspicion.

I have tried to look into the hearts of Frank and Laurel Gilford, of Lucille McLauchlan and Deborah Parry, and into the hearts of their friends and families. Much there is obscure. All have attempted to put gloss on their opinions, dressing them up as fact. But fact is as elusive as goodness. There is truth in those hearts; there is good, even in the guilty. There could be a greater truth, and certainly more goodness, if those hearts spoke to each other. Yet in a world of doubt, fear and hate, I don't believe that will ever happen.